Sto[illegible]e

And Other Short Stories

by

Bill Haworth

DCL Publications, LLC

www.dclpublications.biz

First Edition May 2010

DCL Publications
1033 Plymouth Dr.
Grafton, OH 44044

ISBN 978-0-9844615-6-1

This is a work of fiction. Names, characters, places and incidents are the product of the author's imagination, and any resemblance to any actual persons, living or dead, events, or locales, is entirely coincidental.

Cover design by Annie Marshall, Beyond the Book Productions

PUBLISHED IN THE UNITED STATES OF AMERICA

Reviews for Bill Haworth

Stonehenge :
"a story of love, sacrifice and magic centred around the great stones..... For a man who claims he doesn't write romance, Stonehenge, the story of these teens will pull at your heart strings." - Rose Brungard – Romance at Heart Magazine

Ice Palace:
This is a beautiful love story and excerpts of this book may actually someday be in the various elementary school readers and be compulsory reading for generations to come. Yes, the story is that good and hopefully will not get lost among the many other published works. - Sylvia Cochran -Roundtable Reviews

"Have read with great pleasure" - actress Joanna Lumley

The author adds a surprise ending to this delightful tale that made me clap with glee. For an almost magical tale of good vs evil 'The Ice Palace' is the book to read! - Natasha@ Romance Junkies.

Armistice :
".....a poignant story, this time of men at war, their thoughts on home and those they left behind. The story of these courageous men will pull at your heart and your soul. Well done Bill. the movies couldn't do it any better" - Rose Brungard – Romance at Heart Magazine

Whitby: Vampires Return?:
"A classic detective tale with all the right stuff, and the hint of love as well. I hope he decides to bring Clare around again, because she is one classy lady, as well as being a good cop. This is a must read.... Whitby is definitely on my must keep list" - Rose Brungard – Romance at Heart Magazine

Dedication

I would like to dedicate this set of tales to those who love variety in stories.

Acknowledgements

With grateful thanks to DCL publishers Stuart Bazga & Pam Seres. To Ashley Roland - Pearson for her inspired cover work on the e-books and to Annie Marshall for this book's cover. To editors Jan Douglas and Jean Watkins & Pat Kempe for their patience and clear sightedness and not least to my friend and fellow DCL author Kate Hofman for her wise counsel and support. I would like to add, also, my special thanks to Tracey Bell of Scream Management Blackpool U.K. for her early encouragement.

B. H.

My website
http://www.billhaworth.com

Table of Contents

Stonehenge

"Are we there yet Daddy?" asked Jesse, the younger of the two girls who were sitting blindfolded on the car's back seat. The Jack Russell terrier sitting on her lap also sported a small blindfold. Jesse thought it looked cute.

"Well, if you take that silly blindfold off, you will be able to see where we are," her father said.

"But Holly is wearing one," Jesse complained.

"That's because it's her birthday and her surprise," her mother explained.

"All right," Jesse grudgingly agreed, and turning to her sister said, "Holly, you keep yours on and I'll read you some clues. You have to guess where we are."

"Okay," said her elder sister, her blonde hair draping the top of her blindfold and her freckles underneath.

Jesse removed her frilly handkerchief blindfold, and rubbed her eyes in order to focus. She looked out of the car window and read out loud the road sign as they whizzed by, "We are on the A303. It's the road to...."

"Sshh!" her mother interjected, "Not too many clues now."

To any passersby they must all have appeared a strange sight what with the blindfolded dog and all; but they were a happy family perhaps with a trace of healthy eccentricity running through their genes, but where's the harm in that? The fact that Professor Bush, eminent history teacher at the prestigious Fulchester University, had decided upon *Holly* as the name for his first born confirmed that tendency toward the slightly eccentric, though he preferred to call it *Thinking outside of the box.*

Upon Jesse removing the Jack Russell's blindfold, it immediately stuck it's head through the window to smell the sweet country air rushing by and see what was going on.

"Say a town or village, not a number," insisted Holly, as she played with a gold chain, holding a gold letter '*H*' around her neck. Holly loved her birthday present from her parents and was secretly pleased that they saw her now as almost a grown up. *A gold necklace*! *Wow!* For her fourteenth birthday she half expected something sensible from them such as shoes or a frock, but a gold necklace! Now that was grown up! That was proof enough that her parents were acknowledging their child was leaving girlhood behind. How pleased and grown up she felt, despite her freckles.

Although Jesse loved her sister and fully appreciated that this was her birthday, she couldn't help feeling a twinge of jealousy at Holly receiving so much attention.

"Mum," she asked, "why does Holly get a gold necklace for her birthday and for mine all I got was a pair of shoes?"

Her mother formed her answer as delicately as she could, "Darling, it's not really the gift that matters so much, it's the thought behind it, and your sister being older than you deserves a present befitting her age."

Jesse thought for a moment then replied, "But Mum, she will always be older than me! Does that mean she will always receive better presents?"

"No darling," Mum replied, "you will get what is appropriate to your age, now be a good girl and be happy for your sister. She is growing into a young lady as you soon will and she will be of help to you in so many ways."

"What ways?" demanded Jesse.

Mum answered, "Never mind for now," and kissed her on the forehead.

Holly was also thrilled to know that this day out was planned as an extra treat; not only for the birthday girl but for the whole family as well. '*Where are we going?*' she wondered. '*Will I like it?*'

To give her eldest daughter a clue, Mum asked, "What is the date today darling?"

"Why you know what day it is. It's my birthday," said Holly.

"Not the day," corrected Mum, "I said the date!"

"Well, it's the twenty first of June of course," answered the bemused girl.

As they turned a corner, Holly heard the sound of what she thought was an outdoor rock concert in the distance. "Hey! What's all that noise?" she asked. "Rock music? Oh – I've got it. I know where we are; we're at the Glastonbury music festival, aren't we?"

"Nope," said Dad, "We're miles away from Glastonbury, anyway it's the wrong month."

Jesse piped up, "Between Amesbury and Winterbourne Stoke."

"So?" asked Holly, a confused frown furrowing her brow.

"Not far from Salisbury," Dad said.

"What else happens on the twenty first of June?" Mum asked.

As the car carrying the family of four through the Wiltshire countryside on that sunny summer's day, the penny dropped and Holly suddenly cried out, "The summer solstice! I've got it! I know where we're going. It's Stonehenge isn't it?"

"Aw, Jesse, you gave it away," said Dad.

"No, you gave her too many clues," Jesse cried.

With that Holly took her blindfold off and took in the amazing view that greeted them.

As the car came to a halt by a large wooden farm gate Mags, their Jack Russell, yapped excitedly at the scene that greeted them. The gate led onto a great field of acres and acres of open downland. There seemed to be hundreds of people there milling around treading and ploughing up the once green field underneath them.

Luckily there had been no rain or the ground would have suffered more. Cars and vans of all makes and models were parked in a disorganised and haphazard way.

Dad noticed that in the distance people were cavorting to rock music from a band, which had erected a makeshift stage in the field. Noisy diesel generators powered the amplifiers. Were it a colder day the hot fumes could rise above the crowds but as it was a warm day they had to endure the smelly fumes polluting the sweet country air.

"Why are some of the people dressed in those long robes, Dad?" asked Jesse, "They look more like those worn by medieval folk."

"Oh, I guess they will be the Druids," explained Dad.

"Real ones?" asked Jesse.

"Some take it seriously," said Dad, "but not these characters; they're just dressed that way for the occasion."

Mum commented, "I don't know about you, but they look drunk to me!"

"Aw, they're just having fun, Mother," Dad said, "The public are only allowed on to the field once a year. It's a big day for the Druids."

"Druids off their heads?" observed Mum, "I've seen nothing like it!"

"Well, what does it matter?" asked Dad, "They're just getting into the spirit of things."

Witnessing the crowd's drunken antics, Mum said, "I guess the *spirit* of things is right. Fluid Druids, is what I would call them!"

Holly and Jesse looked on the scene with excitement. "It's so cool!" cried Holly, "It's the summer solstice; and on my birthday too. Oh wonderful. Thank you Mum, thanks Dad!"

The crowd of merrymakers parted to allow the vehicle to pass and there straight ahead about fifty yards from them was the great monolith itself; the massive series of stone structures that had defied centuries of battering from the elements. There it stood as it had for thousands of years as if defying people to figure out, not only its original purpose but how on earth it was constructed in the first place. There in all its ancient, brooding glory for all to see and marvel at; stood the mystery that is...........*Stonehenge.*

"Happy birthday, Holly," said Dad and hugged his eldest girl.

"Happy fourteenth, darling," said Mum.

"Oh this is so cool!" cried a delighted Holly. "I've been studying Stonehenge for my 'A' levels. I know lots about it, really I do!"

"C'mon," said Dad as he drove through the gate and found a place to park. "Let's get out and take a stroll around and see what's going on."

Working their way past the cavorting gangs of hippies and road travellers, they made their way towards the mound that surrounded the monument.

Dad explained, “The public are normally denied access any further because of a riot they had in 1985, but the council gave way and decided that once a year on the day of the solstice they would permit limited controlled access.”

“Well, I guess it attracts that many tourists bringing in all that revenue, they had to give in a little,” added Mum, “I notice we have a police presence just now.”

“That’s par for the course these days,” said Dad, “for public order as well as safety. Apparently a while back the place was never cordoned off and souvenir hunters tried to chip off bits of the stones. It is owned by the crown and managed by English Heritage with the surrounding land owned by The National Trust and they are not about to allow louts to desecrate the site like what happened in 1985.”

“Why? What happened then?” asked Mum.

Dad went on, “Well, apparently there had always been a Stonehenge Free Festival but in that year the place was swamped by hippies and new age travellers and turned it into a real fiasco. They trashed the place, got off their heads with drink and drugs and generally ran amok. The police had to be called in and by all accounts things got pretty heavy. Since then the council and the English Heritage said no way was that going to happen again.”

“So, how come we have such a crowd today?” asked Mum.

“Well,” replied Dad, “Like you said, I guess the powers that be relented as now Stonehenge is a great source of revenue from tourists.” Taking a look around the massive site full of travellers, hippies, neo-Druids and members of the public, he added, “But by the looks of things, today it could get out of hand again.”

Amidst the noise of the blaring rock music and boisterous assembly, a man stood on a soapbox and was attempting to give a speech. He was dressed in the style of a neo-Druid in that he was robed and hooded. He carried a staff in one hand and a microphone in his other. Around his mic was wrapped a sprig of mistletoe, and having a less powerful amp than the rock band meant he was struggling to be heard.

He addressed the crowd. “I am Rowan,” he said, “Arch-Druid and High Priest of the Celtic Neo-Druids. We are philosophers, doctors, seers, judges and astronomers from pre-history and have been entrusted to look after this henge for millennia.”

“Rubbish!” shouted a voice from the crowd, “You lot came around the second century B.C. This place is three to six thousand years old!”

“Who’s to say?” asked Rowan with a benign smile.

Jeers and guffaws went up from the man’s cronies. “Not you, pal!” said one.

“You want to learn your history, mate!” shouted another.

"Nevertheless," Rowan went on, "we were here before the Romans and are even pre-Celtic."

Another drunken voice shouted out, "You look more like pre-*historic*!"

Loud jeers and guffaws almost drowned out the Arch-Druid's words. He continued, "The religious beliefs and practices for which Stonehenge was first built are ancestral to those of the later Celtic Druids."

"Yaah – get lost!" shouted another crowd member, "No one knows who built it or why. You lot just took it over so you could have your heathen sacrifices."

"There are no sacrifices nowadays my friends," replied the Arch-Druid, "and as for the reason for its construction, we have many scholars exploring the possibilities of it being an ancient astronomical observatory, as well as a religious meeting place. So please, be welcome one and all to this sacred plot on Salisbury Plain. To those of you who arose early to witness the sun rising and also to those who have arrived later, we entreat you all to respect and revere this auspicious occasion of the Summer Solstice."

Rowan, the Arch-Druid, attempted to explain the rituals involved at the summer solstice, but the crowd were too drunk, boisterous and bored with him to pay any attention. Looking up at the clear sunny sky, he noticed a dark cloud and stopped to judge which way it might be going. '*A downpour would be most welcome about now,'* he thought, '*might induce those idiots to clear off and leave the day to those serious about the event.*'

Policemen in twos mingled in the crowd and kept a wary eye out for potential flare-ups of violence or bad behaviour. They came upon a group of louts kicking a football. One policeman immediately confiscated it, much to one lout's displeasure.

"You can pick it up from our mobile patrol van when you leave," one officer told him.

Jesse herself found it difficult to concentrate on the Druid's boring sermon and instead played with her dog.

"Stop throwing that frisbee around, Jesse, or else that policeman will lock you up," Dad warned her.

The family of four moved through the crowd and headed towards the mound surrounding the site of Stonehenge proper.

In defiance, Jesse threw the frisbee for Mags to chase. It flew over the earthworks surrounding a circular setting of large standing stones.

Behind one of them were a couple of new – age travellers/hippies in a sleeping bag. Nobody thought this unusual as most people had been up very early that morning to witness the sunrise on this day of the summer solstice and were no doubt tired or drunk or both by now. It turned out, however, that the two pretend Druids were both drunk, or stoned up to the eyeballs, and were in fact indulging in frantic sex within the limited confines and privacy of their sleeping bag.

Dad reached the spot where the engrossed couple lay before the others did. Upon being confronted with the scene, he immediately turned around and walked back in the opposite direction. "Not this way kids," he said, "let's go round that way," he said pointing to an alternative route to the centre of the henge.

Mum was horrified at the disgraceful spectacle. "The dirty beasts! That's disgusting!" she said.

"What is?" asked Jesse, her interest aroused by her mum's remark.

"Never you mind," Dad shouted and dragged her away so she wouldn't witness the obscene spectacle.

"In broad daylight, too!" Dad fumed, "The bloody pigs!"

Jesse asked her sister, "What were they doing, Holly?"

Holly was of an age and education enough to understand the goings on within the sleeping bag. She was also aware that her younger sister should be kept in complete ignorance of such matters.

"Oh, they're just drunken idiots messing around. Don't pay them any attention."

That satisfied Jesse's curiosity and she ran off ahead with Mags, the dog, throwing the frisbee for him as they went.

Mum and Holly said nothing but just exchanged a half smile and slightly embarrassed looks. '*What a wise little girl her daughter was,*' Mum thought.

To Dad's dismay the hurled frisbee did a u-turn in mid-air and landed in the vicinity of the engrossed hippies in the sleeping bag.

"I'll get it!" shouted Dad, "You three go on. I'll catch you all up."

By now more sightseers had made their way to the mound and saw for themselves the cavorting couple thrashing around inside their sleeping bag. Blind drunkenness, the effect of drugs or just sheer concentration on satisfying their lust made the couple oblivious to all the jeers and catcalls from onlookers.

Dad retrieved the plastic frisbee but the dog kept jumping up at him in an attempt to effect its release from his strong grip. This gave Dad an idea. He tormented Mags by offering it to him then refusing to let it go. The dog was becoming annoyed and started growling.

When he thought the Jack Russell was suitably enraged, Dad deliberately threw the plastic frisbee at the couple in the sleeping bag. Dog and master made a bee-line for it. The dog barked noisily as he again was refused his toy, but skilfully Dad drew the angered dog's attention away from the frisbee directing it rather to the rapidly moving lump within the sleeping bag which was in fact the male partner's backside.

Enraged and frustrated, the mad hound sunk his teeth into the flailing backside. Its sharp gnashers penetrated the sleeping bag and amidst feathers flying the hippie on the receiving end of Mags' annoyance let out an almighty "Aaaaagghhh!"

The dog, enraged at being denied his favourite toy, was now startled and aggravated more by the hippie's pain-induced hollering and so bit again.

The sleeping bag's screaming male occupant thrust his hips forward in an involuntary movement to escape the hound's savage buttock chomping attacks. "He's biting my arse!" he yelled in pain, "Get 'im off! Get 'im off!"

The recipient of the said pelvic thrusts squealed in delight and yelled out, "Oooh no! Bite him again! Bite him again!"

The gathering crowd were in hysterics and encouraged the dog to bite the hippie's ass some more.

Feeling pleased with himself, Dad grabbed Mags and dragged him off the distressed hippie, who could only make pleas for the first aid man to hurry and attend his shredded posterior. '*Serves the bugger right*!' Dad thought to himself, and threw the frisbee towards his family up the hill.

Finding extrication from the sleeping bag somewhat difficult, the injured hippie struggled to wriggle out of it.

In passing, the Arch-Druid Rowan also displayed his rage at what he thought was the hippies' continued sexual shenanigans in the sleeping bag, and so he stomped down hard on the male's already severely lacerated buttocks. "Take that from me, you heathens!" he cried.

This prompted another death-curdling "Aaaaaaggghhh!" from the male followed by a satisfied "Aahhhh!" from his lady partner.

Upon catching up with his family, Dad was pleased to see Holly reciting her knowledge of the area to Mum and sister Jesse.

Dad and Mum were both teachers, she in the infant's and junior's school and Dad was a History professor at Fulchester University. That he gave Holly extra lessons on her and his favourite subject was now paying dividends as her school exam marks testified, which meant she had an excellent chance of attending his university after she left school.

He stood back and with glowing pride and admiration listened to his eldest child engaging in conversation with one of the official guides at Stonehenge.

"This collection of structures was not all built at the same time but rather over a period of some three thousand years," the guide said.

Confidently and authoritatively Holly added, "And if you include the very earlier wooden version of the henge, then the construction phase could be said to have lasted between three to six thousand years!"

Much to Mum and Dad's delight the gathering sightseers appeared impressed by Holly's knowledge.

The official guide seemed less so.

"Hmm; quite," he agreed begrudgingly, "we are standing within a raised circular mound known as the earthworks; which in archaeological terms refers to any artificial changes in land levels. They can vary in height from a few centimetres to over forty metres as over on Silbury Hill and run along for miles in a linear fashion as in Offas Dyke; which was the old border between England and Wales."

"What are these holes in the ground?" asked one of the sightseers.

"Oh – I know the answer to that!" Holly piped up. "They are Aubrey holes and were used to support wooden posts when Stonehenge was all made of wood. Isn't that right?"

"You are correct girl," confirmed the Arch-Druid Rowan as he approached and joined the small gathering. "When wooden posts were not required the holes were filled in with, er...well, do you know what?" he asked her.

"As a matter of fact I do, sir," replied Holly confidently, "they were filled with the ashes from cremations."

The official guide was becoming impatient with these two high-jacking his little speech. "No doubt from the ritual sacrifices your lot got up to, you heathens!" he accused the Druid.

"Which confirms my theory that this was a site of a religious order in ancient times," the Druid answered.

"Nonsense!" the guide said, "it is scientifically accepted that first and foremost Stonehenge was an astronomical observatory of some kind."

Holly interjected, "Why could it not have been used as both? You know, at different times, I mean?"

Not wanting to get in a heated discussion with a mere child as well as a druid, the guide gave a haughty sniff and bade the crowd follow him as he made his way further into the site.

Dad gave Holly an affectionate hug as they all followed behind. He was pleased at his daughter display of reasoning as well as knowledge of the subject which showed she could hold her own with not one, but two adults; and professionals at that. He knew a lot of her knowledge and education was down to him giving her extra tutoring and to some degree it might have been passed down through the genes, which only served to make him doubly proud of his bright daughter.

Moving along, the guide answered no more questions but concentrated on delivering his schpiel in *parrot–fashion* manner which only served to confirm to Holly his boredom with the subject. Even so, interesting facts couldn't help but spill through his dreary monologue. The crowd learned that the Sarsen circle was at one time comprised of thirty trimmed sandstone blocks, only seventeen of which now remained.

They learned that the Sarsen Circle originally had shaped lintels on top of their uprights forming a continuous circle around the top. One of the lintels lay alone on its side and it had been decided this was the Slaughter Stone for ritual sacrifices. The guide couldn't help but inform them of this possibility without a sneer in the direction of the Arch-Druid.

The interested crowd also learned that two of the four Station Zones were surrounded by circular ditches causing the interior of those circles to appear mound-like and have lead to the notion they were burial mounds or *barrows* as they were known, that sacrificed persons were entombed in.

In mute response to this suggestion, Rowan looked at Dad and shook his head.

"Mum," said Jesse, "I'm bored."

"Be quiet, darling," Mum urged, and pointed over to a solitary object a way off. "What's that?" she asked.

Rowan told her, "That is the Heel stone. At the time of the solstice the sun rises directly above that stone and shines into the open arms of the Horseshoe arrangement. Very mystical, don't you think?"

"Not really," said Dad, "more like an astronomical calendar if you ask me."

The guide gave the pair a dirty look. '*Another expert!*' he thought to himself, '*That's all I need! I have three of them at it now!*' With an audible sigh he proceeded with his talk. "Now folks," he continued, "within the Bluestone Oval stands an arrangement of stones called the Trilithon Horseshoe, ten upright stones arranged as five freestanding pairs. Each originally had a horizontal lintel, but now only three Trilithons were complete with such, and as the two gentlemen pointed out, the sun rises over the Heel Stone a ways off over there, and hits the centre of this horseshoe arrangement. It is mind-boggling to know how such accuracy was calculated in those far off times."

"It must have been a sight to see back in the day," mused Dad.

Others in the crowd agreed, but by this time Jesse had lost all interest in the guide's talk.

She fancied the two pillars of the upright Bluestone Trilithons with its horizontal piece might have been a goal post for an ancient soccer team. That's what she would use it for, if only she had brought a soccer ball.

Bored with the guide's droning talk and uninterested in the music festival of the would-be hippie/druids in the fields behind them, she resorted to throwing the frisbee for Mags. '*At least that would be more fun than listening to the guide's boring old yapping about a bunch of old stones,*' she thought. She reached back as far as she could and - Whooosh! With a great lob, away went the frisbee soaring over the stone lintels far off towards one of the Station Zones, the supposed burial mounds.

It landed in a pile of loose stones that appeared as though they were a collapsed structure of some kind. The Jack Russell wasted no time in darting over there to retrieve it.

Just then the dark cloud that Rowan had noticed looming earlier passed over the sun and darkened the sky. The sudden rainfall caught everyone unawares as it lashed down fiercely on all and sundry. In a matter of moments everyone was soaked to the skin and enmasse they all ran for whatever shelter they could find.

"Hurry, kids!" shouted Dad taking Mum's hand as they raced back to where the car was parked.

"Come on, Mags!" shouted Jesse, but the dog was determined not to go without his precious toy.

"I'll get him!" shouted Holly, "I'm closer. You get in out of the rain."

As she ran to get the dog, Holly hardly noticed the Arch-Druid Rowan standing stock still in the pouring rain absolutely soaking wet and laughing.

The drenched Druid raised his arms aloft, "Have I done this?" he shouted. "Have the powers that be finally listened to me?"

Laughing insanely, he took great delight in witnessing dozens of soaked and sodden hippies churn up the muddy field in a mad scramble to reach their vehicles. '*The sacrilegious swine*!' he thought to himself.

"Mags! Mags! Come here, boy," cried Holly.

A crack of thunder and a blinding lightning flash made the dog yelp in startled surprise. The brilliance of the light from the flash momentarily illuminated the scene. An upright sandstone column with its horizontal lintel was reproduced in shadow on the ground.

The panicking Jack Russell appeared to run through the non-existent opening and Holly followed Mags into the optical illusion.

"There you are, you silly boy," said a relieved Holly. As she watched the family pet shake himself dry, she was suddenly aware that it had stopped raining as quickly as it had begun. The sky was clear and sunny again. "I've got him!" she shouted, as Mags jumped into her arms; but as she turned around she was shocked to see that the scene had completely altered. There was no one in sight, at all; no family, no rushing sightseers, no hippies, no vehicles – only the still silence of a warm summer's day. Momentarily confused, Holly stood on top of the stone rubble to gain a better view.

She could neither see nor hear any traffic in the distance; what was more disconcerting, there appeared to be a small wood where the road should have been. "*I don't understand*," she said to herself.

"Oh!" said a startled voice in the distance. It belonged to a young man wearing a long robe and carrying a staff. They were the only two people on that lonely moor. '*This is most strange,*' thought Holly.

As the young man dropped to his knees and made the sign of the cross, a loud crack of thunder scared the dog so that it jumped out of Holly's arms. He darted back across the pile of rubble at the same instant the lightning cast the same shadow of the monument on the ground. Holly tried to follow but the shadowy entrance had gone. "Mags! Where are you? Mags!" she yelled.

Appearing on the other side of the rubble Mags jumped back into the scene he had left only moments ago. The rain was still lashing down and all the people were frantically running for cover.

Upon finding Jesse, the Jack Russell barked wildly at her and ran back to mound of rubble where last he had seen Holly.

"What is it, Mags?" asked Jesse.

The dog continued barking furiously at the pile of rubble.

Sensing something was wrong, Mum and Dad joined Jesse at the mound.

In tears, Jesse blurted out, "It's Holly, Mum, she's disappeared!"

"What?" cried Mum, "she can't have!"

Dad grabbed hold of Jesse, "Talk sense, girl!" he shouted, "Stop crying. What do you mean *disappeared*?"

The sobbing Jesse pointed to the pile of rubble at which Mags was barking frantically.

"What's he barking at; the idiot?" demanded Dad, "There's nothing there!"

"Holly went to fetch the frisbee and she just disappeared; there!" explained his sobbing daughter.

Mum cradled the distraught girl as Dad dug furiously around the mound, thinking she might have fallen down a hole. Try as he may, he could find no holes.

As the lightning flashed once again, he briefly caught a glimpse of a girl as though in a mirage. "Holly!" he cried in stunned surprise.

"Dad! Dad! Help me!" Holly cried out, "I can't get back!"

Rowan the Arch-Druid ran over to survey the scene. An eerie glow of static electricity had formed on the wet upright stones. With one hand he rubbed one of the wet stones. At once he realised what had happened. "Holly!" he shouted, "When the lightning flashes again, run back through the same place you went in."

"Help me, please!" cried Holly from the other side. "Mum, Dad, help me!"

The official guide turned up, demanding, "What's going on?" He turned a deathly pale as he saw the fading mirage like image of Holly by the mound.

No more lightning flashed as the wind blew away the black cloud. Dad stood helpless as the mirage that was his daughter faded. Racking his brains, her father shouted, "Think Holly, think. Use your brains, darling."

"What can I do?" came Holly's faint reply.

"Find a holy man," Rowan shouted. "We'll try to do something from this side."

As the sun broke through and bathed the scene with light once more, the mirage was gone. The devastated Mum and Jesse clung to each other while a few shocked onlookers tried consoling them.

"What just happened?" Dad yelled to the Druid, "If you know what all this is about tell me, now!" he demanded.

Rowan put his hand on Dad's shoulder and calmly told him, "Your daughter has fallen into another dimension; another time zone!"

Mum, Dad and Jesse stared at the Druid in disbelief.

"What?" demanded Mum, "What are you telling us?"

Rowan pointed to the pile of rubble and explained, "These are not simply a pile of old stones. They are the remains of a dolmen, a burial mound."

"So? What does that mean?" asked a worried Dad.

"Known as a cromlech, or dolmen or as I believe to be in this case, a *portal* dolmen. Originally it had three uprights which supported a cap of rock, a roof; then it was covered by bark and earth to form the dolmen; an above ground tomb in fact."

Mum, Dad and Jesse were confused, distraught and speechless, yet hung on to his every word.

The Druid continued, "And not just any old tomb. The stones were believed to have magical properties in themselves and placed on lines of energy these *portal* dolmens were supposed to convey the spirit of the deceased to the next world." He paused, then added, "Or another world!"

"Oh no!" cried Mum, "my baby!"

"Well, that's just bloody dandy!" moaned Dad.

Rowan took his cloak off and covered Mum with it. "Better sit her down before she faints," he advised.

Dad and Jesse helped her to sit on a rock, but she refused, preferring the wet ground instead.

"What rubbish!" snapped the official guide, "Stonehenge is an ancient contraption for working out the dates and seasons for the planting and harvesting crops. It's a calendar, that's what it is!" he insisted.

"You saw what just happened!" snapped Dad.

Patiently, Rowan explained, "This great structure at Stonehenge is of a multiple purpose. The stones themselves are of near indestructible quality and erected at this particular site of terrestrial energetic powers and celestial significance." Turning to the guide he added, "It is indeed an astronomical observation device as you say, but it was used on those particular periods in the annual cycle when the Earth's energies were most highly influenced by the sun, moon and stars. Festivals of renewals were held at those charged, energetic periods which had been determined by astronomical observation."

"Wow!" said the guide, "So it was a matter of science being used in aid of the mystical?"

"That's one way of putting it, yes," affirmed the Arch-Druid, "and all these stones of special qualities are positioned in such a way as to create a specific form of sacred enclosure which functions as a type of battery for gathering, storing and expressing earth energies of the site on festival days."

"But what can we do to get our daughter back?" begged the distraught mother.

Putting his arm around Dad he said, "The Professor and I shall go to work on it, right away."

Mum scolded Jesse, "You and your blasted frisbee!" she said.

"Mum, I'm sorry, so sorry!" cried Jesse.

With tears streaming down their faces, they hugged each other.

The official guide had listened intently and realised that this could mean great publicity for Stonehenge with the possibility of more government or indeed private funds being made available to research this new phenomena.

In response to his call on his mobile phone, the police and ambulance arrived on the site. Mum was treated for shock and Dad, the Druid and the official all tried to convince the somewhat skeptical police of the fantastic event.

* * * *

The frightened young man on his knees begged Holly, "Spare me, please. Are you a Draugr or a witch?" The goats he had been tending had run off in a panic when Holly appeared.

"Don't be stupid!" said Holly, gaining confidence now she could see the lad was obviously terrified; of *her*. "Who are you and what's a *draugr* when it's at home?" she demanded.

"An un-dead creature which haunts the burial mound," answered the scared lad.

"I'm not un-dead, and I'm not a witch. I'm lost and I want to know what's going on!" she yelled.

"But, but the magic koun?" he stammered.

"Magic what?" she queried.

"The koun," he repeated, "the hound, the dog!"

"Oh! You mean my dog? But he's not magic."

"Yes," he said, "The one that disappeared. You called him *magic*."

"Mags!" she said, "I called him *Mags*."

"Does that mean *magic* where you are from?"

"No, you stupid boy," Holly remonstrated, "that's just his name. Now tell me, what is this place? What's going on? Where am I?"

"You just appeared out of thin air, my lady," explained the lad.

She thought for a while and said, "Yes, it's weird. I saw my father disappear, over there. It's not raining here, either. I don't know how it happened but I've been conveyed to, to where?" she asked. "The place looks the same. Perhaps I'm in another dimension."

"I do not understand your words, my lady," pleaded the lad.

Holly had an idea. She lifted her arm to show the lad her wristwatch. "Have you ever seen such as this before?" she asked him.

"Is it a jewel? An adornment of some nature?" he asked.

"It tells the time," she said.

Looking puzzled he asked, "A small hour glass?"

"Thought so," said Holly to herself, as a creeping realisation dawned on her that time had played a trick.

"Look boy, what's your name?"

He replied, "Alan, my lady," then after a pause, added, "it means *handsome.*"

"Yes, quite," she said, "my name is Holly."

"Aagh! No!" he cried. "As I thought, you are *Hallawes,* the witch goddess!"

I am no such thing, you fool!" Holly snapped. "My name is Holly – Holly Bush. Get up off your knees and listen; I need to know what year this is!"

"Hollybush?" the lad asked. He noticed the gold necklace with the letter '*H*' around her neck. "You are the hollybush? The hollybush that protects the sacred mistletoe? You are a good witch sent by the Druids?"

"Yes, if you like," answered the girl, "now I know *where* I am, but not *when;* please answer me."

He accepted her hand and rose to his feet. He was somewhat pleased and relieved to feel she was solid and not an apparition as he had at first thought. Puzzled, he answered her, "Why my lady, it is the year sixty in the year of our Lord."

"Oh my word!" cried Holly, and thought to herself, '*I have travelled back though time. What to do, what to do. What did Dad say – think. I am thinking. The Druid! He said find a holy man.*'

"Alan, tell me; do you know of any holy men?"

Alan answered, "Since the Romans came upon our shores they have brought their holy men; the priests. A lot of our people have converted but many still remain loyal to the old ways of the Druids."

"Where are the priests?" asked Holly.

"They march with the army to the east to put down the uprising of the Iceni tribe and Boudica their fierce queen. I know of no others nearby, but my father, Corann, has some knowledge of holy verses; if you deem Druids to be holy that is."

"Of course!" said Holly, "Druids! Can you take me to him?"

"Yes, my lady. My family live but a moment away over the brow of yon hill; follow me."

Shortly after, Holly and Alan arrived at a building of meagre construction.

'Probably mud brick. Wattle and daub perhaps?' Holly thought.

The two youngsters were met by a stocky grey-haired man of around sixty years of age or so it appeared to Holly.

Wearing a look of amazement on his grizzled features, the man looked Holly up and down. He pondered while his wife came from the house to join them. She was a plump woman with a happy face. The wife stared at Holly's strange clothes. Presently she asked, "Where have you come from, child?"

"Well, I..." Holly began.

Alan interrupted, "She came from yonder, Mother," and pointed to the henge.

The pleasant faced old woman smiled at her then to her husband and her son, Alan, in turn. Holly felt reassured by her demeanour.

The old man introduced himself as Corann, Alan's father. "Corann means *Magical Druid,*" he explained, "which I am neither but my family were steeped in the old beliefs. These days it is best to keep one's head down as they say; bad enough the Romans fostering bad feelings amongst all the villagers.

They cannot take out their anger on an army but they might use a druid as a scapegoat. I am known as Llwyd," he told her, "it is because of this." Smiling, he stroked his full head of grey hair.

"Oh, I see; it's a nickname!" said the perceptive Holly.

Unfamiliar with the term, Llwyd just smiled and invited them all to enter the house. "Now tell me, child, where do you come from?" he asked.

"I don't know how this will sound, but I think I am from another time," she told Alan's baffled parents.

The mother asked Holly, "Were you playing by the stones? Did a rock fall on you, is that what happened, child? Did you bang your head?"

Realising this was not going to be easy for them to understand, Holly simply answered, "Er, well... possibly."

Alan's parents exchanged a knowing look and with that all entered the house.

With an arm around his son's shoulder, Llwyd whispered to Alan, "Looks like your prayers have been answered, son."

Over a bowl of *cawl* soup – made from the previous days leftovers followed by a basic meal of offal, the less valuable parts of a carcass such as heart and liver; supplemented by lentils and beans and other such seeds and pulses with plenty of bread and goat's milk, Llwyd explained to Holly that he and his wife, Olive, had moved to the area from nearby Wessex after the Romans seized their property to house troops. Thinking they would escape them, they moved on and settled near the town known as Old Sarum, an old village now taken over by the Romans. Fearing the move to the busy garrison town might be a case of jumping out of the frying pan and into the fire, Corann/Llwyd decided they ought to try to placate the

Romans if possible for the sake of his family.

Despite owning but one cow that meant they had milk, a means of tilling the soil and beef when the cow was calved. They acquired a few goats, which subsisted on the most meagre of grass and produced good milk and cheese. Being of Celtic stock they were well used to foraging from the land and providing for themselves, producing not only enough food for themselves but enough left over to offer the Roman commander of the town. That way they had been left in relative peace, although this meant the neighbours harboured feelings of distrust and even jealousy toward them.

Despite this, Llwyd knew it was for the best and he would worry about his so-called friends and neighbours later; right now his main concern was the welfare of his immediate kin. The Roman army had no qualms over putting down any form of resistance to their new order in the most cruel and terrible way. With the burning of villages, executions of Celtic kings and leaders; and mass murders that could only be described as genocide; any notion of resisting the interlopers was aggressively swept aside. The last of the battles to break the Celts resistance was at that very moment taking place in Colchester where Boudica, the widow of the Iceni king Prasutagus was fighting in vain for a way of life never to return.

Reneging on their promise to allow Boudica to remain Queen upon her husband's death, the Roman army had whipped her mercilessly and raped her two daughters. Guerrilla strikes, battles and reprisals were now taking place in that unfortunate part of the country, which necessitated the presence of more troops and therefore their priests.

Over a hot drink of nettle tea, Holly told her hosts, "You appear to be a nice family. Can you help me? I am lost and need to find my way home again."

"Don't worry, child," said the kindly matron, Olive, "sleep now and we can tend your problems on the morrow."

Holly was tired and somewhat strained after the ordeal of that strange day. She gratefully accepted the use of Alan's room.

As she undressed and climbed into the straw-packed cot, Alan entered the room, his way lit by a burning candle. Smiling at her he put the candle by Holly's bed then took a sheepskin rug from the floor and lugged it over his shoulder. He said, "I shall sleep by the hearth. Good night, Holly."

"Er, good night, Alan," she answered timidly.

Before he left the room, he smiled at her and said, "Don't worry. You'll be fine.........I'm glad I found you."

****

Mum had taken to her bed, suffering from the stress of her lost daughter. The doctor had prescribed a strong anti-depressant to prevent her condition worsening. He feared the freeing of hormones and enzymes such as cortisone and adrenaline within her system could severely affect her heart rate and breathing. As she refused to go into hospital, Jesse stayed off from school to attend her, and be there to phone the hospital should an emergency arise.

While Mum agonized over Holly's fate, Dad and Rowan were busy searching for any information from any source to help them.

Dad immersed himself in his University library, with its books and computers able to access the best information possible from some of the world's most eminent authorities.

Meanwhile Rowan and his Druid fraternity scoured old parish records and manuscripts for anything that might give them clues to finding a solution for this terrible happening that had befallen the once happy family.

Church records, magistrate's records, old books relating to Stonehenge, witchcraft and druidism; all were scrutinised. Interpreters were brought in whenever they were unable to decipher old Celtic words phrases or references.

For over two months they struggled with this almost seemingly insurmountable problem. Mum grew weaker, Dad became more withdrawn as he concentrated his search, and all Rowan could do was to accept that only a miracle was going to bring Holly back from wherever or *whenever* she was.

****

Holly's new life in an old world passed slowly for her. There was so much to acclimate to apart from the seemingly impossible bridging of time itself; the lack of electricity, of running water; the strange beliefs of the locals; the feeling of being so alone yet cared for by her surrogate family. Worst of all, the soul searing anguish that came from realising she might never return to her own time.

She busied herself by helping Olive with the household chores and was amazed to learn from her that she used items very familiar to her.

"Olive," she said holding a small bulbous root, "You have garlic. I am surprised!"

"Oh yes!" said Olive, "The Romans brought such here to our land. It flavours the food and is supposed to purify the blood."

"In my time," said Holly, "we have discovered that garlic is one of nature's greatest antiseptics."

"Anti – what?" asked Olive.

"It's as you say, Olive; it keeps the blood pure. In fact with foods such as garlic and honey as part of a regular diet, you won't go far wrong."

They took to discussing the foods they knew in common. They found they knew old remedies such as '*Knitbone*' was the old word for comfrey whose leaves could be boiled and drank as a tea or applied as a poultice to repair damaged bones.

Holly was delighted to learn that even as long ago as in Olive's time honey was used topically on the skin as an aid for burns. Olive prided herself in telling Holly that making a poultice from mouldy bread would draw any poisons from wounds of the flesh.

"I know," said Holly, "but Olive, would you believe me if I told you that no harm would come to you if you ate the mouldy bread?"

"Why on earth would you do that, child?" asked the bemused matron.

"For internal infections, Olive," explained Holly, "it's what we call an antibiotic. It kills micro-organisms that infect your insides."

"Such words! Such words!" cried Olive, "I don't understand them."

Holly assured her that fevers could be brought under control with such a treatment. What assuaged Olive was Holly stating that many of the future medicines were discovered by tinkering around with old remedies such as Olive knew of and used regularly. To convince her she asked Olive, "What would you give a person if they had a headache?"

"Ah!!" cried Olive, "I would strip bark from the willow tree and boil it and administer as a hot drink. Believe me, child, there is no better cure."

"I do believe you, Olive," said Holly, "We have a pill or tablet called an aspirin which does exactly the same thing."

"Why, are there no more willows in your time?" Olive asked.

Holly laughed and explained that the aspirin was actually made from the same substance found with the willow bark. For heart problems we use digitalis which you know as *Foxglove*. To combat stress and palpitations we use *feverfew* as you do in these times."

This delighted Olive and she and Holly danced around the kitchen.

"We are from different times, child, but we are not so different are we?" said Olive.

"Indeed, no," said Holly, "We wouldn't have advanced so if it weren't for people such as yourself."

That drugs of one age were still in use in another delighted Olive, making her happy that their worlds were not so far apart after all.

They danced some more. They were still dancing when Alan entered the kitchen. "Oh! We have time for dancing do we, when I have the goats to milk?"

Holly laughed, "Come on, Alan, I'll help you. Show me how to do it."

With that she took his hand and rushed out to the field.

Placing a wooden pail under a female goat Alan showed off his milking skills, delicately teasing the teat and squirting the milk into the pail.

She admired his expertise in getting the milk efficiently and with no discomfort to the animal.

"The villagers think the goats are evil," he told her.

"That's just silly!" she said, "Why?"

"Well, it could be because of their funny-shaped eyes," he said, "or it could be because they have a habit of doing this!" With that he turned the teat upwards towards Holly and squirted her full in the face.

"Aah – you horror!" she yelled and chased him trying to pull his hair. They stood in the field larking around, pulling at each other's hair, followed by nips on the skin.

"Ow!" Alan yelled, "That hurt!"

"It was supposed to," laughed Holly.

The chasing and nipping and trying to avoid the nipping turned into tickling each other. Alan had got the better of Holly and she was being tickled mercilessly.

"Stop, stop. Please stop!" she laughed.

"Only if you give me a kiss!" he demanded.

"I certainly will not!" she cried.

With that Alan carried on with his tickles.

Holly was aching with laughter so to put a stop to him she kissed Alan quickly on the cheek.

He stopped. They both stood there looking at each other and getting their breath back. Without warning Alan grabbed Holly and kissed her passionately on the lips.

Holly pulled away. "What are you doing?" she cried.

A red- faced Alan apologised. "I don't know what made me do it," he told her.

"Well, don't do it again!" she snapped.

She and Alan had become very friendly as might be expected with youths of their age, but this was a step too far for the young Holly. She was confused and a little frightened by his actions and possibly, her own feelings.

"I'm sorry, Holly," said Alan, "I meant no harm. I am embarrassed."

"Alan," said Holly, "you are a nice boy and we are good friends, but I am not ready for this. There is too much confusion in my life already. I don't need this. We are just friends."

"But I have feelings for you that go beyond friendship," he told her.

Holly gave it some thought then said patiently, "Alan, I don't know what to say. I'm flattered, but how can this be?"

"I prayed for you, you know," he told her.

"What?" she stammered.

"The day you appeared to me, I had been praying to one of our Celtic gods for a love of my own. Then as if by magic you appeared. I took it as a sign."

"Now now, Alan," said Holly, "to begin with you don't believe in the old gods do you? You told me yourself how your whole family have now come to embrace Christianity."

"Well," said Alan, "the Romans are no example of what they preach, but in spite of their cruelty, we kind of believe in both," replied Alan. "We're just hedging our bets I suppose," he laughed

"You can't do that!" snapped Holly, "it's either one or the other!"

Alan showed her a small stone tile about twelve inches square. Chiselled onto the face was a depiction of a holly bush with the letters *H* and *B* either side of it.

"What's that?" asked Holly.

Alan told her, "Father and I are building a place to pray, near the house. He still has some of the old beliefs, but we must keep them secret lest the Romans or even the villagers take offence."

"I see what you mean by *hedging your bets*," said Holly. Stroking the chiselled tile she said, "It's quite beautiful really."

Alan declared his love, "Holly," he said, "I have grown to love you. You are a wise and lovely girl and I am a strong, hard working goat-herder. We are perfect for each other and anyway, are we not of age?"

"No, we most certainly are not!" said Holly.

Bemused by the forcefulness of her answer, he said, "But I am fifteen and you told me you have just turned fourteen years of age!"

"Well, then," said Holly, "there's your reason."

"I don't understand," Alan complained.

Holly explained, "Look Alan, we are far too young."

Alan laughed out loud, "Oh, I see it is a jest?" he asked.

"No jest!" Holly replied.

The confused lad asked, "Too young? At what age do you think a couple *should* marry?"

"Oh around twenty three or four I should think," was Holly's considered reply.

Alan was taken aback, "Marry in middle age? Why that is ridiculous Holly! No, no; we are of age now. We cannot wait until we are half dead. Now is the time for such as we to jump over the broomstick."

'Hmm – I wondered where that saying came from,' thought Holly.

She asked him what he meant. Why did he consider the age of twenty four to be middle–aged?

He answered, "Well, Mother and Father left it very late. They didn't marry until they were of the age you say is correct, and look at them now; almost at death's door."

This puzzled Holly greatly. “If they were wed at twenty four or thereabouts and you are fifteen, just how old are your mother and father?” she enquired.

“Father is forty two and Mother is now forty,” he told her.

Holly was shocked. They looked to her as though they could have been Alan’s grandparents.

“And how long is a person’s life expectancy in these strange days?” she asked

“Holly, my love, you ask very odd questions,” Alan said. “Look, let me explain; we marry at any time from early teen years onwards. Some couples are betrothed even earlier. Our mid twenties is middle-aged as we usually don’t last past forty odd years.”

Holly was shocked.

“Although I have heard that some last until very old age like sixty or so, but I don’t believe it.”

“Alan,” said Holly, “It appears your life span in this day and age is roughly half of that in my own age. We don’t die until our eighties on average and with advances in medicine it is thought that figure is likely to increase.”

“My goodness!” said a stunned Alan.

Holly thought to be diplomatic with the lad so as not to upset him. She said, “So you see Alan, fourteen is too young for me. I want a career. I want to do things first before I settle down. I am very flattered. You know I like you, very much.”

“Do you?” he asked earnestly, “Do you really?”

With a slight blush she answered, “Yes, silly. Of course I do.”

This satisfied Alan, but moments later he stated, “But you forget one thing my love, you now live in my times; therefore your life expectancy will be as short as mine.

“We should marry while we still can have relative good health. What do you say, my sweet?”

“I do care for you, Alan,” Holly told him, “but I miss my family so much. I have to find a way to return.”

“And if you cannot?” he asked, “Will you think about it?”

She smiled sweetly and promised the love-struck boy that she would think on the matter if her efforts to repatriate herself to her own times failed.

He tried once more, “I know we could be happy together, but I understand your dilemma. I do love you, Holly.”

She smiled tenderly and told him, “I know, Alan. I know.”

“Then the gods will decide,” he said confidently, “I believe they have brought you to me, and only they could take you away.”

‘*Good Lord!*’ thought Holly, ‘*this would be a matter requiring deep thought and wise counsel in any time period. I have enough to think about without all this.'* She resolved to put the matter of Alan's infatuation right out of her mind and concentrate the immediate problem of being a girl lost in time.

It did occur to her though, that in other circumstances things might have been different. Although certainly not ready for him, she did like him and allowed herself a wistful little smile at the thought of what might have been in another time or place.

Later, at supper Corann, or Llwyd as he liked to be known, asked Holly if she would like to write an account of life in a Celtic household, for posterity. She said she would enjoy this very much as she knew it would be of help to later generations of history scholars.

With Llwyd's help she would write of the old Celtic beliefs and traditions, but pleaded that she be allowed to write in her own words as in time his native tongue would disappear and other new languages would emerge.

"Oh, we know about Latin," Llwyd said, "A very difficult tongue."

"Latin will last through the ages," Holly told them, "but the English language shall prevail around the world."

"How do you know these things, child," asked Olive, "are you indeed a witch?"

"No, not at all," replied Holly and over the evenings talks by candle light, she persuaded the family that she had indeed slipped through a portal in time and for Holly this was almost two thousand years in her past.

"I am amazed, child," said Llwyd, "but not entirely disbelieving of your tale. Many a strange thing has occurred by the Stonehenge; but if that be true, Holly, you could tell us of many wonders to come, surely?"

Holly thought for a moment then told the family, "Without proving them you would find what I could tell you very difficult to believe. However, I am certain my limited knowledge of my own world would help you in this age."

"Oh really?" said Llwyd. "How so?" he asked.

"Well," Holly started, "Alan informs me that the average life span is only forty or so years."

"Alas, that is so," said Olive.

Holly told them, "I believe that is because of basic mistakes you are making, like not boiling impurities out of your drinking water."

"But we collect only running water from the stream," said Olive, "It is fresh, yet we still filter it through a sack cloth to remove even the smallest of things. No dirt can be seen in it, I assure you. We are clean; after all cleanliness is next to Godliness, don't they tell us?"

"Please, don't be offended at what I say," said Holly, "Your cleanliness is of a high standard but it needs improving, even as in my own time. There are germs, bugs or small animals if you will, that are so small they cannot be seen with the naked eye. Take my word for it that if you strain and then boil the drinking water first, you will eliminate many, many of today's illness and diseases to say nothing of the stomach gripes.

Also, and very important, is that you wash your hands before touching food, especially after performing your bodily functions. That has been the cause of many deadly illnesses. Please believe me. Remember my people live far longer than yours do today, and this is one of the reasons. Try what I say. What is there to lose? Judge me after a few months."

"Small animals?" laughed Alan.

"Your words have wisdom girl," said Olive, "We shall try your ways."

The father and son both nodded in agreement. Llwyd asked, "What can you tell us of the monsters that live elsewhere in the world?"

"Monsters?" asked Holly, "What monsters?"

"You know," said the father, "the dog-faced men, the elves, the fairies and giants who roam the forests."

"Well, have you seen any?" asked Holly.

"No," said Alan, "but we have heard tales."

"And that's all they are," assured Holly, "tales; folklore like this is common even on the other side of the globe. It's not true I tell you."

"The other side of the globe?" asked a confused Alan, "what globe?"

It occurred to Holly that they were not aware that the world was in fact round. When told this there was an outcry of disbelief.

Olive laughed, "Why child, people would fall off!"

"Or walk upside down!" laughed Alan.

Llwyd could see Holly wasn't laughing, "Do you jest with us, child?" he asked her, "We have met travellers, monks, merchants and such who have journeyed many, many miles, and everywhere they went the world was flat. This I believe."

"Well, if I had a ball I might convince you," said the girl.

"We have that animal's bladder the old crone found, don't we Father?" asked Alan; and hurried to fetch it from under his bed. "See? It is as round as a globe. It must have come from a strange animal indeed."

Holly looked at the object in amazement. "It is a soccer ball," she said. "It is a plaything for kicking around as in a game. Where did you get it?"

"Ursula the old healer says she found it one day by the Stonehenge," explained Olive, "but I don't trust her, she's a witch who conjured it up from a monster's bowels."

"No, it is from my world; my time," said Holly. "Look," she said holding the ball in the air, are not the sun and the moon the same shape? Then why not our world also?"

Llwyd humoured her, “It’s been a long day, child. Rest now; we shall talk more later.”

Holly thought it best not to bombard the family with too many new thoughts in one go. Intrigued and excited that a football could find its way to the past as well as herself, she asked if she could meet Ursula the healer sometime. The old woman might be able to throw some light on what had happened to her. At first opposed to the idea, Llwyd eventually agreed only if he and Alan went with her, armed with swords.

Over the next few days, Holly settled down to write Celtic recipes and tales of druid life in a journal for Llwyd. Whilst doing so, her mind raced for a solution to the problem of her being trapped in time. Based on her limited knowledge of Stonehenge and its myths, she asked herself *‘What if this were a special time when the earth’s energies were all building up into one place – this place just as that Rowan fellow had said? Would there be any more tricks in time? What conditions would apply? When would they manifest themselves? Under what conditions?’* She vowed to find out with the help of Llwyd and perhaps this the so-called old witch. Whilst writing, she had a brainwave of an idea, and began to scribble furiously in the journal.

****

Dad, Jesse and Rowan were at Mum’s bedside. She was very weak from not eating due to loss of appetite. Although semi-conscious, she could hear her husband say, “You must eat darling. The doctor will only admit you to hospital if you don’t and there they will feed you by a drip if they have to! Now come on. We are not going to lose another in the family. For our sake, as well as your own, please take some food.”

“Why should I bother?” Mum asked in a feeble whisper, “I have lost my child to another dimension. How will I ever get her back?”

There was no answer to that question. Dad and Rowan simply exchanged looks.

“We are doing all we can darling,” said Dad, “Rowan reckons we might be able to reproduce the same conditions as when she disappeared.”

“What good will that do?” asked Mum.

Rowan explained, “Scientists think stored up energies of some kind are released at the solstice. You never know. We have to consider everything.”

“But that is next year!” she cried, “I can’t leave my baby there a whole year!”

“It might not be a year, darling” Dad said, “We are studying the winter solstice in December. The same conditions might apply then.”

“December!” Mum cried, “Anything could happen before then.”

"At least it is not next summer solstice. It gives us some hope," Dad told her, "It's better than nothing."

Mum responded in grief-stricken groan.

"We have the best brains in the world working on it, my dear," said Rowan.

"And if they are not enough?" came the hoarse reply.

"We always have the power of prayer," he assured her, "It was a miracle of nature that took her, perhaps we ought to pray for a miracle to bring her back."

Mum partook of a spoonful of soup Jesse held to her mouth. With a groan she waved the rest of it away and laid her head back on the pillow.

Mags, the Jack Russell terrier, slept by her on top of the bed as he had done from the day they lost Holly, and would not be moved from Mum's side. Just then, Rowan's mobile cell phone rang.

"Oh, excuse me," he said to the family and went outside to take the call.

It was a colleague of his. "You should get down here right away," said the voice on the other end of the phone line.

Moments later an excited Arch-Druid rushed back into the bedroom. "You won't believe this!" he shouted.

Mags jumped up.

"What?" demanded Dad.

"What?" asked Jesse.

A feeble "What?" issued forth from Mum's lips.

"Well," said Rowan, "you know they are doing an archaeological dig about half a mile away?"

"Well, what of it?" snapped Dad.

The excited Rowan told them, "Let's just go there; right now."

"What is it for crying out loud?" demanded Jesse.

Rowan smiled and told her, "Not sure yet, child; but it might be that miracle we were praying for."

Five minutes later, Dad and Rowan were at the site of the archaeological dig. Rowan's friend, Callum, who had made the recent urgent phone call said, "Come this way, gents. I think you'll find this most interesting."

They climbed over the barrier tape and proceeded to climb down into a hole about ten feet square. "We found an ancient book," he told them, "we put it back inside under cover until you arrived."

At the bottom of the hole were two men delicately brushing the last of the loose earth away from a stone floor. Engraved onto the face of a stone flag was a diagram of a holly bush. Gently prising the stone away they uncovered the cavity it had sealed for thousands of years.

Wearing fine latex gloves, Callum carefully reached in and bought out a dusty and somewhat flaky parchment scroll with words that looked like Latin and Celtic written on it.

Dad and Rowan looked on with great concern and some confusion.

"Can it be read?" Rowan asked.

"Oh sure," confirmed Callum, "but it's what is written at the back of the manuscript that I think you will find surprising! Just take a look at this!"

At the back of the parchment scroll were strange words written in another language other than Latin or old Celtic. Rowan read out loud, "'*M plus D PLS HLP MNAD60 MOK.MLKD FTR.BY N/FMLY. PLS.HLP. MV : - (ILY.YDTR.XHOLLYX'* Is it Roman numerals?" he asked.

"It's gobbledegook!" said a disappointed Dad, "Just nonsense!"

"Far from it!" laughed Callum, "Why a child of five or six could read it."

"What are you talking about?" asked Dad barely able to conceal his annoyance at the flippant remark.

Callum went on, "Have you noticed it is written in a different coloured ink? That would be to draw attention to it, separate from the rest of the text."

"Is it a sort of code, then?" asked Dad eagerly.

"Sure is," Callum confirmed, "Notice I said *'from the rest of the* ***text****?'*"

Dad looked confused.

"It's a text message," said Callum, "from your daughter."

"What?" gasped Dad, "How? What do you mean?"

The archaeologist smiled and said, "She's written it in text speak. Look, I'll translate. It's easy, '*M plus D.*' That's '*Mum* ***and*** *Dad*'."

Dad and Rowan looked on amazed.

Callum went on, *"PLS HLP* is obviously '*Please help.*' *MNAD60 'Am in A.D. 60.' MOK* means *'Am O.K'. MLKD FTR BY N/FMLY* is *'Am looked after by nice family'* then that '*please help'* again and lastly, *M.V. : - (which means 'Am very* – then the sideways face, meaning - *sad.*' then *ILY.YDTR.XHOLLYX* which is obviously her saying *'I love you your daughter Holly'* with a kiss either side.

"My God!" gasped Dad, his eyes filling with tears as he realised it was in fact a message across the ages from his beloved daughter. "That's incredible!" he said, "But why did she write in text speak?"

"I would say," guessed Rowan, "in order to confirm that it is indeed from her."

"Also," added Callum, "that style supported by a different colour differentiates it from the rest of the manuscript. It stands out and makes it easier to spot."

"Of course!" said Dad, "How clever. That's my girl."

"You have a very bright daughter there, sir," Callum told him, "She guessed that you would search for her and so made her message on stone and buried it probably in a church of some kind.

Floors are always the last to go; she knew that. What we think we have uncovered are the remains of an ancient Celtic prayer house. The roof and walls long gone; but the stone floor remains."

"Amazing!" said Rowan.

Dad and Rowan embraced each other in happy delirium. "At least we have contact," said Dad, "Let's go back and tell Mum the news."

"But how do we help her?" asked the Arch-Druid.

"First things first," replied Dad, "Mum needs to know this. Come on."

****

While Mum was receiving the good news that would revive her broken spirit and give her the hope and strength she was badly lacking, elsewhere in a far off time a hand knocked on a door.

"I am Ursula," said the old crone whose bent scrawny body framed the doorway, "the healer."

"Please enter," said Holly.

Despite looking older than her years, the woman was fit enough to have trudged across a mile of rough fields from her home. She set herself down on a kitchen chair and spoke to Holly. "Well, my girl. I've been hearing a lot about you," she said.

"And I, you Miss Ursula," replied Holly, "You are a famous healer. Shall I make us some nettle tea?"

"Where is Olive?" asked the old woman.

"Tending the animals outside," replied Holly, "I think she tends them to allow us some privacy while we talk."

"Allow me," said Ursula and dug around in one of her many pockets. "I have brought my own leaves," she said, "no offence to the house but I concoct my own herbs to suit my own taste and many others will testify I make a delicious brew."

"Not at all," said Holly, "I should like to try some."

Allowing Ursula to make the tea, she watched her go through the procedure of filling a pot from the water jug, setting it on the open fire in the range and preparing two drinking mugs. This gave time for Holly to study the crone without seeming to intrusive. Holly thought that her guest could not look more like the archetypal witch of legends and folk tales if she tried. With a hooked nose, wrinkled skin and bad teeth she appeared more as a comedy caricature rather than a real person. '*Whatever skills this woman has,*' thought Holly, '*she is not a good advert for her so called healing potions; why she even has a wart on her chin! Her name sounds so glamorous too. 'Good Lord, she is anything but*!' It was all Holly could do to suppress a laugh, then charitably she thought, '*Well perhaps it's the local water.*'

"I know where you come from child!" said Ursula.

Holly was taken aback. "You do?" said asked.

"Mmm," she said, sipping her hot brew, "the same place where that bladder came from. I found it you know."

'So that window into the future must appear regularly' thought Holly. '*It wasn't just a one-off occurrence!*'

"I fell over it in the mud," she explained.

"Mud?" Holly queried.

"Yes," said Ursula, "it was a filthy September day of terrible weather; rain, thunder and lightning. I always go to the stone henge whenever it rains to wipe the water from the stones and collect it. They have healing properties you know?"

"Did you say September?" asked Holly.

"Why yes," replied Ursula.

"Not June?"

"No, child. Why do you ask?"

Holly racked her brain to make sense of what little information she had. '*So, that portal in time may appear at times other than the solstice,*' she thought, '*and there always appears to be a storm.*'

"Look, Ursula, can you help me return?" pleaded Holly.

"Alas, no child," the old crone answered, "That is not within my powers, but you could do very well here you know."

"What do you mean?" asked Holly.

"You could work for me," Ursula explained, "or *with* me if you'd rather I put it that way."

Ursula poured Holly more of the brew which tasted so good Holly thought it likely folk could become addicted to it.

The old woman went on, "I know people from far and wide; from many villages to legions of the Roman army. With your knowledge of future medicines and treatments and my connections, we could become quite wealthy."

Holly said, "But I want to return home."

"You must make this your home now," said Ursula.

"But my knowledge is not that great anyway, just a few things I picked up from the Girl Guides."

"The *guides*?" asked the old crone, "so you admit to knowing *guides* from another world?"

"No, no!" said Holly, "you misunderstand."

"And so may others!" warned the old woman. Ursula brooded over her drink, fixing Holly with a malevolent stare which made the girl feel quite uneasy. Finally she said, "You know, just appearing as you did from the henge, from nowhere; some folk might think you are a witch or one of those heathen draugrs that haunt the druids sacred burial mounds."

"But I'm not!" protested Holly.

"I know that, child," said her guest, "but would others be so ready to believe one who has appeared out of thin air...and spoke of *guides* from the other side?"

Recognising the veiled threat, Holly told her, "I am not afraid of you!" said Holly, "And it won't do to threaten me. I am quite prepared to share with you all I know of things of my time; but I will not stay!"

"Have it your own way!" snapped the old crone, and with that threw her brew on the floor and stormed out of the house.

Holly was glad to see the back of her. '*It wasn't long before she showed her true colours,*' she thought. She was just about to take another swig of the hot brew when she looked at the spilled drink on the floor that Ursula had cast away. '*Why, it's almost a full bowl!*' she thought, and realised the old woman hadn't drunk any of it. Suspicious of what the drink might contain; a potion to slow her wits perhaps; Holly got rid of her drink also and placing the fresh water jug to her lips, drunk as much she could so as to dilute anything harmful she may have ingested from the old crone's brew.

Outside a small group of villagers were waiting. A fat man chomping on an apple said, "Well, Ursula, is she a witch?"

Shouting at Holly through the closed door, the old woman said, "These are my friends from the village. Wachabe and his wife, Birog; also Hesperus and her husband, Lug. They are friends to me but not to witches; they have burnt witches before!"

"Aye we have!" snarled Lug.

"Are you a witch, girl?" shouted Hesperus.

Holly opened the door and said, "You are all fools!"

"Will you answer their question or shall I?" asked Ursula.

The angry group shouted as one, "Tell us girl. Are you a witch?"

"Well, are you?" asked the crone

"Go to blazes!" shouted Holly and slammed the door shut.

"Oh my goodness!" said Birog, "She condemns you from her own lips! She invokes the devil!"

"'*Go to blazes*' she tells us," gasped Wachabe and with that he began to choke on the apple he had been greedily devouring.

The angry group banged on the door and screamed and shouted for Holly to come out. "Show yourself witch or we will burn the house down!" shouted one.

"Aye give yourself up!" shouted another.

The noise alerted Olive who had been tending the animals at the rear of the house. She in turn had run off to find Llwyd and Alan.

Alan and his father ran to the house with swords unsheathed. "What's going on?" Alan demanded to know.

Lug answered, "We have no swords. We shall go, but you haven't heard the last of this!"

Seeing the stricken Wachabe doubled over and gasping for breath, Alan said, "What's the matter with him?"

"He's choking! He's choking!" yelled Birog, "Help him!" she cried desperately.

Holly darted from the house and grabbed Wachabe from behind. With her arms around him and her hands locked together over his stomach, she pulled inwards and upwards in a sharp motion. A piece of apple flew out of his mouth, but he still gasped for breath. Suddenly, he collapsed on the floor and lay quite still.

"She's killed him!" Lug accused her.

"Shut up you fool!" Holly snapped, and kneeling beside the collapsed man put her cheek to his mouth. She felt no breath.

Feeling for his carotid artery she ascertained there was no pulse, and so immediately took hold of Wachabe's head and tilted it back so as to extend his neck. Peering into his mouth and seeing no other obstructions, she took a small breath, bent over and sealed Wachabe's mouth with hers. She blew gently and steadily watching his chest rise thus confirming the successful transfer of air from Holly to the stricken man.

"What on earth is the witch up to?" screamed one of the crowd.

"Let her be!" demanded Alan, "She knows what she is doing!"

After two such ventilations Holly still felt no pulse and so placed a hand about one inch up from the base of the sternum. The heart underneath thus located, Holly placed one hand on top of another and applied pressure to the rib cage in a straight downward action. Assessing the man's rib cage had depressed about one and a half inches, she felt confident her actions had the desired effect of squeezing the heart muscle. She continued this external heart massage combining it with two breath ventilations for every fifteen compressions.

Moments later and to everyone's amazement, Wachabe groaned and opened his eyes.

"Lie still!" ordered Holly and asked that the man be propped up so as to avoid any undue strain on his heart. Lug obliged, supporting Wachabe in a semi–upright position.

"Thank you! Thank you!" cried his tearful wife, Birog.

Unhappy at the crowd's seemingly subdued mood, Ursula tried stirring them up again. "That proves she's a witch!" she cried, "Only a witch could bring someone back to life!"

"Nonsense!" cried Holly, "His heart had stopped momentarily but I simply restarted it."

"But with what magic?" asked Lug.

"No magic," answered Holly. "I was taught it by the Girl Guides. It's easy, I could show you all how to do it."

"From the *guides* eh?" asked Ursula, "Would they be the guides from the *other side?*"

"Of course," said Holly.

"Does that not show she is a demon amongst us?" the old crone asked the mob; but for the moment the confused mob chose to ignore the crone's accusations.

Four men picked up the heart attack victim and carried him on their shoulders. "Come on," said Lug, "let's get him home." And with that the group departed for the village.

"Thank goodness for that!" said Alan sheathing his sword.

"This will mean trouble!" warned Llwyd, "so much trouble it will be dangerous to stay now. We must make preparations before they return. Gather what things you wish to take; we shall leave at daybreak," said Llwyd, "Alan, you and Holly try to get as many goats in as you can."

"Yes, Father," said Alan. "Come on, Holly!" he urged.

She was busy writing on a piece of parchment. "I'll meet you at the prayer house," she told him.

****

Dad spoke rapidly on the phone to Rowan, "Do your hippie pals have those bonfires in place yet?"

"Yes, we have four big ones spread around Stonehenge," he confirmed.

"And all constructed from local wood from the forests?"

"Certainly!" Rowan replied, "But the National Trust people are going mad about it!"

"No matter," said Dad, "we have clearance from the English Heritage people and the government. The trees will grow back, eventually."

"What's happening, Dad? Mum wants to know, so do I," said Jesse.

"Wait a moment, darling," Dad urged her.

Continuing his call to Rowan he said, "Set the fires now and keep them burning all day and night and as long in to tomorrow as we can. Tell the T.V. crew that the giant Arc light must be set up to shine its beam directly at the Heel Stone."

"Dad! Dad, please tell me!" said Jesse.

"I'll be right with you, darling," he told her.

"Will do," said Rowan.

Grabbing Jesse Dad said, "Right Jesse, let's go see Mum."

Dad, Jesse and Mags the dog, all bounded excitedly into Mum's bedroom. Clutching the roll of parchment Dad showed Mum the last entry. It was in a red dye ink and of the same letterings as before.

Dad could hardly contain himself, "Look at this, dear" he said, and showed her the new message from Holly. It read, 'M + D. DNT. W8.4 SLST. FX SAME.@ NXT. EQNX. POC.DOLMEN. PLS.HLP.ILY.XHOLLYX'

Dad was almost breathless trying to translate it for Mum. Jesse helped him, and together they uttered the words, *Mum and Dad don't wait for the Solstice. The effects are the same at the next Equinox. Point of contact the Dolmen. Please help. I love you. Holly.*

"Oh my God!" shouted Mum, "What can be done?"

"It's a little complicated but I'll explain on the way. Come on, we're camping overnight at Stonehenge."

Their hired camper van reached the fields just as the first of four great bonfires were set alight by dozens of hippies and friends of the Arch-Druid Rowan.

"We got enough wood to feed those fires?" Dad asked Rowan.

"Yes, indeed," he confirmed.

As the T.V crew set up their equipment in the hope of witnessing some hitherto unrecorded phenomena, Dad asked. "You got that searchlight thing lined up?"

"Yes, sir," a crew member shouted back.

"Enough diesel to keep it powered up?"

"You betcha!"

Dad was joined by Callum and Rowan. "All in place and looking good," said Callum.

"Please! Tell me what's happening!" implored Mum.

"O.K. This is weird!" he said, "But it might work. You know thousands of people had contributed information and advice via the internet? Well, it turns out that when burnt, the local willow trees give off smoke that has properties of potassium and sulphates obviously drawn up by the trees from the soil."

"So?" asked Mum.

Dad continued, "This rang a bell with me and so I looked up information on 'Battles of the American Civil War' and sure enough, there it was."

"What was?" asked Jesse.

Dad continued excitedly, "It turns out that a scientific report was made into the phenomena of why rain would fall only hours after a major battle had occurred."

"I don't get it," said Mum.

Noting the anguished looks on their faces he implored, "Stay with me. It is thought there is an effect that agitates weather conditions and triggers the build up of water molecules in the air. Perhaps the sulphur or potassium stimulates things in some way. Anyway, enough of all this agitation and stimulation could bring about freak weather conditions such as thunder, lightning and rain!"

"That's unbelievable!" said Mum, "But I still......"

Dad interrupted, "It only means we might be able to control the weather to some degree! How does that grab you?"

"It sounds impossible!" said Mum.

"Maybe the Red Indians and those old rainmakers of American legend might have known something we don't?"

"Who's to say?" asked Rowan, "I didn't believe in water divining until I saw it with my own eyes."

The throng of hippies, neo-Druids, T.V. crew and police kept a vigil all night as they maintained the burning bonfires. No-one knew if anything would happen but Dad and Rowan had convinced the authorities that if anything were to happen it was calculated to take place on the following day of the autumn equinox, September the twenty third.

Truckloads of wood and willow branches were bought in a continuous stream to maintain the bonfires throughout the night. Rowan looked quite foolish as he danced and sang encouraging all the new-age travellers, neo-Druids and hippies to sing and chant during the long vigil. Most complied as they genuinely wished to help, while others were there merely for the fun and spectacle.

Rowan was aware they were secretly laughing at him and his antics behind his back, but he didn't care if some thought he looked foolish. The end justified the means as far as he was concerned. He would gladly prance around all day and night encouraging people to pray and chant if it meant getting Holly back safely. The T.V. crews patiently waited for something - anything to happen.

As the September dawn broke Dad asked Callum, "What's the weather report?"

"No change as yet," he answered.

"O.K. Keep those fires topped up," instructed Dad.

****

Alan harnessed the cow to the cart carrying Llwyd, Olive and Holly and as many of their belongings as it would hold. Leading it out and down the muddy pathway they noticed a large fire in the distance burning fiercely. They chose to go in the other direction of it as no doubt people would be there and witness them attempting to leave. However, and much to their distress, they found their way ahead blocked by a mob of angry villagers, lead by Wachabe and Ursula.

"Seize them!" the old crone ordered.

Surrounded by so many of the villagers, the family had no choice but to allow themselves to be pushed and jostled until they reached a small pond by the stonehenge.

The baying crowd dragged Llwyd, Olive and Alan from the cart and held them fast with their arms behind them. The cart was positioned close to the bank and a long log was brought over and laid across it.

With one end of the log on the ground the mob tied the struggling Holly to it. Now with the cart acting as a fulcrum, two big men lay on the other end of the log pulling down which raised the screaming Holly at the opposite end, in the air.

"You have been condemned as a witch!" shouted Ursula.

"Duck her! Duck her!" shouted the crowd.

"No!" screamed Olive, "She will drown!"

With that the two men eased their weight off the end of the log and lowered the desperately thrashing Holly into the freezing pond water.

Before she went under, Holly had managed to take a deep breath. The cold water came as a shock to her system, but she controlled her urge to panic and not lose the precious air in her lungs. She knew she could hold her breath for a minute as she had timed herself in the swimming baths, but that was in warm water not this perishing murky pond.

She had counted to thirty seconds or thereabouts when she felt herself being raised up. When her head was above water she took full advantage and gulped in as big a lungful as she could.

"Duck her again!" came the cries from the baying mob, "She still lives".

The two men were not so gentle this time and just let the log go so that Holly entered the water again with a terrible splash.

She knew they meant to kill her and her mind raced for ideas to survive this mad ordeal. The heavy ducking pole's violent crash into the water had broken of some long reeds that Holly could just make out in the limited vision of the murky water. Trying to bite off the other end of the reed without sacrificing the precious air in her lungs was not easy, but off it came and Holly blew a small amount of air through it to see if it was in fact hollow, and clear any small bits of debris that might be inhaled.

The reed was about twelve inches long and protruded above the surface just enough to allow Holly to breathe and expel through the same tube. She focused her mind and prepared herself for many minutes under the freezing water. Exhaling through the same reed meant no bubbles shown on the surface, which after several minutes had convinced the mob that the *witch* was dead.

****

Rowan, Dad and Callum noticed that dark clouds had indeed begun to form and pushed their way over to where they stood.

"Here it comes!" said Dad, and with that a heavy downpour was suddenly let loose on them.

Everybody cheered.

"It works! It works!" Dad shouted, "Now shine that arc-light on the Heel Stone. That should agitate things!"

****

Holly was dragged up from the pond and untied. Olive ran to her and covered her with a cloak.

"Not so fast!" old Ursula said," I will check her first before you take her."

The cloak prevented Holly from losing any more body heat and when Ursula nipped her arm she gave herself away by wincing at the unexpected pain.

"Aha!" cried the old crone, "She lives!"

"She lives! She lives! She must be a witch!" yelled the mob.

"Aye, and a pretty cold one at that," snarled Ursula, "but never fear girl, or demon or whatever you be; we shall soon warm you up! To the fire with them all!"

The wild mob dragged the terrified Holly, Alan, Olive and Llwyd towards the fiercely burning fire.

"Wachabe!" shouted Holly, "I saved your life! Is this how you repay me?"

"Only a witch could do that!" shouted the miserable Wachabe, "you are condemned by your own actions!!"

"Holly!" cried Llwyd, "If you are a witch, cannot you save us?"

"I cannot," she said, "for I am no witch."

"Let them go! Let them go!" shouted Holly to the mob.

"You all burn together!" yelled the old crone, "and well rid of you we are too. We want neither witches here nor those who trade with Romans. You all burn together!"

"You are an evil woman, Ursula!" cried Olive, "A curse upon you. A curse upon you all!"

"Ah so! Another witch by her own admission!" shouted one of the mob as they dragged them towards the fire.

****

The Arc light powered by the generator shone a powerful beam onto the Heel Stone, but nothing happened.

"On no!" groaned Dad, "Maybe it's not strong enough. It was supposed to light up the dolmen and produce the same effects as before."

A flash of lightning suddenly hit the metal frame of the arc-light, illuminating the whole scene and bathing the henge in a strange eerie glow. The combination of all the earth's energies once again in alignment at this time of the Equinox and the lighting agitating those energies began to reproduce the conditions at the Summer solstice.

"Of course!" shouted Dad, "Even better. That's what was needed!"

****

The heat from the fire felt unbearably intense as Holly was dragged towards it.

Without warning, the bolt of lightning that had illuminated the modern day scene also lit up the ancient one. The stones of the henge glowed their eerie light in the modern day as well as the old days. Time had been spanned.

A downpour of rain hit the fire and it steamed and spat as it was extinguished.

The eerie glow from the stone henge caused someone in the mob to scream in terror.

"What's happening?" yelled Lug.

Amid the violent crackle from the weird lightning Holly heard a dog bark. Holly turned to the direction of the bark and saw the strange mirage – like effect like blurred vision over the dolmen.

"Mags! Mags!" she cried.

The Jack Russell bounded towards her and promptly set about those holding her.

"Aagh! She hails a magic koun from hell!" they shouted as Mags ran amok and sank his teeth into any one between him and Holly.

From the area of the portal dolmen two figures emerged as in a mirage. This caused the crowd to descend into a mad panic. Some ran away in fear of their lives, others tried to attack the visions.

"Demons!" Lug shouted, "From another world!"

"Kill the girl!" Ursula shouted, "They shall not take her!"

Alan and Llwyd took advantage of the confusion and set about members of the mob with their swords.

"Holly!" shouted one of the visions.

"Dad! Dad!" Holly cried and ran to him.

Rowan, the *other vision,* went to the aid of Llwyd and Alan. Pulling out a strange tool from his cloak he zapped Lug and he fell to the ground in a fit.

Without delay he also zapped the miserable Wachabe and he also fell to the ground trembling unconscious.

Everyone stood still and looked in awe at the Arch-Druid.

"A taser!" exclaimed Dad, "Where the hell did you get that?"

Rowan tapped his nose and smiled, "I know people," he answered.

The lightning continued flashing intermittently. When it flashed the portal was visible; when it ceased it was not.

"*You* are the draugr!" the old crone accused Rowan, then grabbing Alan's sword from him raised it above Olive's head and told Rowan, "I do not fear you, demon. Give me your magic wand or I'll kill the woman!"

Calmly Rowan said, "By all means woman, take it," and handed it over to her.

The old crone took it in her hand and pointed it at Rowan.

Unable to operate it, she asked, “How does it work?”

“Like this!” replied Rowan as he brought another taser from under his cloak and shot fifty thousand volts into the old crone.

She also collapsed in a trembling heap.

“She won’t die,” explained Rowan, “High voltage but low amps. They will all recover soon. I suggest you get gone!”

“What about you?” asked Holly.

“I think I belong here,” Rowan said, “It is an interesting time period and at least I will be taken seriously.”

“Are you sure you want to?” asked a concerned Dad.

“I have friends here,” he said exchanging smiles with Llwyd and Olive, “now go! Before the lightning ceases, or we will all be stuck here!”

Dad took Holly’s hand and raced back through the portal that had opened by the dolmen.

“Don’t go!” Alan shouted and tried to follow.

“No!” screamed his mother.

Dad and Holly were on one side of the time divide and Alan on the other.

While Dad ran off into the rain and lightning to bring Mum, Holly and Alan just stared at each other from their own respective time zones. She was in the modern day, Alan was in the past. The stones glowed as the lightning flashed and crackled.

“What about us?” Alan asked.

Holly told him, “It was not meant to be Alan. We are of different eras. I belong here, and you belong there.”

“But I love you, Holly,” he said

“And I love you,” she said.

“You do? Then come back,” he pleaded, “or I shall come to you!”

With that he attempted to get through the barrier, but the lightning ceased as quickly as it had begun. Alan seemed to fade away like a ghost, and Holly was only half visible to him.

Quickly she took the gold chain from around her neck and held it through the time portal. “Take it,” she said, “It is solid gold. It will finance you in starting up a new life elsewhere.”

Alan told her, “Holly, I don’t want to be anywhere without you; you are the love of my life.”

She hesitated for a moment then cried, “Can’t you see it wouldn’t work, sweet boy? Please take it, quickly.”

Alan reached out and took the gold chain. For a brief moment in time, Alan and Holly were able to hold hands. Not in his time nor hers but in a time of their own

The glow from the stones subdued and their visions of each other slowly disappeared.

“I love you, Holly Bush,” she heard Alan say.

"Goodbye, sweetheart," answered Holly, "perhaps we shall meet in another life."

The moment was gone. The rain stopped and all returned as it had been.

"Holly!" shouted Mum, at which mother and daughter ran to each other and embraced.

One of the T.V. camera men asked his colleague, "Boy! Tell me we got that on film!"

"Not without that arc light we didn't!" his colleague groaned.

Mum, Dad, Holly and Jesse were reunited and laughing and crying at the same time. Despite all being soaking wet their joy was immense. Picking up Mags in her hands she became covered in wet mud from the dog.

They all laughed. "At least its modern day mud!" laughed Jesse.

Holly noticed the frisbee in Jesse's hand and grabbing it from her said, "And we can get rid of that thing!"

She was just about to hurl it away.

The dog looked in eager anticipation.

Jesse looked in surprise.

Mum looked in horror.

"I'll take that, thank you!" said Dad, to everyone's relief and secured it within his shirt.

They all laughed.

"I'm sorry, Holly," said Jesse, "Is it alright with you and me?"

Holly put her arm around her younger sister and told her, "Of course it is, silly."

"Come on," Dad said, we'll all have a hot drink in the camper and you can tell us all about it."

****

Rowan helped the family to straighten out the cart and said, "Best make haste friends," and pointing to the confused mob added, "there's no telling what they will do when their wits return."

"At what age is it right to be wed?" Alan asked.

Rowan answered, "In Holly's case, I would say that another four or five years is quite soon enough."

"Ah, then I should be twenty or twenty one and she would be nineteen or twenty. Is that better?" asked Alan.

"That would be better," agreed Rowan.

With a beaming smile Alan confidently stated, "Then that is when we shall meet again!"

"How so?" asked Rowan.

"Well you know the secret of the Stonehenge, don't you?" asked

Alan, “If it can be done once, it can be done again!”

His mother and father hugged him. “What do you think Rowan?” asked Llwyd.

As they left the brooding spectre of the stone henge behind them the Arch-Druid simply smiled his benign smile and replied, “Who’s to say?”

The End

The Ice Palace

(A fictionalised account of a true event)

Chapter One

ITALY

There was a fresh Alpine breeze that spring morning of 1739. It gently blew away the morning mist that hovered over the waters of the Italian Lake Garda, and revealed shimmering reflections of shoreline hamlets dotted along its banks. Embedded in the mountain foothills, the lake area was protected from the worst of the weather from above while still enjoying a warm Mediterranean climate down by the lake side. Palm and olive trees flourished, as did tomatoes and vegetables in great variety. The scent from the apple orchards, and the orange and lemon groves charged the air with a sweet pungency.

The lake had an abundance of freshwater fish such as carp, pike and tench, while salmon abounded in the rivers and streams. Wild boar and deer roamed the nearby forests, and a small herd of cows grazed the rich green slopes. Domesticated ducks and geese played at the water's edge. The mountain streams provided clean, sweet drinking water, filtered through many layers of rock.

With the ambient weather, it was an idyllic oasis; a veritable Garden of Eden tucked away in the mountain slopes; a happy healthy environment for raising families, or recuperating from illness. The folk living there blessed their good fortune, and led a contented existence. Life was, indeed, sweet.

In a log chalet, on a slope overlooking the lake, the dawn sunlight streaked through the bedroom window, casting illuminating fingers of light upon the faces of the young couple still at slumber. The bed and bedroom were littered with rice and confetti. A garland of flowers hung from the corner post of the headboard. On the wedding bed, were partly opened gifts. Clothing and empty bottles of wine were strewn in happy disarray, about the floor. While songbirds twittered merrily outside, the flickering tentacles of light played on the young man's eyelids. He gradually awoke, and when his sleepy eyes became clear, he focused them on the beautiful young woman lying alongside him.

He smiled, and playfully caressed her long golden locks of hair spread across the pillow. He marvelled at her voluptuous form. His caresses, plus the dancing rays of sunshine on her face roused her from her sweet slumbers. He blew gently in her ear.

Her eyes flickered without opening. “Good morning,” she said sleepily. He kissed her tenderly, full on the lips. At that moment he was a happy man and knew he had everything in the world he would ever want. *Life could not possibly get much better than this,* he thought.

She responded to his passionate ardour, and both became locked in a loving embrace. He resisted the temptation to make love yet again. Instead he teased her, “Guess who?”

Her vibrant hazelnut brown eyes opened. “Oh,... you!” she cried, and proceeded to hit him with a pillow. “’Guess who?’ indeed!” she laughed.

“Ouch! Christina!” he cried, grabbing the pillow from her, kissing her again.

“I am so lucky. I dreamt of a handsome young prince, and here you are.”

Smiling, he answered, “A Prince by birth, perhaps. Your *husband* by choice. That is the title I cherish above all else.”

She smiled lovingly, then when he was off guard, whacked him with the pillow again. Now it became a free for all.

Whacks from the pillows were compensated for by tender kisses and giggles. Their playing was interrupted by the sound of a male voice singing by the lake.

“Who is that, Mikhail?” Christina asked

Her husband replied, “It’s that nincompoop, Oleg, I’ll be bound.”

By the water’s edge, the Prince’s manservant and lifelong friend, was bathing and frolicking with Eva, a buxom wench from the tavern, and the rakish Oleg’s latest *conquest*.

“Oleg!” Mikhail shouted, “Colazione!”

“What?” Oleg shouted back.

“Colazione!” Mikhail repeated louder.

“Oh! You mean zantrak,” corrected Oleg.

Mikhail shouted back at him, “You are in Italy now, you heathen. Come on. Zantrak or colazione — it’s still breakfast in any language. Come on. We’re famished.”

“Bathe first, you pleb!” laughed Oleg.

Mikhail smiled at Christina, “*Pleb,* he calls me?” With that, he leapt out of the bedroom window onto the sloping kitchen roof, and from there, dropped to the ground. He dashed a few yards to the water’s edge and dived in. The two old friends wrestled and splashed each other, and were generally larking about with gusto.

Eva came out of the water, drying herself. She informed them, “I shall attend to the Lady Christina.”

Ignoring her, the two men continued to splash and duck each other. "Brrr! It's damn cold!" said Mikhail.

"Cold?" said the frolicking Oleg, "This good living has softened you up, my Lord. Why, it's a warm bath, compared to swimming in the Neva or the canals of St. Petersburg."

The Prince agreed, "You're right. Even at this time of year it's still freezing back there."

Oleg laughed. "Even that whale of an Empress, with all her blubber, would freeze in those waters!" They both laughed and carried on frolicking, as Eva waved to Christina and made for the lodge.

Later, that morning the newly married couple enjoyed an outdoor wedding breakfast with Oleg and Eva. All were in high spirits, as Eva danced around the table serving the food, while Oleg played the mandolin, eyeing her lustfully.

Despite the Prince being, by far, the most handsome of the two men, it was Oleg who was the unashamed womaniser. His roguish Russian charm was of great renown in the lakeside hamlet, and was the source of much amusement — amongst the females, at least.

He relied on his brazen grin to diffuse possible reactions when faced with sullen looks from husbands, brothers, or fathers. The cheeky, lovable rogue was, for the most part, accepted as just that.

Strumming his instrument he said, "It's not the balalaika, but if it makes the ladies sway like that, who cares?" Nodding towards Eva, Oleg asked Christina, "What do you think of her, then Milady?"

She answered, "I like her. She's a good cook and very helpful in the house."

Mikhail observed, "Looks like we'll be employing more help, then. Handy for you that eh, Oleg?"

Eva poured everyone a cup of cold milk. As she did so, the grinning Oleg slapped her on the rump, and asked the Prince. "What do *you* think of her, Sire?"

"Well..." said Mikhail thoughtfully, "...she's certainly better than that old bag I saw you with last week!"

The two men laughed out loudly. Eva looked most displeased. When they noticed Eva's sour expression, the two men looked at each other, and burst out laughing again.

Poor Eva knew she was the butt of the joke but couldn't figure out what exactly they were laughing at.

Had there, in fact, been another 'old bag' earlier? she wondered.

The men knew she was pondering this, and her annoyed confusion caused them to laugh even more. The two men were merciless in their teasing.

"Enough!" cried Christina, "Leave the poor girl be."

Without warning, Eva poured the jug of milk over Oleg's head.

At this, Mikhail fell off his stool helpless with laughter. Eva chased Oleg, swinging the milk jug wildly at his soaking wet but elusive head.

"Darling, cease!" Oleg implored, "You know you are the only woman for me."

Eva mellowed. "I had better be!" she warned, setting the milk jug down.

Taking his seat again, Oleg pulled her onto his lap and kissed and fussed with her. "Well, for today at least!" he added, with a wink to Mikhail.

Eva struggled to get free and hit Oleg again, but he held her fast. All four of them were laughing heartily at the antics.

"You're a rum beggar, Oleg," said Mikhail.

"Well, I look at it like this, Sire," laughed Oleg as he pulled a ridiculous face while grasping the struggling Eva.

"You clown," said Mikhail, then turning to Christina he smiled and asked, "Are you happy, darling?"

Before Christina could answer Oleg said, "Yes thank you, darling."

"Not *you*, you fool!" said Mikhail, throwing a bread roll at his friend.

The four friends laughed heartily.

The laughter was interrupted when Christina suddenly clutched at her chest. "Oh!" she cried, and tried to stand up. She swooned and sat back down again.

Mikhail rushed to her side. "What is it?" he asked anxiously.

Christina breathed deeply and tried to bring her rapid gasping under control. "It's my heart. Too much excitement. I need to lie down for a little while."

"Stay calm, darling. Breathe nice and easy. We'll get you inside. Just relax."

Now most concerned, a worried Oleg asked, "Was it us, larking about that brought it on? Please forgive me."

Christina's face was pale. She smiled at the other three. "No, Oleg. It's not you. I like you both being boisterous. You are happy. There is no pretence or affectation. It is my heart, I'm afraid. I just need rest."

"What can we do?" begged Oleg.

"Nothing," she smiled. "I just need rest. Here, in this place of beauty, peace and fresh air. That, and the company of good friends and," pausing to look into Mikhail's eyes, she added, "of the one I love. That will help me most of all, and put strength back into my ailing heart."

Mikhail picked Christina up in his strong arms. "Let's get you inside the chalet," he said. The concerned Prince carried her up the slope into the chalet and laid her on the bed. "Come take the herbs the doctor prescribed for you, "he said, "Then you must rest."

"What about the villagers?" she asked, "they will be expecting us."

"There's no rush to do anything," Mikhail told her, "Sleep for a while. We have all the time in the world."

Theirs had been a whirlwind romance, marrying within weeks of meeting; but it seemed so right to them both. As Ambassador for Russia, he had travelled to Italy, and met with politicians and tradesmen at a Guild in Verona. There he met Abramo, the mayor of the lakeside community of Garda.

Abramo had been accompanied by his beautiful daughter, Christina. For her, and Mikhail, it was instant attraction. Mikhail was aware of her illness, but was convinced his love for her would be the cure. Now, it was being put to the test.

In the nearby village, a fair was in progress. The place was a hive of activity. Stalls were set up for traders to ply their wares. Pots, pans, fine linen and drapes were displayed, while other stalls had farming and fishing equipment for sale.

Laughing children helped grownups to chase geese and pigs into makeshift pens, while others danced around poles, holding attached ribbons, to tunes from an accordionist and a fiddle player. There was happy turmoil in the market-cum-fair. It was loud, brash, busy and fun.

Tents had been erected for the supping of ales and wine. The townsfolk were celebrating the fact that a new road had been opened, which made for improved trade connections between them and the *outside world.* A small dirt track up into the mountains had been widened enough to allow adequate passage for carriages and carts instead of just mules.

This meant vital trade links between the lakeshore villages and the towns of Bardelino and Trento across the mountains and, ultimately, Verona. Now visitors attended the fair, some arriving by boat from across the lake while others from farther away came via the new road through the mountain pass.

One man had made the town's growth and prosperity possible: Prince Mikhail Golitsyn. It was he, who as Russian roving ambassador, had met the town elders at the Trade Guild in Verona the year before. Corresponding by carrier pigeon, he had asked for, but been refused permission from the Russian court to commit any of his country's money to a road widening scheme through the mountains. He thought it such a wise move, though, that he invested his own limited capital in the project. Improved trade routes could only be a boon to all he reasoned, and he was now being proved right.

There were many royal families in the various Russian provinces, and although a royal himself, Mikhail was way down the list of those in order of succession to the throne. He had secured the post of ambassador from his Empress, the Tsaritsa Anna Ivanovna, due to his ability to speak foreign languages. His fine intellect and tact made for impressive diplomatic skills. His charm and handsome good looks were no hindrance either; however he was not vain, but a serious politician and astute businessman who recognised potential when he saw it; all qualities ideal in an ambassador.

His scheme to widen the mountain track to accommodate wagons and carriages, met with the village elders' approval and the obvious benefits of an improved route through the mountains was apparent to all. Indeed, it was necessary if trade, development, and prosperity were to be brought to the region.

With the offer to finance the undertaking himself, there was no opposition and when Mikhail fell in love with Abramo's daughter, the beautiful Christina, it was as if fate itself had decreed it and the deal was set in stone.

The villagers took the handsome benefactor to their hearts, for not only providing the means to bring progress to the area and enrich their lives, but because he, a Prince, loved a woman so much he was prepared to leave his native land for her and make the Italian lakes his new home.

Mikhail had decided long ago that this would, in fact, be no sacrifice. He had virtually no chance of succeeding to the Russian throne, and although he was not impoverished, his small personal fortune wouldn't go far.

He thought it best be utilised on such a project as he now embarked, rather than try to maintain servants and a grand house in St. Petersburg. When given the job of roving ambassador, he saw it as a godsend. Russia was fine, but he saw little opportunity there for him. He vowed to find a place where he could develop a business, and live in peace and relative comfort for all the days God allowed him.

He had spotted a business potential in Italy, and was happy in the knowledge that he had done the job his country had asked of him. He had given the Tsaritsa first rights to his project to connect the villages. Since she had rejected the idea, he decided he was free to act independently. As far as he could see, everyone was happy. His future was here, and it would be a happier and more productive one than at home.

In Russia he would have no wealth; here he would have prospects. At home he would have to face the numbing Russian winters. Here, he could bask in glorious summers and milder Alpine winters. Food was plentiful, with no mass crop failures, as occasionally happened in his homeland. He loved the land of his birth, but realised his future was not there. It was an easy decision to abandon his land of inhospitable weather, for a new home in the sun. There he would struggle; here he had a future. There, he had no one; here, he had Christina.

Later in the day, Christina felt a little better. Oleg drove her and Mikhail in the carriage to the fair. In the makeshift square, Christina and Mikhail stepped out to a great cheer from the villagers. They, indeed, made a beautiful couple.

The Prince carried his delicate bride to the main tent where he sat her at a table. He shook Abramo's hand, who bade him be seated.

Abramo, addressed the gathering. "Friends, we give thanks to the newlyweds for sparing time to visit us today. *I know they are busy.*"

Laughs and cheers went up from the crowd.

Turning to Mikhail he continued, "We cannot thank the Prince enough for the good works he has done since arriving here last year. That day was a very fortunate one for us all."

The crowd cheered again.

"The new road, that for years, was only a track, has now been cleared and widened through the forest and up into the mountains, linking us with our neighbours, many who honour us with their company here today. That, plus with the new jetties and boats for our lake, will mean our future, as a trading post *and* tourist destination is a distinct possibility. Prince Mikhail's enterprise will allow our towns to grow and take their place in the world of commerce."

More cheers.

He continued, "But I am doubly grateful that he not only chose to stay to preside over our welfare, but that he has not deprived me of my only daughter, Christina. Her frailty means that she would not fare well in a harsh environment. To show his great love for her, and his commitment to these valleys, Mikhail has turned his back on the land of his birth and has taken Italy as his adopted home. I have, indeed, as we all have, now not lost a daughter, but gained a true and loving son. Three cheers for our esteemed benefactor, Prince Mikhail. Hip — hip!"

The crowd cheered ecstatically.

With a hand resting on Christina's shoulder, Mikhail addressed the gathering. "I love the land of my birth, but I love this woman more."

This produced robust cheers from the men in the crowd and tears from the women.

He went on, "I would live wherever she chooses, even if it were on the moon. After all, it cannot be as cold as the Russian Steppes!"

The elated villagers laughed and roared out their approval. The festivities re-commenced. Abramo shook Mikhail's hand and embraced him. Then both, in turn, they kissed the smiling Christina.

The mood was a happy one that spring morning.

Oleg was drinking himself into a stupor and dancing with Francesca, Marietta and Eloisa in turn and any other pretty girl he could until Eva stepped in.

As she slapped him about the head and began dragging him away, the delighted crowd went into hysterics.

"Are you happy, darling?" Mikhail asked Christina.

Smiling, she answered, "More than I have a right to be, my love."

They gazed around the fair watching people enjoying themselves.

Children were playing, running in and out of the stalls. Traders were bartering their wares. There were games and competitions, jugglers and minstrels and folk just milling about, enjoying the day.

"Who are those men?" asked Christina.

Draining his goblet of wine, Mikhail asked, "Which men?"

"Those, over there," Christina gestured to some dozen men in cloaks standing by their horses and wagons.

"Oh, I don't know. What would *you* think? Traders in ugly faces, perhaps?" Mikhail joked.

She scowled disapprovingly at his silliness, then, smiled at him, to show it was just pretend scorn.

The strangers spread out and circled the fair's small enclosure.

A tall, well-built man approached the main tent. As he passed the newlyweds, Mikhail thought there was something familiar about the man's bearing and purposeful stride. In a thick foreign accent the man addressed Abramo, "You are leader?" he asked.

Abramo nodded.

The stranger continued, "I am General Lev Leonid, Master of the Royal Guard of St. Petersburg."

Mikhail was within earshot and at the mention of his Russian home, the surprised Prince begged his leave of Christina and went over to join Abramo and the General.

Lev acknowledged the Prince with a smart salute, "Greetings, Your Highness. Forgive me, I did not recognise you in the crowd."

"What is it you want?" asked Abramo.

Lev answered sternly. "We are here on the express orders of our beloved Empress, Anna Ivanovna, Tsaritsa of all Russia and its territories. It has come to the Palace's notice that Prince Mikhail intends to marry outside of his faith, and without seeking the blessing of his Empress!"

Mikhail interrupted, "It is no intention, my friend. It is a fact. I have already wed the lovely Christina, yesterday."

The General paused momentarily; his shifty eyes darting back and forth. He said, "In that case, it is, er – *requested* that you and er, – your bride accompany us back to the Royal palace at St. Petersburg, so that our gracious sovereign can congratulate you in person."

This didn't sound right to Mikhail. With his suspicions raised, he recapped the General's story back to him, "So, she complains I didn't ask her permission to wed, and therefore er, *requests* my presence at her court to explain myself; and when I tell you the wedding has already taken place you then inform me of Her Majesty's wish to congratulate us in person! Hmm. You can see why I ponder, General?

The General looked a little uncomfortable. He added, "And, to offer you a position at court."

Puzzled, Mikhail told him, "I already have a position. I am

ambassador to this nation. What do you think I am doing here? However, it would be nice to see the old country again. You may inform the Tsaritsa that we shall pay a visit after our honeymoon."

"When the Tsaritsa says to come, she means now!" growled the General.

Mikhail brushed him off with, "Perhaps... after the honeymoon."

"No!" shouted Lev, "You will come, now!"

His men all threw back their cloaks and drew their swords.

The startled crowd gasped and backed away.

"What is the meaning of this?" cried Abramo.

"The meaning is simple," said Lev, "The Empress demands the Prince's presence at court. Immediately!"

"No!" shrieked Christina.

"My wife is not well," Mikhail told them. "The journey would be too much for her."

"We have no need of the Italian peasant!" said Lev's lieutenant, Pavel. "Leave the bitch here! She would only slow us down."

With that, Mikhail knocked the lieutenant on his back, and grabbed his sword. As the Prince and the General became locked in fierce combat, the villagers all grabbed what they could to defend themselves. Although pitchforks, scythes and axes were no match for professional troops with battle weapons; the villagers fought bravely and fiercely.

When Pavel noticed that Mikhail's superior swordsmanship was getting the better of the General, he grabbed Christina by the hair and dragged her from her chair. She fell onto her knees. He raised a sword above her head in a threat to strike.

"Cease!" bellowed Abramo.

Everyone froze to the spot as the sword hung perilously above Christina's neck.

Mikhail lowered his weapon.

"Take him!" ordered General Lev. The Prince's hands were bound, and he was manhandled into a carriage.

Christina was not faring too well and lay gasping on the ground, being attended to by the other girls.

"You intended all along to take me. Why?" demanded Mikhail. "What have I done?"

"You have incurred the displeasure of our monarch, and in so doing, of the Russian people also," said Lev.

"Nonsense!" cried Mikhail, "I have done my duties as ambassador. I told you I had informed the Tsaritsa of the great opportunity to add to the royal coffers, as well as to create good will between the two countries. I have been a good ambassador."

General Lev mounted his horse. "The Empress cares not for your silly business ventures. That is not your crime you fool!"

"Then what?" demanded the Prince.

General Lev explained, "You have married a Catholic, and what's more without royal permission. Our Empress is outraged. You will explain your actions to her."

Pavel's face broke into an evil grin as he made the motion of a knife drawing across a throat.

"This is ridiculous! "Can't you see my wife is ill? Let me stay until I know she fares better."

Lev slashed at the carriage door with his sword in anger, making Mikhail jump back. The General motioned to the driver with his sword, "Move out!"

With that, the driver slapped his reins and the horses moved off with a whinny.

"Christina!" cried Mikhail from inside the carriage. "I will return."

The unhappy villagers, who only a few moments ago were celebrating their good fortune, looked on in dismay as the Russian party drew out of the village with their captive and set off towards the foothills.

From a distance the Prince was heard to plead, "Abramo! Take care of her. I will return."

The carriage containing its royal abductee disappeared over the brow of a hill.

Helping Christina up from the ground Abramo instructed Oleg, "Take her back to the chalet. I will bring the doctor." Looking around he cried, "Is the doctor here?" as Oleg started to pick her up..

The doctor was on hand at the fair. "No! Don't move her!" he shouted as he ran to Christina's side.

The doctor advised Christina to lie down on the ground but with her head and shoulders raised slightly. He placed his hand in the centre of her chest. "Her heartbeats are irregular."

A girl peered into the tent and saw Christina was deathly pale and in a cold sweat. "What's wrong with her lips?"

Christina's lips and the tip of her nose had turned slightly blue.

"Her blood does not circulate properly. It does not take fresh air with it through the body," the doctor explained.

"What can be done?" asked the concerned Abramo.

"Rest, and fresh air, and no exertion!" the doctor instructed. "Possibly some herbs to widen her arteries to help the blood flow; but she is a very sick girl."

"The blood *circulates*?" asked an onlooker.

"Indeed yes," replied the doctor. He explained, "Some years ago an English doctor by the name of Harvey discovered the heart is but a pump that sends blood fused with good air coursing through the arteries to feed the tissues. In Christina's case, I'm afraid the pump is damaged."

The villagers knew the doctor to be a knowledgeable man, and respected his grim diagnosis.

Christina's face was pale and waxen, with blue tinges around the nose, lips and earlobes. The doctor continued, "Her breathing is now laboured. Her body is in distress... I fear the worst!"

"Those blasted Russians!" exclaimed Abramo. "My daughter's young heart should be happy with love and excitement today; not injured through distress brought on by those vagabonds! I curse the day I first met a Russian!"

Christina's eyes opened. She was very weak. She held her father's hand, and smiled at him as he kneeled at her side. "You don't mean that father. Mikhail is a good man. Don't blame him for what the others have done. He has improved our lives. Think well of him."

Abramo smiled at his daughter and stroked her golden locks.

Smiling back at him she said, "Think well of me, father. I fear I am at the end. My time has come."

"No!" exclaimed her grief stricken father. "It cannot be!" Turning to the doctor he pleaded, "Do something... please!"

The doctor felt the irregular rhythm of Christina's failing heart. It grew weaker by the second. With spittle on his fingers he applied them to the side of his face, then leaned close to his patient. The moisture on his cheek detected only the slightest of breaths from the stricken girl. He could say or do nothing for her now. No words were necessary. The grim look on the doctor's face relayed to the distraught Abramo all the information he did not want to hear. It confirmed his worst fears.

Still smiling, Christina squeezed her father's hand, sighed then closed her eyes for the last time. All the villagers were still and hushed as Abramo made the sign of the cross, then fell down alongside her, crying as he hugged his daughter's now lifeless body.

****

Beyond the village, Prince Mikhail was being ungainly bashed about inside the carriage as he and his Russian captors drove up into the high foothills.

"Blame yourself for your discomfort," said General Lev, "You built this road!"

Lev's men laughed.

"It was not intended that travellers be trussed up like animals. Let me out. I cannot endure this treatment all the way to the nearest port," the Prince retorted. "I am a Prince, not an animal! How dare you?"

"You are a prisoner! That's what you are, right now... Sire!" said Pavel, with a sneer. "Sit tight. Let's see how good your workmanship is."

They carried on, ascending as they went. The once rough mountain pass had been widened, and stoned, was now well suited to accommodate large carriages. Wearily Mikhail prepared himself for a long journey.

Hours later, as the hills became steeper, the Prince was puzzled that the carriage did not head in a westerly direction but seemed to carry on northwards. He asked the General, "Do we not travel through France?"

"Why would we?" asked the General.

"To get a ship at Calais," Mikhail said, "Surely that is the easiest way?"

"We do not sail," the General told him, "We go overland." Mikhail was puzzled by this long route home. *Why not go by sea?* he thought. It would be one hell of a trek across land, and he set his mind to figuring the route the General intended taking. He guessed that once through the mountains they would have to head for Treviso and the Adige valley in the north, which connects Italy to southern Europe. From there it would be a long slog through Austria, Bohemia, and across the Carpathian mountains into Poland before entering his gigantic homeland of Russia some fifteen hundred miles away. By his calculation, it could take up to eight weeks; but only if they managed an average thirty miles a day. He was baffled as to the reason for the extra effort that a land journey would involve.

"But why not head for France, and sail from Calais then into the Baltic via Copenhagen?" he asked the General. "That would save a lot of time and effort."

The General explained. "We have friends along the way. Staging posts where we can rest and change horses."

"Rubbish!" said Mikhail, "Why, it's just like the Tsaritsa to choose the hardest passage; for everyone, I might add. We have enough ships in our navy to transport us."

"You would do well to be silent, my Lord," General Lev warned him. "We obey our Empress, not question her."

The Empress's reputation as a cruel and vindictive woman was well known. Mikhail was not in the least surprised she chose to make his journey back to the motherland as uncomfortable as possible. *But what had upset her so?* he wondered. *Surely, getting married is no crime? That cannot be the reason.* He wondered what he had done to warrant her making her General take a three thousand mile round trip just to bring him back? And, more to the point, what was in store for him when, or indeed *if,* he ever he got there?

For the Prince, the day had begun happily, with optimism and a sense of fun. Both had now rapidly deserted him. His thoughts sailed back to his beloved Christina: his beautiful bride, and the crazy, happy, unlikely whirlwind romance that had brought them together. He prayed for her recovery. When would he see her again? Time alone would tell. The carriage bounced along up the increasingly steep track.

****

By the time Oleg had caught up to the Russian caravan, they were high into the mountain pass and the weather had changed dramatically. Wind and snow now prevailed.

"Hey! Wait! Wait!" cried Oleg, speeding his horse onward.

Viktor, one of the guards spotted him in the distance. "General!" he called, "Someone approaches."

With that, the caravan halted. The guards drew their swords and archers took aim.

"I have news! I have news!" cried Oleg.

"Don't fire!" said Mikhail. "It is Oleg, from the village. He is on his own."

Breathlessly he addressed the General. "General. I have some bad news from the village."

"What is it?" Lev asked.

Turning to Mikhail inside the carriage, he said. "Master, it is your lady wife."

"Christina? What's wrong?"

Oleg's courage failed him. He couldn't speak. His heavy breathing formed white clouds and disappeared into the air.

"Speak man!" shouted the General. "Why have you stopped us in our journey?"

Mikhail turned pale as he sensed what he was about to be told. "What is it? Tell me, old friend."

Oleg composed himself and told him, "It was very sudden. A heart attack — with all the excitement. She is gone, my Lord."

The shock hit Mikhail like a blow from a sledgehammer. His heart sank to his boots. He put his head in his hands.

Oleg turned to the General, "The villagers request you postpone your journey until after the service for the Lady Christina."

Pavel piped up. "I thought you said you had bad news? So she is dead. So what? Who will miss just another Italian peasant?"

"You bastards!" yelled Mikhail. "She'd be alive if it were not for you knaves!"

Oleg drew a bow and fired off an arrow that pierced Pavel's side. "Take that from another peasant!"

The Prince dived from the carriage but was immediately felled by one of the guards.

The wind was whipping up the snow and provided Oleg with the chance to escape. Archers fired off a volley of arrows, but the wind blew them all awry.

The enraged Pavel shouted: "Allow for the wind! Aim just ahead of him!" he ordered, and when he judged it to be right, cried, "Now!" The archers fired off another volley. Oleg's horse was hit and it reared up throwing the rider off.

A bowman took advantage of the still target. An arrow found its mark in Oleg's back. He fell. His body slid face forward down the slope and out of view.

With a grimace, Pavel yanked the arrow from his bloody side and threw it after where Oleg was last seen. He spat on the ground in contempt.

Mikhail groaned. "Oleg! Oleg."

"We go on!" the General commanded.

The guards manhandled Mikhail back into the carriage.

Looking back at the spot where Oleg fell, all the Prince could say was, "Not you as well, old friend! Not you, too, on this accursed day."

The Russians just grinned at him in his misery.

"You bastards!" shouted Mikhail. "You unearthly devils! A curse upon the lot of you!"

Ignoring him, the General raised his hand and shouted, "Forward!"

Mikhail slumped to the floor of the carriage with his head in hands. The party carried on its way up into the mountains.

Chapter Two

The Trek North

For Mikhail, the rest of the journey was like a bad dream. In the space of less than one day he had lost his new bride, his best friend and his adopted country. It was too much to take in. He was shattered; nothing mattered now. His despair turned to depression. Jumbled pictures of the day's events jostled in his mind. He thought of Christina, taken from him so suddenly. Her young life lost — their future together stolen from them. Although they had not known each other long, they did love each other. *Christina deserved a longer, happier life,* he thought. He knew he could have given her that. Now, she was gone. Gone forever. Mikhail struggled to grasp the reality of the situation. His mind was in turmoil.

Images of his dead bride were replaced by those of his lifelong friend, Oleg. He tried to recall their many adventures in happier times, but he felt only half alive, and began experiencing a mental decline into a living nightmare that robbed him of his energy and senses. He felt terribly weak, and laid himself down in the carriage to rest. Mikhal's bleary eyes located in the sky above, wild geese winging their way north, returning home to Mother Russia. He prayed that Oleg's soul was flying with them. The thought of escape played upon his tired mind, but he felt physically drained of energy. First he needed rest before he could even consider escape and the effort it would take.

General Lev sensed Mikhail's frame of mind and ordered two guards to sit alongside the Prince in the carriage at all times. Others would take over in shifts around the clock to ensure Mikhail could not escape or harm neither himself, nor others.

The stress of the day's events had sapped his energy and Mikhail's tired brain rejected the planning and seeking of opportunities to flee. It was pointless.

His mind tried to make sense of what had happened in such a short space of time. His life had changed, for the worse certainly, but for how long? He was mentally exhausted. He had neither the will nor the inclination to resist any more. He became passive. His only thoughts were to survive and to think of an explanation the tyrannical Empress would accept.

Trying to second guess a mad woman was only adding strain to his heavy heart. He tried to sleep, but Christina and Oleg haunted his dreams.

The two people in the world who meant anything to him were gone. *What was real? What was a dream?* Mikhail slept poorly and knew no peace, yet realised he had to conserve his mental and physical strength for what lay ahead.

The party followed the route over the still snow-capped Alps and skirted the beautiful and unearthly spires of the Dolomite mountain range; then through the length of the Adige valley. Day after monotonous day passed. They slogged onward, journeying through Austria and Bohemia stopping at their pre-planned staging posts for refreshments and new horses. The Prince was under constant guard and had no chance of escape, or even putting up a fight for that matter.

The journey was hard and tedious. Made roads gave way to tracks then to bogs and back again to made roads. Wheels broke on the carriages. They were fixed. Horses broke legs. They were killed and left where they fell for the wolves.
Replacements were obtained at the next staging post. Nothing stopped the relentless trek onward.

The journey continued day and night through all weathers, through forests and across plains. Italy was just a fading dream to Mikhail now. It was as though his life there had never happened. No more fight was left in him. His world had collapsed. Nothing lay ahead for him. He sank into a black melancholia. All he had left were his prayers.

****

Since Russia had been at war with Turkey from 1735 it was obvious that unprotected overland travel was a very risky undertaking for any Russian, and thus caused Mikhail to wonder why they had chosen such an obviously dangerous passage.

The route took them through parts of Hungary and Yugoslavia, then known as Bohemia and perilously close to Turkish military outposts. Russian attacks on Turkey were mainly from the Crimea on the edge of the Black Sea but, as a backup strategy, allies had been cultivated in the Bohemian countries such as Bulgaria, Romania and Hungary. The staging posts were run by people friendly to the Russians, providing them with not only rest and a change of horses, but a chance for them to stay informed of the Turkish Army's movements.

As the days passed, Mikhail gleaned information from gossip and snippets of conversations between the guards.

It transpired that the reason for Prince Mikhail's abduction was not only to explain himself to his Empress, but she also intended to make use of him on the journey home. He was to assess the political and military situation at close hand.

His diplomatic skills, and talent with languages meant he could hold dialogues with local leaders, to evaluate wisely any information that might be gleaned. General Lev would serve as an escort only. Wit and wisdom were required for such a task. Mikhail would be the brains — General Lev and his men, the brawn.

Reports were to be sent back to St. Petersburg by carrier pigeon, and if, in carrying out this task, the Prince fell foul of the Turks, his death, and those of his escorts, would result, usefully, in more outrage to justify the Russian aggression. All were dispensable to the Tsaritsa.

What the tyrannical old Empress had not reckoned with, however, was the death of Mikhail's wife, and therefore his understandable unwillingness to cooperate. *Why should I?* he thought. His wife had died, and now he was expected to be all charm itself on what amounted to a spying mission.

He refused to speak to any local leaders or mayors, and was determined to be of as little help as possible in their mad war games.

Upon leaving one of their overnight lodgings in Bohemia, the Russian party was chased by a small band of Turkish soldiers, who had been informed of the Russian presence by a traitorous agent at their last staging post. The Russians made good their escape only because they had fresh horses, unlike the Turks who had been riding hard all night in an effort to reach the Russian group. Only one Turk on a fast horse, managed to catch up with them. In sight was a Russian who, despite riding a fresh horse, was lagging behind the others.

A painful injury in his side prevented the rider from committing his horse to full gallop. This proved fatal as the Turk released a bolt from his crossbow, which accurately found its target in Pavel's neck, killing him outright.

The Russian riders gave chase. The lone Turk turned his horse about and raced away. He was confident his speedy mount, and knowledge of the local terrain, would soon put some distance between them; but his horse stumbled and fell. He was immediately surrounded.

As the carriage drew alongside Pavel's body, Mikhail spoke out loud to it: "To hell with you, you bastard! Oleg; you are now avenged!"

General Lev told the Prince, "This would not have happened if you had done your job properly, and used your wits as you were supposed to!"

Rebuking Lev, Mikhail said, "My job? You have abducted me from my job! In Italy! Not only am I to face trumped up charges for having wed, but I am expected to serve as ambassador, spy and intermediary along the way back!"

General Lev sneered, "Let us just say it is payment for your passage!"

"You are as crazy as the mad bitch who sent you here!" said the

Prince.

"Be warned sire!" Lev snarled, "Insult our monarch, and you insult Russia! I don't care where you die; here or in St. Petersburg!"

The defiant Prince answered, "What difference does it make with my wife and best friend now gone?"

The General fumed, "Insulting our monarch will do you no favours, Sire. As for your grief, I suggest you hurry up and deal with it! We have work to do!"

Mikhail was unsure of the General and so thought it best not to carry on the heated exchange between them.

Pavel's killer had been captured and was in the process of being summarily executed by Lev's men, seething for revenge over the loss of their lieutenant.

"Wait!" cried Mikhail, "Don't kill him, you fools. We need him for information."

The General thought for a moment. "He is right!" and ordered that the poor Turk be tortured to find out the size of the Turkish army's strength in that area. Stabs, cuts and vicious blows to head and body soon had the Turk parting with the limited information he possessed.

Apparently, his party was only about twenty strong, and one of many patrols scouring wide areas to see if the Russians did, indeed, have plans to attack from any other direction. The main Turkish force was still encamped by the Crimea.

Having divulged all he knew, the Turk looked to Lev hoping to be spared. The brutal General ordered him killed anyway, and watched without pity as the Turk died defiantly under a terrible rain of hacking, bloody blows from the Russian swords.

Aghast at their cruelty, Mikhail rebuked the General. "You evil swines! There was no need for that!"

"He had served his purpose," the General told him, happy his mission had met with partial success. Getting the Prince back to face charges would complete his task.

The Russian abductors continued their hard journey across Europe with their Royal charge.

Eventually, the weather showed signs of improvement as the spring gave way to early summer. Although the hike across the Carpathian Mountains into Poland was gruelling, with its share of biting, penetrating winds, thankfully to all, it proved safe and uneventful. Now, they were on the last leg of their long journey.

During the endless slog northwards, Mikhail had become stoical as he reflected on the recent terrible, life changing events. *Life goes on*; he thought, not for Oleg and Christina, but it still goes on. He must put his grief behind him and adjust to matters. Either that or be overwhelmed by it all. Try to forget and just get on with things. Adjust, adapt; be stoical.

He saw the sense of it and made a determined effort to put his young bride, and his friend out of his mind; to coldly remove the sadness. It was the only way Mikhail could survive. He took this forced medicine, but it was indeed a bitter pill to swallow.

Chapter Three

St. Petersburg

Two months to the day of leaving Lake Garda, the weary travellers looked down from a hill to view the wide expanse of the majestic city of St. Petersburg, illuminated by the morning sunshine. The chilly offshore breeze from the Gulf of Finland confirmed how far north they were.

Mikhail was glad to see his city again. It looked so different in the early summer: grand and welcoming. He admired, all over again, the haunting magnificence of its vast crystalline squares, the new wide roads and old canals. Beauty and practicality existed side by side in the Russian capital.

He admired the many tree-lined avenues and beautiful parks, most of which had been the work of Peter the Great who, having travelled extensively, had brought new innovations back to his homeland. The Winter Palace was not built yet, but in the very early stages of development.

Tsarskoje Selo was a beautiful palace set in a magnificent park and had been the summer residence of Crown Princess Elizabeth. Now, when not in Moscow, it was the residence of Tsaritsa Anna Ivanovna – Romanov daughter of Ivan V, and niece to Peter the Great.

She was made Tsaritsa in 1730 on the death of Peter the Second, with the help of the Russian aristocracy who had supported her ascendancy to the Russian throne. In their own interest, the Supreme Privy Council members chose her over Elizabeth, a teenage daughter of Peter the Great.

The council imposed on Anna a constitution modelled after Sweden's, which restored some of their lost privileges. She agreed not to marry again, and giving up the royal right to declare war and levy taxes; and allowing the Privy Council to name her successor. However, if they expected her indebtedness to the nobles for her good fortune, they were mistaken. After coming to power, the Tsaritsa enlisted support of the opponents of aristocracy, rescinding all prior concessions. The articles she signed, limiting her powers, were but a minor inconvenience. Anna soon established herself as an autocratic ruler, using her popularity with Imperial guards and lesser nobility.

One of her first acts to consolidate power was to restore the security police, which were used to intimidate and terrorize those who opposed her and her policies.

Opposition to the ruling government was punishable by torture, death and exile. Mikhail was wise to be somewhat apprehensive of his fate.

Conversely but nonetheless to her credit, the Tsaritsa had established ballet and opera in Russia to bring culture into her realm. She held many parties in both Moscow and St. Petersburg. Although she considered herself attractive, at forty-seven years of age, she was bloated and suffering kidney ailments through gluttony and the consuming of large amounts of vodka. Though hardly a beauty; the Tsaritsa was vain, arrogant and self-indulgent. She surrounded herself with foolish and ignorant maids whilst enjoying the false flattery of the servile males who sought to enhance their position at court.

Crowds of onlookers lined the route to Tsarskoje Selo. Mikhail peered out from a carriage window at solemn faced men. The only reaction was from the women who cheered and waved at the handsome young Prince. Some young girls even swooned.

Mikhail smiled. It lifted his spirits.

The gates closed behind the carriage and its escort as they entered the grounds of the Royal summer residence.

On either side of the grand driveway lay exquisitely manicured lawns and landscaped gardens displaying trees and exotic flowers, which exuded a heady sensual perfume.

The carriages pulled up at a side entrance to the grand building. When be-wigged footmen opened the carriage doors, Mikhail alighted and stretched himself.

"Well, here at last," he remarked.

"Yes, indeed, Sire," said the General. Unsure of the Prince's fate and so hedging his bets, General Lev asked, "Will you give a good report of your journey my Lord? We treated you well."

Amazed at Lev's audacity but noting his uneasiness, Mikhail merely shook his head and said, "General, you and your men were responsible for three deaths, and were even prepared to take my life; now you are concerned for your own. You oaf!

"We were just following orders, Sire." the General offered as an excuse.

The Prince gave an ironic grimace. "So you were, General," he said resignedly, "So you were."

With an apprehensive smile, the General smartly saluted the Prince.

Two ranks of Palace guards lined up either side of the entrance.

Lev was about to accompany the Prince into the building when an armed party of secret police appeared quickly surrounding them.

With hand held high the officer in charge silently motioned the General and his men to stay put. Without speaking, the secret police escorted Mikhail into the building. Upon passing through their ranks, the Palace guards, in turn, followed the party inside. The joint escort conveyed Mikhail to the Great Hall, to await the arrival of the Empress. Tired and bewildered, he stood flanked by the palace guards standing rigidly at attention. The secret police guarded all the exits.

Mikhail gazed at the ornate decorations on the ceiling and walls of the Great Hall. Patiently waiting were ministers, courtiers and servants of all ranks dressed in finery. The ladies at court gave the handsome Prince admiring glances and tittered as he smiled back at them.

The great jewel-encrusted hall doors gradually opened, and four trumpeters blasted in unison, hailing the arrival of the Tsaritsa and her entourage.

A startled Pekinese dog barked excitedly upon hearing the fanfare.

The monarch entered the large hall. With layers of pearl necklaces covering her goitered neck and jewels sewn into her billowing gown, Anna was overdressed to such a degree Mikhail thought she resembled an excessively decorated Christmas tree. With a glower from her, the dog whimpered and ceased his yapping.

A long-gowned official announced in a loud clear voice, "Her Highness, Anna Ivanovna — Tsaritsa of all Russia and its territories."

All bowed as her ungainly waddle conveyed the monarch to the royal throne in the centre of the hall. Haughtily, she cast an eye about the room. As she stood there, the silence was eerie.

She appeared to Mikhail, to be the personification of arrogance.

This Tsaritsa lived a life of luxury and opulence, while many of her subjects lived in fear and squalor. She didn't need her secret police to instil terror; her countenance alone exuded sheer malevolence. The privileged life had obviously been wasted on her, Mikhail thought. She could do a lot of good for her country instead of ransacking its treasury just to keep her in fine clothes, jewels, and parties.

She selfishly indulged her every whim and he loathed her and all she stood for; but as many did, wisely kept his opinions to himself. Critics had a habit of vanishing or being made an example of.

The Tsaritsa's swivelling eyes located the Prince. She looked pleased; then seated her large rump on the throne. She snapped her fingers, motioning to the guards, who marched Mikhail briskly before her.

Her counsellor spoke quietly in her ear. "Your Majesty, before this business, there are urgent matters of state!"

She waved him away.

"The chancellor is in need of an audience," he said, "It is arranged. This man can wait. His business is not urgent."

The Empress bellowed, "It is urgent to ME! All else can wait until I have dealt with this matter of my *roving* ambassador!"

Suitably admonished and a little pale of face, the counsellor bowed and stepped back, "Of course, your Majesty."

Prince Mikhail knelt before his Empress. She eyed him up and down. After a long pause, she said, "So, Prince Mikhail, you deign to honour us with your presence? What have you to say for yourself?"

With cool calm the Prince replied, "I do not understand, your Highness. What is it I have done that I should explain myself?"

Wildly, the irate Tsaritsa slammed a fist into the open palm of her other hand. "What have you *done?* You have married without my permission!" she bellowed, "That's what you have *done*!"

"I was not aware I had to have it, your Majesty," pleaded the Prince.

The court gasped at his brazen reply.

"You need my permission to marry a *Catholic*!" she ranted. "How dare you? How dare you disgrace me?"

"But I..." he began.

She interrupted, "You are my roving ambassador. You represent me and my wishes, where so ever you travel, and my wish is that there will be no intermarriage of faiths by my subjects. You didn't even ask permission to wed a woman of our own Orthodox faith — let alone a Catholic! What am I to do with you?"

"I apologise for offending your Majesty. I didn't know."

"Well, you should have!" she roared. "A good ambassador would have kept his monarch informed of all she needs to know."

All he could think to say was, "I plead I am your good ambassador and loyal servant, your Majesty. I fulfilled my role even as I returned to Russia. We have valuable information on our enemies' movements."

"Only because the General had the good sense to torture it out of the captive Turk!" she exclaimed. "You would have taken all day!"

He protested, "I could have got the information without resorting to torture, your Majesty."

"Bah!" she cried. "Your tact and diplomacy could have meant a dangerous delay! Time was of the essence."

"The General and I may have different methods, but I still served you rightly Ma'am," he pleaded.

"That is your duty!" she snapped. "As is your informing me of any *personal* arrangements you might have!"

All was quiet for a moment as it sunk in that the man before her had indeed, attained valuable information. She was grateful for his political skills but still fumed at his marriage without notice, let alone consent. "You show mercy to my enemies. Is that because you hope for mercy yourself?"

Mikhail thought a moment and answered, "May your Majesty's will prevail."

"Exactly!" she growled. "That's exactly what will happen!"

The atmosphere was tense.

God she has a fiery temperament, Mikhail thought.

Warily he ventured, “Is your Majesty aware I am widowed?”

“What of it?” the Empress snapped, coldly.

“I mean, am I not punished enough, Ma’am?” he asked

Menacingly, she spat her reply, “I shall be the judge of what is fit punishment! What you have done is an affront to your Tsaritsa and to your country!”

“I assure you, your Majesty,” Mikhail pleaded, “no affront was intended. I merely fell in love.”

“What!” she bellowed. “You hardly knew the girl! Wed after a matter of weeks! Love? Hah! When I made you Ambassador, you pledged your love for *me*!”

She paused. As the court looked on, slightly puzzled she quickly added, “To the Crown that is; and to your country!”

Mikhail sensed something else was going on in the Tsaritsa’s mind. He realized his position was precarious and had to think quickly. “The love for my country, and my Tsaritsa, is absolute.”

Before she could reply, he added, “It was always so.” He dared half a smile at his Tsaritsa. “Tell me what I must do to prove it.”

All was silent. The crowded court looked on apprehensively. The Tsaritsa was well known for her capacity for petulance and cruelty; but she also had a lustful reputation and Mikhail gambled it may be well founded. If ever he needed his charm, it was now. Her subjects had died for a lesser crime than flirting.

Her demeanour softened. Unknown to all, the old Tsaritsa had long harboured affections for the young Prince, but first, she decided, he had to be taught a lesson. She thought for a moment then said brusquely, “Get this handsome charmer washed down and rested. This matter is not ended. We will speak later.” She waved him to go, and turned to her chancellor. “Now, to other business,” she snapped.

Mikhail bowed graciously and retired from the hall. There was an audible sigh of relief from the court, but none was more relieved than Mikhail. Whatever he had said had got through to the mad old Empress. He had struck some kind of chord, and for now he was reprieved.

A manservant led the Prince out of the hall and along the corridor to his room where a hot bath was drawn for him. “Aahh! At last, a hot soak,” the Prince exclaimed, and hurriedly undressed.

For a full half hour he luxuriated in the hot tub, which the manservant constantly topped up with piping water and aromatic oils. The memory of that grinding, slogging journey faded as Mikhail felt the heat from the water draw the aches and pains from his tightened muscles and jarred bones.

He was towelled down and dressed in a nightshirt. In the

bedroom, the covers on the large comfortable looking bed were turned back. After eight weeks sleeping at staging posts no better than old barns, he felt suddenly very fatigued. He was mesmerised by the large feather bed and it's promise of a luxuriously deep and peaceful sleep.
The manservant informed him: "Her Majesty requests you join her for supper. It is now noon, sire. I shall awake you at six o' the clock."

Mikhail was hardly listening. The sumptuous feather bed beckoned the weary Prince who fought to stay awake until he could reach it. He flopped ungraciously into its comfy depths pulling the large eiderdown cover over himself. A warm veil of slumber swept over him.

The manservant drew down the blinds to shield the sleeping Prince from the daylight then, closing the door behind him, left Mikhail to thankfully drift away into his long awaited and first proper sleep in weeks. He slept deep and sound and dreamless.

At exactly six o'clock the manservant and a maid entered the bedchamber. He placed a jug and bowl of hot water on the dressing table; and shook the Prince; who merely groaned and pulled the covers back over his head.

The maid giggled, causing Mikhail to open his bleary eyes. The pretty girl placed the clothes that she had been carrying, on a chair. Mikhail smiled at her.

"You may go!" the manservant told her sharply.

She smiled at the Prince and left the room.

"There is hot water, sire, shaving soap and a blade. Also, a change of attire. Do you require any assistance?"

"No. I can manage. Thank you."

"Then I shall return in half an hour, Sire, and escort you to the Royal suite."

"The Royal suite?"

"Yes, Sire. Her Majesty commands you to dine with her in private."

"Why?"

The manservant did not answer but merely raised his eyebrows.

"Hmmm, and I thought I was in trouble," Mikhail mused.

The manservant spoke up. "Sire, if I may be so bold. It is a fact that you are well liked in the court and there are many who pray your diplomatic skills and, er... charm will assuage Her Majesty's, er... let's say, ...capricious temperament."

"What are you saying, man?"

The manservant struggled to find the right words, but eventually told him, "There is concern over your predicament. I hope I am not speaking out of place, my Lord, but your fate may well rest in your own, er... hands, if you know what I mean."

"My fate?" Mikhail studied the manservant, trying to grasp the meaning of his words. It was well known the Empress Anna was a strange woman with a volatile disposition. She could just as easily have a man's head lopped off, as shower him with gifts. All were wary of her. The manservant was taking a risk in advising the Prince to be cautious.

After a moment the Prince smiled. "I understand. I know of her odd ways. I shall watch my step." As the manservant walked to the door, Mikhail said, thoughtfully, "Thank you for your support. Thank you all."

The manservant bowed, and left the room. Within the half hour, the two men were walking down the great majestic corridor to the Royal suite.

Mikhail felt refreshed after his sleep, glad to be washed, shaved and rid of his travelling clothes.

Upon knocking, the grand doors to the Royal suite were opened by two footmen. Mikhail noticed they both wore their swords, and rightly guessed these two impressive hulks also served as bodyguards to the Tsaritsa. They all entered the suite and the Prince was beckoned over to the Tsaritsa seated at her throne.

In attendance was the same handmaiden who had brought him his fresh clothes. He glanced at her but did not acknowledge, instead bowing to kiss his monarch's outstretched hand.

"Now you *look* like my ambassador, Mikhail," she said pleasantly, "Well scrubbed and freshly attired. Let us dine. You must be famished. How was your journey? Did my guards treat you well?"

Mikhail was caught off guard by her apparent change of mood. "Er... yes, your Majesty. They treated me as well as I would have expected, and the journey was very, er... long."

Anna clicked her fingers and her maid immediately opened an adjoining door. In came kitchen servants carrying hot steaming trays of food.

Mikhail led the Tsaritsa by the hand to the banqueting table where dinner was served. "I thought you might prefer it to a boring old sea journey."

"It was very thoughtful of you, Ma'am," the Prince graciously replied.

The aroma of the appetisers of cold sauerkraut with gherkins and traditional borscht beetroot soup, plus the heavy black rye bread hit Mikhail's taste buds, and told him he was well and truly back in his home land. Although his palate had been exposed to more exotic food of late, this was what he had been brought up on, and he welcomed the change back to familiar fare. He had especially enjoyed *blini,* the traditional Russian pancakes with sour cream fillings, and the caviar ladled onto heavily buttered bread. However, after so long away, it all now tasted different.

The main course of mutton and pork stroganoff, with an assortment of boiled and baked potatoes and cabbage — all cooked with copious amounts of butter, and served with sauces and garnishes; was a little too rich for him and he found it somewhat *over - facing*. It had been a long time since his stomach had experienced such rich fare.

He was glad the kitchen had prepared salted, boiled herring. *Why not diversify from the traditional Russian diet of high carbohydrates and fat?* he thought. They were situated by the sea after all, which produced cod and herring by the ton.

Though most was used to sell and trade, the wealthier locals had a highly developed a taste for seafood, and the intake of vital protein manifested itself in the healthier complexions and general well being of all those who included it in their diet. It was also easy to identify those who had stuck to the old fatty diet — either through habit or, as in many cases, not being able to afford anything but the cheapest, and most basic, foods.

The Tsaritsa was a glutton and Mikhail thought she overindulged in the less healthy types of fare. Despite being a sea trading port, fresh fruit items like oranges, grapes and limes and vegetables were seldom seen in St. Petersburg. The time it would take to bring such items from the warmer climes meant the food would perish long before it arrived in port.

The Prince wondered if her stodgy diet might also be, in some way, responsible for her fiery disposition and mood swings. On his travels he had heard that an unhealthy diet could affect the mind as well as the body. *Could poor food cause a kind of brain poisoning*? he wondered. It made sense to him, but thought it unwise to include it as a topic at dinner.

As the Tsaritsa greedily devoured a huge piece of pork, the Prince smiled wryly to himself. The revolting spectacle prompted a thought. It occurred to him she, herself, was one piece of pork devouring another. *A fine example of cannibalism,* he mused; but this was no time for humour. He must not relax, but keep his wits about him, and not encourage the wrath of this unbalanced woman.

To that end, Mikhail wisely drank only the non-alcoholic beverages of kvas, a bread-based sweet drink; and kompot, boiled water with fruits and sugar, served cold. He felt a little uneasy throughout the dinner though, as the Tsaritsa's gorging of her meal, was punctuated by meaningful grunts, growls, slurps and looks, which Mikhail could only interpret as being of a lustful nature. He felt she might be a glutton in more ways than one as, with her every mouthful, it seemed she was devouring him as much as she was the pork. With any other woman, this behaviour might be slightly erotic, but at the moment it was all he could do to keep his disgust under control.

The meal continued. Mikhail doing his best to avoid stodge such as the pelmeny, little balls of minced meat wrapped in pastry, as tasty as they were. The desert was just as rich and un-nourishing. Pumpkin oladi, a thick pancake ladled with honey, and rich Russian chocolate and cakes.
Throughout the meal the Tsaritsa swigged copious amounts of strong Russian beer and Samogen, the homemade vodka.

"So what was this business deal you kept all to yourself, Mikhail?" asked the Tsaritsa, between mouthfuls.

Mikhail immediately corrected her. "Your Majesty, It was no secret. I notified you that the widening of a road through the Italian mountain pass could increase trade and good will. The remote villages would then have a link to the bigger towns. I sent word by carrier pigeon. You replied saying you had no interest in such a project, so I felt free to make a personal investment."

She thought for a while, chomping on a piece of chocolate. "So you did," she smiled. "I forgot. Used your own money didn't you?"

"I did, your Majesty" Mikhail replied. "I thought: why let a good opportunity go to waste?"

"Quite wise," said the old Empress, deliberately sucking on her chocolate in a sexually provocative manner.

Mikhail felt somewhat shocked and embarrassed at her explicit and unashamed display of sexual intimation. He was at a loss at what to say next.

With slow deliberation she stroked his thigh and fixed her gaze on him. "You recognise an opportunity when you see it then, do you — my handsome ambassador?"

Mikhail was alerted to his worst fears. The tyrannical old girl had a reputation as a sexual predator, and as Tsaritsa, her demands would be impossible to refuse. *Was he being set up for a night of lust or for the chopping block?* he wondered.

The Tsaritsa poured him a glass of the Samogen. He hadn't noticed a small amount of white powdery substance in the bottom of the glass. "Drink!" she ordered. "Calm your nerves!"

As he grudgingly swigged the tasteless drink, she clapped her hands and bade the servants remove the items from the dining table.

"Come," she ordered, "We will sit and talk."

She waddled over to a large comfortable couch and plonking herself upon it, she beckoned Mikhail to join her. Smiling at him, she loosened her button on her jewel-encrusted blouse. "Don't you think it's warm in here?" she asked.

Mikhail was in a mild panic. His brain raced to find a way of changing the subject. *Be wary,* he said to himself, but the suspect alcohol had dulled his normally sharp wits. He struggled to concentrate.

Indicating the things still left on the table she barked at the servants, "Clear that lot up tomorrow. Get out!"

Thus dismissed, the servants all left. Only the handmaiden remained, and the two guards.

"You leave, also. Out!" she told the girl.

The handmaiden curtsied. She and Mikhail exchanged the shortest of glances as he and his Tsaritsa both watched her leave the suite.

When the girl had gone the Tsaritsa asked him "Tell me, why did you smile at her?"

"Who, your Majesty?" asked Mikhail, surprised.

"The girl!" she spat, "The girl! What do you take me for — a fool?"

Alarmed at her sudden change of mood Mikhail said, "You are mistaken, your Majesty. I politely acknowledged her. That is all." He nervously eyed the guards looking on, as he tried to persuade the Tsaritsa of the innocence of his gesture.

She calmed down. Slurring her words, she said, "Yes. You're just Mr. Innocent aren't you?" She held his face in her hands. "Mr. Goody-Goody. Is that what you are, Mikhail, a good man?"

Mikhail felt awkward and cast a glance at his guards. They looked ahead, aloof. "I try to be, your Majesty," he said.

Stroking his face, the Tsaritsa drunkenly sighed, "I have always had a soft spot in my heart for you, Mikhail."

Loosening another button, she eyed Mikhail hungrily, like a wolf about to strike for the kill.

The Prince was racking his brains for a way out of this potentially very dangerous predicament. *'This woman is crazy'*, he thought. The wrong word or action now could mean his life. What to say or do to bring the conversation back onto a normal track? She was difficult enough to reason with when sober. How much more so when drunk?

She screamed at the guards, "Get out!"

"But... your Majesty," uttered one.

"Get out!" she ordered. "Can't you see we have urgent matters to discuss?" she slurred.

The two guards immediately clicked their heels to attention and marched briskly out of the room. Outside they positioned themselves at the door, hands on swords.

With the guards gone, Anna relaxed. "What are your feelings towards me, Mikhail?" she asked him, her bare foot caressing his groin.

"Your Majesty," the Prince began cautiously, "I love and respect you. You are the Tsaritsa, the Empress of all Russia."

"You love me?" she asked coyly, planting a big slobbery kiss on his cheek.

"And respect you, Ma'am," he added. "...as my Empress."

"I am also a woman," she answered, undoing another button on her blouse. Her large bosom heaved as her excitement grew.

He could see the two large pendulous orbs inviting themselves to be touched. Mikhail strived to keep his senses about him. "Ma'am, you are known for your sense of humour and love of practical jokes," he lied, playing for time.

"Am I indeed?" she asked, "and what if this were not a joke my handsome stud?"

He was a young and healthy man. Despite her years and fullness of figure, he thought there was a strange eroticism about her. The Tsaritsa's brazenness and animal sexuality tantalized him. Mikhail forced himself to be strong. What was he thinking? Was it the vodka? Was there something in it? Had it tasted normal? How would he know? He hardly ever drank the stuff, but something was making his head swim. *Concentrate, you fool!* She was there for the taking and he knew it. *Such an opportunity might be welcome to a drunken man on a cold night, but a sober one?* He was glad he had not drunk much of the vodka, and lost control of his libido. *Who knew what would happen?* Yes, he could have her, and he would enjoy it also; and he would damn well make sure she did, too. *But at what price? To hell with that!* What was he thinking of? Fighting the effects of the drug-laced vodka he was determined not to risk losing his head, just because this maniac wanted sex with him. But animal lust pulled at Mikhail's loins. He mustered all his self-control not to take her there and then. *Pull yourself together man,* he told himself as she fondled him. *Keep your wits about you.*

"Tell me your feelings, Mikhail," Anna purred seductively.

"Your Majesty," replied Mikhail carefully, "I have not allowed myself to think of you in any other way but that of my Tsaritsa. How could I? It would not be proper."

Anna stared at him hungrily. "Well tonight I am not your Tsaritsa. I am your woman! If you want me, take me!"

Well, there it was in a nutshell. *Get out of that — if you can*, he told himself.

"Your Majesty," he said, "you are a lovely and voluptuous woman. Any man would love to have you. I am deeply honoured, but I still grieve for my lost wife. Surely you can see that?"

"Pah!" she coughed. "You barely knew her!"

"Your Majesty, please!" implored the Prince.

Ignoring him, the lusty old Tsaritsa stood up and removed her underclothes. Mikhail gulped. She straddled the seated Prince.

With her blouse fully undone, she buried his head in her heaving breasts. "I am not your Tsaritsa tonight. You are not my subject. We are young lovers. Don't be afraid, my darling. We are equals. Take me, Mikhail," she gasped, pouring another vodka down his throat. "Take me. Now!" she cried.

Mikhail's brain was swimming. He felt his blood boil, and his manhood about to explode. He could not control his urges. She did not deserve making love to. What she deserved was just a damn good screwing, plain and simple. *I could do it to her just out of spite*! he thought. *What the hell? It might be my last moments on Earth*, his drunken mind told him. He would give in to her wishes and take this madwoman, this Tsaritsa.

Ripping at his shirt in a state of sexual frenzy, she screamed, "Do it to me! Do it now! I order you!"

Alerted by this, he mind momentarily cleared. "You order me, Anna? I thought you said we were equals, now you *order* me to take you!"

"Just do it!" she yelled. "Do it, or I'll have your head!"

With those words ringing in his ears, Mikhail lost any kind of sexual feelings towards her. His ardour was well and truly dampened. The seriousness of his predicament sunk in. *She is a madwoman.*

"So that's it?" he said, "You mean to punish me. I see it now. First you will gratify your sexual urges, then it's off with my head is it?"

Going wild with lust the Empress told him, "It will be *off with your head* if you *don't* do it!"

"So you say. And what's to stop you having me killed after we're done?"

"Come on. Come on. Come on," she ranted, her loins bucking away on the Prince's lap. "I won't kill you. I promise!"

"How do I know that?"

With that, she shouted for the two guards.

They burst into the chamber, their swords drawn.

This is it, thought the Prince, expecting to feel cold steel upon his neck at any instant.

With swords raised the guards were about to strike.

"No!" yelled the Tsaritsa. "You are here as witnesses to my words. If he *doesn't* do it to me, you are to take his life! Do you understand?"

The guards were speechless. They were aware the old woman was indeed mad, but this had them both flummoxed. Eventually, one said, "We understand, your Majesty."

"And what about afterwards?" the Prince demanded.

"Afterwards, he shall be free to go," she screamed impatiently.

"You are witnesses to that!" Mikhail urged the guards.

They both nodded.

The mad Tsaritsa warned the guards, "But you two *shall* be executed... if word ever gets out!"

"I swear," said one guard.

"You have our word of honour, your Majesty," said the other.

"Good! Now get out!" she yelled at them.

The guards hurried out of the chamber.

"Satisfied now?" she asked the dumbfounded Prince

"I am so nervous, I cannot perform, your Majesty."

"Drink!" she ordered, giving him the vodka bottle.

He took a long swig.

Whilst he drank, the sex-crazed old woman had got to her knees in front of the Prince and was struggling to get his manhood out of his breeches. Eventually she exposed his flaccid member and taking it into her mouth, skilfully brought it back to its full power, by moist tender licks and caresses.

The Prince was almost out of his mind with pleasure. His will to resist had waned by the effect of her actions and the vodka. He felt his blood rise again. He knew he shouldn't, but now there was no doubt that he would.

Mikhail was convinced he was entertaining a lunatic, and not likely to survive in any event, and so resigned he thought *what the hell?*

He decided to give in to his baser instincts — to have his way with her and gratify both their raging lust. *To hell with the consequences,* he thought, *and to hell with her, the mad bitch!*

Throwing caution to the wind, he took her from behind and savagely slammed into her in a steady, deliberate rhythm that had her squealing with delight. He gradually quickened his pace.

Anna panted breathlessly as his hips slapped ruthlessly against her ample buttocks. The air was charged with sexual frenzy. Mikhail's lovemaking was cold and deliberate. She was delirious with pleasure.

However, the alcohol, his mixed feelings and the tension of all the events that had brought him to this moment, suddenly deprived him of any feelings.

His head cleared. He thought to himself, *What the hell am I doing? I don't want this. This is not me. What's happening? Is it the vodka? Am I mad?*

Mikhail was aroused and hard, but could feel no sensation. She, on the other hand could, and delighted in his ability to keep going and going mechanical-like, without climaxing.

He carried on — his mind not willing but his body still strong. It was a function, merely a duty now. He derived no pleasure from it. In his half intoxicated state, Mikhail even entertained the notion she might expire from exhaustion.

The Tsaritsa showed no signs of wishing to stop. Her appetite was immense. Eventually though, after what seemed like ages of frantic sex, Anna's lust was sated. Exhausted and perspiring, she lay back on the couch and gasped for breath.

Outside, the guards peeped through the keyhole to make sure all was well. They grinned at each other. "Unbelievable!" said one of them.

"That was good!" said Anna taking another swig of vodka. Looking down at Mikhail and noticing his state, she asked, "Why are you still hard? Did I not please you?"

"Yes your Majesty. Of course," replied the Prince. "It's just that I am still enamoured of you, Ma'am," he lied.

She thought about his statement then laughed. "Ha, ha. A true diplomat. I chose well to make you my ambassador." Still eyeing his erect manhood, she took another swig from the bottle of vodka. Mikhail thought for a moment that he was going to be asked to do it again, but her demeanour suddenly altered. Her unsettled mind could turn on a rouble.

"You're a liar!" she bellowed. "You are not spent. You can't do it because you don't love me. You never did!"

"I never said I did, Anna. I said I love you as my ruler," pleaded Mikhail.

"Liar!" she yelled. "I made us equals. You were free to love me as an equal, not as your ruler."

"You ordered me!" Mikhail shouted at her. "You forced me to drink vodka!"

"Do you need drink to love me?" she yelled.

Mikhail shouted at her. "But you *ordered* me!"

"You bastard!" she screamed. "You can love a Catholic peasant, but not your Tsaritsa! I'll have your head! Guards!"

For the second time that night, the two guards were obliged to burst into the chamber.

"Execute him, at once!" she bellowed. Covering herself up, she added, "Your Tsaritsa has been ravished!"

The guards stood there dumbfounded, not knowing what to do.

"Do it!" she ordered, "or you will be next!"

One guard stammered, "But, Your Majesty... your orders were..."

Without waiting for the guard to finish, Anna took his sword from him and raised it against Mikhail.

"Stop! Anna! Stop!" cried a voice. Into the bedchamber walked the Tsaritsa's Chamberlain and chief advisor, Ernst Johan von Biron. Assessing the situation, he attempted to calm her down. "Come, come, dear woman. What's all this talk of executions? Such fuss. What has the boy done, but give you the pleasure you crave? Give him a milder punishment, I pray."

"He has humiliated me," argued Anna.

"Nonsense! Your little indiscretion should not upset you. What would the people think if he were executed?"

"What do I care what the people think?" the Tsaritsa bellowed.

Biron replied, "In case your Highness is not aware, your popularity flags somewhat and such an impulsive act might not go down well. Showing a little compassion might improve your standing with your subjects."

The Tsaritsa pondered his words.

"But if you are upset Ma'am," her advisor continued. "May I suggest that I ask the physician to give you some more of his special medicine? Would you like that?"

This brought the old Tsaritsa to her senses, and she calmed down. She knew Biron had powerful friends at court, and he was the only person she really feared. Even her secret police feared him and his connections.

She thought it best not to make a direct enemy of him just yet, but made a mental note to deal with him at a later time.

"No one must ever know," she insisted.

"And no one ever shall, Ma'am," replied Biron.

Now calmer, the Tsaritsa said, "I bow to your common sense as always Master Chamberlain. What would I do without you?"

"All is well, then," said Biron. He took the sword from Anna's hands and laid it on the couch.

Mikhail was indebted to him and the astute advisor knew it.

"I suggest you come with me, Sire," Biron told him.

The Prince nodded and rose to leave.

"Not just yet!" cried Anna. "The dog is in need of *some* punishment!"

"What are you punishing him *for,* your Majesty? Is it because he had the nerve to marry a Catholic, or is it because he refused your love?"

"He has made a fool of me!" she cried.

"No, he hasn't."

"Well, he *sought* to make a fool of me!"

"Nobody will know!"

"I will know!" the Tsaritsa shouted.

"What do you propose then, Ma'am? The stocks? A whipping?" the Chamberlain asked.

The Tsaritsa thought for a moment, then smiled. "I propose that I make a fool of *him*!" Turning to Mikhail she told him, "You are hereby appointed to be the court jester, to appear at my side at all occasions. You will act foolish, be foolish and do all I command a jester should. You will endure laughter and ridicule at my pleasure."

"I refuse!" said the Prince.

"You cannot!" she retorted. "I order it! Besides, you will need a job to pay for your keep. You shall reside here, within these walls, where I can keep an eye on you! You have no money to live elsewhere, so be grateful of my employment — Fool!"

"I am your Ambassador, your Highness" Mikhail pleaded, "and paid as such."

"Not any more!" Anna bellowed. "You are a fool, my fool."

"Send me away to foreign parts," he pleaded, "I will acquire land and trade for Russia. What good would I serve staying here as a foolish jester?"

"It would be good for me! I would like it!" spat the Tsaritsa. "You may thank the Chamberlain for your life, but don't risk it yet again. Your new position at court is settled. You will be guarded day and night.

"Try to escape, and you will die, very slowly!"

She waved to the guards, "Take him away. Lock him in his room. Then wake up the court seamstress, and tell her to make a costume for our new jester. Present him to me in the morning. We will instruct him in his duties as a Fool."

"Yes your Majesty" said one of the guards.

They were about to leave the bedchamber, when yet again she called them all back. "Wait!" she cried. "Bring him here!"

They did so.

She bade Mikhail to kneel before her.

As he knelt, she grabbed the guards discarded sword from the couch, and before anyone could move she had it raised in the air. The thunderous look on her face changed to a sneer. She looked at the concerned faces on everyone and laughed.

Gently, she dubbed Mikhail's shoulder. "Arise. Arise, Mikhail, Prince of Fools. Jester to the Court of Tsaritsa Anna Ivanovna – Empress of all Russia. Now go away, and thank your stars you leave with your head still on your shoulders!"

The guard motioned him to the door, "If you please, my Lord."

Mikhail staggered drunkenly, and placed himself between the two guards, who then escorted him to his chamber.

Chamberlain Biron put his arm around Anna and patted her. "What a wise Tsaritsa you are."

It was rumoured that Biron himself had been one of Anna's lovers for many years, and had used this to advance himself at court. While he sniffed curiously at the Prince's empty vodka glass, old memories stirred in the loins of the lust crazed Tsaritsa.

She sprawled back on the couch and with a lustful leer said, "Close the door and come over here."

Chapter Four

A Fool For All Seasons

Throughout the summer months, Mikhail was paraded at court as a jester. He had no option but to comply with the mad Tsaritsa's wishes. She delighted in making him do the silliest of things; hitting visitors to court with an inflated pig's bladder, piggyback races with dwarves and midgets, telling inane jokes, falling down, running and walking backwards, and reciting stupid verse.

She humiliated and scorned him at every opportunity. "Behold Prince Mikhail Golistyn, former Russian Ambassador, and lover of Catholics," she would tell people. "His talents now more suitably employed as your very own Fool!"

The scared and servile crowds would cheer and applaud.

Mikhail tried not to let it get to him; but instead made an effort to become philosophical about his lot. He reasoned that a lot of folk have worse or even no employment, and many would jump at the chance to pay for one's lodgings this way. He also appreciated that things could have gone a lot worse for him, had the Chamberlain not intervened; and was thankful for that. Meanwhile, he would plod on in his role as Court Fool whilst figuring out a plan of escape.

The summer seemed endless. The many festivities regularly went on well into the early hours. The Tsaritsa made sure he attended all the fairs and balls at court, never missing a chance to have him derided as often, and as publicly as possible.

However, Mikhail had gained a lot of support and sympathy from people at court and beyond. Being handsome, he was popular as always with the ladies which did not go unnoticed by the jealous old Tsaritsa. Every time she saw him chatting to a wench she ordered he put his three-pointed coxcomb hat back on his head and clown's makeup on his face; and go running about ringing a bell declaring his stupidity.

Servile courtiers laughed with the old monarch at the Mikhail the Fool making himself look ridiculous.

Laughing at a fool however soon became boring to the townsfolk of St. Petersburg, and only did so in order to placate the eccentric Tsaritsa. Sympathy was growing for their handsome ex-ambassador, the man who once commanded respect and the confidence of his nation now reduced to ridicule and scorn.

Although he felt undeserving of the treatment, he was alive at least and grateful for that no small blessing; and still being able to flirt with a pretty woman gave his ego a much needed boost, which made life just about bearable.

He began to notice that when some people laughed, they tended to laugh not at Mikhail, but at the Tsaritsa — albeit behind her back — and never to her face. Although a Fool, life was not altogether so bad for Mikhail that summer.

Eventually, the balmy summer gave way to short lived autumn, and the onset of what was forecast to be a very cold winter. Ships arriving into port brought the city and indirectly Mikhail, the news of unusually bad weather at sea, with even parts of the Baltic Sea freezing. It was the year 1739 and by November, Europe was in the grip of one of the worst winters on record. Rivers, including the Seine, Rhine, Danube and Thames, froze solid for months. Old folk perished in their homes. The streets were littered with the carcasses of dogs, cats and pets who had succumbed to the low temperatures.

Canals linking the city to the Volga River froze, denying the transportation of goods by barge and so became of no use but for well-wrapped children to play on and folk to indulge in skating and curling.

It was along the 2,300 mile length of the Volga during medieval times that the ancient trade routes of Russia developed, giving rise to a whole string of trading posts, fortresses and towns along its banks. Access to these was now denied.

If it were not for the ice-breaking ships getting through the Baltic and the Gulf of Finland, St. Petersburg would have suffered the same fate as many other towns and cities; that of being cut off with no supplies.

All this mattered not one jot to the Tsaritsa. As long as she could have her parties at court, she cared nothing for the plight of her subjects. Her only concern was that she might be prevented from going to and from Moscow for more fun.

Travel by barge was out, but wisely, her ministers ensured that sea salt and shale was dumped and spread along the St. Petersburg to Moscow road thereby enabling stagecoaches and carriages to keep their grip, and so ferry people and goods between the two cities.

The citizens of St. Petersburg stoically put up with deprivations the weather had brought. They prayed in their churches that the cold spell would not last long, and gave thanks for supplies from the sea not being cut off.

As in times of adversity, people of fortitude have a trait of *soldiering on* and making the best of things. The hardy Russian folk with their innate stoicism are no different and, perhaps, more adaptable than most at getting on with life despite what is thrown at them.

In place of wheeled carriages, sleds and troikas were used. Draughty doors and windows were sealed with cloths soaked in whale blubber and animal fats.

The latter, along with the likes of goose grease could also be applied to the body as insulation from the terrible cold. That had saved many an infant and old folk when the fires went low and the cold was felt even under the duck and goose down quilts.

The roads and walkways were gritted with sea salt and shale. From shale, paraffin for light and heat could be made. People were resourceful in play, also. Whereas the cold weather meant the end of some games and activities, it brought with it other forms of amusement. Adults, as well as children, took part in skating, curling, tobogganing, skiing and even snowball fights. It was fun, exercise and kept the spirits up; although some preferred to sit indoors hugging a hot brew of tea or a glass of vodka.

Mikhail witnessed such goings on with the Tsaritsa, as she attended them or wandered around with her fool in tow inviting children to throw snowballs at him.

The craftsmen and artisans of the city took to sculpting amazingly intricate designs and images from blocks of ice. So realistic were the ice effigies of trees, flowers and animals that sculptors, with plenty of time to spare, improved their skills and competed with each other for prizes.

It was at one such prize-giving that the Tsaritsa had her most grand and bizarre idea ever. *It would be a magnificent project* she mused and would hopefully impress her subjects enough to restore her dwindling popularity.

The marvellously involved and intricate work of the craftsmen and artisans working the ice had given Anna the idea. The intense winter was indeed severe and by all accounts not due to let up for a long time. Therefore, the notion took hold of her, to construct a castle or palace made out of nothing but ice.

She enlisted the help of the famous Russian architect Peter Eropkin, who had been responsible for construction work in St. Petersburg. Now, in enforced redundancy, the eccentric Anna could put Eropkin's knowledge and building expertise to good use.

After testing the depth of various canals, lakes and rivers running through the city, Eropkin informed her that the project was quite feasible. The many temporarily idle citizens would make up the work force; the craftsmen and labourers. Finance was available, and the whole project had the blessing of the citizens of St. Petersburg.

All was in place to build a marvellous structure made completely of ice. It would be a grand winter attraction, as long as the Baltic was passable.

Visitors could come from afar to marvel at the spectacle, thereby developing a winter tourist economy. It was frivolous, yes, but also practical. There would be commerce and fun even in the depths of winter. Also, Anna thought it wouldn't hurt to help win over her people by providing such an unusual amusement.

Each block of ice was to be transparent, so Eropkin decided that the still waters from one of the many lakes would be perfect; unlike the canals, which were shallow and murky. His idea was to cut blocks of ice from a deep lake, and build the edifice on a sloping bank. When the thaw came, he reasoned, the waters from the melting ice palace will drain back into the lake; but Anna wanted it placed on the river Neva itself, practically in the centre of the city.

"Your Majesty" Eropkin said. "The river will not withstand the great weight of the intended structure, not to mention the weight of hundreds of sightseers walking in and around it."

"Nonsense!" she replied, "Is not the river deeper than a lake? See how the river splits into several branches, before it joins the Gulf? It forms a delta where downtown St. Petersburg is situated and thus ensuring easy access to all. When the structure eventually melts; so would the river it stands on, and all will safely run downstream; thus posing no harm to the surrounding conurbation." She smirked at Eropkin and tapping her head, informed him, "I am not just a pretty face!"

"But your Majesty," the architect pleaded, "As deep as the river may be, it is still a tidal river, an estuary composed of salt water, which will not freeze as thick as fresh water; and, for all we know, there may be tidal movement underneath it. It is too dangerous Ma'am. The lakeside is a safer choice of location."

The Tsaritsa ranted at him. "I say it is safe! Why, all the rivers in Europe are frozen and we are situated even farther north. The ice is probably thicker here than anywhere else for goodness sake. Also the palace will be sited far up the estuary; even safer."

Eropkin explained again that ice-breakers were sailing all along the Baltic keeping the shipping lanes clear, which in turn meant that there would be tidal movement in the Gulf and therefore the estuary. His patient and rational caution however, was wasted on the stubborn and determined Tsaritsa.

"If all the greatest scientists educated guess is that this winter will last for months, we must believe them," she told him.

Eropkin produced a glass tube etched with numbers on it. It was encased in a wooden frame. "Perhaps we can leave guesswork out of it Ma'am.

"Thanks to this recent development of the thermoscope by Mr. Fahrenheit, we shall *know* what the weather is doing."

"It *will* last for months, I tell you!" the Tsaritsa spat. "I want the palace to be seen from far and wide; from the surrounding hills as well as from the port entrance. It is safe, I tell you!" Before Eropkin could speak, Anna raised her hand and cried, "Build it where I say; on the river. Get on with it!"

So, with plans drawn and agreed to, an army of construction workers, artisans and craftsmen commenced their labour of love; and commerce.

Eropkin would not allow the river ice to be cut into. Instead, huge ice blocks of crystal clarity were sawn out of a deep lake, by teams of workers.

The blocks were skidded and dragged to the riverside by teams of men and horses. There, in an area laid out for cutting and fashioning the blocks, they were measured and cut precisely to size before being manhandled on to the frozen river into the pre-arranged positions as laid out in the architects' plan. Men and horses heaved and struggled to get one block on top of another with the help of ramps, ropes and pulleys.

As the blocks of ice were lifted into place, they were cemented together with water, spilled straight onto the joints, which instantly froze. The watering of all the blocks this way, meant the whole structure would become one single piece of ice, and therefore, structurally very sound.

Within a short while the edifice took shape. It was over eighty feet in length, some thirty odd feet high, and about the same deep. Rather than making it a tall building and thus concentrating all weight in a small area; Eropkin built it low and wide, to better displace the weight. It was classical in design with its roof topped off with towers, turrets and battlements, to make it more castle-like.

The outer walls were lined with faithfully reproduced ice sculptures.

If the outside was as a castle, the inside was as magnificent as a palace. It had grand doors on great stud hinges, a large hallway leading to a ballroom with ice-chandeliers hanging from its ornate ice-carved ceiling. The bedroom had an elaborately curtained four-poster bed, with mattress, quilt and two pillows. All were carved out of ice.

Windows were not really needed as enough light penetrated the ice walls themselves, but by including them the architect showed how he strove for the realism the marvellous edifice deserved.

The windows were thin sheets of ice displaying immaculate engravings of saints and Russian heroes. Amazing ice furniture, and even a meticulously carved model clock adorned one of the walls.

Outside, the castle/palace had its own garden with sculptured ice trees with painted ice birds sitting on the branches. Fantastic examples of the craftsmen's skill abounded; like a life-size ice elephant ridden by an ice man dressed in a Persian costume. From the elephant's trunk spouted a 24-foot jet of water during the day; to be replaced at night with petroleum so that the animal spouted flame. Even a trumpeter was concealed inside its body to simulate the elephant's roars.

Competing with this was another marvel of the artisan's work. Six cannon and two mortars made of solid ice.

The correct amount of gunpowder it required to successfully discharge a blast, without damage to the guns or to the public, was measured to the finest calculation. The whole edifice was an amazing piece of construction and craftsmanship.

No one had seen anything like it before. It's fame spread far and wide. The grand opening had all citizens, and as many visitors who could get there, wonder at the marvellous spectacle.

Giant braziers burning wood and coal on the ice served as gathering points for folk to enjoy hot drinks and roasted nuts and meats, and to warm themselves before charging away to various games on the ice.

Inevitably, the Tsaritsa wanted fairs and parties unending, and she organised a massive opening day: a Buffoonery Masquerade where everyone dressed in ridiculous costumes, and clowned about like idiots. Of course, it was another opportunity to ridicule, scorn and poke fun at the unfortunate Prince, but by this time he had adapted to his lot. Mikhail was making the most of it, simply enjoying the festivities like everyone else.

Tsaritsa Anna realised that for her subjects, the novelty of ridiculing her ex-ambassador had lost its appeal. He had genuine sympathy at court, and in the country, and could count many courtiers and maids as his friends.

Whatever tomfoolery Anna had him engage in, he took it in good part and even his friends joined in making fools of *themselves*. The handsome, good-natured Prince was now popular, not the figure of derision as she had intended. The plan had backfired, and the bad-hearted Anna was not happy.

Biron, her advisor, had noticed her foul mood and enquired of her, "What ails Her Majesty? Is this not a happy time for St. Petersburg and all its citizens? Look, we defy the worst the weather can hurl at us. Everyone is happy and they have you to thank for it."

The evil old Tsaritsa snarled at the Chamberlain, "But, I don't want everyone to be happy! Do they laugh *with* me at the jester — or with him at me?"

"My beloved Tsaritsa, are you still upset over the ambassador? Hasn't he paid for his crime of marrying the Catholic? Forget about him."

"I cannot forget!" she snapped, "and NO! He has not yet paid for his crimes against the state and me. But for you, he would be rotting in a dungeon now, or his body floating in the Neva!"

"Banish him if he offends you so much, your Majesty — but death? No. He is much loved here by powerful people. I humbly suggest neither death nor torture would be appropriate, nor indeed wise, Ma'am. Tact and thoughtfulness are called for on this matter. Banish or exile him; but death — no Ma'am. The people love him. They might revolt!"

"But I detest him so!" the old Tsaritsa complained.

"Why, your Majesty? You had your way with him; he served a purpose, now be done with it!"

"I cannot!"

"It is because he rejected *you* not your advances, for he was under orders. He rejected *you*! You could not order him to love you. That's what sits badly with my Tsaritsa. Am I right, Anna?"

The wily old girl mulled over Biron's words, then laughed out loud. "So, jester or no, my handsome Prince is loved at court, is he? I want him dead; and you wish him banished. Well, my friend, the answer stares us in the face. Loved is he? Then let love be his undoing!"

She laughed crazily as they both stood in front of the ice palace, Anna with her arms open, embracing a diabolical idea known only unto herself. Biron looked on scratching his head and wondered what crazy vision his Tsaritsa had seen in her disturbed mind.

A couple of days later, she summoned Mikhail to the grand hall. It was full of courtiers, dignitaries and guards all making small talk. Anna was engrossed in conversation with her advisor when the Prince arrived dressed in his jester's costume.

The Tsaritsa's cronies sniggered at him and some, seeking to gain favour, beat him about the head and shoulders with inflated pig's bladders. They ceased upon the silent command of Anna raising her hand.

"Now, my fine Prince," said the Tsaritsa, "tell me, have you had enough of wearing that foolish costume?"

"If your Majesty decides my punishment is over, I shall be happy to discard it," Mikhail replied.

"You're playing the fool pleases me no more. Anyway, I have other plans for you. Go away, and come back to me dressed as befits this court."

A manservant stepped forward holding Mikhail's royal regalia of tunic, breeches, hat and medals.

Mikhail couldn't believe his luck. Perhaps the capricious old monarch had mellowed at last. It was possible. *Anyone can change,* he thought. He bowed and departed the hall with the manservant.

He dressed quickly. Mikhail thought what a pleasure it was to be out of that stupid costume.

Six months of acting the fool and being ridiculed just for marrying a Catholic was unbelievable, but at last it was over. He vowed never to incur the Tsaritsa's displeasure in future. Perhaps now he might salvage something of his career. Light hearted and optimistic, he bounded back to the great hall.

As he approached the throne, Tsaritsa Anna spoke. "Prince Mikhail, I have been giving your circumstance some thought of late. The reason for your problems was your marital status. You are an impulsive young man, but even I can see you were meant for holy wedlock. It will probably settle you down. I think a romantic such as you, *ought* to be married. It would be good for you."

"But, your Majesty" Mikhail stammered, "I am profoundly honoured, but..."

Anna interrupted him with a laugh. "No, no you fool!" she cried. "I am not proposing that you and I..." She laughed out loud as did everyone present.

"No," she continued, "I have chosen a wife for you, from here at court. What do you think of that?"

Mikhail was perplexed. *What madness now?*

"You see, my boy, I do have your interest at heart. You chose unwisely last time. That was the problem. Trust *my* judgement now, instead. Come."

Mikhail had to play along. He knew there was no choice, and warily stood by her side.

The Tsaritsa clapped her hands and a group of young ladies-at-court, lined up alongside each other. She paraded up and down the line of women with Mikhail in her train. There were courtiers, handmaidens, maidservants, and secretaries and, oddly Mikhail thought, even cooks and cleaners were made to stand in line.

Mikhail's eyes picked out the pretty Polya, and looked at the Tsaritsa for confirmation. She smiled and shook her head side to side. She delighted in seeing the Prince tantalised and curious. It amused her greatly to see him ogling this line of beautiful women, and wondering which he was to be offered. She fancied he looked like a little boy at a party, not knowing which gift to open first.

She shook her head when he pointed to a buxom blonde. The same happened when he stood in front of Olga, Katya and Lyudmilla; all beauties in their own right.

No. It was to be none of these. Anna suddenly clapped her hands and shouted, "Avdotya! Come forward!"

From the rear of the line up stepped forward a very unattractive Kalmyk kitchen servant. She was the plainest girl Mikhail had ever seen! Plainer than the Tsaritsa, and that was saying something.

The look of horror on his face made Anna shriek with delight. "Look at his face!" she cried. "Look at it!"

The girl stood still, expressionless.

"Come forward, girl!" demanded Anna. "Don't be shy. I have a handsome young prince for you!"

To describe Avdotya Ivanovna Buzheninova as plain was a kindness. Apart from her wild Mongolian features, she had a poor complexion, lank hair, a podgy shapeless body, and discoloured teeth. There was absolutely nothing feminine about her. Even her youth did not help her appearance. Today the poor wretch was young and ugly, in time she would simply become *old* and ugly.

Mikhail was horrified that Anna would want to force him into a marriage with this woman. "Will Her Majesty never tire of humiliating me? Haven't I been punished enough?" he bravely questioned his Tsaritsa.

"Silence you ungrateful oaf!" she roared. "You are lucky to be alive." She paused, "And anyway... you will hurt the young lady's feelings!"

With that, everyone burst out laughing.

"Isn't she a beauty? The prettiest Kalmyk in all Mongolia. You see?" Anna said, "I reward my handsome Prince for his loyalty. Nothing but the best for you, my lad."

Mikhail's heart sank. The kitchen girl didn't look any happier.

"You are pleased with my choice?" Anna asked Mikhail sternly.

The forlorn Prince was in yet another predicament of the mad monarch's design. Although nature had not seen fit to bless the girl with any grace or attractiveness, Mikhail still felt some sympathy for anyone who had to go through life so disadvantaged. He needed time to think. His life or death, and the girl's, could be decided on a whim. The forlorn prince answered with a lie. "Yes, your Majesty."

"Good," said the gloating Empress, "because I am very pleased!"

With another clap of hands, a priest from the Eastern Orthodox Church entered the hall followed by choristers, some holding the train of his robes, others carrying the Holy Bible and hymn sheets. Mikhail looked aghast.

"There will be a wedding, NOW!" the Empress bellowed. "Come. No time to waste!"

There followed what must have been one of the shortest wedding ceremonies of all time. The Tsaritsa removed a ring from her bloated finger and urged Mikhail to take it. She pointed to the Kalmyk girl.

With a heavy heart, Mikhail placed it on the girl's third finger of her left hand.

The priest made the sign of the cross and babbled on with the incantation.

Mikhail heard little, and understood less. His mind was numb with shock.

His head was swimming. With the placing of Avdotya's rough hand in Mikhail's, the ceremony was complete.

The crowd cheered and applauded the couple, as the trumpeters sounded a celebratory fanfare; but the newly-weds looked for all the world, like a condemned couple.

"Smile!" ordered the Tsaritsa. "It's your wedding day. You may kiss the bride."

Mikhail looked at his bride, then at his Empress.

The old Tsaritsa said, with menace "I said, kiss her. That is an order!"

Mikhail lifted his bride's veil, viewing her coarse features. Her face was expressionless, her eyes half closed. Her youthful skin blotchy and dry.

Putting his revulsion to one side, he thought she must be as fearful, if not terrified to be in this position as he was. She hadn't asked for this. She was just as much a pawn in this mad woman's game as he was. Their eyes briefly met. He was surprised to notice that her eyes were quite blue; as blue as a robin's egg, and perhaps her only saving grace. Though expressionless, he thought he saw them slightly moisten, as if holding back tears.

Mikhail could offer no passion in the brief kiss, more like compassion for his fellow victim of a despot's indulgence.

The capricious Tsaritsa smirked, "What a lovely couple," then yanked the ring harshly from Avdotya's finger. To Anna, in her desire for revenge, this was the pinnacle to which her mad dreams could aspire.

The most handsome man in the court had rejected her; now he was paid back by being forced to wed the ugliest woman in the land.

The bad – hearted Tsaritsa delighted in the evil irony of her sick plan, and told them, "And NOW, you will find that no expense or consideration has been spared for you to enjoy your, er... honeymoon."

Cheers and guffaws went up from the crowd.

What torment and humiliation was in store for them now? Mikhail wondered. *Would they suffer? Would they both survive?*

Chapter Five

The Ice Palace

Avdotya looked solemn, detached. The couple were ushered outside where, on the grounds of the royal residence, a large crowd had gathered. To the couple's amazement, an elephant had been decorated with elaborate adornments, and upon its back was a cage with two seats inside. Its trainer made it kneel, and the newlyweds were ordered up a set of steps and inside the cage.

The guards made them sit on the chairs inside the cage and face each other. The elephant rose to its feet and, on command from its trainer, began walking. Following them, were groups of grotesque human beings; freaks, misfits, oddballs, cripples, dwarves and members of despised ethnic minorities, with the swelling crowd jeering at the whole entourage.

Locked in their cage atop the elephant's back, Mikhail and his new bride headed the weird procession.

Following them was the open troika sled pulled by three horses abreast, transporting the Tsaritsa who was wrapped in heavy furs for protection against the harsh, cold air.

Along the way, the bizarre group were joined by even more people. Some playing balalaikas and accordions, some banging drums, others blowing flutes and tin whistles, whilst onlookers and bystanders laughed and ridiculed the caged newlyweds.

Arriving in the downtown area, the whole procession marched out onto an area of the frozen river Neva.

Mikhail and Avdotya could not believe their eyes at the spectacle in front of them; and were astounded by the magnificence of the awesome edifice that was the ice palace. They gasped in amazement at the surreal structure and all its marvellous adornments of ice statues of trees and animals in its grounds.

The nervous couple were manhandled down from the cage on the back of the kneeling elephant and brought before the Tsaritsa as her troika pulled to a halt.

Pointing to the grand edifice, Anna said, "A wedding present to the handsome Prince and his lovely bride; your very own palace! As you deserve! A bed has been prepared in the honeymoon suite. All made from ice, naturally."

The servile crowd laughed, along with their Tsaritsa.

Mikhail tried to speak. Holding her hand aloft, Anna said, "Do not thank me. It is the least I could do for a subject as loyal and obedient as yourself."

The Prince pleaded, "Your Majesty, we will surely perish. Let the girl go, she has done you no harm."

"How sweet and thoughtful you are to your lovely bride," was her sarcastic reply. "You two love-birds will be happy together. Now go on; get inside."

"We shall perish!" insisted the Prince.

"Not at all," replied the mad Empress, as the guards grabbed them, "You will have your love to keep you warm!"

Back slaps, belly laughs and uncontrollable hysterics issued from the crowd at the Tsaritsa's remark.

The frightened couple were sick to their stomachs at the prospect of being entombed in the icy edifice.

"You are a man with too much love, Mikhail," the Tsaritsa continued. "Love for the girls at my court? Oh, yes. Love for a Catholic? Indeed; ... but love for your Tsaritsa?" She shook her head. "I don't think so. Nevertheless, a man with so much love deserves to share it with the prettiest wife, and in surroundings of luxury. A Prince and his Princess in their own palace."

Biron, her advisor, interrupted her. "Ma'am. You cannot!"

"Cannot?" she bellowed. "How dare you?"

"Your Highness, it amounts to a virtual death sentence. The people will not forgive you if they die."

"What care I about the people?" she snapped.

"There could be an uprising, your Majesty!" said Biron.

The mad Tsaritsa barked, "Then the dissenters may join them. The palace is big enough!"

Biron pleaded. "Please be wise, your Majesty. I beg you."

"See. The people are laughing. They love this sport. They love me! They don't hate me."

"They will if the couple perish, your Majesty," replied her advisor.

Anna thought for a moment. "If they survive the night, they may go free. If not, we can say it was an accident."

Biron reluctantly agreed, but begged, "Give them some protection, at least Ma'am. Let the crowd know it be a jest. That you do not seriously intend them any harm."

Anna spoke to the crowd. "Let them be given a cloak each, to preserve their modesty through these transparent walls."

The crowd laughed.

The couple, now terrified at their imminent incarceration were given a cloak each by someone in the crowd, then bundled through the tall icy doors, and into the ice palace. The doors swung on stout icy hinges, and closed behind them.

With Mikhail and his wife inside, the guards threw buckets of water at the door hinges, freezing them almost instantly. They were now locked inside their icy tomb. Despite protection from any breeze, the low temperature inside crept into their muscles and within minutes they were shivering. Dread filled them both.

The Prince took both their capes off and, placed the two capes, one atop the other, over their heads and around their shoulders, doubling what insulating capacity they might have.

The couple could see the Tsaritsa and the crowd through the transparent icy walls, goading and cajoling them to lie on the icy bed in the bedchamber.

Guards waved their swords at them.

Mikhail thought it best to obey for now, as the mad Anna could merely have the walls smashed in and them both put to death.

Anna smirked and the crowd roared its approval as the couple lay on top of the massive piece of ice that was their nuptial bed. As they huddled together for warmth, Mikhail's brain raced for ideas.

Outside the party continued. Drunken revellers jeered and catcalled at the newly-weds, freezing inside their glacial tomb. The Tsaritsa peered in through the frosty windows to see how they were faring.

Her gloating face was a picture of malevolent glee as she witnessed the two cuddled up together, rubbing each other frantically trying to create heat by friction, and hopefully delay their inevitable, shivering end.

Two burly, armed guards in sentry boxes were posted outside the big frozen doors. Others were positioned every thirty feet or so around the castle's perimeter, each standing by their own lit brazier and a small supply of wood to last them through the night.

Inside the palace there was no heat of any kind; not even a small candle.

As the evening drew on, the crowd realised there was nothing to see and, becoming bored, began gradually to disperse.

The fur wrapped Tsaritsa sat in her troika drinking hot wine with Biron. That and the half dozen lit braziers on either side of them kept the freezing night air at bay.

He checked the time by his pocket watch. "They have been in there for two hours now, your Majesty. Let them out. You have had your pleasure."

"Not yet!" snapped the Tsaritsa.

"But they might be dead already!" Biron exclaimed.

"Let's wait and make sure then," insisted the mad old monarch. With an evil smile she said, "I'll wager you a hundred roubles they don't last another hour."

He answered, "Sadly, Ma'am, I would not take that bet. But how will we know? Why not take them out every hour or so? That way we shall know to the closest hour when they died. We could all take bets."

"Do you think me a complete fool, Biron?" Anna spat. "You just want to give them more chance. No! They stay until sunrise! If they survive, they go free. That's what we decided. It is fair, is it not?"

Eventually, the cold night and lack of activity within the ice palace bored the spectators and so went home to their warm beds. The Tsaritsa was smug in the certain belief her handsome lover would pay the ultimate price for her perceived rejection by him.

Inside their icy chamber, the couple shivered. Mikhail was suffering most as he had less body fat than Avdotya.

She noticed it had gone quiet outside and getting up off the frozen wedding bed she went over to a frosted ice window. Peering through, she saw that only the guards were outside now, stamping their feet and patting their arms. She thought to do the same. She hurried back to the bed and got Mikhail to his feet. He was now quite drowsy from the effects of the cold.

"Sain by noo. Sain by noo," she said in her native tongue. "Hello. Hello. Wake up. Do not sleep. Do not sleep," she told him, her breath forming little white clouds in the air. She walked him around the chamber, hugging him tightly under the cloaks forcing blood to circulate into Mikhail's numb brain.

"What are you doing?" he asked in a daze.

"Sorry my lord if you find me loathsome, but we must cuddle up to make more heat."

"I understand," he mumbled.

"Keep walking," Avdotya instructed, guessing correctly, that her extra mass could help them both; if only she could hug him close to her to convey her body heat.

Slowly, Mikhail responded as they paced around sharing each other's warmth. From a pocket in her dress, his co-prisoner produced a small pot jar.

"What's that?" he asked.

"Is goose grease. It seals heat in," she informed him. "There's not much," she added, and rubbed it into his neck, then undid his shirt and rubbed some more onto his chest and spine. The remainder of the goose grease was spread thinly on her own head, neck and chest area directly over the heart; saving the last small measure for their feet and fingers.

Avdotya put the two capes back over them, and they carried on shuffling around on the ice floor, hugging and rubbing each other all over hoping to generate enough heat by friction to stay alive.

"I forgot your name. What is it?"

"Avdotya."

"You are a resourceful woman, Avdotya."

"I come from the Steppes. Now *that* is a cold place!"

Mikhail forced a laugh at her remark. "Ha, not nice and warm like here then, eh?"

"Also, I am not used to the salty sea air of St. Petersburg, so I use the grease to stop my face being chapped raw. It's lucky I had some on me."

"Well, we deserve a bit of luck," said Mikhail, smiling at this ugly woman who he realised had probably just added vital hours to both their lives.

She told him, "Well, I don't intend to die here, so come on; cuddle up! Let's rub and pace around. Keep walking."

He knew she was right and so complied, hoping her perseverance would pay off. *What time was it? How long will this night last? If only we could fight this numbing cold and manage to stay alive until the sun's rays came up.*

He cursed the Tsaritsa for condemning the kitchen girl as well as he; yet was thankful for her being there as he knew he would have perished already without her.

****

Outside, in the dark, a beggar was relieving himself near the castle wall.

Suddenly, one of the guards grabbed him. "What are you doing?" he shouted angrily.

The beggar answered timidly, "Begging your pardon, sir. I meant no harm I am a poor beggar. I was just relieving myself."

The guard pushed him and said, "Then relieve yourself somewhere else, old man." He reproached him, "What if I let every beggar relieve himself against the wall? Why, the whole castle would melt from the heat from your foul fluids! Wouldn't it? Wouldn't it?"

"So it would, sir," agreed the beggar, "So it would."

"Then, be gone, before I crush your skull!" the guard shouted. As the old man stumbled away down the path, flaying himself for warmth, the guard called him back.

Ordering the beggar to hold out his hands, the guard ripped off a piece of the beggar's coat and said, "Hold this!" He placed a hot ember of burning wood into the old man's covered hands.

The old man smiled at his kindness.

"Now go!" said the guard, and laughing, kicked at the beggar's backside as he turned to leave.

The old beggar disappeared around the corner of the castle, leaving the guard to sit in his sentry box huddled by his brazier.

With his great furs preventing loss of body heat soon enough warmth was generated to make him feel a degree of comfort. Thus relaxed he was able to kill time by marvelling at the wonder that were the Northern Lights. Witnessing their shimmering hues of green and violet hanging like drapes billowing in a silent breeze, he wondered to which gods he should pray and give thanks for such an awesome spectacle. The dancing shapes against the black, star studded sky provided fascinating entertainment. He thought, *How much more terribly cold it must be up there where they flash and cavort across the heavens and how they must envy my little world of meagre comforts. I have my brazier, my furs and a nip of vodka. What do the gods give them? I'd much rather be me down here looking up at them than them up there looking down at me'.* With that he gave a shiver and greedily swigged the last drops of his vodka then, warming his hands by the brazier's flames, he settled in as best he could.

When he was out of sight of the guard, the beggar stopped outside an ice window and looked around. Although perimeter guards had been posted every thirty feet or so, fortunately wall buttresses on either side of the window meant it was in a blind spot to them. Taking advantage of this, and the dark night, the beggar took out the ember of wood and blew at it furiously to maintain the hot end. When it glowed red, he placed it against the window and drew it down the ice, in an attempt to cut the ice window.

However, the melted ice simply dampened the hot ember, compelling the old man to blow hard at it again to try to reproduce its hot tip. It was useless. It simply went soggy.

The beggar took off his cloak, and placed it against the window thinking to break the ice-glass by hitting it with the lump of wood.

He re-thought this strategy however, when he heard one guard call to another. He realised the ice window was thick and it would make too much noise in breaking.

The beggar stood stock still until he saw the guard 'about-turn' and start pacing away.

When the guard was out of sight, the freezing beggar hurriedly put back on his cloak, patting himself to beat some warmth back into him. He gave up on the idea of breaking the window, and tossed the old ember away.

Over three hours had passed since the couple's incarceration. Inside the bedchamber their condition was worsening. They huddled together on their knees so as to make as little contact as possible with the ice. Both were pale and the blue tinge of cyanosis began to show on their lips, noses and ears. Their fingers and toes were also suffering badly.

Avdotya wiped a smear of grease from behind her neck and applied it to Mikhail's blue extremities. "Lips, ears, nose; they go blue, then black then fall off," she explained then cradled the shivering Mikhail in her arms and mumbled through her rattling teeth, some old Mongolian chant.

"What are you saying?" asked Mikhail. "Are you praying for God's help or praying for death?"

She told him, "I am Kalmyk woman. We never say die. Death will come anyway. Why pray for it? I pray for life."

Mikhail smiled at her. She had given him at least some hope of survival. He was thankful of her positive attitude, but he knew the reality of their situation.

"Zoo gear." she said.

"What?"

"It means *don't worry*."

Mikhail gave her a smile and silently cursed the Tsaritsa again for involving this poor woman in this terrible situation. Why should *she* be punished as well as he? He knew they couldn't last much longer and despite feeling sorry for this blameless wretch, he was grateful he at least had the chance to die in the arms of a decent woman.

"How long before dawn?" he asked.

"Long time. Come, let's rub." With that she continued with her attempts to increase their body temperature by the friction of frantic rubbing. "Fight Prince, fight, never say die!" she ordered.

"Oh God," cried the freezing Prince as he felt the freezing paralysis taking over his body.

Rubbing him frantically she said, "It is said that God helps those who help themselves."

The energy it took also increased their heart rates and breathing, thus raising their rate of metabolism. It all helped.

"You're a good woman, Avdotya," he told her.

She smiled. "Yes, I know. There are not many of us left."

The suffering Prince let out a short laugh. "How can you joke at a time like this?" he said through chattering teeth.

"If not now, when? Shut up and rub." she ordered.

Outside the castle one of the guards standing watch stamped his feet on the thick river ice. A woollen scarf wrapped around his head and face prevented the bitter night air from freezing his lungs. The cold air affected his bladder so, with a wide spray, he relieved himself, careful not to catch the palace walls.

He did not notice in the distance, the woman approaching the castle. She was bundled up in heavy rags and carrying a wooden pail containing some bottles. Her quiet approach startled the guard as he was dressing himself.

"Who are you?" he demanded.

"I am Galina," she said, "from the tannery."

"Don't you know better than to creep up on a guard in the middle of, er... his duty? I might have killed you!" he said with boastful self-importance.

"With one hand?" she asked. "I doubt it."

Quickly rearranging himself, the guard asked her, "Well what do you want, Galina from the tannery?"

She laid the wooden pail by his feet, and removing the two bottles, spoke through her heavy muffler. “Here. Drink. There is vodka and beer to help you through your vigil.”

The guard snatched at a bottle, paused and sniffed at it, then greedily took a large swig. “Aaaahh!” he gasped gratefully, “You are a Godsend, woman.”

“You drink. Keep warm.” Pointing at the bucket, she told him, “Then use that. In there. Not on the ice. I will come back later to collect it.”

“Why? What on earth for?” asked the puzzled guard.

She told him the tannery valued human waste water, as the uric acid could be used in the leather curing process. The drink would keep him warm while his urine would help tan the hides. “Anyway,” she told the guard, “you must not relieve yourself against the wall.”

“I know. The heat from urine will melt the ice, and the Tsaritsa would not be very happy if that happened.”

“You could also *get stuck* to the ice wall — if you know what I mean; and *you* wouldn’t be very happy about that!”

The guard winced at the thought. “Thank you, Galina. Glad we can be of help to each other.” He waved at her as she trudged off into the night. He warmed his hands again by his brazier, and happily took more swigs of his vodka and the beer.

The guard thought this arrangement of free ale, in exchange for vital chemicals needed by the tannery, was marvellous. This symbiotic relationship made him feel important and more useful than just having to guard two frozen bodies, on this terrible night. He toasted himself and his efforts. Within a short while, the combination of the beer, and the cold night air had their effect on his bladder. He gratefully relieved himself in the bucket provided.

From out of nowhere, it seemed to him, there again appeared the wench from the tannery. She swapped the guard’s now full pail for an empty one, and from beneath her cloak she produced another bottle of beer.

“Good old Galina,” slurred the guard swigging his vodka.

She disappeared around the corner and administered vodka and beer to each guard in turn. When sure she had given them enough to get drunk on, she disappeared into the darkness.

By the ice window between the buttresses the beggar shuffled uneasily. He called out to the tannery wench in a forced whisper: “Galina! Over here!”

She joined him in the dark by the ice-window where she set down the pail of warm urine. She gave him a small jug which he then filled with the waste water, and gently trickled the fluid down the top of the half inch thick ice window, first on the left, then on the right.

The window’s icy surface melted a little from the warmth of the urine. The beggar scratched at the weakened ice with his knife blade, gouging a groove.

He produced a wooden ruler from his jacket and laid it horizontally across the top of the pane, trickling the warm fluid across its straight edge. It bit into the ice in a straight line and softened it enough to be able to gouge some out with his blade. He did the same on the bottom edge, then, quickly repeated the whole process, trickling the warm urine on the ice and while still soft, gouging a groove in it.

"This certainly takes a lot of waste water," said the beggar.

"Don't worry, we have an unlimited supply. I have men working on it as we speak!"

The beggar gave a wry grimace, and carried on pouring and gouging. With persistence they eventually saw a gap form all around the window.

Only small stubs of ice at the corners now held it in place. With his fingers inserted in the gap at the top of the window, he applied gentle pressure. The whole pane came loose and the beggar gently eased it out and laid it to one side against the wall. "And there we are!" he told Galina proudly.

After he had climbed into the palace through the hole, the wench passed him a large bundle. He then helped her to climb inside. Once inside, the beggar produced a flask of water from inside his cloak. While Galina held the ice window back in its frame, the beggar spilled some water onto its four corners. It immediately froze, thus holding it in place in its frame once more.

The two of them walked very carefully on the slippery floor, passing through amazing halls and rooms replicated in ice. They marvelled at an immaculately sculpted reproduction of a grand piano and a beautiful ornate chandelier.

They were awe-struck at the perfect ice replicas of settees, chairs, tables and lamps, exact down to the last detail. Lifelike ice statues stared down at them as they carefully edged their way along the hall.

When they reached the bedchamber, the old man pulled back the cloak around the couple's heads. They were still breathing. He wrapped them, and himself, in a large fur so they would share his body heat. Under the wrap, he vigorously rubbed the couple, both in turn.

With some oil-soaked kindling wood, Galina had started a small covered fire on a grid to keep it up off the ice, and soon had a pan of the flask water boiling in it.

With the beggar's help, she sat Avdotya and Mikhail up, and began forcing a hot mixture down their throats. Coughing, gulping and spluttering they gradually responded.

Galina quickly opened up her bundle and produced a thick oilskin cloth, which she spread on the ice bed, and laid a large fur on top of it. One at a time the couple's frost encrusted outer cloaks were removed and their heads and bodies covered with more dry furs. Thus protected from the icy bed beneath them and with the heat retaining furs on top, the deathly effects of the cold were held at bay.

"Come on. Drink!" commanded the old beggar. The hypothermia had stupefied them both, but they now responded to the combination of hot brew, furs and body heat. The old beggar kept on urging Mikhail to drink. "Come on," he repeated.

"Ugh! What is it? It stinks!" coughed Mikhail, coming round.

The beggar told him, "Its herring liver oil with vodka, hot water and honey. It will raise your temperature and sustain you. Drink. It will save your life."

"Uugh! It's vile!"

"Never mind all that," said the beggar, "Drink it! It will create warmth from the inside."

Galina, put a cup of the hot brew to Avdotya's lips. She sipped it readily without complaint.

"Uugh!" Mikhail spluttered, as more of the brew was forced down him.

The beggar urged him, "Never mind '*Uugh.*' Drink it! Come on, drink — you pleb!"

Mikhail's brain registered the familiar insult. He slowly pulled at the beggar's head covering and was stunned to see a face from the grave. "Oleg!" he gasped.

The two men stared at each other. The half-dead Prince could not believe his eyes. There before him was his old friend Oleg, not only alive and well but giving him succour in his desperate hour of need. "It can't be! Is it really you?" Mikhail cried.

Oleg smiled his villainous smile. "It is no other, Sire." The two old friends embraced.

"How can this be?" asked Mikhail, "You are supposed to be dead."

"You also, by the look of things here," laughed Oleg. "C'mon drink this."

"But how?" asked Mikhail, almost in tears.

"Get under the warm furs, Sire, and I shall tell all."

Snuggled under the large furs, with their bellies full of the hot drink and their frosted capes discarded; Mikhail and Avdotya at last felt the life returning to them. Oleg explained that Pavel's arrow had, indeed, pierced his shoulder but laying in the cold snow had prevented him from bleeding to death. Abramo had sent men out to search for him. They eventually found him and returned him to the village to be cared for.

"Thank God for Abramo," said Mikhail.

"Thank God for the cold," Oleg said. "It saved my life."

"I do not thank it now. This night it could take our lives, not save it; but it is good to see you old friend. How are Abramo and the villagers? It seems a lifetime since I was there."

"Abramo is well. It was he who sent me to St. Petersburg to see what had become of you once I had recovered. I travelled in better style and comfort than you, I dare say."

"A better carriage?"

"No, Sire. I travelled across land through France as far as Calais, then took a ship through the North Sea and the Baltic. It took a mere four days. The winds were kind."

"That's the way to travel, but that must have cost you a pretty penny."

"Er... well, actually," Oleg said, "it cost *you* a pretty penny, Sire, not I. Abramo paid the fare from your estate."

Mikhail laughed. "And well spent it was, too!" he cried.

"Also, my Prince, I brought plenty with me," Oleg told him. "I anticipated you might have need of a few roubles." He patted his pocket, which issued forth a welcome chink-chink of silver coins.

"Good thinking, Oleg. What a friend to have in such times."

Oleg told him that he had been in St. Petersburg for weeks, waiting for an opportunity to contact the Prince, but there were too many guards and secret police around. He had spent the time ingratiating himself into the company of the ladies at court, and learning what he could.

Galina brought a pot of grease from within the bundle, and proceeded to smear it all over the couple.

"Ah! Goose grease," said Avdotya, helping Galina to partially undress Mikhail and quickly smear great dollops of it on his head and back first, then all over his body, sealing in the warmth, before speedily dressing him again.

It was then Avdotya's turn. She turned her back, and with Galina between her and the two men for privacy, she undressed. Galina lit a candle to see better.

"No!" cried Oleg. "The light may be seen outside." He went blow it out, first taking a peek at Avdotya. Unimpressed with her looks, he pulled a face to Mikhail and shook his head.

Mikhail smiled and said, "Oleg, you're terrible."

"Well, she *is* a bit hard to look at. She has a face like a bulldog chewing a wasp!" He blew out the candle. "That's better," he laughed.

In the dark, Avdotya elbowed Oleg hard in the ribs. He let out a stifled yell. "Listen who is talking!" said Avdotya. "You are no oil painting, either. You have a face only a mother could love!"

Grunts of suppressed laughter, guffaws and giggles issued forth from the quartet. Mikhail and Avdotya were, by now, warm from the effects of the drink and combined body heat, and were feeling a lot better.

"Good for you, Avdotya!" cried Mikhail. "He is my friend but he is also a rum beggar. Aren't you, Oleg?"

Rubbing his side good-naturedly, Oleg replied, “Well I look at it this way, Sire,” and pulled a ridiculous looking face.

“You clown,” said the Prince as he repositioned himself and Avdotya between Oleg and Galina.

Turning to Avdotya, Oleg said, “You give as good as you get. I like you.”

He went to give her a hug, but Mikhail’s arm shot around her in an involuntary movement and pulled her away slightly in a subconscious act of protection.

Oleg looked quizzical.

“I think we are warmed up enough now. Shall we go?” asked the Prince.

“No your Highness,” said Oleg, “I’m afraid you must stick it out until dawn. Your lives wouldn’t be worth one rouble if you were found escaping. We’ll stay with you as long as possible. You’ll make it. Don’t worry.”

“He’s right,” said Avdotya, “We’ll do fine now. Just a few more hours.”

“A toast!” said Mikhail raising his mug. “To my three companions, who I know have saved my life this night. I shall be forever in their debt.”

They quietened down and enjoyed more of the hot brew, all four of them snuggled up together and sandwiched between the great furs.

Outside, the guards were pacing up and down, then, warming themselves by their braziers. Eyebrows and beards were heavy with frost.

Inside the palace, the life-sapping cold had been temporarily abated. Under their furs, their combined heat and stomachs full of the hot beverage meant that for Mikhail and Avdotya, their chances of survival in the icy halls had greatly improved.

Oleg and Galina were fairly certain that the couple would now be able to sleep rather than drift off into a cold-induced coma.

Before they were allowed to doze off, Galina produced thin strips and panels of fur instructing Mikhail and Avdotya to wear them under their clothes for added insulation. “Just an afterthought,” she said, “otherwise you could be back where you started.”

Once attired in their new underwear they were allowed to sleep, but with Oleg and Galina snuggled up to them and keeping an eye on their breathing.

The flickering from the guard’s brazier, outside formed strange dancing lights around the walls of the icy chamber. Oleg thought it was decidedly eeric. *How weird*, he thought as he snuggled up to Galina, *What crazy person could have imagined a place such as this?*

The hours passed in the freezing palace. Eventually, sensing a slight change in the light outside, Galina roused and got busy brewing another pot of the herring liver oil, vodka and honey brew. She woke the newlyweds, and bade them drink. With apologies, she started packing the oilskin cloth and furs into a large bag.

Meanwhile, Oleg was hacking away at a piece of the wall and away fell a large chunk of ice. While the couple drank and paced around, Oleg melted the lumps of ice in the pan. Galina refilled Oleg's jug with the water, then made a hot brew for the couple to keep them going after she and Oleg had gone.

"We can leave you a flask of hot brew," Oleg said. "Hide it in your clothing. That and your fur undergarments should sustain you until the guards release you at dawn, but keep pacing. Exercise; it will keep your blood circulating. Keep moving your fingers and toes, or the frostbite will attack them first."

Having packed the oilskin and furs to remove all evidence they had been there, Oleg and Galina made their way back to their point of entry; where Oleg took a small saw and hacked at the frozen corners of the ice window. It gave way.

He and Galina scrambled back outside through the hole. With Oleg on the outside and Mikhail inside the two friends shook hands through the open window.

"Thank you my friend," said Mikhail.

"See you soon," replied Oleg.

From inside, Mikhail held the ice window up into place within the frame.

Outside, Oleg splashed the water from his jug around the edges of the window to re-seal it as it froze. The guards to either side of them were sound asleep in a vodka induced stupor.

With the window now secure, Oleg and Galina looked around, then silently disappeared into the darkness.

Mikhail and Avdotya paced up and down with their arms around each other and heads under the two capes; every now and then taking sips of the brew Galina had left them. They paced, drank and talked as the dawn started to break, and rays of early morning light pierced the ice walls.

"Avdotya," Mikhail said, "I am sorry."

"For what, Sire?"

"This is my problem. You would not be here but for me," he explained, "and for that, I am truly sorry."

"Oh, it's all right, Sire, we'll get through this now. Anyway, it's not your fault we are here. It's that pig of an Tsaritsa!"

Mikhail gave her a surprised look.

She immediately apologised to the Prince in case he was offended by the insult to the Tsaritsa.

Mikhail smiled and told her, "You called her a pig. Well, I ate a meal with her, once. She was eating pork, and I thought she was like a cannibal eating her own kind."

Avdotya's laugh came as a pleasant surprise to Mikhail. It was attractive, and quite feminine in its own way, he thought.

"Pork, eh? Well, you know what they say. *You are what you eat*!"

With that Mikhail roared with laughter. "Well said, woman! I like your sense of humour. It's so refreshing."

They both laughed and continued pacing as the sun began to rise.

"How long have you been at court?" he asked her.

"A few months only. I was a teacher in my village near the Volga. I came to the court to improve my skills."

"A teacher, no less!" Mikhail exclaimed. "I am impressed. Intelligence as well as...." He paused.

"Beauty, my Lord? You don't have to say it. It does not apply to me."

"Now I am embarrassed, Avdotya. You are right. I have said such words often in order to flatter. It is shallow and I apologise."

"No matter," she replied, and then, with a straight face said, "I have thick skin."

Mikhail stared at her, not knowing what to make of the comment. Her face creased into a wide smile and she laughed out loud. Mikhail realised Avdotya was teasing him and laughed with her. He didn't know how to take this woman. She was intelligent with a dry sense of humour he liked.

They drank another sip from the flask that Oleg and Galina had left them, and continued pacing the floor to keep their circulation up.

"What did you teach in your village?"

"Cookery."

"Cookery?" he said, surprised. "I thought you said you came to improve your skills?"

"So I did, Sire."

"But surely, a cook is a cook? How much skill is required to cook food?"

She gave the Prince a wry smile. "Sire, there are many ways to improve most things. As for food, well, if it is undercooked it can cause illness, stomach-gripe and worms. If overcooked, the essential nutrition may be lost from it. Either one of these means your body is not assimilating the goodness of the food. You may as well be eating grass."

"Fascinating! I see you have made a study of the matter."

"Indeed, my Lord, there are experiments I would like to conduct to see the effect of certain foodstuffs on the human body."

"For instance?"

"Well," she continued, "in a port, such as St. Petersburg, ships bring in different foods from afar. I wish to see such things as do not grow here, like limes and oranges and lemons. The British Navy, apparently, issue these to their sailors to protect them from the scurvy. Have you witnessed such, my Lord?"

"No, I haven't," he said, "But I once lived in a place where these fruits grow naturally and no one there had scurvy. In fact they all appeared well and healthy. Mind you, the weather was always sunny, and there was always an abundance of fresh foods: fish, and fruits and suchlike."

"That is my point, Sire; eat well, and you will look well. I would hope to improve my looks by changing from a poor diet of mutton and borscht. All Russians are lumpy. They consume too much stodge to help keep them through the winter months. They pile on pounds of flesh like hibernating animals."

"You are right, Avdotya," observed Mikhail.

Pacing up and down, the couple kept talking, partly to distract themselves from the bitter cold, but nonetheless interested in each other's views.

Avdotya continued, "I fear the Tsaritsa's diet may be her undoing."

"Really?" asked the Prince "How so?"

"Her diet is also that of greasy food, with little or no fresh vegetables or fruit. That, with her high consumption of vodka, may account for her bloated appearance. The alcohol is impairing the function of her kidneys, thus creating water retention. That alone will bloat a person, and the food is just stodge with poor nutritional value. If she changed her diet, her health would not only improve, but it might also change her appearance."

"Fascinating! You are, indeed, well read. Tell me, can diet also affect one's disposition? I mean, can it affect one's mental health as well as the physical?"

Avdotya thought perhaps the Prince might think her vain in displaying her knowledge and intellect. Not wanting to risk his displeasure she decided to lighten the mood. After some thought, she advised the Prince, "Yes, some believe it can, my Lord. For instance, I believe she consumes far too much grass in her diet."

Mikhail looked perplexed. "She is greedy, and it turns her nasty," Avdotya continued, suppressing a little smile.

"Too much grass?" the puzzled Mikhail finally asked.

"That's right. She ought to leave some for all the other cows!"

Mikhail roared with laughter. He had almost believed her. They both laughed heartily at her teasing.

Avdotya was good company, and intelligent as well. He had decided she was witty, bright and resourceful, and he could have done a lot worse than to share such a night with a woman like her. He was also taken with her nice smile and speaking voice, which came as a surprise. It was a great shame her appearance did not fit them.

Outside the palace wall, the laughter had not gone unnoticed by the bemused guards. It was dawn now, and the Chancellor Biron was out front with dozens of townsfolk, curious to see what had become of the newlyweds.

With the arrival of the Tsaritsa and her entourage, Biron ordered the doors be hammered until they broke into several pieces, and entry could be effected.

"Go inside and bring out the honeymooners!" ordered the sneering Tsaritsa.

Before the guards could act, the couple, still huddled together for warmth, their cloaks and heads covered in frost; shuffled out from inside their frozen prison.

"They're alive!" gasped one of the crowd.

Mikhail and Avdotya looked up at the sun in the sharp, cloudless winter sky. "I'll wager you never thought you would see that again?" the smiling Biron told them.

"Indeed no, my Lord Biron," replied Mikhail.

"It feels so warm," remarked Avdotya.

"Well, compared to being in there, I suppose it is!" noted the Chamberlain.

"I still feel cold enough to perish," said Mikhail, blowing and rubbing his hands.

Studying his Fahrenheit contraption, Eropkin informed them, "The thermoscope today does, in fact, give it slightly warmer by half a degree."

"Perhaps, a thaw comes at last?" wondered the Prince out loud.

"Who knows?" answered the smiling Biron. "It could not come soon enough, eh?"

The joyful crowd gathered around the couple, patting them on the back, and offering them food, hot drinks and extra cloaks to cover them.

Tsaritsa Anna was furious. "He was not supposed to see the sun... ever again!" she blasted. "The woman must be a witch. That's it. She's a witch! They will be executed immediately! Guards! Seize them!"

Biron raised his hand high. "Hold fast!" he bade the guards.

"How dare you?" Anna spat.

The officer in charge of the secret police produced a hand pistol.

"Leave it to me, your Majesty." he said.

"Leave it to *you* – you thug?" snarled Biron. "This is not an easy murder in the night. Could you face a crowd that size?"

"Take care," warned the officer, "my men out number yours."

"Not for long," said the Chamberlain, "I have the people on my side, and from them I can recruit more guards. You and your men are more despised than our monarch. It is you who should take care. Put your gun away, you fool."

As if responding to a silent command, a number of the palace guards surrounded the officer. Nervously, he re –holstered his pistol.

The angry townsfolk surrounded the couple and would not allow the guards or the secret police access to them. They began to boo and hiss at the evil old Tsaritsa.

Sensing danger Biron said, "Your Majesty, think wisely, I urge you. You promised to release them if they survived the night. Well, they have. Now, show the people you are a monarch of your word."

Even Anna could see the large crowd could easily overpower the guards should they wish.

She also was painfully aware that the fickle crowd displayed more love for the couple than they ever would for their ruler, but could not risk a riot with her guards outnumbered. Fuming at her missed opportunity to satisfy her vengeance, she complained to her chamberlain, "But, he committed a crime!"

"And a night in that place was his punishment, your Majesty," insisted Biron. "They have suffered enough. Why, it is a sheer miracle they both survived."

"A miracle!" gasped the eccentric old monarch. "Y-e-s. That's what it must have been! See how well they appear. How fresh and unharmed. If she is not a witch, then the palace must have magical properties!" she ranted. "Yes, of course. It all makes sense!" she reasoned, as she stood transfixed, mesmerised by the imposing great icy structure.

"Your Majesty," pleaded Biron, "Let them go. Show this crowd you are a magnanimous ruler. Do not have them hate you any more than they do already!"

Anna was lost in thought. "Er... yes. Yes, yes. Let them go!" she instructed.

The crowd roared its approval and carried the couple off shoulder high.

The mad old Tsaritsa told her advisor, Biron, "They are banished from court; both of them. I wish to have no further dealings with them."

"Thank you, Ma'am." replied Biron, "Most wise. Most wise."

The Chamberlain whispered instruction to one of the guards. A short distance away were two elaborately sculptured ice coffins. Standing guard over them were several members of the sinister secret police.

"Out of our way!" one palace guard ordered.

"By whose orders?" asked the officer.

The palace guard nodded in the direction of Lord Biron who waved back at the small group.

The surly officer acknowledged the Lord Chamberlain and begrudgingly bade his men to allow the palace guards to access the ice caskets.

Two guards quickly hacked at the coffins with their swords, until they were unrecognisable rubble.

It would not do for the crowd to see their Tsaritsa had not

intended to keep her word. Even in death it seemed, Mikhail would not have been spared one final humiliation; that of his and his wife's dead bodies encased in the icy coffins for all to gape at as they waited for the thawing river to carry them off.

"I shall spend the night in the palace!" the mad Tsaritsa declared.

"But, your Majesty," her advisor cried, "You will perish!"

She rebuked him, "I will do no such thing! Did they perish? No. Why, they look none the worse for their ordeal! If *they* can survive, so shall I. And, if they can emerge looking healthier than when they went in, then I shall also. Don't you see, Biron? The palace is magical. The magic sustained them!"

As the Tsaritsa convinced herself, her face was lit up in wonder as a child witnessing its first magic show.

There was no putting her off her deluded notion, and what's more, the wily old Chamberlain had no intention of doing so. "I think your Majesty may well be correct," he told her. "It may indeed be an enchanted palace, and if it can improve the health of our beloved monarch, why not try it?"

"I shall spend a day and night in there. Get me some blankets, and on no account let anyone else in. This is not for the likes of commoners. If anyone deserves to be rejuvenated, it is I!"

Biron agreed with her. "Quite so, Ma'am. Our monarch should, indeed, be the only one to take advantage of the, er... of the magic."

A guard arrived with extra blankets for the Tsaritsa. "My Lord," he said to Biron, "is this wise?"

"Her Majesty's wishes will be carried out," the Chamberlain ordered, then pausing for thought added, "Who knows, a night inside that place might prove a blessing to us all!"

Chapter Six

Mikhail and Avdotya

Through the crowd, Oleg appeared driving a troika. The newlyweds were lifted on to the open cart, and covered in more furs, then driven through the ecstatic crowd and away to the city outskirts.

Shortly after, they arrived at a small dacha cabin, overlooking the city. Inside, Galina opened the door and greeted them, bidding the three of them enter. She informed them, “There is hot water a’plenty, and a hot steam bath has been prepared.”

“A Banya!” Mikhail exclaimed, “How wonderful!”

“You get warmer, faster,” said Galina, “this is to raise your body temperature back to normal; then hot food and into a warm bed with you both.”

“No cold dip in the river afterwards?” asked Oleg.

“Don’t be stupid!” Galina replied.

“Then what kind of banya is this?” Oleg teased. “I suppose there’ll be no whipping with birch bark either?”

“Certainly not!” said Galina.

“Pity,” said Oleg, with a wink to the couple.

Mikhail laughed at him, wagging his finger.

Oleg quietly replied with a cheeky grin, “Worth a try.”

Avdotya insisted Mikhail use the banya first as he was slimmer than her and, therefore colder. She patted her rump and told everyone, “He does not have my protection.”

They all laughed. “Isn’t she a marvel?” Mikhail asked Oleg.

Unusually for Oleg, he was stumped for words. He could see the Prince admired Avdotya but, unable to summon up an appropriate reply, all he could think to say was, “Well, she has nice eyes.”

Mikhail shook his head and smiled. “My friend, have you not heard the saying that *beauty is in the eye of the beholder*, and that *looks are not everything?”*

Oleg pondered this. “There is another saying, my Lord: *If it were not for vodka, ugly women would get no passion!”*

Mikhail rebuked him, “Now, now Oleg! She cannot help her looks. She is a good woman, and God knows there are precious few of those around.”

Oleg replied meekly. “Yes, my Lord.”

As Mikhail went to his banya, Oleg looked at Galina, and pointing to his head told her, “Perhaps the cold has shrunk his thinking matter.”

With Mikhail in the steam bath, Oleg decided to quiz Avdotya. “Well, then, my Kalmuk beauty, you have certainly come a long way in a short space of time.”

“Yes, from the Volga,” Avdotya replied, “and it is pronounced Kal*myk*!”

“I don’t mean from the Volga, and well you know it!”

“Then, what *do* you mean?”

“You have really landed on your feet, haven’t you?” said Oleg accusingly.

“Meaning what, exactly?”

“Meaning,” said Oleg, “Mikhail is a Prince, and, therefore, you are now a Princess.”

Avdotya corrected him, “Mikhail is a Prince in name only. He has no wealth or property.”

“Ah! But he may amount to something again. After all, he was an ambassador once. You know he is well thought of at court.”

“Not by the Tsaritsa, He has no future at court; he is banished, as I am.”

“Well, then,” smiled Oleg, “if he is to be as poor as a church mouse, you have no need of him. Agree to a divorce and go your own separate ways.”

“But we are only just wed.”

“That was no wedding,” said Oleg “That was just a fiasco, a shambles.”

“Shambles or not, it was a wedding the Tsaritsa herself ordered. That crazy woman would have our heads if we married one day and divorced the next. She would be insulted enough to kill. The lunatic intended our deaths last night, anyway. We were never meant to come out of that place alive!”

Oleg patted his bag of silver. “There might be a little something for your inconvenience.”

Eyeing Oleg coldly, Avdotya replied, “I did not ask for this marriage. I was forced into it, as he was. We both had no choice so do not mark me down as a gold- digger, you oaf! If I were sure of no reprisals, I would gladly divorce the Prince right away. I know this is a poor match for him and there’s no sense in making two people unhappy, but we must be careful of the Tsaritsa.”

Again Oleg patted his bag of silver.

Avdotya reproached him. “*And* I would take no coin for doing so! I have my pride if nothing else! You can choke on your silver!”

“Come, come girl,” protested Oleg. Looking for support he asked, “Galina, what do you say?”

“Don’t ask me,” Galina answered. “I think they both have had a lucky escape. Now they need time to rest and think what to do."

"Thank you, Galina," said Avdotya.

Galina sorted out some fresh clothes for the couple for when they had bathed.

"I think they should as least split up when they leave here," said Oleg.

Galina admonished him, "Let *them* decide. Not you! Why should you decide? The one whose brain works the least well!"

Avdotya smiled.

"I am only thinking of what is best," pleaded Oleg.

"Don't try thinking. You know it hurts you!" laughed Galina.

Avdotya laughed with her, then turning to Oleg, she said accusingly, "You would have us put at risk again. You know what our beloved Tsaritsa is capable of! To ask for a divorce now, would mean our certain deaths. A good time for divorce is when it is safe to do so. Let us all *use* our heads, not *lose* them!"

"Yes, you oaf!" said Galina.

"I apologise, Avdotya," Oleg grovelled, "I just wanted to make sure about you. I'm sorry I ever mentioned divorce!"

Mikhail came into the room still towelling his wet hair. "What is all this talk of divorce?"

Instead of answering, Avdotya asked Mikhail, "Is there enough hot water left?"

"Why, yes."

"Good. I shall take a bath."

Mikhail gently grabbed Avdotya's arm. "I asked you a question!"

Curtly, she answered, "Ask him," nodding at Oleg. "I am taking a bath." With that she left, and slammed the door to the bathroom behind her.

"What was all that about?"

"I merely suggested, you might divorce, Sire," explained Oleg.

"Oh, I see. What did she say?"

"She said the Tsaritsa would execute you for insulting her again."

"Well I suppose she is right about that. After all the trouble the Tsaritsa went to with that stupid wedding, she would go berserk if we tried divorcing so soon. I agree with her, it would not be sensible, yet. Er... what else did she say?"

"Well, just that she was, in theory, agreeable to a divorce. She said she had no wish to make two people unhappy."

Mikhail pondered a moment. "She said that?"

"Yes, my Lord," Oleg answered. "The cheek of the Kalmyk woman!"

Mikhail was lost in thought for a second. "Well, of course, she is correct about our mad monarch. She would certainly have our heads after such a snub. Best to wait a bit, I suppose." He paced the room towelling his hair in silence, then, said, "It would make *two* people unhappy, eh?"

"That's what she said," confirmed Oleg, " and she says, if nothing else, she has her pride."

Mikhail scratched his head. "Well, she has that alright. She is a strange one, but no fool. Go easy on her Oleg; she intrigues me. I would find out what makes her tick."

Rising to his feet, Oleg said, "*Intrigued* is it? Anyway, Sire, I must take my leave of you to attend my pigeons."

"Pigeons?" asked Mikhail.

"Well, yes," affirmed his friend. "I brought pigeons. I promised to let Abramo and the villagers know of your fate. Enjoy your breakfast, sire. Will you attend the tavern this evening? The people have asked to see you and the Kalmyk, er... your bride, that is." Facetiously, he added, "They are *intrigued* about your ordeal."

"You go and we shall see you later. I need more rest. Also, I need to speak about things with Avdotya."

Galina opened the door, and left the room.

As Oleg prepared to follow her, he looked back at his master. He was uneasy. He said, "Yes, Sire. You need to straighten things out. See you later."

"See you later, my friend," answered the smiling Prince.

Mikhail and Avdotya ate breakfast in silence. He was tired and drained from the night's ordeal. His mind was confused.

Eventually Mikhail said, "Oleg told me what you said. You are right about the Tsaritsa. She would have us killed if we asked for a divorce so soon. We need to wait."

Avdotya just nodded.

"You know," said Mikhail, "in that horrid place, when you think your number might be up — well, it focuses ones mind on... well, er... that is, it concentrates one's thoughts. I mean about life — and er, about what is, er, well, about what is right."

Avdotya listened attentively.

"About, er, what is important" he continued, "Have we done all we might have in life? Have our dreams been fulfilled?"

She fixed him with a clear blue eyed gaze, "I think I know what you mean, my Lord."

"Do you? What are your thoughts, and dreams, Avdotya?"

She answered, "I merely wish to go through life, without hurting anyone.... or being hurt."

"A fine sentiment," Mikhail observed. "A bit like: '*Do unto others as ye would be done by,*' eh?"

Avdotya pondered his words then observed, "In a perfect world, perhaps, my Lord, although the sad reality is, more like, Do unto others first, *before* they do it to you!"

They both laughed at her witticism.

Mikhail yawned and stretched his arms. Smiling at her, he said, "Well, we have many things to talk about, but first let us get a decent sleep in a proper bed."

He noticed a slight blush on Avdotya's face.

"Do not panic," he told her, kindly. "I just wish to sleep. We are man and wife, it's true, but not of our own doing, and I would never take what is not given freely. Besides, I am tired."

At first, thinking he might have caused offence by intimating they would sleep together, Mikhail now feared he caused offence by saying they would not. He stammered, "But, er... that is, not to say that I would not do my duty as, er... as man and er... that is, er... wife."

He was obviously flustered and cleared his throat.

Avdotya was relieved at his embarrassment and found it endearing.

He continued, "We must discuss what to do about this strange situation, later. But first, sleep. Come."

Avdotya dutifully followed her husband to the bedroom where they both fell asleep the moment their heads touched the pillows. Together, they soundly slept the sleep of the innocent.

The hours passed and it was dark when Mikhail slowly awoke from his slumber. He looked at her asleep beside him and tried to assess his feelings for this intelligent, funny and decent woman. He felt some pity, some kindness, and some thing he could not quite put his finger on.

Avdotya opened her clear blue eyes and looked at him without speaking.

"Did you sleep well?" he asked.

She smiled and nodded.

"I was dreaming," he told her.

"Was it a nice dream?"

"Well, sort of. It was about you."

"Oh! Well, I hope it was nice then," she whispered.

"I dreamed about all the beautiful women I have known, and then I dreamed of you."

She turned away.

"No Avdotya, you don't see. You are no ordinary woman. You are not like the others. The things you say are so, well... intelligent."

"You make it sound like an affliction. I told you I was a teacher back in my village."

"Yes, you did," he replied, searching for words that might explain his thoughts about her. "Many have academic intelligence, but you also have wisdom and kindness. You have, you have.... goodness, Avdotya. It shows, and I like you for it."

She answered him, “Only someone with a good heart would see that, Mikhail.”

In silence they stared into each other’s eyes. Finally, she asked, “Is something the matter?”

“It’s just that your eyes...” he hesitated, “...are so blue.”

“And you were thinking: why cannot the rest of her be as attractive?”

Once again she had hit the nail right on the head. Mikhail was glad she couldn’t see his blushing face in the half-light. He explained: “Good looks can be as much of a curse as plain looks. People are so shallow. We never see past the image into the soul. But God made us this way, and we must do the best we can. You are not to blame for the way you look. That’s as unjust as taking credit for the beauty God bestows on a person. Don’t you see? Neither is a cause for shame or pride. We didn’t make ourselves, God did.”

She smiled at him. “So, I do not humiliate you?”

“No, no. Of course you don’t,” Mikhail assured her. “I am ashamed I used that word, but that was the Tsaritsa’s intention. I was accusing her. I should never have said it. I apologise, deeply. I didn’t mean to hurt you.”

“I am not hurt, Mikhail,” she said smiling, “not now.”

“Anyway,” he continued, “is it not said that beauty is in the eye of the beholder. That it is only skin deep, anyway?”

Avdotya took her time to ponder his words. “In that case,” she said, “perhaps the good Lord has turned me inside out!”

They both laughed.

“You silly thing! I love your sense of humour. And I love the way you....”

He hesitated. Their eyes fixed on each other’s. Mikhail realised that was twice he had used the word *love*. He felt self-conscious, unsure of his feelings. He knew he respected this woman — this Kalmyk. He appreciated her intelligence, and her drive in wishing to make something of herself. He enjoyed her teasing, her quirky sense of humour, her resourcefulness, her honesty, and her good nature.

Despite her lack of beauty, he sensed there was something drawing them together. He reasoned that most of the beautiful women he had met were just shallow and vain, and only concerned with themselves.

This woman beside him could not be accused of that. She had the qualities all women should have. She just did not have the looks. Perhaps that was a blessing. *Would she be as good a person if she were beautiful?*

Avdotya was attracted to him, how could she not be? He was a handsome man, and a prince, to boot, but more importantly to her, he was a kind man. Even without a crown it was obvious he was a man who could rise to importance in other fields. Unusually for a royal, there was no arrogance in him. Mikhail was a good and considerate man, and Avdotya could see that in him. She knew it was their qualities that were drawing them together, and she believed him when he wisely said that looks don't really matter in the long run. Mikhail was a rare find. She could give her heart to such a man.

And, he was attracted to her. True, he did not realise it fully himself yet, but she did. Avdotya made her mind up not to prompt him in any way. He had to reach his decision about them both, all by himself.

They stared at each other in silence. In the half-light Mikhail gazed at her lovely eyes and her smile.

"What are you thinking of?" Avdotya asked.

"I have been doing a lot of thinking lately," he told her, "you know, sort of weighing things up."

"Oh, really?"

"Last night, in that freezing tomb. I thought it would be my last night on Earth. It makes a person think, Avdotya, about mortality. About what is really important in life. About what makes it all worthwhile."

"They say love makes it all worthwhile, at the end of the day, that's all there is."

"I believe that also," he replied, "It's just that I have loved before... and lost."

She thought for a while and said, "He whose love has gone away, shall live to love another day."

"Sounds like you just made that up." he said.

"I did," she told him with a smile.

They both laughed. Something about her had definitely got under his skin. Mikhail couldn't explain it to himself. Perhaps, she could.

"Something is happening, Avdotya."

"What do you mean?"

"Well, it's just that I feel kind of different to how I did yesterday."

"Do you mean, warmer?"

"No, silly, I am a wiser man today. I was, er... getting my values straight, in my head."

"Values?"

"Er... yes," he replied, "you know, worthwhile things."

"And have you? Got them straight?"

"I think so," he said, in a low voice. Hesitatingly he said, "Also, I was wondering..."

"Wondering what?" she whispered.

"Why I am so attracted to you," he admitted.

"Oh — I see," she said in a low voice. "And are you attracted?"

"Yes. I am," breathed Mikhail.

"It must be my raving beauty. Or, your poor eyesight," she teased.

He laughed.

They laughed together.

Touching her arm he told her, “You are a good woman Avdotya. There are many beauties, but not so many really good people; and you are a good person.”

She whispered, “It takes one to know one. You could have many beautiful women, Mikhail.”

“I have had my share of beautiful women;” he confessed, “most are as shallow as a puddle and a lot less interesting. When their looks are gone there is nothing left, except perhaps the goodness they might have inside them, and you already have that. You are a rare woman, Avdotya; anyway, I want quality, not quantity.”

“You’re a good man Mikhail.”

“Avdotya, I think I love you.”

“You only think?” she teased.

“I know it,” he answered.

“Are you sure, Mikhail?”

“You’re like a breath of fresh air, Avdotya. You’re like rain upon a barren desert.”

“But I am plain,” she insisted.

“Not to me.”

“But you can do so much better,” she said.

“No – I can’t,” he told her. “I can see beyond looks. You are a lovely person; and you have many worthy qualities. I can see you are a good woman, Avdotya. A man could spend a lifetime looking for one so good.”

“I wish I could be beautiful for you,” she whispered.

“You *are* beautiful,” he told her, “in more ways than one.”

They gazed lovingly at each other.

He said, “I’ve just realised what it is that I love about you.”

“What’s that?” she whispered.

“All that you are,” he answered.

Avdotya’s heart was racing. “Don’t say it if you don’t mean it,” she begged.

“I do mean it... darling,” he said, and kissed her tenderly on the lips.

She responded gratefully. As their bodies pressed closer together Mikhail’s head reeled. It was delightful.

The chemistry between them was perfect. He knew they were right for each other. His initial respect and admiration for this woman had turned to affection, and in turn that had turned to love.

He knew he was right to love her, yet cursed himself for appreciating the dark. Yet, for now, he needed it to concentrate on Avdotya, the woman, so beautiful in mind and spirit.

He would not be distracted by her plainness. He craved not only touch, but feelings and emotion. He yearned for that unseen inner beauty, which his wife had in abundance, and of which he wanted more. *It's what's inside that counts,* he thought, *What would others have at the end of it all, when their looks faded? Nothing, if their love were based on looks alone. Others could have their temporary beauty, but Avdotya had what they did not; she had the goodness, and that would last. That is the foundation stone of a perfect relationship, and we could build on it. Anyway, aren't the plain also entitled to love — or is love only for the beautiful?*

As their passion grew in intensity, it was almost unbearable. Mikhail had loved before, but not like this. This was a deep, sacred, almost spiritual love. *He didn't deserve it,* he thought. *Where had these thoughts come from — and so soon? Was he under some kind of spell?* he asked himself. If he was, he didn't care. He was not his own man. They were as one person, in mind and body and spirit. It was an experience he had never had in his life before, but now couldn't imagine life without it. His love and deep affection for this strong, determined yet vulnerable woman outweighed any other factor.

The two lovers felt the same, and both surrendered to their feelings.

Mikhail realised he was leaving behind the immature, shallow love so many mistook for the real thing. He was upgrading his emotions to where all should aspire... to real love. Avdotya would help him.

The intelligent and perceptive woman that she was, Avdotya knew that with Mikhail, trust, friendship and love had a real chance. He was the man for her. She cared for him for the right reasons. She cared for the man, not his position. They were kindred spirits who could now join forces and face the world and all it had to throw at them. Avdotya trusted her instincts. If a man could love her in spite of her looks, then he was a good man, and that was all she wanted. She didn't need a Prince, only a good man to go through life with, and she had found him.

Things could now only get better. Apart, they would have drifted for years, then, no doubt, have died lonely deaths; never having known real love. Together they had more than a chance of a happy life.

They had overcome the hardest obstacle, that of finding each other. The rest would be easy. They marvelled at this new experience for them both, and enjoyed it, appreciated it, and thanked the Lord it had not passed them by.

"We can have a good life, Avdotya," he told her.

"I believe it, too."

"It's about caring, not just about beauty or making love."

"It isn't?"

"Well, no," Mikhail teased, "I mean, making love is all very nice but what would we do for the other twenty three hours and fifty nine minutes?"

The silly joke made them both giggle.

"We'll have to work on it," she whispered. "Mr. and Mrs. Mikhail Golitsyn," she mused. "Now, I feel married."

"Actually, we could be called *Prince* and *Princess* Mikhail Golitsyn."

They looked at each other and said in unison, "Naah!"

The happy couple laughed. They both sensed they would do a lot of laughing together.

"But you deserve better," she told him.

"I deserve *you*! Look, we're in love, aren't we?"

"Yes," she breathed.

"Then that's all anyone can ask for. We'll make it," he reassured her. "I love you."

"Really?" she asked.

"Really," he answered.

"And I love you, Mikhail."

"No more mention of divorce, eh?" Mikhail asked.

Teasing him, she said, "We'll have to see."

"Alright; let's give it fifty years or so before we make a decision."

"Agreed!" Noticing the hour, Avdotya asked, "Don't you wish to join your friends in the tavern? Oleg will be there."

Mikhail kissed her and sighed, "Not a chance. The tavern will always be there, and more than likely with Oleg in it! Anyway, I don't think my friend *is* there."

"What do you mean?"

"I mean I don't think he is *all there*!" he joked, tapping his head.

They laughed.

"He is a good friend, Mikhail," she said, "he saved our lives."

"*You* saved my life, Avdotya. You brought something worthwhile into it. You are my light in a dark place!"

"But he *was* there for you in your hour of need."

"And so were you," he answered, "as you are now."

"I shall be always there," she told him.

Mikhail smiled at her. "Good, Avdotya. Good, good, good!" he said, in between kisses.

Chapter Seven

When Fate Lends a Hand

Inside the palace, Anna lay freezing on the solid ice bed. Although wrapped in cloaks and blankets, she was suffering. To stave off the intense cold she drank copious amounts of vodka, little realising that was only adding to her problems.

"I'll show them," she ranted to herself. "I'll show them all! Fate decreed I build this place. Now I know why, it's magic. My magic palace."

Vanity, stubbornness or just plain stupidity persuaded her to endure the perishing temperature convinced she would emerge a younger, healthier woman.

Before long, the combination of the vodka and icy bed that was robbing the heat from her had a devastating effect on her already ailing kidneys. The vodka put her to sleep, and the kidneys, contracting in the cold, could do only one thing; they began to shut down. Her health was now in an irreversible decline. She gave a cry of pain as her kidneys' blood vessels shrank back and became unable to function. The Tsaritsa Anna slowly, but inevitably, slipped into a coma.

Outside, the guards could see her asleep on the bed but were none the wiser of her predicament. At the same time fate was taking a hand with the weather. The outside temperature had only increased half a degree but it was the start of a thaw, the rate of which could be anyone's guess in the freakish climate. Also, strange things were happening under the water, noises and movements, that shouldn't be.

The architect, Eropkin, had been right about the condition of the waters in the estuary. Salt water took longer to freeze, and to a lesser depth than fresh water. The sailing vessels fitted with ice breaking metal bows had done a good job keeping the shipping lanes free by chopping the ice up, but that allowed the high tide the night before, to gather up in a big swell. The iced over river could only offer token resistance as it raged up the estuary.

The weight of the rushing water under the frozen river caused massive cracks in the ice base that supported the palace. The positioning of fires in braziers every thirty or so feet did not help, either, making the ice even thinner in those places; and soon the braziers were all connected by one large crack encircling the palace.

The townsfolk in their beds were awakened by ominously loud reports and booms, as the ice began to crack and break up. The tidal surge under the ice had undermined the palatial structure, which began to dislodge itself and buckle under its own weight.

The guards stared in disbelief as they witnessed great slabs of ice shudder and dislodge. In horror they saw the ice palace buckle and deform before their eyes.

Inside, the sleeping Tsaritsa did not move. The Chamberlain, Biron, and architect Eropkin, were sent for.

Meanwhile, the guards tried to smash down the large icy doors of the palace. As they breached them, part of the roof caved in, blocking their access to the sleeping Tsaritsa.

Within minutes, townspeople and guards were risking their own lives trying to reach their monarch; but the ice shifted under their feet dislodging more of the construction.

"It's like an earthquake on ice!" one shouted.

Many thought better than to put themselves at any more risk, and got off the slowly shifting frozen base.

"Why is it breaking up?" someone asked, "It is still freezing!"

Biron informed the man, "No doubt our good friend the architect can explain, but first we must do all we can."

A massive slab of ice gave way from a wall and crashed on to the frozen river, smashing a great hole in it. The turbulence it caused upon hitting the ice then the water below caused great instability to the wall the block had fallen from. The unsteady wall teetered then all fell away and upon pounding the river shook the whole structure.

Chaos and panic ruled the night as the surging tide caused the ice to crack and shift. People worked like an army of ants to rescue their blissfully unaware monarch from the crumbling edifice. Some men darted onto the unstable ice palace base which now mimicked the motions of a raft. Only a few small blocks of ice could be tackled before the men had to escape for their lives as the moving ice buckled under foot.

The unconscious Tsaritsa could be seen in the chamber, but no amount of shouting could wake her.

Men seized their chance to leap once more on to the moving ice to pull away as much rubble as they could; but their efforts were ineffectual as the ice deformed all about them. Everyone began to realise they were fighting a losing battle.

****

Later at the dacha, the early morning peace was disturbed by a breathless Oleg as he burst into the bedroom. "You'll never guess what's happened!" he cried.

Alarmed, the couple sat bolt upright in bed. "What is it? Speak man!" said Mikhail.

Regaining his breath he told them that the Tsaritsa was trapped inside the palace.

"What happened?" Avdotya asked.

"Apparently, the crazy old woman spent the night in the ice palace," Oleg explained, "She was convinced it was a magical place because you two had survived it. The guards heard her cry out in pain but could not bring her out because the river ice has shifted, and the palace has partially collapsed in places. She is trapped."

"Good Lord!" exclaimed Mikhail. "Is she injured?"

"She just lays on the bed, Sire. She is breathing, but no one can wake her, or get to her — and the palace is crumbling!"

"Hmm," said Avdotya, piecing the grim details together in her mind. *Vodka, freezing cold, frail kidneys, — coma.* "What a disaster," she muttered.

"For her, maybe, but a lot of people are rejoicing."

"Oleg!" snapped Avdotya. "Please, have some feeling."

"Why?" he asked, "After the old bitch tried to kill you both, I thought you would be happy at the turn of events."

"She is a sick woman," Avdotya pointed out, then pointing to her head, said, "In here, also."

"Well, obviously," said Oleg "otherwise the old trout would not have been so evil! Anyway, to hell with her! She deserves what she gets. Hurry up and get dressed. Meet Polya and me in the tavern. Everyone is down by the river trying to help."

"Well," said Mikhail, "she *has* been a cruel tyrant to many, including us. Perhaps she does deserve what befalls her."

Avdotya asked Oleg, "Did you say — *Polya*?

The grinning Oleg answered, "Well. You know how it is." He then gave the couple a wave and rode off to the city. As he galloped away Mikhail said, "Come on. Let's see if we can help." They quickly dressed.

The day was milder than before and the sun shone brightly in the winter sky. The extra degree of heat, plus the movement of the river under the ice palace had accounted for the partial collapse of the structure.

At the site of the Ice Palace, the army and townsfolk were desperately trying to drag away the great fallen slabs of ice that once were the palace walls, in order to get to the Tsaritsa. Many slipped as they grappled with the huge chunks. Through the transparent walls, the Tsaritsa could be seen inside still laying on the ice bed. The sudden surge from the high tide plus the thinner river ice had made the total collapse of the edifice inevitable.

"I told her! I told her!" screamed a distraught Eropkin. "But she wouldn't listen!"

The integrity of the whole structure was compromised by the shocks and tremors caused by the falling blocks of ice and the combined effects of the tidal surge and the movement of the river current. It now appeared to be in a most precarious state.

The guards, the army, and the throng of helpers shouted in terror as parts of the palace broke up and began to sink into the icy waters of the river Neva.

"Get out! Save yourselves!" shouted Biron. As the panicking people scrambled to the shore, the great edifice noisily broke into great pieces.

The thinning river ice had failed to sustain the weight of the palace. The once magnificent building was now a pile of ice blocks collapsing into the river, carrying its unconscious occupant with it.

The Tsaritsa's dumbfounded subjects looked on helplessly at the sight of the monstrous mountain of ice slowly drifting on the current and out to sea. Some fell to their knees and crossed themselves, others smiled and waved at the floating tomb. The mad Tsaritsa was no more.

****

Later that day, a party from Tsarskoje Selo, the royal residence arrived at the newlyweds' dacha.

Lord Biron stepped out of his carriage, as a guard banged on the cabin door.

Mikhail answered it. "My lord Biron!" he said surprised, "What is it? Please, come inside."

Biron declined, "No need for that, Sire. I have news. We have found the body of our Tsaritsa! It was a terrible way to go, even for the likes of her."

Avdotya spoke up, "If it is any comfort, my Lord, the Tsaritsa will have died before the palace collapsed."

The puzzled Biron asked, "Why would you think that, woman?"

"She was a heavy drinker of spirits," Avdotya replied, "and known to have suffered with kidney problems. She probably fell into a coma while she lay on the frozen bed. She would have felt no pain."

"You see, Biron," Mikhail said, "this *woman*, as you call her, — this Princess in fact, is a very astute person, and in case you didn't know, was far too bright to be working as a mere serving wench in that old drunkard's kitchen!"

"Forgive me, Sire."

"What now, then?" asked Mikhail "Have you come to arrest us?"

"No, not at all, Sire." Biron said with a smile. "I have come to offer you a position."

"A position?" queried Mikhail.

"You may be reinstated as Ambassador. You are too valuable to be banished from court and made to scratch out a living. You have diplomatic skills and a talent for languages. The Ambassadorship is yours for the asking."

Mikhail pondered upon this sudden change of events.

Biron informed the Prince, "Sire, now that the conditions that forced you into marriage no longer exist, a divorce from the Kalmyk woman can be arranged. The church is reasonable. They would accept it on the grounds of non-consummation."

Mikhail eyed him with a cool stare, "Are there any other grounds?" he asked.

Biron felt shocked and embarrassed. Momentarily at a loss for words, he thought better than to ask whether or not the marriage had in fact been consummated. "Er... yes, my Lord," he said, "On the grounds that you were both forced into marriage. It can be annulled. Shall I arrange it, Sire?"

"You shall not!" answered Mikhail, his arm around his wife. "As strange as it seems, we actually get on quite well. I'll bet that evil old Tsaritsa never banked on that!"

"Indeed, Sire," replied the surprised Biron.

The embarrassed silenced was broken by shouts from Oleg riding furiously on horseback towards them. He waved a piece of paper at Mikhail. "A message, sire. A message," he gasped.

"From who?" asked Mikhail.

"From the pigeons."

"The man is a fool!" cried Biron, "Now about your position, Sire."

"Wait!" ordered the Prince. A smile creased his face as he read the note. "It is from Abramo." He read it out loud. It read: **Business booming thanks to new road. We need a Mayor. You have the vote. Signed — Abramo.**

"Your Highness, we are in need of you at court," Biron pleaded. "Your diplomatic skills would be most useful, as we now have to find a successor to the throne. Every royal in the land will be beating at the doors. It will be chaos!"

"Nonsense," said Mikhail, "It's obviously Crown Princess Elizabeth who is next in line."

"Would you serve another woman, my Lord?" asked Biron.

"There's only one woman in my life right now," he told him, "Anyway, there are Romanovs a-plenty yet. Ivan for one."

"It's just that your diplomacy would be invaluable in the midst of all the squabbling," said the Chamberlain.

"Well, Biron," Mikhail laughed, "best of luck to you, with that little problem!"

"What is your answer, Sire?" pleaded Biron.

"I shall think about it, my Lord Biron," Mikhail said, holding the message from Abramo in his hand. "I shall think about both offers. Thank you."

With that, Biron bowed and got back in to his carriage. He and his guards returned to Tsarskoje Selo, the Royal residence

"What is there to think about, husband?" asked Avdotya, "You are reinstated."

Mikhail told her, "I have had enough of royalty; of politics and intrigue. I just want a peaceful life."

"Then we are for Italy, Sire?" asked Oleg eagerly.

Mikhail took Avdotya by the hand. He had to be fair to her. She had to know the full story.

He explained that he had been married to Abramo's daughter for but a day, when she expired from a heart attack. "He, nor any of the villagers, knows I am wed again, or the circumstances thereof," he told her.

"I see," said Avdotya. "Would it be too insensitive of us to tell him of our marriage? Would he understand?"

"I do not know, Avdotya. I must ponder. As yet, he is not aware."

Producing a pigeon from his pocket, Oleg said, "Well, he soon will be!"

"Fair enough." said Mikhail, "Let us wait to hear what he says."

Taking his hand, Avdotya told him, "Where we live is not important. If we can survive that palace, we can exist anywhere in this country. Although we may prefer warmer climes, if we expect the worse, we are prepared for it and it will come as no shock."

Mikhail held her. "This is our home. We are used to it and its ways. We know Russian people are good people. It's just that life is short and I want to give you the best I can; in somewhere other than this freezing land."

"There are those who have it worse than us," she answered. "We'll survive."

"You are a good woman, Avdotya," Mikhail told her.

"Did you love her?" she asked.

"Christina? For the short time I knew her, yes, but so much has happened. It's all in my past. You are my future."

"Her father still feels the pain. Will he accept us? Will he accept me?"

"I don't know," he answered, "it depends on him. Perhaps, if he believes in fate. Who knows? But he is a good man."

She smiled at him and asked, "Do you love me?"

"Yes, I really do," he told her.

Taking his hand she said, "Then let us make the most of whatever happens. We can fare as well here as anywhere. Just as long as we have each other, we'll do fine."

Mikhail answered, "I agree," and kissed her cheek. With their arms around each other, Mikhail and Avdotya watched Biron disappear and Oleg's pigeon taking flight.

"What news will you bring back, little bird?" said Mikhail, looking up.

Oleg mounted his horse and bade them farewell.

As he rode off, he stopped and turned to the couple. He laughed. "It comes to something when our future is decided by a blasted pigeon!"

They all laughed. Mikhail and Avdotya waved as he galloped off into the distance.

From their position, the cabin looked out over the city of St. Petersburg. Avdotya and Mikhail could see the port and the river estuary, blocked by the gigantic frozen mound that had once been the ice palace.

Avdotya said, "That poor woman; freezing to death like that."

"Bless you, Avdotya, but she planned that very fate for us."

Avdotya nodded.

"Anyway," Mikhail grimly observed, "she will not be cold where she is bound."

Avdotya crossed herself.

As their eyes swept across the vista of the great, cold, majestic city, the newlyweds pondered their future. What would it hold for them? So much had happened. Which way would their lives turn? They were both from hardy Russian stock, and were stoical even fatalistic about what could lay in store. They knew this country; and if their love could survive here, it could survive anywhere.

Whatever was to be, they decided their future depended not on *where* they were, but the fact they would be *together*. If Abramo would not accept them, then, at least they knew Russia and understood how to fare in that harsh environment. All that mattered was that they would be together, wherever fate took them. *Together* they could face the future. Together, they *had* a future.

Epilogue

Five years later, on a sunny summer's day, two blue-eyed children were running up a hill overlooking Lake Garda in Italy. They laughed with glee as their puppy chased after them.

The boy shouted, "Look! There's Daddy!"

The girl raced to meet him, as the boy stopped to grab the puppy in his arms. The father embraced the children one at a time, then gently scolded them for running off out of his sight. "Now children, I told you don't run too far off. Your mother is worried."

"We were chasing after Chico, Daddy," explained the boy.

"Where is Mummy anyway?" the girl asked.

From over the hill came a shapely young woman, with a lovely peach complexion. Her clear blue eyes complimented her glossy, raven-black hair. She was a picture of health and beauty. Her lovely smile exposed gleaming white teeth.

"There she is!" cried the girl, and both children ran to her.

The mother swept the little girl up in her arms.

The boy wrapped his arms around his mother's waist.

"You two are so naughty," she said. "You gave me a scare. You were meant to help Mummy in the orchard. Now don't run off again!"

"We won't, Mummy," they both promised.

The father sneaked up behind the children, and picked them both up in his arms. They squealed with delight as he swung them around.

Chico, the puppy, was barking excitedly, and tried to snap at their flailing legs. Becoming tired, they all fell, laughing, on to the grass.

The father breathlessly said, "They are OK, Ava. See? They're fine, my Princess."

To their delight, he kissed and tickled the children, then kissed his wife on her forehead.

The mother produced oranges from her apron pocket, giving one each to the children.

The girl asked the father, "Daddy, why do you always call Mummy *my Princess?*"

"Because that's what she is, darling; my beautiful Princess," he explained. Turning to his wife, "Most beautiful people have nature to thank, but I have a clever wife who has helped nature."

"Oh, it was simple enough," said the wife. "I suspected the change of diet would help the skin and hair."

"And, the figure!" the husband said playfully.

She added, "And the fresh mountain air and mild climate. They have all played their part. Thank you for this place, darling." She kissed him on the cheek. The children giggled.

What a difference a few years had made. The healthy Mediterranean diet, the replacing of lard for cooking with olive oil, the plentiful fruit and vegetables, and the sweet, fresh Alpine air and waters had worked wonders. Their happy new life as a family in this sunny, stress free environment had produced a minor miracle in Avdotya. Her once wild Mongolian features had now softened into what could only be described as exotic. She was now beautiful, in looks as well as disposition.

"You deserve to look as beautiful outside as I know you are inside," Mikhail said. "Also, it is a bonus for me!"

She kissed him sweetly on the lips. They both smiled. "Are you happy Avdotya?"

"Yes, Mikhail. More than I ever thought I had a right to be." In her native Mongolian language she told him, 'Bi chamd khairtai' — *I love you.*

Mikhail smiled and shook his head. In Russian he said, "Ye tebya liubliu" — *I love you.*

She smiled and shook her head. They both laughed then said in Italian "Ti amo" — *I love you.*

Abramo's reply had been just what they had wanted to hear. Once he was aware of the full story, the young couple were welcomed back to the Italian lakes with open arms, and the kindly old mayor was soon captivated by Avdotya's winning personality. Her cooking skills in producing mouth-watering examples of Mongolian and Italian recipes soon helped her establish a popular restaurant and a reputation as a gourmet chef.

Upon Abramo's retirement as the town's Mayor, Mikhail had taken over the office during which time the area flourished as tourism and trade developed under his astute management. Small businesses were encouraged, allowing many of the folk to prosper by developing what used to be mere cottage industries.

The widened road through the mountains allowed regular passage of goods to and from the area. Fishermen could pack their catch in the mountain ice and transport them to a larger market via the new road. The same applied to the wide variety of fruits and vegetables.

Tourists came to ski on the slopes and sail on the lakes. The hunters became mountain guides for hikers; fishermen hired their boats for angling trips. Prosperity had come to the region, and all due to Mikhail's foresight.

Upon the birth of the twins, he himself stood down as the town's leader, concentrating on raising his family and running a grand lakeside hotel. He employed many of his friends in his large orange orchards and lemon groves. Life was good for all.

"You have a right," Mikhail said. "All good people have a right to be happy. I know we are very lucky. It could have gone a lot worse for us."

"Yes," she said, "I am a lucky woman, and you are a lucky man."

They smiled and kissed.

The kids joined in the game. The girl cried, "And I am a lucky girl, and he is a lucky boy," she said, pointing to her brother.

The boy grabbed Chico and yelled, "And he is a lucky dog!"

Just then, they heard laughter and singing from a boat passing close to the lakeshore. On its hull were the painted words: ***Oleg's Pleasure Cruises.*** Two giggling young women were rowing while a grinning Oleg lay sprawled out, playing a tune on his mandolin.

"Now, *there* is a lucky dog, for you!" said Mikhail.

His wife gave him a dig in the ribs.

"Avdotya!" he yelped, feigning injury. He grabbed her and began to play-wrestle. The kids and the dog all joined in.

Avdotya pretended to scold him. "Mikhail! Behave yourself. You are as bad as the kids."

The young girl said, "No, no. Not Russian names. Italian! Mummy is, Ava..."

The boy jumped in, "...and Daddy is 'Miki!' Miki, Miki, Miki!"

"Ava, Ava, Ava!" cried the girl.

The father grabbed them and tickled them both.

The children's laughter was more like screaming.

Chico the puppy jumped from the boys arms and barked excitedly.

"Children!" said the mother, "Not so loud. They will hear you in Russia!"

"Tell us a story about Russia, Daddy," said the little girl.

The boy joined in, "Yeah. A story. A story. A story."

The father hushed his children, "One day, if you are good, I will tell you how I met your mother."

"Tell us now!" pleaded the girl.

"We have no time," the father said. "Uncle Abramo is coming to visit today. I shall tell you later. I promise."

"Please, Daddy," begged the girl, "Tell us now."

The father teased them. "Oh. It's a very long tale."

"But a very nice one," said the mother, smiling.

Returning her smile he agreed, "Yes, it is."

They all got to their feet and began to walk up the hill to their home.

The grand wooden chalet overlooking the lake bore the sign: **The Kalmyk Lodge Hotel**, underneath it said: **Proprietors — Miki and Ava Golitsyn.**

The father patiently ignored his children's constant request to relate the story to them.

Swinging from an arm each the children kept up the pressure.

His smiling wife shrugged her shoulders and said, "You'll get no peace until you tell them. Anyway, you're outnumbered. I would like to hear it too."

The father relented. "I know when I'm beaten, "he said, "but first; payment." With that he placed his forefinger to his cheek to suggest a kiss.

Ava dutifully obliged.

"Well," he began, "It is the strange tale of a cruel Empress in a land far away where, one freezing cold winter, she built a huge palace all out of ice!"

The wide – eyed children gasped.

"Ice?" the girl asked.

"Pure, solid blocks of ice," the father explained, "and once, she imprisoned Mummy and Daddy in there, all night long."

"Brrrr!" said the girl, in a pretend shiver. "Were you frightened?"

The boy picked up his pet dog and hugged him closely.

"A little," said the father.

"Wasn't it cold, Daddy?" the boy asked.

"I'll bet it was," said the girl, "was it, Daddy? Was it awfully cold?"

"Yes, it was," the father told his children, "Awfully cold. Bitterly cold,"

Giving a loving smile to his wife, he continued, "...but children, we had our love to keep us warm."

"Aw," said the boy in feigned embarrassment.

The father and mother exchanged smiles then he ruffled the boy's hair who, in turn, ruffled his dog's head.

All holding hands, the happy family made their way up the steps of the Lodge and entered their home.

The End

Armistice

The cold, dark November morning all along the Western Front began with 'Stand To' as usual one hour before dawn. On both sides night observers and snipers were relieved of their posts on the trenches fire step behind double rows of wet and rotting sandbags. This was a favourite time for both the British and Germans to take pot shots and many a rookie Fritz or Tommy had succumbed to a sniper's bullet after foolishly looking over the parapet to take a peek across no-man's land.

Life in the front line trenches was a grim existence. Even without the gunfire, many a man found their physical and mental fortitude being sapped by having to endure the disgusting conditions that prevailed. Instant death by enemy fire was considered preferable by some to all the other possible ways a man's life might be snuffed out. If one escaped being buried alive by shell bursts or dying a slow death from blood loss caused by lice and ticks, he still had poison gas to contend with to say nothing of diseases brought by rats the size of cats, and the overfilled, rotting latrines. Painfully debilitating Trench foot, the fungal infection caused by wet and damp, was a constant plague. The smell of creosote and lime, used to stifle the constant threat of disease and infection from rotting carcasses, would pervade the air - even getting into the food and water supplies. Morale and courage under fire was never before so tested.

In the distance could be heard the boom of artillery fire from the American Expeditionary Force. This was their contribution to the one hundred days offensive which had begun in September. The Allies were intent on pulverizing the German Hindenburg Lines into submission or at least softening them up for another massive push. The A.E.F.'s rapid taking of St. Mihiel and then Ephey combined with the recent success of the British at Havrincourt, convinced the British Commander-in-Chief Sir Douglas Haig of the decline in fighting will of the German army. It was the general consensus that after such massive losses sustained from four years of advances, retreats, and the stalemate of stagnating trench war-fare; combined with now facing enormous Allied reinforcements, the German Army was now all but beaten. Both sides knew this and frantic negotiations were being made to bring the carnage to a conclusion.

British squaddies of the First Infantry troop manning the sloppy mud trenches stomped their feet on the wooden duck-boards to generate some warmth. After an hour of the usual obligatory exchange of fire between snipers hoping to get lucky, it was normal practice for the men to stand down for breakfast, leaving one in three to man the parapet until they in turn were relieved for food. The relief observers and snipers took over their stations still gulping steaming hot mugs of cocoa and a shared fag brought a modicum of cheer on that cold morning. The makeshift sign over the dugout which read, "The Savoy" was evidence of the soldiers' ironic sense of humour, and the hungry men jostled and pushed their way in to the rough canteen to wolf down whatever was on the 'Savoys' breakfast menu.

Swigging a mouthful of his hot cocoa one of the soldiers out on the parapet made use of the resultant hot air by blowing hot breath into his cupped hands.

Another did the same then stuck his fingers into his hot brew.

"What are you doing Private Ashton?" asked Sergeant Jack Bennett. "Drink the bloody stuff; don't play with it!"

"I'll have it if he don't want it!" said Corporal Kerr snatching it away from him and taking a great gulp.

"I was trying to warm up my trigger finger," Ashton complained.

A voice from down the line yelled, "Why don't you stick it up your......?" His last words muffled by the sound of jeers and unkind laughter.

Ashton watched the last dregs of his hot cocoa disappear down the Corporal's throat before confiding, "I already did that!"

The Corporal coughed and splurted out the drink, retching violently to the great delight of the rest of the men.

"That'll teach you, you greedy bastard!" shouted one.

"Alright. That's enough of that!" barked the Sergeant, "and keep your bloody heads down lads! You new blokes are going to learn the hard way, I'm telling you! I've told you before just use your periscope to look over the top. No sense in getting shot at until it's necessary. And don't let Fritz see your cigarette end for crying out loud!"

"They know our position already Sarge!" said Melhuish the departing sniper.

There was a mutual respect between Sergeant Bennett and the men, but now and again he discovered there was always one idiot to get him angry.

With forced patience he explained, "I know he knows our position lad. He's known it for days, but what he wants to do now is to pick us off one at a time and if old Fritz happened to be looking along his rifle sights and saw a solitary little ember from the tip of your *gasper* don't you think he'd be able to put two and two together and realize there was a great thick 'ead like yours at the end of it? Well wouldn't he?"

Private Melhuish could only reply with a meek "Yes Sarge."

"Aye lad, 'Yes Sarge' is right. So don't be an idiot!" Then menacingly raising his voice but in such a manner only those unaccustomed to his ways might fear, yelled, "You dozy bugger! You'd better smarten up soon or I'll punch your bloody arse for you! And you won't like it! I kid you not, you will definitely not like it!"

"Yes Sarge!" grovelled the now thoroughly intimidated Melhuish.

Addressing the rest of his troop he emphasized, "Now listen you lot. Those German Mausers can fire a round that will penetrate six inches of solid wood!" Then with a smile added, "So just keep your heads down, eh?"

The men laughed at Bennett's dry witticism and Melhuish's apparent lack of comprehension.

"It's gone right over his head that one Sarge," shouted Private Ashton

With a wink, Bennett replied, "Let's hope the bullets do as well, eh?"

The men looked enviously as the sergeant checked the time by his wristwatch, a relatively new innovation.

Private Ashton piped up, "Great idea wearing your watch on your wrist ain't it Sarge?"

"Damn sight easier than fumbling around in all your clothes for a pocket watch, especially with numb hands," Bennett replied.

"I thought only officers were issued them Sarge?" asked a squaddie.

"Lieutenant Young gave it to me. Said I had more need of it while he's ill. Very considerate gentleman, he is."

The fumbling due to the creeping arthritis now gnawing at his hands was of great concern to the thirty-seven year old veteran of almost twenty years service. Constant exposure to wet and damp resulted in great pain at times as well as loss of digital dexterity, and he secretly prayed the condition would not let him down. Pain he could endure but not being able to do his job was more than his pride could bear.

A commotion further up the trench line forced the men to make way for a gasping runner who breathlessly fought and skidded his way along the trench's slippery duck-boards.

"Begging your pardon Sarge. Orders from H.Q. Where's Lieutenant Young please?"

"He's in the sick bay son," said Sgt. Bennett. "Out of action with dysentery. I'm in charge. What is it, boy?"

"All units to stand down until further orders," he said.

"Do you mean stand down for breakfast?" asked the Sergeant.

"No Sarge," came the reply. "Until further orders!"

With land-lines damaged, the only way Sgt Bennett could contact his senior officer was via the runner's message.

"Let me see that signature!" he demanded.

The runner handed it to him.

Convinced it was genuine and not the work of a joker or malcontent, Bennett said, "Hellfire! What's all this about?"

"Dunno Sarge," the runner answered, "All I know is we stand down until further notice. All officers to report to Command H.Q. at 08.00 hours, Sarge. The same message has been sent up the line to all the other units also."

"Blimey!" said a squaddie.

Turning to the men on the trench parapet he ordered, “Right lads. I want one pair of observers and snipers every twenty feet. Use periscopes only. Do not, I repeat do *not* display your thick heads to old Fritzy. Look for anything different to yesterday out in no man’s land. A tree stump, a mound of earth, the slightest movement. On a cold day such as today a sniper might give his position away by his breath looking all white – like. Got it? Right, carry on. You'll be relieved later. The rest of you, do what you're told. Stand down until further notice.”

A great cheer went up from those within earshot and passed the word along the trench line.

“That'll do for me,” said Ashton racing ahead of the others to the warmth and safety of the dugout.

Someone shouted, “Get out the way!”

Someone else replied, “Get stuffed!”

Happy profanities resounded as the cold wet soldiers jostled through the dug-out entrance.

Shouts of “Get that bloody kettle on Pete!” and “Who's got a smoke?” were countered by the calm deliberate instructions from the Sergeant. “Easy, lads, easy now. You're kicking mud all over the place! You dozy articles!”

“How many lumps do you want in your coffee, Jack?”

“What lumps? Sugar?” asked the surprised Sergeant.

“Nah! Mud!” laughed Melhuish.

Pushing him along Sergeant Bennett replied, “Go on, get inside clever dick. And less of the *'Jack'* ...it's *Sergeant* bloody Bennett to you my lad! And get me hot brew. This cocoa tastes like friggin' mud!”

“There's a coincidence,” replied the cheeky Melhuish. “I'd say this mud tastes a bit like friggin' cocoa!”

“Get along with you!” said Jack Bennett, raising his hand in a mock gesture of an impending swipe.

Inside the cooks had to endure the usual run of insults from the men. One shouted, “Hey Cookie! What's this crap? Mutton?”

“No, it's rotten!” shouted someone else, producing laughs from the men.

Looking at the disgusting fare on his tin plate, one soldier said, “Uugh! This looks like it's been eaten once already!”

“Here Cookie!” shouted a voice, “You could eat your bleedin' stew through a straw!”

“Shaddup and get it down yer!” bawled the cook. “Or you'll be wearing it in a minute!” he threatened.

“Oi! Who called the cook an ar*eshole?” said a voice in the crowd.

Another voice answered, “Who called the ar*eshole a cook?”

This produced gales of laughter from the men.

In times of severe stress it doesn't take much for men to grab with both hands the slightest excuse to behave or act in a silly fashion so foreign to their normal nature.

Partly to *rag* the cook and as much to enjoy a happy distraction from what faced them outside, they all burst into song:

Boiled beef and carrots,
boiled beef and carrots.
That's the stuff for your 'Derby Kell',
It makes you fit and keeps you well.
Don't live like vegetarians on food they give to parrots.
From morn; 'til night, blow out you kyte......... on boiled beef and carrots!

This was followed by a great rousing cheer.

"Leave him alone," bawled Sergeant Bennett, "and get yer grub while you can!"

Outside he struck a *lucifer* match on the dugout's wooden support beam and lit a cigarette. Inhaling a lungful of smoke he wondered about the strange order to stand down and decided to discuss it with Lieutenant Young in the Regimental first aid post.

****

Fifty yards behind the front line, inside the officer's dugout, the Company Colonel addressed the gathering of all the Troops' officers.

"I'm afraid we're a bit cramped for space gentlemen, but make yourselves as comfortable as you can."

Collins, the Colonel's batman, squeezed his way through the tightly packed group with glasses of whiskey crammed onto a small tray.

Sergeant Bennett entered the dug-out and saluted the Colonel. "Beggin' your pardon Sir," he said, "Lieutenant Young is medically indisposed right now and I'm here in his place."

Detecting an atmosphere and hearing grumbles from the assembled officers, the Colonel rebuked them sharply, "Gentlemen, I am surprised at you. This NCO is deputizing for Lt. Young. I'm sure you all know or have at least heard of our Sergeant Jack Bennett - holder of the Military Medal. A most valued member of our troop."

A snotty Captain Etheridge sneered at the Sergeant but looked away when Bennett returned his stare.

The Colonel wouldn't stand for the deep rooted social snobbery rampant in the Armed Forces. As far as he was concerned, a soldier's value and esteem was based on merit and not on his having a commission bought by one's rich family. Jack Bennett had proved over the course of a dozen battles he was worth his salt. The Colonel knew it and insisted the officers knew it.

No one argued with the Colonel's decision which prompted the Sergeant to brazenly help himself to a shot of whiskey. He looked at the Colonel for approval of his action, to which the Colonel simply nodded in mute reply.

"Are we celebrating, Sir?" asked Bennett.

The Colonel replied, "Well, er, yes and no, Sergeant," and holding up a piece of paper, he told the assembled group, "I have received a telegraphed message from General H.Q."

"Is it good news or bad, Sir?"asked Captain Neal.

"A bit of both, I'm afraid, gentleman," replied the Colonel, "Come on, drink up."

An air of expectancy pervaded the cramped dug-out. All the men there were veterans of many horrible conflicts during this so called 'war to end all wars'. Tough and battle-hardened though they were, some were almost at the end of their endurance.

'*What now*' many wondered.

After one big slug of his whiskey, Captain Neal said, "Come on, Sir, let's have it."

Clearing his throat the Colonel read from the paper in his hand. "At five a.m. this morning, in his personal railway carriage based in the forest of Compiegne some sixty-five kilometres north-east of Paris, the Allied Supreme Commander Ferdinand Foch met with a delegation of the German Army."

With baited breath the officers in the dug-out hung on the Colonel's every syllable.

He continued, "Gentleman, an Armistice has been signed by representatives of all sides.........."

He was interrupted by gasps from the officers. Those gasps soon changing to a great cheer but were immediately silenced by the Colonel holding a hand high.

He continued, "This Armistice being conditional on Germany not deviating from any of the terms and conditions on pain of hostilities being resumed within forty-eight hours."

The room stood silent.

Eventually an officer asked, "What's that mean exactly sir? Unconditional surrender?"

The Colonel replied, "No, technically it's an armistice but it amounts to the same thing. Just a face-saver for Fritz. I suppose that would mean war reparations, and the relinquishing of territory and safe return of prisoners of war." With a pause for effect the Colonel added, "Another condition is that Kaiser Wilhelm abdicates!"

More gasps and a roar of approval as this information was taken in.

Someone shouted, “Old Kaiser Bill to go? Bloody marvellous!”

The Colonel continued, “As I say, the articles have been agreed to and signed this morning and therefore I an tell you that particular condition has already been met.” With a beaming smile he raised his glass and said, “It means gentlemen, that to all intents and purposes, the war is at an end! It's over. It's finally over.”

After a moment’s silence for the shock and relevancy of the Colonel’s words to sink in, a deafening cheer filled the dug-out. A most un-officer like hysteria took over the whole room as backs were slapped, men hugged each other, some danced and screams of unbounded joy spilled out into the trenches. The Colonel was manhandled onto the shoulders of two junior officers amid yells of delight from all.

One or two officers just sat down in a kind of shock unable to comprehend that the years of carnage and misery were finally over. The built up strain of four years of hell on earth produced no tears of laughter in them but instead ones of shock and incredulity. Minds almost too numb to absorb the information and comprehend that the death and destruction and sheer carnage was at last to end.

“It's over? It's really over?” asked one. “It's too much to believe. Too much to ask for.”

“I knew they would collapse!” shouted Captain Etheridge. “We've had them on the run all year. Their blitzkrieg doesn't work so well now with the rest of the world against them. I wonder how they like it?”

The Sergeant looked on, quietly sipping his whiskey and saying nothing.

Despite his protestations, the Colonel couldn't quieten his officers’ ecstatic roars of unrestrained joy and relief. “Gentlemen,gentlemen. Please!” he shouted from his rather undignified position aloft.

Sergeant Bennett shouted over the din, “You said there was good news *and* bad, Sir.”

The room suddenly went very quiet. The officers lowered the Colonel to his feet and awaited clarification.

Soberly the Colonel told them, “Our celebrations, though perfectly justified, are I'm afraid, somewhat premature.”

The men, now quiet, stood with solemn apprehension as the Colonel explained. “Due to the rapid advancement of our troops, and shell damage it has not been feasible to have intact land-line communications all over the Western Front. It is of highest priority that HQ relay this morning’s welcome and long awaited news to the whole of the British Armed Forces and its Allies on active duty throughout the entire European theatre of war. Therefore any means possible, telegraph, morse, semaphor, vehicle messenger, runners, bugle call and drum and even carrier pigeon if need be, is now being utilized in great haste to inform all concerned. It is anticipated that it will take several hours to ensure that all of the forces on both sides are aware of today's epic proceedings."

"So?" piped up a solitary voice.

The Colonel continued, somewhat sadly, "So, it has been agreed upon that at eleven hundred hours today the hostilities will *officially* cease."

Captain Neal said, "Sir, you say the Armistice has been signed and it comes into effect at eleven a.m. yet you say there is also bad news. What is it Sir?"

"Unhappily gentlemen, I have to inform you that although hostilities will indeed officially cease *at* that appointed hour, I'm afraid, they will not............ *until* that same hour!"

Gasps of astonished disbelief rang through the dugout.

"I don't understand," said one officer.

"What madness is this, Sir?" cried another.

"I am much disheartened to inform you, but the sad fact is that some of our most influential generals at H.Q. as yet not familiar with the experience of active service, are eager to, well ...eager to earn their battle honours shall we say."

Another officer asked, "You mean to say they want to carry on fighting until the very end Sir? Until eleven a.m.?"

"Unhappily gentlemen," said the Colonel, "I have to tell you, that is the case!"

An audible moan of despair spread through the assembled men. There were cries of "I don't believe it!" and "It's incredible!"

Captain Neal asked, "Sir, so this war is being prolonged just to satisfy a few desk-bound generals who want their moment of glory on the battlefield? To get 'bloodied' in war like primitive savages? These same men who no doubt have already contributed to the war lasting this long due to such stupid strategies and insane reasoning as they display now?"

"Nonetheless," the Colonel replied, "They wish to experience battle before it's too late and to give them credit, they will be laying their lives on the line."

"And everyone else's!" Neal objected. "It's lunacy!"

"As I say gentlemen, they are very influential!" said the Colonel.

Neal asked, "Sir, this decision wouldn't have anything to do with the recent American successes at Ephey and St. Mihiel?"

"I fear that is a distinct possibility," said the Colonel sadly.

"Well that's bloody good, ain't it?" said the Sergeant. "They just don't want the Yanks to grab all the glory! It's just a game of one-upmanship to them. Haven't they had enough blasted killing?"

"Apparently not!" sighed the Colonel.

"Bloody Top Brass!" said someone

Captain Neal pleaded, "Sir, surely we are not going to sacrifice men for a strip of land we can simply walk across and take in a matter of a few hours?"

Shouts of, "That's right!" - "Let's just sit it out!" and "Why risk our necks now?" issued forth.

The grim-faced Colonel held up his hand and replied, "H.Q. has agreed we make this last push, so those not already bloodied might attain their portion of glory."

"What does the cabinet have to say?" asked one officer.

"It is not a political decision ..... I'm told," the Colonel replied.

With lusty voice the enraged officers cried out their vehement objections.

"Bloody ridiculous!" said one.

"It's an outrage!" said another.

Shouts of "Damn glory hunters!" and "Blasted imbeciles!" resounded.

"It's immoral!"said Captain Neal

"It's bloody criminal that's what it is! Criminal!"said Sergeant Bennett.

"Nonetheless!" the Colonel boomed, "Those are our orders from H.Q. and we shall carry them out! May I remind you we are still all subject to military law and are obliged to obey orders upon pain......."

He stopped short his words.

"Upon pain of what Sir?" asked Captain Neal, "Of court martial? Of death? Don't say it, Sir. We don't need to be ordered. There isn't a man in this unit, officer, N.C.O. or other ranker who hasn't put his life at stake for his country and regiment more than once in this blasted war to end all wars! We are not cowards Sir and have proved that many, many times over. We don't need a bayonet in our backs to advance. We don't need to be ordered to fight on but we *shall* fight on, simply to show that, yet again, what our country asks of us, we shall not be found lacking."

Great cheers erupted from the assembled officers.

Sergeant Jack patted Neal's shoulder, "Well said, Sir. Good for you!"

Neal continued, "So, with all due respect Sir, may I suggest.... you respect us?"

The Colonel said, "Gentlemen, I shame myself in the eyes of some of the bravest officers and men I have served with and I respectfully request that you, that is, *we* comply with H.Q.'s orders."

"We, Sir?" asked Neal.

"If we go," said the Colonel, "we all go together!"

All stood to attention and raised their glasses.

"To the Colonel!" shouted Neal.

"To the Colonel!" they all shouted back in reply.

"And to the regiment!" shouted someone.

"And to good old Blighty!" shouted another.

Sergeant Bennett stuck two fingers in the air and shouted, "And to the Top Brass!"

The robust cheer from the men endorsed his crude gesture.

"Permission to speak sir?" requested Sergeant Bennett.

The Colonel nodded his approval.

The Sergeant began, "Sir, for everyone's sake, could we now employ tactics that would ensure minimal casualties... on both sides I may add?"

"What?" questioned Captain Etheridge. "The Hun are finished! We can counter anything they throw at us now. We just charge ahead surely?"

"They are still extremely dangerous," said Bennett, "perhaps more so now knowing there is no need for this last push. They will fight ferociously and who can blame them?"

Etheridge sneered, "Well if you're not up to one last good fight, Sergeant..."

The fuming sergeant bit his tongue to contain his anger at the insult. He continued, "I am thinking of my men and all the unnecessary slaughter both sides will face!"

"Ah nuts!" said Etheridge with a dismissive wave of his arm. "It will be a walk over. What's the matter with you man? Got battle fatigue?"

"Now really, Etheridge!" said the Colonel.

Bennett stared menacingly at the officer and said, "Battle fatigue eh? You admit there's such a thing do you? I heard you claim there was no such thing. Why you're the despicable swine who had poor Gunner Graham face a firing squad for having that *non-existent* malady. Go to hell, Sir!"

"How dare you talk to me like that?" yelled the captain. "It's sheer insubordination!"

Bennett told him, "Look mate, we are roughly three hours away from either death or glory here. I'll talk to you any way I like. You can't do a thing to me!"

"I could have you shot!" Etheridge bellowed.

"Oh no you could not!" shouted the Colonel. "Think of the publicity surrounding an execution just two hours before a ceasefire, and for what? For not agreeing with a battle we are only engaging in to satisfy our generals' blood lust? Can you imagine it? The whole regiment would be criticized, probably the whole Army and its leaders. There would be questions in the House! No Sir, you will not have Sergeant Bennett or anyone else shot. Besides, I want to hear about these tactics."

"But Sir," said Etheridge, "surely H.Q. devises tactics not NCO's?"

The Colonel replied, "H.Q. has offered no overall strategy except allowing us to proceed as we see fit. All they care about is a forward advance. Sergeant Bennett has won battle honours at Paschendale and Ypres and his experience goes as far back as the Boer War. I trust his suggestions are worth listening to. Go ahead, Sergeant."

Bennett began, "We may proceed as we see fit eh? Well, with respect sir, that's been a bloody long time coming! If H.Q had allowed local commanders to adapt to changing conditions on the ground instead of ordering ridiculous strategies, this war might have ended a long while ago!

Sir, I am not advocating that we do not fight. If they are our orders, so be it. All I'm saying is let us not all commit suicide by marching into a wall of machine gun fire as so many have done before. Admittedly, that was not our fault as we were obeying orders from High Command, but surely we could conduct this battle in a way that gives everyone a fighting chance of getting home in one piece? I maintain we can comply with our orders with honour whilst keeping our casualties to a minimum."

"We are listening, Sergeant, "said the Colonel. "What are your suggestions?"

Bennett went on, "Well, I suppose the best idea would be to stay here and finish this whiskey and sod taking any more risks! But seriously, Sir, can I ask will we have the use of our tanks?"

The Colonel informed him, "I believe they are now repaired but by the time they get here, the deadline will have passed."

"Well then," the sergeant continued, "Without any working tanks at our disposal, I would suggest that the artillery provide a rolling barrage beginning fifty yards from our lines. Any closer and there's danger of our own side being hit by shrapnel. With luck they will take out a lot of the barbed wire and mines we know are laid in no man's land.

While the barrage is keeping Fritz busy, we go over the top keeping that safe distance from the creeping barrage. We should be able to advance behind this as Fritz will be busy keeping his head down. When we are within range, the barrage will have to cease so as not to hit us, but by then we will have moved into a closer position to allow us to locate and target the Huns' machine guns. We concentrate all rifle fire and mortars to knock those out. Half of us race forward zig-zagging making it difficult for the enemy to train his sights on us while the remainder, from the protection of foxholes made by the barrage, provides cover for them.

We alternate like that... advancing under cover, hitting the foxholes and then covering the next wave in leap frog action. When the German trenches are within throwing distance of our grenades, we give 'em the lot then it's a mad dash to get on top of them. Once there, they will either surrender or take as many of us with them as they can. But the combination of bombardment, zig-zagging troops, the early disposal of their machine guns and leap-frog cover by use of the fox-holes is a better bet than marching headlong into their guns."

Recalling earlier orders to do just that one officer sneered, "Yeah *that* was a brilliant tactic!"

"Why not use gas if the wind is in our favour?" asked Captain

Etheridge.

Bennett replied, “Because Captain, as we know from past experience, the wind can change and we'd be gassed by our own side, and we don't want any cock ups at this stage do we? Besides the Hun has no gas left otherwise they would have used it on us by now, so why should we use it on them? Personally it's a method I never favoured. It's such a vile weapon.”

Pleased with the Sergeant’s suggestions the Colonel said, “I approve of the Sergeant’s tactics. Unless any of you can come up with as good a plan in the next five minutes, I suggest you inform your men as soon as you can that we go over the top at nine a.m.”

The officers' silence was an endorsement of the sergeant’s plan.

Captain Etheridge sneered at Bennett. “Daddy’s favourite! Hmpf! Military Medal ....my eye!”

Draining his whiskey the Sergeant leaned closer and whispered in the Captain’s ear, “Hey pal, go pile sand up your arse!”

Knowing it was pointless replying, the snotty Captain simply stood and fumed.

The Colonel raised his glass and said, “And with that gentleman, I wish us all good luck in this last battle of the war.”

As they trundled out of the dug-out, Captain Neal called out to the Colonel, “Once last suggestion, Sir.”

“What is it?”

With a smile he asked, “Could we commence battle at five minutes to eleven?”

Everyone laughed good-naturedly at the captain’s joke then shuffled out to get themselves organised for the coming fray.

****

Within fifteen minutes of the officers meeting, all the men of the First Infantry Troop were kitted up and at action stations in the trenches. The first line stood on the parapets awaiting the whistle for battle to commence.

“Check your weapons now lads,” said Sergeant Bennett. “There won't be much time when we get over the top.”

The senior NCO’s had been informed of the nearing Armistice and also of the reason why the push was still on, but it was decided the other ranks be kept in the dark about it for fear of them not committing themselves fully to the battle and their possible indifference proving fatal.

'Poor buggers' thought Sgt. Bennett as he ran up and down his section of the line checking his men had all their correct equipment and ammunition. *'If only they knew.'*

Private Melhuish gave a startled yell as a bullet ricocheted off his helmet.

The Sergeant screamed at the soldier, "Bloody idiot! How many times have I told you to keep your head down at all times! Use your bloody periscope if you want to do some sight seeing. Bloody fool!"

The shocked but uninjured Melhuish fingered the hole left by the round. "Well stuff my old boots!" he exclaimed whilst another squaddie gave a low whistle.

For the next half an hour all that could be heard was the deafening noise of Allied artillery pounding the German defences in an attempt to soften them up before the advance. The air was filled with the stench of cordite from the exploding shells, wafting towards them on a slight breeze.

If we had decided to use gas, thought Sergeant Jack, *that same breeze would be delivering to us death on a grand scale now.*

No-mans land, stretching a mere two hundred yards to the German lines, was pock-marked like the surface of the moon. The relatively short distance to the enemy lines meant that a 'creeping barrage' was extremely dangerous to the attacking side but it was a chance they had to take and if done within the safety limit would enable a mad dash across no man's land.

On the officers' signals, ladders were placed against the trench walls and the first wave of soldiers stood on the rung awaiting the order to go over the top.

Suddenly all was quiet as the big guns fell silent. The men knew the sights were being realigned to commence pounding a mere fifty yards ahead of their position.

The tension in trenches was electric. A pale-faced Private Ashton was looking definitely the worse for wear.

"Are you O.K. lad?" asked Bennett.

"To be honest Sarge, I'm crapping conkers! I think my number will come up today."

"Tommyrot! You won't die. That's the last thing you'll do!"

"How can you joke at a time like this, Sarge?"

"When better son? You'll be fine," the Sergeant assured him.

"There's a rumour going round that there's to be an Armistice soon. Is that true, Sarge? I mean if it's true, why are we going over the top? It's crazy!"

Trying to calm him Bennett said, "I don't know about that son but what I do know is that we've got old Fritz well and truly on the run. They're outnumbered, low on ammunition and demoralised as hell."

"I know how they feel!" Ashton moaned.

"Ah rubbish! Get through this one last big push and there'll be a nice big parade for all of us when we get back to Blighty."

"A parade?" said the Private. "A bloody parade? I'm not doing this all for a poxy bloody parade!"

Sensing his near hysteria the Sergeant calmly said, "Then do it for us, Pete lad. Do it for your mates. We've got to look out for each other just a while longer yet."

This appeal to Private Ashton's conscience brought about a look of resignation on the lad's previously strained face.

Capitalizing on the mood change he sensed, the Sergeant went on, "It won't be long now, I promise. Pretty soon you'll be swigging a pint of best ale in my pub in the East End. You'll love it there. What a riot we have on a Saturday night. All the music hall stars come in my place after their shows. There's Dan Leno, Florrie Ford, Little Tich and as for Harry Champion, he brings the bloomin' house down, he does, when he sings 'Boiled Beef and Carrots' and 'Any Old Iron'... it's hilarious. People will pay good money for a show like that and we get it for nothing. Bloomin' marvellous!" he enthused.

Private Ashton gave him a quizzical look and said, "Harry Champion? Are you kidding me, Sarge?"

"Not at all, lad," he assured him. "We've had all sorts in there. The pub is located near quite a few music halls. Even before my time it had Fred Karno before he went to the States with Charlie Chaplin. They all come from around there you know. Oh yes. They come in there to let their hair down have a few pints and end up giving a free performance. It's grand I tell you. And when the Pearly Kings and Queens arrive it's a riot, I tell you!"

"Pearly Kings and Queens?" Ashton asked.

"Yeah, you know... they have all these fancy buttons sewn into their clothes, hats, jackets, trousers and so on. When they parade up and down the street with the barrel organs playing, they look a million dollars, they do."

"Sounds grand," said the private. "Tell me, have you ever had Marie Lloyd in your place?"

"Marie Lloyd? Why of course," boasted Sergeant Bennett. "We've that little songbird in loads of times. Wonderful woman, she is. A heart as big as Waterloo. Why, she even sang to me herself."

With that, Sergeant Bennett began to sing, "Oh, the boy I love is up in the gallery, the boy I love is smiling down on me...."

"Oh, that's my favourite!" exclaimed Private Ashton. "Or rather my fiancée's - my Alice."

"Alice?" queried Bennett. "You don't mean that sweet little bird who used to work for the 'Sally Army' doling out hot mugs of tea?"

Ashton explained, "She worked for the V.A.D. Sarge. The Voluntary Aid Detachment. It's made up of St.John's Volunteers and members of the Red Cross. Worth their weight in gold, they are Sarge, especially her."

"Ha ha!" the Sergeant laughed, "That's why you lost your 'bottle'.

You've got something to risk losing now, haven't you lad?"

"*Bottle,* Sarge?"

"As in *bottle and glass* - Cockney rhyming slang, ain't it? What rhymes with glass, eh? You work it out!"

"I haven't lost my bottle at all!" complained the Private."It's just that now I've got something to live for... my Alice. Suddenly all this killing seems so bloody stupid. I mean, those Germans over there are just like us. Conscripts. They're probably just like us, decent lads one and all with wives and mothers, too."

"You're right son, but if you want to see your sweet little bird again don't fool yourself into thinking old Fritz won't kill you stone dead. Good lads or not, they will kill you. They'll have to won't they? It comes down to just us and them lad. Now keep it together for just a short while longer. "

"O.K. Sarge. Thanks. But I'm no coward. I ain't lost my bottle!"

"I know that. Anyway the only *bottle* I'm interested in is my first bottle of brown ale back in my pub. First pint's on the house. How does that sound?"

With a half smile the Private said, "I'll take you up on that Sarge."

Private Ashton was day dreaming of how he and his Alice came to meet as she served tea to the troops in the reserve trenches. He marvelled at how they had just '*clicked*' and got on so well together, relaxed and happy in each other's company despite the carnage around them. That cold night and with the sound of bombing in the distance when he kissed her sweet lips for the very first time, he felt he could float on air. It was so odd and out of place having a little darling like her over here in France and within death's reach. She shouldn't be there. She should be home and safe - and but a picture in a soldier's wallet to take out now and then to hearten him in lonely times, to kiss, caress and dream over. But he was glad she was with him now and in the flesh. As they embraced, he in his harsh khaki uniform which embodied horrors and death and she in her nurses uniform symbolizing goodness and life, it felt so incongruous. Their love drew them together yet their uniforms seemed to repel them. Life was so strange, emotions so intense. Their kisses so sweet he felt they represented something unexplainable, something so sacred that carnal thoughts had no place yet in their newly awakened emotions. Perhaps it was because they were both virgins and unsure of even how to feel. He just knew that when the time came it would mean so much more to them than it had ever done to anyone else. She was special to him and he felt so special when with her, that he vowed from that day onwards he would do his utmost to survive this bloody war and spend the rest of his days with his true love. *Was that too much to ask? To grow old together in safety? Not if I can help it,* he swore.

The Sergeant smoked a cigarette musing with some confidence that Ashton's jitters had passed. '*He probably thinks I gave him load of old tripe about the pub. Any way he's O.K.* now. *He's accepted his lot. Resigned to whatever fate has lined up for him. Fair play to him, I say. He might not be confident – who is for God's sake? - but at least he won't be going over the top scared useless. He's right though. It is crazy, but what difference does it make if you get knocked on the first day of war or the last? You're still just as bloody dead! Tomorrow is promised to no one. I don't know. What a caper!*

Sergeant Bennett checked his wristwatch and at 08.45 hrs he took from his breast pocket, a photograph of his wife and two kids. Allowing himself a brief but loving gaze, his mind wandered back to his last leave when he and his wife finally secured the tenancy on their East End public house. '*The Crimea*'. Years of scrimping and saving, salting his Army pay away while his wife and son worked long hours to maintain a modest home, meant they could all now enjoy a more secure life. With a small pension and gratuity to look forward to for his twenty-two years of service Sergeant Jack was looking forward to a happy working retirement with his family upon his imminent demobilization. A happy end to a long, hard career in service to King and Country. He couldn't wait to get back to his friends and family in London and resume his carefree career of sloshing beer to happy customers.

He quietly sang a little ditty to himself, *Any old iron? Any old iron? Any, any, any old iron? You look sweet. Talk about a treat. You look dapper from yer napper to yer feet. Dressed in style wiv a bran new 'tile' and yer father's old green tie on. Well I wouldn't give yer tuppence fer yer old watch chain. Old iron...old iron.*

He hadn't been as quiet as he thought and his little song brought smiles to a few faces that had been close enough to hear. He didn't care and smiled back at them.

He kissed the photograph and carefully secured it back in the buttoned down pocket. With one last drag, he dimped the end of his 'fag' and stuffed it in a pocket to be enjoyed later.

The moments before a battle is due to commence can stretch out making it seem like time itself is slowed to a standstill. In such moments, soldiers must grab this opportunity to reflect for there may be no opportunity to do it later. If there is, then they have even more to reflect on, but in case this is the last time possible, such moments are sacred. They reflect on their lives, their loved ones and events that had brought them to this dangerous crossroad in their existence.

****

Not all was doom and gloomy apprehension among the ranks though as at 08.50 hrs., Corporal Kerr reminded them.

"Oi Sniffer! Was you at Hellfire Corner that first Christmas in 1914?"

"Which one?" Sniffer asked. "There were a few. I was at one in Armentierres. Where were you?"

"I was at St.Yvon," said Kerr. "There must have been more than one Christmas truce along the lines."

"Dare say they were all along the Northern France and Belgium lines. Good old stuff it was."

Corporal Kerr related his experience of that strange first Christmas under fire. "It was Christmas Eve," he began. "Freezing cold it was and old Fritz was only a couple of hundred yards away, a bit like here. Well, they had some Christmas trees planted in the trenches and decorated with lights. We thought they were preparing to fight so we opened fire didn't we? They returned fire and the battle was full on. Relentless artillery barrages, mortars, whiz bangs, rifle, grenades and machine–gun fire. It was real ding dong! Both sides were shouting and screaming blue murder as they fired. *Bloody Germans!* and *Bloody English*! and such. No doubt both sides thoroughly cheesed off that they had to be fighting at such a time."

For his pals entertainment Kerr made up the dialogue as he went along. "So a British squaddie lets go a mortar round and yells, '*Take that you filthy Hun! I hope you get blown to Kingdom come you Kraut gits!*'

Then a German machine gunner fires a burst and yelled back, '*Und you take zat, you Tommy Schvienhunt.*'

The Tommys yell, '*Square heads!*' and the Germans yell back, '*Scheisenhauser! English pig-dogs!*'"

"Here, how do you know what the Germans said two hundred yards away?" asked Sniffer.

"Well, I've got good ear-sight, haven't I?" said Kerr, his nonsensical explanation convincing no-one.

Kerr continued, "Any way, the firing ceases after a while and we use the time to clean and reload our weapons. While we're getting a fresh brew going we hear a distant sound of a German singing. '*Stille nacht, heilige nacht. Alles schlaft, einsam wacht.*'

'*What's he saying? He's still knack'd?*' asks a squaddie.

'*The whizz bang must have found it's mark,* one answers, '*he must still be knacked!*

'*No!*' says an officer. '*They're singing Christmas carols! Holy Night!*

'*Lord love a duck!*' I says. He sings it beautiful he does and we can hear him all the way across no-man's land. When he's finished we all give him a big round of applause. '*Very nice Fritz*' we shout across.

'*Now you Tommy!*' he shouts back. So we gets Taff Jones to sing him one back. Lovely baritone is Taff. Sang with the Male Welsh Voice

Choir, didn't he? He gives it, ' *Once in Royal David's city, stood a lowly cattle shed...*' Lovely job he makes of it and all.

Well, "said Kerr continuing his tale, "we carries on like that all night, singing and relaxing with not a shot fired between us. Then as it grows light one of the Gerrys gets up out of his trench and marches straight towards us. He carries no rifle but when he gets within chucking distance he lobs something straight at us. Well, we all duck for cover, don't we?

"*'Get yer 'eads down'* someone shouts and we all cocks our rifles and take aim. But there's no explosion. *What's their game,* we think.

Then Fritz shouts, *It's schnapps Tommy. Merry Christmas!*

I grabs it and has a taste. *'Blimey! It is alcohol!'* I says.

I remember an officer saying, *I suppose it's the same for them. We'd all rather be somewhere else tonight.*

"'I know where I'd like to be,' says Chalky White, 'Watching the kids unwrap their present while I polish off the wife's Christmas pud.'"

"Or playing football after a belly full of brown ale! Lovely!" says I.

Jock wraps a bottle in some rags and prepares to throw it to the Kraut. '*Same to you Fritz,*' he shouts. '*Best Highland whiskey. Single malt coming right up*!'

Then instead of allowing him to throw the bottle to Fritz, the officer tells Jock to hand it to him, then proceeds to climb out of the trench and stroll over into no-man's land.

We are all shouting at him to come back. *Too risky* we says, but he ignores us and carries on. Then blow me, if a German officer doesn't climb over his parapet and the two officers walk silently towards each other. *What's all this?* we thought. We hadn't seen anything like it! Well they meet in the centre of no-mans land, salute each other and shake hands! Next minute they are sharing a cigarette!

Within a few minutes us Brits and Germans, all cautious like, climb over the top and walk towards each other. It was weird I tell you, face to face with the enemy but within a few moments we were all swapping fags, stories, showing each other family photographs and sharing what beer we had. And lots of hand shaking, back-slapping and laughing. It was marvellous. They were just like us.

Before long somebody brings out a soccer ball, from where I don't know, but it's decided we should have a football match, so we makes goal posts with our helmets and greatcoats and away we goes at it. An energetic game ensues, all men and officers alike getting stuck in and having a rare old time of it. Everyone is as happy as Larry. You wouldn't think there was a war on. That's all forgotten for the time being. Wonderful, it was.

Well wouldn't you know it, a slight altercation develops when one of the Fritz's accuses Nobby Clark of being offside.

'*Get lost,' says Nobby. 'Offside my a*se!'* and words to that effect.

'*You vant to learn how to play zer football*', says one of the Fritzs.

*'B*ll*cks!'* says Nobby. *'We invented the game, mush!'*

Of course old Fritz had never heard of the term 'mush' so he says, *'Moosh? Vot iz dis* 'moosh'? *You sink I am ze friggin' dog? You Prittish schveinhunt?'*

So both teams begin a lot of pushing and shoving and exchanging of insults like, *'Sod off square head!'* and *'Getten ze shtoofed you, you fish and chips you!'* Well this gets worse and a fight breaks out. It's a right free for all with plenty of fists in the face and boots up the a*se. Officers on both side try to calm the men down but they become involved also. All descends into mayhem over a bloody football game!

Suddenly a German officer fires a round into the air to get everyone's attention, but everyone's so jittery that when the shot rings out Brits and Krauts alike grab their helmets and coats and scarper back to their own lines. The German officer frantically firing his pistol into the air to quiet things down only panics the men even more. Us Brits are racing back to our lines swearing and shouting and lobbing stones, clumps of frozen mud, and anything we can lay our hands on.

Chalky White boots the football towards the German lines in a last act of defiance and it lands on the spiked helmet of the German officer who, enraged at being made to look foolish, fires at Chalky but misses.

From the comparative safety of our respective lines both sides resume hostilities. The temporary display of peace and goodwill now totally dissipated, anger and hatred is re-instituted in full venom.

A German soldier fires a rifle and shouts, *'Take zat you John Bull. You English pig-dog!'*

One of our lads returns fire with a mortar and shouts, *'Here you are Fritz. You can stick this right up the Kaisers...........!'*

Then we are back where we started from, us giving it things like, *'Bloody Krauts! I hope you get blown to Kingdom Come!'* and Fritz yelling back, *'Take zat you Tommy Schwienhunt!'*

I couldn't hear the rest as the noise drowned everything out, but the point is that previous to the football match both sides felt they had nothing to fight about. *Now* they had a reason to fight! They didn't understand war, but they understood football!"

Upon finishing his tale, the men in Corporal Kerr's trench laughed and gave him a round of applause.

"You ought to be on the music halls with that kind of spiel, Corp." said one voice.

Sergeant Jack said nothing. He was happy that his men could find something to laugh about before the imminent bloodbath. *Better they be in good spirits than in nervous apprehension.*

****

At 08.55 hrs Captain Neal, satisfied all preparations were in place, allowed his mind to wander back to his last evening in England. The dinner party at his country home had been somewhat of a disaster. Supposedly organised by friends and family to wish him good fortune upon his return to the front lines the day after, he had found himself having strong words with his father-in-law; a general in the War Office in London.

"Well it was a wonderful dinner, Muriel," said the General.

"As always darling," Captain Neal added, patting his wife's hand.

Pulling it away rather too quickly for Neal's liking she said, "You two go and smoke those foul cigars in the drawing room will you? I'll keep our other guests entertained."

"By other guests, no doubt you mean that twerp Roger!" said Neal. "Why on earth that man isn't in uniform, I'll never know."

"But you do know!" insisted Muriel. "He's busy running a very large munitions factory. If that can't be classed as a 'reserved occupation' I don't know what can!"

"His *father* runs it, not Roger!" said Neal impatiently. "All he does is swan around enjoying the profits! The man's a skiver. You know I can't stand him!"

"I think you're very unkind to him darling. After all where would I get such a good tennis coach with this beastly war taking all our men away?"

A cold stare was all her husband could offer in reply.

"Oh. I'm sorry darling," Muriel said, "I didn't think."

Putting an arm around his son-in-law the General said, "C'mon my boy. Let's have that cigar."

In the drawing room, Captain Neal lit the General's cigar and then his own. Both slumping in to comfy armchairs, they enjoyed their smoke in silence.

Eventually the General said, "All right, let's have it. What's troubling you my boy?"

"There's no point beating around the bush sir," said Neal. "I think Muriel's having an affair!"

Calmly blowing a smoke ring the General asked, "What makes you think that? Just because she's changed the colour of her hair?"

"No, nothing so trivial, there's much more to it than that. Things just haven't been good lately."

"Hmmm. Sorry to hear it. What do you intend to do about it?"

"Dunno yet sir. Need all my concentration on what's happening at the front."

"Quite so."

"But in all sincerity, it doesn't look good sir. I think we'll have to divorce."

"That bad eh? Do you have the grounds?"

“A friend of mine from the tennis club saw them checking into a hotel. Said he'd recognise her anywhere despite her new hair colour.”

“Hmmm. No chance it was a one off and you two could sort it out?”

“'Fraid not sir. It's been on the wane for a while now.”

“Bad business, divorce. I am not happy to think about what that might mean in the circles I move. It is somewhat of a scandal after all.”

“But it doesn't affect you sir. Just me and Muriel, and that swine Roger!”

“Not so, old son. Mud sticks to the blanket after all. I'm your father-in-law. Family tainted and all that.”

“I apologise for involving you sir but it is no fault of mine. Your daughter has committed adultery, not I.”

“Why not simply continue living together? Keep up the pretence of a happy marriage for appearance sake yet still go your own way?”

“And still be cuckolded by that despicable draft dodger? No thank you.”

Taking a long draw on his cigar the General eyed his son-in-law. Eventually he said, “I can make it worth your while you know.”

“What on earth do you mean, sir?”

“The War Office is always looking for bright young officers. It would mean automatic promotion and an increase in pay!”

Neal puffed on his cigar and contemplated the General’s offer. His marriage to the General’s daughter was in tatters and he had no desire to try to make up with her. As far as he was concerned it was a lost cause.

“Promotion eh? .... *and* accommodation in London?”

“You've got it!”

“All to protect your good name from scandal, eh sir?”

“Look my boy, I've served the Crown for thirty years. I refuse to have my name and good work tarnished!”

“I understand that sir, but I want more.”

“More! Isn't a promotion to the War Office enough?”

Neal took a draw on his cigar and leaned forward. “Hear me out sir. I seem to remember you were no great fan of certain high ranking officers.”

“Well, it's no secret I preferred Sir John French to his deputy Douglas Haig. What of it?”

“After the war sir. If I survive it that is, I intend to rake as much muck as I can over the treatment of the men on the Western Front. You are friends with some editors of prominent newspapers and your name would add great weight to my cause.”

“Now wait a minute old chap.”

“I would even like for questions to be raised in the House!”

“Be sensible Neal. That's far too dangerous. Look, if I would find a divorce too embarrassing how do you think I'd feel about mud slinging in public? We could both be cashiered from the Army. Our careers ruined!"

"Not if we can show evidence and proof. Eye witnesses and sworn affidavits etc."

"But for God's sake, why man?"

"Because our High Command has arrogantly thrown away the lives of thousands of men who took the King's shilling in good faith. I believe they have a duty of care to those men but instead unnecessarily jeopardized their lives by giving ridiculous orders impossible to implement. It took for Lloyd George to threaten to sack half of the staff if proper care wasn't taken over strategies and tactics. You remember, sir?"

"I'm afraid I do son. I recall the fuss they raised when I suggested issuing the men with oilskins and leggings to prevent that blasted trench foot. They even grumbled at the cost of cod-liver oil I wanted. Good stuff, that y'know. Keeps the cold and damp at bay."

"Yes sir. You did a lot for the troops. That's why your support would be invaluable. You know how disgracefully our lads have been treated. Why we were only issued tin helmets after a year of complaints from medical officers. They couldn't cope with all the head injuries, and what about having to concoct fake tablets meant for pain relief? Placebos made of corn starch with no medical use whatsoever except psychologically. Even tried to make use of hypnosis in the absence of anaesthetics. I ask you! The War Office have let down our men considerably; apart from lack of consideration regarding equipment and supplies and their medical well being, they issue diabolically preposterous orders to face down machine guns with cavalry charges? Absolute insanity!"

The General nodded in agreement adding, "And the Hun had three times as many machine guns as we had! *The machine gun is a much over rated weapon* they said. *Same as tanks!* What sheer rot!"

"Quite sir, and it's machine guns and tanks and sensible strategies that are winning the war for our side now. Why didn't they learn that lesson three years ago before the horrors of the Somme, Ypres and Paschendale?"

"I don't know, Neal, but I can tell you there is a lot of sympathy for those brave lads who died blindly obeying those insane orders. One of the worst things was making the men walk, walk mind you, not run, in line against the enemies bullets. Never understood that. Absolute madness."

"Were you aware, sir, that reinforced rubber breast plates had been produced by that fellow Dunlop who makes the car tyres? And that certain officers at High Command disallowed their use, saying that *their men were not cowards* and so made to face the hail of bullets with no protection? I ask you, why on earth was wearing such a garment considered cowardly? Even the knights of old had shields to defend themselves. Those fools at H.Q. allowed our lads nothing. Talk about lions lead by donkeys!"

"You're right Neal, but it's too late. The damage has been done. What can anyone do now?"

"I can publicize it sir. Show those swine up for what they are. Idiotic old dinosaurs who were not fit to command a modern army. I would go so far as to say they are, in fact, *war criminals*!"

The General pondered a while then said, "No. It will never happen. Though I do agree with you, your accusations would never see the light of day. The old boy's network would simply close ranks and shove you out in the cold, with no career and quite possibly prosecuted as well. No you're fighting a lost cause, Neal. Save it all for your memoirs in twenty years or so. When the establishment can't touch you. That's my best advice to you!"

"I can't deny I am disappointed sir, but I suspect you are right. I simply wanted some justice for all those thousands who lost their lives unnecessarily."

"Let someone else write the history books son. Someone who has nothing to lose. Accept your promotion and new position and who knows, you might be more useful within the decision making establishment of the War Office. Put your emotions on hold and Muriel behind you and look to your own future my boy. Your career is everything now."

"I suppose you're right sir."

"Just survive these last few weeks will you?"

Smiling, the Captain replied, "I shall do my very best."

"Meanwhile, I can throw a little bonus your way."

"Oh, really?"

"How would you like that hound Roger to be drafted into your troop? Let the blasted lounge- lizard have a taste of war. It would do him some good!"

"Ha – Ha! Now I would enjoy that sir. He would deserve it, the slacker, but I couldn't accept your offer. It would be like condemning a man to death."

"Nonsense! He'd only be taking the same risk as yourself! Might even make a man out of the bounder!"

"What about Muriel, sir?"

"You're too much of a gentleman for your own good. There'll always be other Muriels! You look to your future, son."

Now having reached an understanding, the two men relaxed into their armchairs and enjoyed their cigars.

****

It was now nine a.m. With a mere two hours to go before the implementing of the Armistice and the end of the Great War itself.

The Allied bombardment suddenly fell silent. The deathly quiet somehow seemed to accentuate the smell of the dank, rotting sandbags.

All the officers down the line looked at their watches, now synchronized to this fateful hour, then blew a shrill piercing blast on their whistles.

"Oh well. Here goes nothing!" said Private Melhuish.

Corporal Kerr didn't realise he was thinking out loud when he said, "I think I would have liked to have known my father."

"I dare say so would your mother!" laughed Melhuish and with that they and swarms of soldiers clambered over the top of the trenches to launch them selves into the fray. Almost immediately they were met by volleys of rifle fire, and the dreaded rat, tat, tat of machine guns spitting death at five hundred rounds per minute.

The artillery recommenced fire now with half the guns engaging the enemy's lines direct while the other half providing the rolling barrage a mere fifty yards ahead of the advancing Brits.

With the Hun thus occupied the men of First Troop grasped their opportunity to employ their tactical advance. At least they could run to the enemy instead of being forced to obey the ridiculous earlier orders to walk abreast and die defiantly en masse. That nonsense had never been satisfactorily explained to them.

First Troop ran, bobbed and weaved their way forward, like side-stepping rugby players trying desperately not to present themselves as an easy target. Fox holes were created by the barrage detonating the land mines. Whether dry or full of stagnant mud, men gratefully dived into them for cover.

Sergeant Bennett's plan was working a treat. The barrage's effect of pinning the enemy down, thus preventing them trying anything too ambitious, enabled a slow but sure Allied advance. The tactic of racing in relays from fox-hole to fox-hole using covering fire meant that within the hour they had gained enough ground that both the static and rolling artillery barrages were obliged to be done away with for fear of making casualties of their own side.

Now the German machine guns were close enough to be targeted with more accuracy by mortars and rifle fire. If the Brits could gain just a little more ground, the trenches would be within reach of their grenades.

A mortar round hit one of the German machine gun emplacements and the resulting explosion blasted out large hot metal fragments killing at least six or seven of the enemy instantly. Without that machine gun to mow down dozens at a time meant that central position was now vulnerable to Allied attack.

The machine gun threat was now reduced to two on either flank but couldn't fire consistently as the mortars had concentrated on their positions.

Their confidence boosted by the central machine gun being put out of action, about a dozen men seized their chance to charge the German lines.

The first two men died instantly as their pounding feet triggered off land mines. The other men stopped in their tracks for fear of the same result, but this only served to provide stationary targets for the German rifles. Two more went down with surprised screams.

"Get down! Get down!" yelled Sgt. Bennett just as another two men were hit and fell with one body on top of another.

Bennett ordered concentrated fire on the positions responsible for the six deaths. With this under way it enabled not only the remaining six men to scramble back to the relative safety of a fox-hole but for Sergeant Bennett to go forward and take cover behind the last two of the fallen men.

From behind the pair of stacked bodies, Bennett was able to use his rapid firing Thompson machine gun to cut a pathway through the minefield.

The mines exploded one after one as the Thompson's bullets sprayed the field. Skilfully ducking behind his dead comrades after hitting a mine he avoided rifle fire and any shrapnel from the blasts as he shot, blew up a mine then immediately took cover again. On the next burst he found he couldn't release his arthritic finger which had seized on the trigger. Rather than waste any time, he simply stood there in full view of the enemy and blasted away. Shooting from the hip, he sprayed a burst of fire from left to right and ahead of him causing explosion after explosion as the bullets found the buried mines.

The shocked Germans marvelled at his display of bravery or perhaps just plain foolhardiness. Miraculously, without a scratch despite all the flying red hot metal, Bennett very soon blew a ten foot wide path through the minefield all the way to the enemy's trench.

With the remaining two guns on the German flanks being attended to by mortars, this left the centre ground exposed and without sufficient fire-power to prevent the seething mass of British Tommys charging forward, lobbing grenades as they bore down on the hapless Huns.

The terrified German soldiers were overwhelmed, some throwing down their weapons, other running to the safety of their underground dug-out.

Looking to his left and right Bennett could see those flanks were now also taken and being overrun by the Brits.

Cries of Kapitulation!" (*surrender*) resounded from the thoroughly trounced German lines.

A beserk Private Ashton had a terrified German soldier at the mercy of his bayonet.

"Bitte, bitte!" the German screamed.

"Ashton!" shouted the Sergeant. "Put your weapon down. He's surrendered!"

The wild-eyed private removed the bayonet from the grateful Germans throat.

"Danke. Danke," he gasped.

Their battle now lost, the Germans had no choice but to lay down their arms and surrender.

A dazed and weary looking German Colonel emerged from his dugout, saluted Sergeant Bennett and handed over his pistol.

As the Sergeant accepted it, a strange quietness spread over the whole area. The silence was eerie. There was no distant rumble of artillery from the other fronts, no rifle fire, no rat-a-tat of machine guns. All was deathly silent. Everyone strained their ears but not a sound was heard, even in the far off distance.

Germans and British looked at each other in confusion when just then a far off single bugle could be heard playing '*Last Post*'.

The German Colonel pulled out an ornate pocket watch and studied its face. With a blank stare he showed it to the Sergeant. The time displayed was eleven o'clock.

Sergeant Bennett slowly raised his wrist to check his wristwatch. It said the same. He emptied the German officer's pistol, handed it back to him then stood back a pace and saluted.

When the German officer returned the salute, ranks on both sides gave up a great cheer tossing hats and rifles up in the air. No attempt was made to stop them revelling and savouring this moment. That was it at last. The Armistice had begun. It was all over.

British and Germans shook hands, backs were slapped and loud, roaring, constant cheers issued from men of both sides grateful for the end of the cruelest of wars that had cost millions of lives.

The German Colonel studied Sergeant Bennett's face and asked, "Why? Why this last charge?"

With a feeling of great shame Sgt. Bennett could only offer, "I'm sorry Sir. All I can say is, it was orders."

"Ah yes," said the officer knowingly and with what appeared great sadness. "Orders. I understand. What happens now, Sergeant? Are we your prisoners?"

Sergeant Bennett shook his head and replied "I wouldn't have thought so. Perhaps if the war was still on ...but it isn't. It's over. I guess we all just go home."

The weary German Colonel said, "That's fine by me".

"Me too," said Jack and the two shook hands before they both turned away and walked back to their lines.

More British troops appeared from behind their positions and came forward to relieve the beaten German forces of their weapons as a safeguard while they waited for instructions from British and Allied H.Q.

Jack Bennett looked around with great sadness at the dead and injured. *This last charge was totally unnecessary* he thought, *a violation of the honour and trust of these brave men; these lions led by donkeys and abject shame on those responsible for what amounted to a crime against humanity.* He thought of a line of poetry he half remembered from somewhere, *Many a mother's son lay down to that eternal sleep, from which there is no awakening.*

Lighting up the remaining half of his cigarette and inhaling a great gulp he could only feel immense sorrow as he looked upon the war ravaged faces of soldiers of both sides. Strolling back to his lines all he could think was, "*Thank God it's all over.*" It was then that he stepped on the land mine.

He never heard the explosion that ripped his body apart and sent him flying twenty feet into the air. Everything went blank for him. All was blackness. He had no thoughts, no feelings, no conception of time. It could have been moments or hours later when he recognized the inside of the regimental first aid post. '*But that's way behind our own lines*' he thought. '*How long have I been unconscious?*'

He watched patiently from a position somewhere above the surgeon.

'Didn't know they had seats up here' he thought. '*Oh well, I'll just hang about until it's my turn to be attended to. Funny, I don't feel any pain at all, not even my arthritis. They must have given me some of that morphine stuff. Boy it works well. I feel as though I haven't a care in the world. Why, I don't even feel cold.'*

Sergeant Bennett looked on happily as the surgeon hacked away at the mangled limbs of a soldier on the operating table.

"He's lost too much blood," the surgeon told his anesthetist. "I don't think we can save him."

'Poor fellow' thought Jack. '*I wonder who he was'*

Upon seeing the man was wearing a wristwatch he thought, '*Ah – it must be an officer. I wonder if I know him.'*

The stretcher bearers lifted the lifeless body onto a stretcher to take it from the first aid post.

"I say, who is that please?" Jack asked but the stretcher bearer didn't answer.

He asked again, this time raising his voice. Still no answer.

He shouted as loud as he could to the doctor and his attendants but no one gave the slightest indication of hearing him.

'*Perhaps the shelling has made them all deaf*' thought Jack and made to tap the stretcher bearer on the shoulder. To Jack's complete shock, his hand passed right through the man's body with neither of them feeling a thing. He tried again but the same thing happened. '*What's happening?*' he asked himself. As the body on the stretcher was carried past him, Jack leaned over to see the man's face. The incredulity and shock of seeing his own face on the man hit him like a ton of bricks. “What's happening? What is all this?” he cried.

A voice from behind him answered, “But you know what this is, Jack, don't you?”

Turning round Jack was relieved to see someone who could hear him. “Oh! Blimey! It's you, Tommy!” he said.

“That's right Sarge, Tommy Barker. How are you doin'?” he asked, smiling.

“Good to see you again mate, but ......I thought you copped it at Ypres last year?”

“That's right Sarge,” he said again in a calm tone, then added, “Haven't you figured it out yet, Jack?”

“I'm a bit confused,” he answered, “I think it's the morphine.”

A small beam of light shone into the first aid post growing fuller and brighter until soon its blinding luminescence filled the whole room.

“Why searchlights?” asked the puzzled Jack.

“Hi Sarge!” came another familiar voice. It was Private Melhuish with half of his helmet blown away.

Pointing to it and grinning he said, “You did warn me didn't you?”

“You can both hear me and they can't?” Jack asked.

“That's right, Sarge,” they said in unison.

As the penny slowly dropped, Jack looked down at the body on the stretcher and said, “That's me, isn't it?”

“That *was* you Jack,” said his old friend.

Jack gasped, “Oh my goodness!” Then asked, “Then it's all over?”

“Yes, it's all over,” confirmed Tommy, “Every thing's O.K. now.”

“No more wars for us, Sarge,” added Melhuish and taking hold of Jack's arm the three men turned toward the light which had re-formed into a beam leading upwards.

“Time to go now,” said Tommy.

“What about my wife? My family?” asked Jack.

Barker told him, “They'll be fine. They are prepared for all this. They'll all be fine. Trust me.”

“I do,” said Jack now overtaken by an all-enveloping feeling of calm and peace.

With that, the three comrades turned and walked towards the source of the bright light leaving behind the first aid post, the battlefield, the *war to end all wars* ....and mortal life itself.

The End

Whitby - Vampires Return?

The train's gradually reducing speed on its approach to the station altered the rhythm of the carriages clunking over the points, making it sound like a giant mechanical heartbeat slowing down to die. The change of pace caused the attractive and elegant young blonde woman to snap out of the daydream she had been lulled into by the passing scenery of serene fields and green hedgerows.

The nervous voles, busy field mice and hovering kestrels continued their business of survival and procreation, impervious to the attentions of the bored travellers gawping from the train windows. Nature's tenuous existence at complete odds with the safe, orderly lives of those cocooned within the cosy carriages. So close in proximity yet worlds apart.

These kind of anomalies mattered to her, from the definite to the indefinite, from the subtle to the obvious and from heat of passion to the coldness of death. Anomalies, comparisons and dichotomies, juxtapositions between one facet and another, puzzles, enigmas, relationships between people, facts and figure... all such matters intrigued her. Her beautiful face and model's body belied a cold analytical mind, easily detached from any urge to act impulsively. Hot passions and cold calculations were under her control to click on and off like a switch when she sought to confront a problem and to achieve the desired result. With a cool, clear-headed ability to compartmentalise subjects and not let herself dwell on or be swayed by emotion, she was a rare woman, in complete control of her faculties and emotions and above all, true to herself.

These invaluable qualities, no doubt desired and coveted by many women, were of enormous significance and advantage in her chosen profession, that of a police officer serving with the county branch of the Criminal Investigation Department, or C.I.D. as it is commonly referred to. With not only beauty but also intelligence and determination at her command, she was custom made for the many diverse requirements of her job. She was indeed all woman but more importantly, she was her *own* woman.

Her interview for selection and transfer from Yorkshire C.I.D. to the capital city's metropolitan force had gone well and what better opportunity to justify her superiors' faith in her than bringing this double killer to book as soon as possible?

Despite having had to make a couple of connections from London to the picturesque north Yorkshire tourist town of Whitby, the journey had not been too long nor unpleasant. Her decision to take the train rather than drive had been a wise one, it having provided the time for C.I.D. Sergeant Clare McKee to bone up on the case in hand and prepare her questions for the local police. More than eager to demonstrate that her deductive skills and instinctive reasoning would produce the results a somewhat baffled local police force struggled to attain, she was, nonetheless, in no doubt that this case would test even her finely honed skills.

One murder would not have fazed the hardened old local coppers; even two only weeks apart was no surprise these days. The unusual thing about this case was the almost identical manner of the victims' deaths, which alerted the gravely concerned local force to the grim possibility a serial killer might be on the loose in their beloved town. The fact that both girls were drained of practically every last drop of blood had given rise to the rumour, no doubt fostered by the press, that more sinister forces were at work.

The quaint ex-fishing village was once home to such distinguished historical figures as explorer Captain Cook and Arctic adventurer and whaler William Scoresby. Locals would have one believe it was also home, for a while, to writer Bram Stokers' notorious creation. The town now prospered from tourism and was in danger of losing its main source of revenue should word leak out of a freak venting his bent whims and fantasies on the local population. A fictional monster was good for business but a real one would prove the opposite... a death knell in fact for the tourist trade in this popular, easy going holiday spot.

In spite of the towns now pleasant demeanour, Whitby had had it's share of excitement over the years. A safe haven on an otherwise inhospitable coast, it became the third largest shipbuilding centre after London and Newcastle in the 18th and 19th centuries. Smugglers made good use of its location and the untaxed wealth soon brought the associated evils of violence, robbery, murder and prostitution to its ever lawless streets.

Vicious press gangs preyed on drunken whalers bashing the unsuspecting drinkers helpless and forcing the King's shilling on their person thereby lawfully justifying the unlucky mens' virtual enslavement for three years' service in the King's Navy. Whitby, in those far off days, was as bad as any of the notorious Wild West towns in the U.S. Life was hard, fast paced and short.

Once the railway arrived it lost some of its wild independence, but from then on the town prospered even more. Fish could now be hauled straight from the docks and transported immediately the length and breadth of the country on a steel network of rails. Fortunes were made, the population grew, businesses boomed; civic pride blossomed as public services, hospitals, and schools consolidated their position. Fine parks, hotels and guest houses were established and before long the once dangerous playground of cut-throats and opportunists matured into civic respectability. When the fishing industry eventually went into decline, the town was pretty enough to sustain tourism and so survived. It always seemed a lucky town in that it could bounce back from any adversities that befell it. Now it was to be tested once again.

Due to her high detection and arrest rate, the local C.I.D. were happy to have Det. Sgt. McKee take over the investigation with approval from London. Her record had been exemplary ever since her experiences in Bosnia when serving with the Military Police where her superiors had been impressed with her strength of mind in not allowing emotion to interfere with the performance of her duties.

Never more so was this demonstrated than when her Lance/corporal boyfriend of six months was killed by a landmine whilst on active service in the war torn Balkans of the late nineteen nineties. Her ability to blot any negative experience in times of stress, was not only advantageous whilst serving in the Army. Later, this attribute was of immense help in aiding a rapid promotion within her home town's local police force; and her subsequent elevation to the famous C.I.D. Her cautious, intelligent approach and painstaking attention to detail had served her and her profession well. Her methodical bent she attributed to her father's genes, but credited her mother with passing on an almost sixth sense. This enabled her to make uncannily accurate assessments of people's personalities, their quirks, traits, habits and indecisions which shone like a beacon for this exceptionally bright girl to pick up on. Once enough of the facts pointed her in a particular direction, she was able to zero in and let that strange and rare sixth sense take over and unravel the rest of many a complicated case. It was with utmost confidence and determination to succeed that Det. Sgt. McKee looked forward to her task ahead.

Slowing to a standstill at the terminus, the train spewed out its passengers onto the platform. Stepping from the womb-like cosiness of the carriage, Clare gave an involuntary shiver as she felt the sharpness of the North Sea breeze on her face.

"Mild for this time of year, love," laughed a ruddy complexioned ticket collector.

"If you say so," she replied with a rueful smile, pressing the outward bound part of her ticket into his outstretched hand. '*The weather forecast had been bad,*' she thought, '*but when was the Met. Office's predictions ever right? The bookmakers might provide a more accurate guess, but more importantly - had it remained mild the night of the murders? Had evidence on the ground suffered because of rain or even mild drizzle?*'

She was carried along with the crowds from other platforms towards the entrance as though the station was haemorrhaging people out of its system, leaving it lifeless as it pumped them outside onto the busy street.

Witnessing the feeding frenzy of taxi cabs swallowing up the disembarked passengers to whisk them away, she realised she was experiencing the mechanics of the first stage of the thriving tourist industry on which this town now placed it's whole dependence.

Within moments a taxi cab had raced to a halt in front of her and with his engine still running, the driver leapt out and grabbed her one large bag. Hastily lobbing it onto the back seat he asked, "Where to love?"

"The police station please."

****

Despite the short journey, the cabbie decided some conversation was in order and so vented the usual cabbies' grumblings about the weather and having to negotiate awkward one way streets and congested down town traffic.

"They need to pedestrianise all this," he moaned, "no vehicles allowed......... except for cabs that is!" he added with a smile. “It didn't take long to start getting busy again. It went a bit quiet-like after Halloween and now it's picking up again. Well, it's coming up to Christmas, ain't it? Always busy here at Christmas. Brrrr it’s cold enough for snow, ain't it Miss? Do you think it will snow? I do. I'm sure it will. It's *taters* out there it is, blooming *taters*. So it's the Police Station, eh? You're not going to report you've seen Dracula as well, are you?" he laughed.

"What do you mean?" she asked.

"Ever since those killings, people reckon they have seen him."

"Oh yeah? Sober people?"

"He lived here once you know!"

"No he didn't," she corrected him. “That was just a story. Pure fiction."

"I'm just telling you what people have said, love!"

"You'll be scaring tourists away with that kind of talk. That won't do your business much good, will it?"

"Not at all, love," he replied," it's just the opposite. People are coming here to see if there's any truth to the rumours. Fascinated, they are."

"And it won't hurt you to drum up a bit of interest, eh?" she asked.

"Well," he smiled, "where's the harm?"

“None I suppose. Unless they become a victim!”

As the taxi pulled up outside Whitby Police Station the cabbie nipped smartly out of the vehicle and handed Clare her large bag.

Looking at the few steps to the main doors he asked, "Need a hand with your baggage, love?"

"I can manage," she told him

"That's £4.50 then, please."

"For driving five hundred yards?" she complained.

"Tourist season rates!" he pleaded.

She scolded him, "I think you belong inside here, you villain!" pointing to the police station.

With a smile she handed him a five pound note and a small piece of paper. "O.K." she said. "Just sign this receipt."

The cabbie was a little taken back to see *Yorkshire Constabulary Expenses Form* stamped on it. As it rapidly dawned on him that she was a police officer, he duly signed the chit and eagerly tried to press a fifty pence coin in her hand.

"Your change er, Officer."

"Keep it," she said and picking up her bag climbed the few steps up to the station's main doors.

Dumping her bag at the desk she rang the bell sitting atop its polished surface.

"Coming, coming," a disembodied voice was heard to say. "Keep your shirt on."

A white-haired police sergeant eventually appeared carrying a mug of steaming hot tea and placed it down upon the hinged part of the counter. Seeing the beauty opposite him, his already heavily lined face crinkled even more as it broke into a grin that made Clare think of the Cheshire cat in Alice's adventures. His grin emphasised his eye bags which now appeared to support his bulbous, bloodshot blue eyes.

"Good afternoon Missie," he said.

"Detective Sergeant McKee!" she corrected.

"Er, no, no. We don't have anyone here by that name my dear."

"That is me."

"Who is?"

"I am."

"You am?"

"The lady in question."

"Oh – oh, yes. Of course you are a lady. No question. Er, What was the question?"

Realising the old boy was not quite with it, she patiently informed him, "I am a police officer. My name is Detective Sergeant McKee."

"A police officer, eh?

"That's right."

"Why are you not in uniform then?"

"I am in plain clothes."

"Oh I dunno. They look alright to me."

With great calm and self-control, Clare reached into her jacket pocket, produced her Identity card and offered it to the desk sergeant. After fumbling and eventually finding his spectacles, he made much fuss over scrutinising first the picture on the I.D. then its owner.

Assuming the old boy was satisfied, she asked, "O.K?"

"W-e-ll." he hesitated still perusing the I.D.

Taking her I.D. back she stated, "Superintendant Norris." It was demand, not a question.

"A – ha!" he exclaimed. "You can't catch me out there! My name is Sergeant Doakes. Old man Norris is our gaffer."

"Gaffer?" she queried.

"Aye, lass. Our boss. He's the Super here. Would you like to see him?"

Patiently she replied, "Oh. That's a good idea. Why didn't I think of that? Thank you. Most kind."

"You hang on here Missie, I'll go get him for you."

The screwy old desk sergeant disappeared for a moment and upon returning to his post, a portly but distinguished looking uniformed officer opened a side door to the reception area.

"Ah. You must be Sgt. McKee?" he said, offering her an outstretched hand. "I see you have met our desk-sergeant."

Clare politely acknowledged.

"She one of ours, sir," he explained to the Super, "but she has no uniform yet."

Hoping to clue Doaksie in, he tapped a forefinger to his nose and said, "C.I.D!"

Doaksie gave him a confused stare then to Clare said, "Welcome to Whitby...... Sid."

"Take care of Ms. McKee's bag will you, please?" asked Norris.

"Will do," Sgt. Doakes replied.

With a smile for the old copper, Det. Sgt. McKee followed Norris into his office.

"Take a seat Sergeant," said the Superintendent he closed the office door behind them. "How was the journey? Fancy a cup of tea?"

"Fine and yes please," answered Clare.

"We have booked you into a local women's hostel for your stay with us. I'm sure you'll find it comfortable," said Norris.

"A women's hostel? I don't think so, Sir."

"Well, you are a woman on her own. I thought you might feel more secure."

Controlling her annoyance she said, "Sir, let's not get off on the wrong foot here. May I speak frankly?"

"Of course,"

"I find your attitude somewhat patronising. I am a Detective Sergeant in the C.I.D. and if you have read my record sheet you will see that I am trained in the use of lethal firearms and unarmed combat. This little lady feels most *secure* - thank you!"

"Well yes of course," spluttered Norris. "I apologise. I didn't mean.....er, well also the thing is we're not made of money up here you know. We have to watch our costs and we thought the hostel would be cheaper."

"There is a small hotel on the corner of this street," she said. "It costs no more than a single room at a hostel. I checked it out on the internet and took the liberty of booking myself in."

"Oh you did, did you?"

"It's closer to the police station than the hostel, and I'll have privacy. I want to concentrate on the job I was sent up here to do."

Suitably admonished, the Superintendant tossed a file on the desk and said, "Here's the latest info on the killings. You will have boned up on most of the details, but have a flick through it anyway while I sort your tea out. Milk 'n sugar?"

"Milk- no sugar, thanks."

"You're sweet enough, eh?" he said in an insincere attempt to be friendly.

Clare ignored him and perused the file while he was out of the office.

Moments later he brought in a tray with tea and biscuits.

"Shall I be mother?" he asked with a smile.

"Yes please," replied Clare and Norris gently poured the tea into dainty cup, which he passed to Clare.

Clare read out loud, "Two murders, four weeks apart. Both young females found in local cemetery. The first murder occurred the night of a Halloween party. Nineteen-year-old local girl, in fancy dress. Second body, a twenty two year old, was found five weeks later, also local and she was dressed normally."

"Yes," said the Super. "We think they attended the Goths' festival, held twice a year here in town. They may or may not have known each other seeing as they were local girls, but it's possible they had the Goth thing in common."

"What's all that about?" Clare asked.

"Oh a bunch of crazy kids get all dressed up in Gothic clothing like vampires and such and parade around the town and have wild parties. The pubs do great business."

"Why choose this town to hold such an event?"

A little embarrassed, Norris replied, "Well, it's all to do with that silly Dracula story. In the book, old Drac was supposed to have landed here, caused mayhem amongst the townsfolk and was chased back to Transylvania where he ended up with his throat cut. It's all fiction of course, but you know kids nowadays - any excuse for a party."

"I see," said Clare, "It's like people celebrating the fictional detective Sherlock Holmes? His fans often roam Baker Street in London looking for his abode."

"That's the kind of thing," agreed the Super. "Old 'Holmesy' never really existed."

"And Dracula *does*?" asked Clare with a half smile.

"Well," said Norris, "both victims have suffered the same fate, that of bleeding to death from wounds to the carotid artery!"

"Carotid?" asked Clare. "Not the jugular vein?"

"That's what the coroner's report says. What's the difference? They're both dead aren't they?"

"The difference is the jugular vein lies close to the skin's surface on the neck. The carotid artery lies further inside protected by neck muscles, but it carries fresh oxygenated blood to the brain. On its return path the blood flows though the jugular just under the skin."

"What's your point, Sergeant?"

"My point is Sir, that blood from the jugular is more accessible. Don't vampires always go for the jugular?"

"I don't know. If you say so," said Norris testily. "I'm not saying it was a blasted vampire but people can become very superstitious very quickly."

"Nonetheless," said Clare, "there have been two identical murders here, real murders not fictional ones. O.K. they're in weird circumstances but no need to let superstition start clouding judgements, is there?"

"No, I agree," said Norris somewhat embarrassed. "I don't believe that crap, but some people do."

"But we are police officers and have a clear minded approach to things, don't we?"

"Of course, of course," he spluttered. "It's probably the local tourist board trying to drum up business!"

"Now really, Superintendent!" said Clare. "Two girls have lost their lives! Let's not make light of it."

"Yes, you're right. I apologise," said Norris.

Clare continued, "Unless we all start believing in vampires, I suggest the style of these murders was in order to give the impression our non-existent vampire has returned. Why, I wonder?"

"Simple," said Norris. "We have a serial killer on the loose and he's getting extra kicks masquerading as a bloody vampire. It's only a couple of weeks before Christmas now so we need this cleared up as soon as possible. Not nice to have this hanging over our heads at such a time."

"Not nice for the parents at *any* time!" Clare chided.

"He's gotta be stopped and quickly!" asserted Norris adding with a thinly disguised sneer. "The local C.I.D. have got nowhere so let's see what the big city detective can make of it!"

"That's what I'm here for," Clare replied. "Now, I wish to see the place they were found. OK? By the way, what were the girls' blood group?"

"It's in the report," said Norris. "'A' negative I believe. I'm afraid the only man we can spare you is Doaksie, but he's really alright. He's a good driver and knows this town like the back of his hand."

Pulling a face at the prospect of being hampered by an old fogey who, in her mind, should have been retired from the force a long time ago she asked, "What's the story with him anyway?"

Norris explained, "Oh we have a soft spot for old Doaksie. He's not as dumb as he looks y'know. Well, he didn't used to be I should say. He was a very good officer until last year when he was injured in an attempted robbery. He not only foiled the robbery but saved a nurse's life at the same time. The Police Force awarded him one of their top commendations. Some say that was a little over the top. After all he was only doing his job." Noting her questioning look Norris added, "That's what *some* people say."

"Well, I am surprised!" said Clare.

"I kid you not Detective-Sergeant. Some thugs thought they would try their luck raiding the hospital for drugs. You see it was like this, at the end of his shift Doaksie here had a habit of calling in for a chat and a free cup of tea with old Joe, one of the hospital security guards. When Joe did not answer his call, Doaksie wandered around the hospital thinking he would catch up with the guard doing his rounds. Instead, he walked right in on a gang trying to raid the dispensary. They had overcome Joe and taken the dispensary nurse hostage, threatening to kill her. Doaksie didn't waste any time, he waded straight into them and in the struggle he managed to bundle the nurse in the drugs room while he and the security guard had a go at three thugs. The guard received a right battering but Doaksie came off even worse, sustaining head injuries that put him in a coma for two weeks. Realising the nurse locked inside the dispensary drugs room had the key in her possession they had no choice but to make a run for it. They made their escape minus any haul leaving Joe badly injured and Doaksie half dead. How he survived was a miracle, but it left him a bit *soft upstairs*. You know, a bit *limp under the cap* as we say in these parts."

"You mean mentally affected?" asked Clare.

"Exactly, but no one had the heart to let him go so he was put on easy duties to ride out his time. He retires soon anyway, at Christmas in fact."

"Were the robbers caught?" she asked.

"No," said Norris, "and identifying them would be a problem, all being dressed the same in boiler suits and woollen balaclava face masks. A couple of things though, when Doaksie finally came round he said one of them had real bad halitosis and thought he detected a foreign accent when they spoke."

"What kind?"

"Don't know. We couldn't get much sense out of him after that and the security guard didn't have a clue either. So we don't know the crooks' nationality, race or colour even. That's one for the 'unsolved' files I suppose."

"Are there many foreigners in the town?" asked Clare.

"Many?" said Norris. "I'll say there are! With the European borders now down we have everyone here from Polish, to Latvians to

Hungarians. The whole of Europe seems to be represented here these days."

"Do I detect a slight touch of Xenophobia, Superintendent?" she asked.

"Not a bit!" stated Norris rather indignantly. "But to be honest, it's bad enough coping with our home grown villains, we don't need to *import* the buggers!"

"I see," said Clare. "Anyway, that's an interesting story, and very considerate of you all to keep him on until his retirement. Under the circumstances I will take him along. I'm sure he will be of some use."

They exited the office only to find Sgt. Doakes struggling to lift Clare's bag over the desk. Lying on top of the desk, leaning over so far that he almost fell into the reception area, he managed to grab the bag but found it too heavy to lift over the desk. Each time he tried to lift it, the weight of the bag almost made him topple over. He abandoned that idea, dumped the bag and, in an ungainly scramble, finally got himself back over the counter.

Without saying a word Superintendent Norris moved Doaksie's mug of tea to one side, raised the hatch part of the counter and opened the small hinged door it rested on. Slinging Clare's bag through the space he said, "Stash it behind the counter Doaksie and then drive the officer to where those bodies were found."

Donning his policeman's helmet, Sgt. Doakes emerged from behind the counter and gave it a bemused glance as Norris pulled down the counter top after him.

Smiling at Clare he said, "A counterbalance would have done it."

"Excuse me?" said Clare.

"I should have weighted my feet down to act as a counterbalance. That's what I should have done! Anyway, no matter. The car is outside. This way Sid."

****

Driving through the winding streets was like being in a maze, which, to Clare's surprise, Doaksie negotiated most skilfully. Deciding she was safe enough to engage him in conversation she said, "Sgt. Doakes."

"Call me 'Doaksie' Sid. Everyone does."

"Doaksie, my name is not Sid. It's Clare."

"But I thought you said......?"

"You weren't concentrating old chap. I am C.I.D. You know.......Criminal Investigation Department?"

"Oh whatever must you think of me? I think I must be getting senile in my old age."

"Well, I suppose that's a good a time as any to get it," she replied.

"And that's why the plain clothes eh, Missie?"

"Correct, but please... it's not *Missie*!"

With a smile Doaksie said, "There's no ring on your finger so I guess it must be M*issie*. Am I right?"

Clare did not reply to his intrusive question. Instead she said, "Good bit of observation there sergeant. You're not as dumb as I first thought you were!"

The backhanded compliment went right over the old fellow's head as he replied with a beaming smile, "Well, thank you Missie."

"Of course you know what we reckon C.I.D. really stands for?" asked Doaksie with a smile that accentuated the bags under his eyes.

"What?"

"Copper In Disguise," he answered.

They both laughed.

"Perhaps you're right, Doaksie."

The police car, having climbed the steep hill leading to the old Abbey cemetery, pulled up just inside of the main gates.

"Bit of a long way round, Missie," said Doaksie, "but easier than climbing those blooming one hundred and ninety-nine steps up from the town. It's like a rabbit warren down there."

"Why are there still people here? It's getting a bit late isn't it?" asked Clare. "They don't look dressed for a wedding or funeral," she observed.

A sour–faced old church curate, carrying a bucket, appeared from behind the row of headstones. "Well it is the second week of Advent in case you didn't know!" he said in a rebuking manner. "Preparations for the Nativity, carol services to be planned, etcetera!"

"Maybe so," said Doaksie, then pointing a finger to a large headstone said, "But they may be here to look at that!"

Clare read the inscription: '*Here lies the undead remains of Count Dracula*'

"What rot!" she exclaimed.

The sour-faced old church curate set down the bucket of soapy water and with a stiff brush began to clean off the headstone. "It's only a mock-up of course," he told them. "There's no-one buried here, supposedly. It's done for the tourists, but there's some say where there is smoke, there's fire!"

Clare and Doaksie watched as the water in the bucket turned a crimson red.

"It's O.K. Doaksie," said the curate. "Your boys from the lab have all the evidence they want and said I could start cleaning it up now."

"Blood group 'A' Negative?" asked Clare.

"Yes, I think so," replied Doaksie.

As he scrubbed away, old sour-face muttered, "There's many think he's back, you know. I think he's back."

"Who's back?" asked Clare.

Pointing to the headstone the curate answered, "He is. Dracula!"

"You idiot!" laughed Doaksie.

"Really!" said Clare. "You do know it was a work of fiction don't you?"

Still scrubbing, the curate said, "So they say, but I'm telling you! He's back alright."

"You're a bit superstitious for a church man, aren't you?" asked Clare.

"If there's good, there can also be evil!"

Running her hands over the headstone she said, "What's all this?"

"Well its blood obviously... isn't it?" said the curate.

"But this patch of blood over on this side appears a little fresher than the other groups of splashes," she noted.

"Don't forget there is a month in between the two samples," said Doaksie.

"It's coming off a lot easier than the other stuff did," said the curate.

"Stop!" shouted Clare. "Don't clean any more off!"

"What?" said Doaksie.

"Why?" asked the curate.

"Get on your phone, Sergeant," ordered Clare. "Get someone from the Forensic Lab down here. I want this blood tested right away."

Turning to the curate she said, "Close the gates now. No more public allowed in the cemetery."

Clare and Doaksie raced over to the gates while the curate went around the grounds requesting people to leave.

At the gate Clare examined the people as they left. "Let me see your hands please," she demanded. "Take names and addresses, Sergeant."

Satisfied no one had fresh blood on their hands and after they had given their personal details to Sgt. Doakes, she allowed the people to leave.

Moments later a police forensic team arrived and began swabbing samples of the fresh blood. After swirling a sample around in a glass test-tube the young Lab. officer told McKee and Doakes, "We'll do a thorough test back at the lab, but right now I can tell you it's 'O' positive."

"Not 'A' negative then?" asked Clare.

"Definitely not," confirmed the young officer, "and it's recent."

"How recent?"

"Very!" replied the young Lab officer, "and there's a trace of some other chemical in it also. As soon as we identify it we'll let you know."

"O.K. Fine. Thank you," said Clare.

"What now?" asked Doaksie.

"Now," said Clare, "you can drive me to my hotel, but stop by the station first so I can pickup my bag, please. Will you call me when Forensic can tell us any more. You have my number."

"Will do," affirmed Doaksie.

With that they all exited the cemetery and left the curate to lock the gates. Returning to the grave he placed evergreen branches laid flat upon its surface then four red candles in a circle around it. With a white candle in the centre, the Advent wreath was complete. He struck a match and lit two of the red candles to signify that it was the second week of Advent. Covering the whole wreath with a perforated glass dome to protect the flame from the wind, he stood in front of the grave, said a short prayer, crossed himself then, with his cleaning equipment, departed to his lodge.

****

After a long, relaxing soak in a hot bubble bath, Clare felt refreshed and hungry. Her choice of clothing was an unflattering trouser suit as it wouldn't show off her great figure and so give out wrong signals. Locking the bedroom door behind her, she made her way downstairs to the hotel's restaurant.

"Table for one, please," she told the waiter.

"Take your pick," he replied his outstretched hand indicated an empty dining room.

"Quiet tonight, eh?" she commented.

"Only one other resident tonight madam," he said, "a young gentleman. Very quiet. Keeps himself to himself."

"Why so few residents?"

"Well we usually go into a quiet period just before Christmas. The crowds tail off a bit then come back in their hordes over the festive season. It gives us chance to complete any renovations and decorations that might need attending to."

"I see."

"Anything to drink madam?" asked the waiter as he handed her the menu.

"Just tonic water please," said Clare and donned her spectacles to peruse the bill of fare.

While looking the menu over she noticed out of the corner of her eye a tall young man with jet-black hair, being fussed over by a pretty young waitress as he took a seat at a table in the far corner of the room.

Despite the distance between them Clare couldn't help notice how remarkably handsome he was. *Without engaging him in conversation it would be difficult to ascertain the man's character,* she thought although she was not about to do that, this fellow with his handsome aquiline features intrigued her. *'He could be a real 'Jack the Lad' with those looks,* she thought, *a real lady killer. I wonder what he is all about? Is he on business? Does he work here? Is he married or single? Can't see a ring on his finger, but that doesn't mean anything.'*

She continued her quick appraisal when he suddenly looked up from his menu and caught her staring at him. His large brown eyes seemed to transfix her, making it difficult for Clare to avert her blatant staring. The polite smile he gave her flashed across the open space of the dining room and instantly triggered in her a mini-shock of embarrassment. Hoping he wouldn't notice her flushed face, she fumbled in her bag for her notes and pretended great interest in them. *I hope he doesn't come over to speak,* she worried. Wearing her 'specs' and trouser suit, she was sure she was not dressed not too attractively and hoped that by staring at the man she had not sent out any wrong signals. She wanted to look, not be looked at.

But she needn't have worried. The handsome man kept his place and carried on studying the menu.

Questioning her thoughts and feelings Clare asked herself, *Why am I thinking along these lines? Am I attracted to this man? Do I fancy him*? She told herself her reaction to this man's looks and demeanour was simply Mother Nature playing her tricks. She had not been with a man for three years since her boyfriend's tragic death in Bosnia and this was nature's way of letting her know that normal desires had not deserted her. Perhaps that flush of embarrassment and quick little skip of the heart might have meant that she could be open to some kind of pleasurable interlude at a later stage. Satisfied with her own explanation, she put such delicious distractions into a mental file and closed the lid on them. She could always re-open that compartment when she felt the time and man was appropriate, but not yet. As always, with her it was 'business before pleasure'.

During starters she glanced up now and then to see if he was, perhaps, looking at her. No, he appeared deep in thought and hardly touched his soup. His sad or even vacant looking expression intrigued Clare. She fancied he was lost in thought as though trying to recall something. It wasn't until his main course arrived that she noticed a bandage around his right wrist.

The fussy waitress delighted in cutting up his rare steak into manageable pieces for him, which he then tackled ably with just his fork.

Clare smiled to herself, and thought, '*It looks like he's on there - if he's interested.'*

Distracting herself by looking out of the window, Clare had a good view of a well-dressed young woman with shoulder length brunette hair, getting out of the red taxi. She noticed her exchanging a couple of words with the rather unkempt and somewhat scruffy looking driver. In that fleeting moment something clicked in her mind. *What was it?* she thought. *Not a problem, just something seeming out of place. Oh well, it will come to me.'*

Looking over at the young man, Clare continued her little game. She thought, *'So what do I make of this character? Young male, well groomed, devastatingly handsome, possibly single. On business I would guess as he is by himself. Obviously not waiting for anyone as the table is set for only one. He is a gentleman I'm certain, otherwise he would have made a pass at me. Perhaps I am not attractive to him. Perhaps he doesn't like women. 'Bats for the other side' as it were. Hmmm. Hope not. What a waste that would be. Commercial traveller? Possibly, but he looks robust enough to be involved in some manual form of work. Engineer perhaps? Why so deep in thought? Is he engaged in a project that requires a lot of attention?*

"Would you like to see the desert menu madam?" asked the waiter.

"No thanks," she replied.

"Coffee?"

"No, it would only keep me awake."

"Very good madam."

As Clare signed the check for the meal, the woman from the taxi entered the restaurant and went straight over to the young man's table and sat next to him. Seeing his clumsy attempt at feeding himself, she took the fork from his hand she assisted him with his meal.

Having to pass his table on her way out Clare couldn't resist a last glance at the handsome young man. *'There is something disconcerting,* she thought, *about the way this woman fusses whilst feeding him like he was a new born chick. Despite the attention he is receiving, it appears as though it is a duty rather than a labour of love, as one would imagine. There's no sense of closeness between the couple. Most odd!'*

To Clare's surprise and the woman's annoyance, the man stood up as Clare passed and with a smile, politely nodded his head to her in mute acknowledgement.

This caught her off guard. *'What a gentleman'* she thought. Hesitating slightly, she gave him the briefest of smiles, then thought as she left the room, *'Oh well, enough of all* this, *I need to concentrate on the job I came here to do. Time for some rest. '*

Upstairs in her room Clare undressed and, catching a glimpse of her reflection in the wardrobe mirror, she appraised her slender and indeed model-like figure, momentarily entertaining the notion of ever being with a man again. *If so, what kind of man would he be? Looks would have to be important, but not as much as good health, kindness and decency; and most of all someone I could really be sure of, who would care about me and only me. Not some good-looking 'Flash Harry' who had women doting on him hand and foot! Oh get to bed woman!* she told herself. *Why am I wasting time thinking of things unrelated to the case? I'm just tired after that journey and not concentrating. Sleep is what I need and here's hoping the old subconscious will start piecing together some obvious facts I can't quite see just now.'*

Clare cleared her mind of the day's thoughts and within moments of her snuggling under the nice warm duvet and her head hitting the pillow she had drifted, thankfully, away into the 'arms of Morpheus' and was soon so very sound asleep.

****

The shock of her bedside phone ringing noisily roused Clare unwillingly from a deep slumber. With a groan and great effort she lifted the receiver.

"Sorry to wake you, Missie!" said the voice on the line.

"Doakes? It's midnight. What is it?"

"It's midnight Missie. You just said. Oh, er, sorry. I mean Norris told me to phone you. Quick! Get dressed. I'll pick you up in five minutes."

"Why? What's happened? Not another body?"

"No not a body. This one's alive!"

"Where?"

"Same place. The cemetery."

Clare leapt out of her warm bed and quickly dressed in slacks and a heavy anorak.

The banging at the door minutes later could only be one person, Sgt. Doakes.

"I'm ready," she said. "Let's go."

Noticing his footwear she exclaimed, "Doaksie, your feet!"

"Yes – they're mine alright," he said.

"No, you twit!" she said, "They're covered in snow!"

"It started around ten o'clock," he said. "Looks like we'll have a white Christmas eh, Missie, er, I mean Ma'am?"

"Maybe we shall have an early Christmas present?" she said, removing her anorak temporarily to put a thick jersey on underneath.

"What do you mean?" asked Doaksie.

"Footprints, Doaksie. Footprints!"

Moments later they had joined Superintendent Norris, two other officers and a laboratory forensic officer at the cemetery.

Inside a stationary ambulance the two-man crew were working on the supine figure of a well-dressed male. A nasty head wound had been dressed and an oxygen mask was being fitted to assist his laboured breathing while the other medic was rigging up an intravenous drip.

The profuse splashes of crimson red blood over the headstone showed up in stark contrast to the clean white blanket of snow now lying all around.

"What's the story?" demanded Det. Sgt. McKee, her breath

forming little white clouds in the cold night air.

Norris told her, “Night security found this guy slumped over the grave, unconscious. His wrists have been slashed.”

“The head wound. Serious?” Clare asked.

One medic answered, “We don't know yet. He's out cold, but he responds to pain stimulus and his pupils are even and dilate when a light is shone into them.”

“Meaning?” asked Norris.

“Meaning no probable brain damage,” the medic told him. “He's concussed is all but if there's any internal bleeding then compression will manifest itself quite shortly, and then it's serious. We have to get him to hospital right now.”

“Any idea how he got it?” asked Clare.

“Perhaps he hit his head on the headstone when he collapsed,” was the medics considered reply.

“Any I.D. On him?” she asked.

“No wallet, no driving license. Nothing,” said one of the constables.

“Can we trace him through his mobile phone?” she asked.

“No mobile phone,” the officer countered.

“What time did you find him?” she asked the night guard.

“About twenty minutes ago, Ma'am,” he answered. “I was just doing my hourly check.”

“So he must have got here between eleven p.m. and midnight.”

“How do you know that?” asked Norris.

With a look of disdain she explained to the Superintendent, “It snowed at ten o'clock. The guard found nothing at that time. No body or footprints in the snow nor at his next check one hour later, therefore this person arrived in between eleven o'clock and now.”

“Er, oh yes of course,” said a slightly embarrassed Norris. Turning to one of the officers he barked, “Constable, go take a look at the steps leading up here. Any footprints must be recent. Off you go!”

“Looks like he lost a lot of blood,” Clare remarked to the forensic team. “Can we find out if it all belongs to him?”

“Yes Ma'am,” said the forensic officer

An ambulance man told them, “He would have lost a lot more but the guard managed to bind his wounds. We have a saline drip into him just now.

We need to cross match him for a transfusion and get him a brain scan.”

“Any neck wounds?” asked Clare.

“No,” confirmed the medic.

With a wry smile the security guard said, “I think he's the kind who would give a neck wound rather than receive one.”

“Meaning?” asked Clare.

"Look closer," suggested the guard.

By the ambulance's internal light Clare and Sgt. Doakes could see that the man was dressed in what appeared to be a costume, a black suit and long high collared cape. His jet-black hair was swept back and highlighted his handsome aquiline features.

"Can you take the oxygen mask off please," asked Clare, "just for a second?"

She struggled to fight an immense feeling of shock and disappointment as she recognised the man from earlier in the hotel dining room.

Calmly she said, "O.K. put it back on him. We'll follow you to the hospital."

"Hospital my eye!" said the curate. "What he needs is a stake through the heart!"

"He's unconscious," said Doaksie. "How can he eat a steak? You twit!"

"A *stake* I said," the curate growled, "right through the heart!"

"Why you idiot," laughed Sgt. Doakes, "that would kill him!"

"Duh, y-e-s," replied old sour-face, "and the problem with that is........?"

The two men exchanged confused stares, each convinced the other was suffering from a deficit of brain cells.

Cutting short their inane banter Clare said, "C'mon Doaksie. Let's go!"

****

Later in the waiting room of the hospital's accident and emergency department, Clare drank her third cup of coffee in the hope it would stave off the overwhelming feeling of tiredness.

Doaksie calmly read a magazine as Norris paced up and down impatiently.

"This is the guy. I am certain of it," said the Super.

Clare ventured to correct him. "Nothing is for certain at this stage, Sir," she said.

"We need this nipped in the bud, Sergeant. Now! Before Christmas."

"Sir, this case deserves as much attention, scrutiny and patience as any other case *without* a deadline!"

"I was merely saying, Sergeant, that time is of the essence."

"I disagree, Sir. Justice is of the essence!"

"Pah!" snorted Norris and continued his pacing.

The duty doctor entered the room and before he could speak Clare asked, "How is he?"

"Still unconscious but stable," the doctor said. "He'd lost around three pints of blood before that security guard found him and prevented him losing any more. Fortunately he's a common blood group so there's no delay with a transfusion."

"A common blood group you say?" asked Clare.

"Yes. 'O' positive is quite common," confirmed the doctor.

"Interesting," she said. "Not 'A' negative like the other victims?"

"Oh, I don't think he was a victim Sergeant, I think he attempted suicide."

"Really?" asked Clare. "What makes you think that?"

"For one thing there are no neck wounds and both his wrists were slashed," he said.

"Now we are getting somewhere," said Norris. "He tried to *top* himself, did he? What do you reckon, Sergeant? An attack of conscience over something? Those murders perhaps?"

Clare pointed out, "I believe the cuts on his right wrist are an old injury."

"Well spotted, Sergeant," said the doctor. "They were."

"Tell me Doctor, would his injured right hand be strong enough to inflict the damage on his left?" asked Clare.

"Yes it's possible."

"Agreed," she said. "Anything is possible. I am looking for the probable."

"How long will he be out for?" asked Norris. "I mean when will we be able to question him?"

"We haven't sedated him," the doctor said. "While doing a cross-match prior to his transfusion, we did a few mandatory tests like for AIDS and diabetes, also for the presence of drugs. We found traces of Rohypnol in his blood stream."

"Rohypnol? The date rape drug?" asked a surprised Clare.

"Indeed, Sergeant," the doctor confirmed. "Not sure how long it's been in his system as it can take a while to break down, but we daren't give him any sedatives on top of that. He's just on Distalgesic as a pain killer. Quite sufficient to do the job but too much can cause respiratory depression, that's why he is on an oxygen ventilator. Plus it helps the haemoglobin take up the O2."

"O2?" asked Doaksie.

"Oxygen," said the doctor.

"Oh .....yes," said Doaksie.

The doctor went on, "He'll be under close watch until he comes around. Don't worry, I think he'll come out of it O.K."

"Why on earth would *he* have a date rape drug in his system?" Clare asked. "The victims, yes – but no trace was found in their systems, was it?"

"Ah! But don't forget," said Norris, "all their blood was drained."

Clare asked the doctor, "Could tests be done on tissue to see if there is any residual remains of the drug?"

"Indeed they can," said the doctor,

"Good. Can you ask the pathologist to look at that?"

"Of course."

"Hmm. We'll have to leave an officer here until he wakes," said Norris.

"Why?" asked the doctor.

"Well, if this man wasn't a victim we have to treat him as a murder suspect."

"Murder?" asked the doctor.

"Possible," agreed Clare.

"But probable?" the doctor asked.

"Why would he try to kill himself?" asked Norris.

As the doctor was contemplating Norris' rhetorical question, a powerful looking police constable entered the room carrying a set of leather straps.

"This officer will stay by the bedside for the next eight hour shift, doc," said Norris. "I want the suspect... er, the patient that is, fitted in this body restraint and secured to the bed in case he wakes and decides to make a run for it."

"Or fly out of the window!" quipped Doaksie.

Ignoring the Sergeant's inane joke, Norris asked, "Has he been fingerprinted?"

"Yes sir," confirmed the burly constable.

"Then Sergeant McKee, I'm off to bed," said Norris. Then to the constable, "You got that dictaphone?"

"Yes sir."

"I want his first words when he wakes up. Mumblings, anything. Got that?"

"Yes sir."

Thus assured, Norris left.

The doctor examined the leather restraint and said, "Yes these are O.K. As long as it does not go near his injuries and it doesn't restrict his breathing, it's fine by me."

"Good," said Clare, "in that case we'll also leave now. Thanks doc."

To the remaining constable she said, "You have a key for this door?"

"Yes Ma'am," he confirmed.

"Right then," she said and turning to Sgt. Doakes, "I'm off to the hotel to see if the desk has any details on our friend here."

"The hotel Missie?" asked Doakes.

"Yes. I spotted this guy earlier tonight at the hotel. He's been staying there."

"That's a bit of good luck!" he said.

"Oh yes. We'll take any luck we can get. Before you turn in, will you see if the forensic guys have come up with anything? Perhaps if his DNA shows up on the computer records we might get luckier. A police record maybe. I'll probably be up for another hour, but don't phone unless it's something positive."

"Understood Missie er, Ma'am," said Doaksie.

With that, Clare and Doaksie took their leave of the A and E doctor and left their mysterious suspect in the constable's charge.

Clare thought to herself, *'Damn and blast! Why did he have to be the suspect?'*

"Do you think he did it, Ma'am?" asked Doaksie.

Clare considered *'I hope not'* as an answer but on second thoughts said, "I would be surprised if all this is as clear cut as the Super would like."

"Clear cut! Ha! I like that one. That's a good 'un!" said Doaksie.

"Good night Sergeant," said Clare patiently.

"G'night, Missie," said Doaksie with a smile.

****

At the hotel a little while later Clare, aching to resume her interrupted sleep, hurriedly chivvied the hotel night desk clerk to find out the suspects' name and address.

"You're not going to believe this Sergeant," said the night clerk, "but we have him down as one Vlad Dracul and address as Transylvannia!"

"Oh blast!" said a tired and irritated Clare. "Let me think. How has he been paying his hotel bill? Cheque or bankers card?"

"Neither Ma'am," the clerk said, "He's been paying for the room and meals by cash. Or at least that woman friend of his has been paying it on his behalf."

'Hmm – more to think about,' mused Clare.

"He may have been staying here only a day or so," said the clerk, "but I have seen this guy before."

"You have? Where?" she asked eagerly.

"He was in town at the 'Goths' festival at Halloween a while back," he said. "I'll tell you what he was doing then as well. He was a dressed up as Count Dracula and joining in the fun. Very popular, he was."

"Ah!" said Clare. "So he was with that lot, eh?"

"Yes Ma'am. I would say so."

'Good,' thought Clare. *'He could be traced through the festival organisers. He probably has a ticket and that might mean a name'.*

"But that was over a month ago at the end of October she said. "Where has he been in that time?"

"Unless he left and came back recently, he must have been staying somewhere else. He's only been at this hotel for a few days," confirmed the clerk.

"Why did you not give the police this information after the first murder?" Clare asked.

"Me and the wife went on holiday after that. Had a month in Florida. Only got back yesterday. We missed all the excitement."

Satisfied she had some useful information at last she said, "Thanks for your help."

"You're welcome, Ma'am."

"One more thing. I'll take the keys to his room. I don't want anyone going in there. It needs to be checked for clues and possible evidence."

The clerk handed her the key to the man's room.

"No-one at all," she reiterated. "That means you, the manager, cleaners, anyone!"

"I understand. Will you be doing that now?"

Stifling a yawn she replied, "In the morning. I'm off to bed now – again!" she said. "Can I have a call at eight a.m.? Please don't let me oversleep."

"Eight a.m. it is Ma'am. Good night."

"Goodnight to you."

****

Despite being dog-tired Clare didn't sleep well. She thought, *'My subconscious must have been working over time on the aspects of the case while the body slept.'*

After being called at eight a.m. she quickly showered then after eating a light breakfast of cereal and coffee, she made her way to the suspect's room. At first glance she noticed the bed was made. *'Who did that?'* she wondered. The bathroom was tidy but the towels had not been changed. *'Good'* she thought, *'That means no-one has been in as I had requested, so the man must have made his bed himself. Very tidy.'*

Moving to the dressing table she eased open each drawer. She noted two shirts, one pair of jeans, a couple of changes of underwear and one pair of trainers. No money, no keys and no I.D. She picked up a hotel brochure welcoming the guests. No marks or scribbling on it. She tossed it back down onto the dressing table where it slid across its polished surface and fell between the table and the wall. About to leave it where it was Clare thought, *'If the brochure can do that, so could anything else',* and so pulled out the dressing table to look behind it. Lying on the carpet near the brochure were two small printed cards. Reaching down for them she realised they were rail tickets. One read:- London to Whitby – Outward, and was clipped to signify it had been used. The other read:- Whitby to London – Return and was unclipped. Both portions of the tickets were date stamped for three days in early November leaving Clare in no doubt that the traveller had intended only a short trip to the Festival but had in fact not returned home.

She searched the rest of the room for a further fifteen minutes, her eyes scrutinising every square inch looking for clues and possible evidence of the room's former occupant's involvement in the crimes. After finding nothing more of any use to her, she left the room and locked the door behind her.

Her mobile phone rang. “Detective Sergeant McKee. Who's this?” she enquired.

An excited voice on the other end told her, “It's Norris. Good news. He's awake!”

“That is good,” she agreed.

“Ha – ha. And the even better news is we've got a confession!”

“What!” she exclaimed.

“You heard me. Thanks for your help but it looks like a short stay for you, Sergeant.”

“I'm coming over. Send Doaksie to pick me up!” she said.

****

At the man's bedside were the Superintendant, the burly police constable and a doctor.

Norris was grilling the suspect. “You can tell us why you did it later you weird-o. Right now you are nicked! You are going down pal!”

The patient looked most unconcerned and just offered a bemused half smile.

Turning to the constable at the bedside the Super went on, “Who needs C.I. bloody D? We've got a result here. What a Christmas present! I can see the headlines now - '*Local police nab serial killer. Streets safe for Christmas*'.

****

Clare shook the loose snow from her coat as she and Doaksie entered the hospital.

"Hello Janice," said Doaksie to a pretty young nurse. "You working over here now, eh?"

"That's right," she said. "Can't chat. I'm busy."

"Me too," he said and followed Clare.

Quickly making her way down the corridor that was now festooned with Christmas decorations, she entered the private ward room. Taking a quick look at the patient, now awake and with a drip in his arm, she noticed he had been fitted with the leather body restraint around his torso and secured under the bed out of his reach.

She asked Norris, “You said you had a confession. Where is it?”

“We have a *verbal* from him,” he beamed happily. "We will get a written one later. But we have a result. He did the murders alright. You can tell. Just look at the horrible little swine!"

Addressing the patient he sneered, "We're going to lock you up and throw away the bloody key, you murdering scum!"

"Yeah," said Doaksie getting in on the act. "We're going to lock you up and throw away the warden!"

Ignoring his stupid remark Norris went on, "The Press are going to have a field day!”

“Not yet they won’t!” said the doctor at the bedside. “I'm sorry but you have hounded this man ever since he woke up. I don't think you're being fair. This man is my patient and I say he's not fit for questioning yet.”

“Fair?” shouted Norris. “Was he fair to those two lasses he killed? I'd hang the bugger if the law allowed!”

“Well it doesn't and we must follow procedure, Sir,” Clare told him.

“You can go home now, Detective-Sergeant,” he sneered. “It seems like your skills weren't required after all. We managed to solve these heinous crimes all by our little old, provincial selves!”

Clare rebuked him saying, “This man is still a patient in this hospital until the doctor passes him fit to hand over. And another thing, I say when I leave or stay. This is a C.I.D. matter and if you try going over my head I will report you for hampering my investigations!”

“Hampering!” Norris squealed. “Rubbish, woman! He did it! He's admitted he did it. He's confessed!”

Ignoring the angry Superintendant she leaned over the patient’s bed, careful not to disturb his intravenous drip and, in a gentle voice, asked him, “Would you be good enough sign a written confession for me please?”

“Of course. No problem,” he said, his smile exposing two canine teeth slightly longer than normal.

“Look at those fangs!” Doaksie exclaimed, and leaned closer to him asked, “Are you a vampire, mate?”

The patient, trying sit up as much as his restraints would allow, gave out a loud roar that made Doaksie recoil in shock.

Upon seeing the sergeant’s reaction the patient laughed heartily. “Glupa!” he shouted then relaxed back into the bed.

An alarmed Doaksie asked, “What are you saying, you Transylvanian twit? Did you hear that everyone? *Glupa* yourself mate!”

“Glupa?” Clare repeated as the tingle of recognition was triggered in her mind. “Who are you calling stupid, Mr. Drac?” she asked him.

“Stupid? Who's stupid?” asked Doaksie.

“He just said you are,” she told the sergeant.

“So you speak Transylvanian now do you?” sneered Norris.

“That wasn't Transylvanian he was speaking,” she said. “That's a Bosnian word.”

“How do you know?” Norris asked.

“Long story. Tell you later,” she said.

“Whatever!” snapped Norris, “Bosnian, Transylvanian. He a blasted foreigner isn't he?”

“Now really!” said the doctor.

“Well that remark says it all about you, Superintendant!” said Clare.

“Well, what I meant was that Bosnia is almost in Transylvannia,” said Norris backtracking as quickly as his prejudiced mind would allow. “I mean they probably have a similar language!”

“And they could have vampires there as well!” added Doaksie pointing at the man's teeth.

“Canines like that are not unusual,” said the doctor, “that doesn't mean anything.”

“Right!” exclaimed a gleeful Norris and producing a sheet of paper said, “Well whatever his nationality, he's admitted to the killings. The constable has made out a statement in long-hand. As long as this confession is signed and witnessed, the job's done.”

Turning to the others he added, “We can type it up later at the station”.

The patient accepted the pen offered to him taking it in his left hand to sign his name on the confession.

Taking the paper from him Clare looked it over then handed it to the Superintendent. “Is this what you were in such a rush for Sir?” she asked,

Norris grabbed the confession and read the signature out loud – “Vlad Dracul - Prince of Darkness!”

“What the hell are you playing at, feller?” he screamed at the patient. “This is no joke, stop wasting my time and bloody well sign it! And properly this time!” he demanded.

The confused patient stared blankly. “But that is my name,” he said.

The exasperated Super asked, “Did you or did you not kill those girls?”

“Of course I did. That's what I do,” the patient nonchalantly replied.

“That will do for me!” asserted Norris. “Get him out of bed. You are coming with us!”

"He's not going anywhere," said the doctor. "There's obviously a psychological problem. He will have to remain here and receive the correct treatment."

"Look, we need to close this case. We don't want all this bull right on top of Christmas!" complained Norris.

"Leave him to me, Sir," said Clare patiently. "Between me and the doctors here, we'll get the truth from him."

"I'll get the truth out of him!" threatened Norris.

"No sir! This is a C.I. D. matter," said Clare. "I know you are keen to get this sorted out but that's why I am here. You defer to me in this case! You can stay and assist me or leave. It's your choice sir, but if you hamper my investigation, I shall report you."

Norris knew he couldn't legally remove the patient. "I'm going for a coffee," he snarled. "The guard stays!"

"Of course," agreed Clare, and with that he stormed out of the room.

With the angry Superintendant gone, Clare smiled at the patient and said, "Now then handsome, let's you and me get to know each other."

"Doaksie, will you find a nurse and organise a cup of tea for everyone please?"

The doctor said, "He'll have to be moved to our Psychiatric Unit, Sergeant. It's more secure. I'll go and arrange it."

"That's fine," said Clare, and turning to the constable said, "If you would like to go outside for a smoke it will be quite alright."

"Well, he is secured Ma'am and I would appreciate a smoke. I've been all night without one. I'm fair gasping."

With that he handed the dictaphone to Clare then nipped out to enjoy a welcome smoke.

****

Clare closed the door and secretly switched on the dictaphone. Hoping to win him over she said with a smile, "Now then, we are all alone."

Appearing more relaxed he answered, "Yes, that's much better. The doc is O.K. but your boss seems a bit intense."

"He's just doing his job," she said, "as he sees fit."

"I know," he replied, then, after a moment, asked her, "Will you be the one?"

"The one?"

"The one who does it?"

"Does what?"

"The one who kills me. I have to be killed don't I?"

"Why do you say that?"

"I am possessed by the spirit of Vlad Dracul. I have killed. My human side wishes to be rid of this evil and the only way is for me to die."

"No – it isn't!" she said firmly.

"Then at least bleed me. Cut my wrists again so that the evil in my blood may be thinned out."

Clare could sense the confusion that was going on behind those clear dark brown eyes. She told him with as much conviction as she could, "Listen to me, you are not a vampire, you're just ill, and you're going to get better. No one is going to harm you. I'll see to that. Now, are you up for a little chat?"

"Aren't you afraid of me?" he asked.

"Not in the least. Why should I be?"

To herself she thought that what she had really wanted to say was, *'Because you are drop- dead gorgeous and I'm convinced you are no killer.'* That thought was quickly followed by another, *'God, I hope I'm on the right track here! Sure he's dead fanciable but that's just the romantic in me. Every instinct of the policewoman in me tells me he's innocent. I promise myself not to be swayed by silly emotions. I'm right about this guy. I know I am. I'd put money on it. C'mon girl. Concentrate!'*

His reply jolted her out of her daydream. "Because I have taken two lives," he said.

"That has not been proven yet."

Shaking his head he sighed, "I'm so confused."

"Of course you are. You have had a concussion and been pumped full of Rohypnol as well."

"I don't understand," he said.

"Try to relax. You are in hospital and are being looked after. I won't let anything happen to you. Look, we think you are suffering from amnesia and all this 'Dracula' thing is a confusion of identities for some reason."

Placing a hand upon his she said, "My name is Clare. What's yours?"

With apparent sadness he told her, "You know my name."

Patiently she tried a different tack. "O.K. then. Just supposing for a minute you were not called Vlad, what would you like to be called?"

After a moments thought he looked at her and, with a vacant smile, said, "Andy."

"Why Andy?"

"I dreamt that was my name."

"You know what I think? I think Andy is your real name and you dreamt you were called Vlad."

"Is it possible?"

"Tell me what you remember Andy."

"Oh dear. It's all so mixed up.

"Start by telling me were you are from?"

"Transylvannia of course................ I think."

"You sound more like a Londoner to me. Tell me, who is the girl I saw you with at the hotel restaurant?"

His dull gaze suggested deep thought.

"Who is she, Andy? Who is she?"

The peaceful atmosphere was shattered by Norris barging into the room and bellowing, "Andy? Who the hell is Andy?"

Andy bared his fangs and hissed at Norris making Clare realise that the special rapport they had was now so rudely interrupted and was, for the moment anyway, gone. His protective barrier had been re-installed. Andy was saying nothing.

"Sir, we need to find out if there are any Missing Persons reported recently from the London area," she told Norris.

"Why? We know where the two girls came from. They were local and not missing."

"Not the girls... him! It's just an idea I had. "

"Don't tell me... it's a hunch?" he asked sarcastically.

"Can we just do it please?"

Behind him the doctor entered with two porters. He said, "O.K. we have a private room in the psychiatric wing. We'll get you over there now."

The burly constable having finished his smoke came into the room and asked, "Can I help? Shall I undo the restraints?"

"No need," said the doctor. "We will move the whole bed. It's not far to go. Just down the corridor a short way."

"I'll bring his things," said Clare and handed the dictaphone to Norris.

With the orderlies pulling the foot of the bed and Doaksie and the constable pushing its head, the bed was wheeled out of the small room and along the corridor. The doctor went ahead while Norris walked alongside with the dictaphone at the ready.

Clare found that the only personal belongings the patient had were his dark suit, cape and shoes. Finding nothing in the pockets, Clare looked inside the jacket for labels. After much rooting and rummaging she found evidence that a small tag, about one inch by a half inch, had been removed from the underside of the turned down collar.

With Andy now removed to the secure unit in the psychiatric wing and under round the clock guards, Clare and Norris decided to compare notes in the hospital coffee shop.

"So, what do we know for sure?" asked Norris somewhat calmer but still impatient.

"Well," said Clare, "he is suffering from amnesia, the doctor is quite certain about that."

"Could he be putting on an act?"

"If it was just the concussion perhaps, but the doc reckons that date rape drug can cause amnesia if over used or mixed with another drug."

"Another drug?

"They also found traces of Valium in his system. So if he had been on that for a while then given Rohypnol, may be the result of that combination is loss of memory."

"Amnesia or not, it doesn't mean to say he didn't do those murders!" insisted Norris.

"That is always possible, but why would he give himself Rohypnol? We have a puzzle here and bit by bit, the pieces are coming together. You'll just have to trust me on this, Super."

"As soon as the doc says he's O.K. that's when I'm going to charge him. So you have until then to get to the bottom of your little puzzle!"

Clare got up and leaving him in the coffee shop, walked around outside the hospital building in order to get some fresh air and to be able to think in some degree of peace.

Walking towards her were Doaksie and the young pretty nurse, her brown hair tied up in a bun under her nurses hat.

Upon seeing Clare he told the nurse "Well, it was nice to see you again. The Christmas tree looks really good. Take care now."

"And you," she said. "See you, Doaksie."

As she walked away, Clare asked, "Who was that?"

"A friend from a while ago," he answered.

"Oh really? She looks familiar."

"Oh no she's not familiar," said Doaksie. "She's a nice girl."

"I don't mean familiar like that, you twit!" said Clare. "Does she work in the dispensary by any chance?"

"No, she is helping to put up a big Christmas tree. Oh er, sorry. Yes she used to work in the dispensary. I think she has transferred to the Path Lab now."

"Is she the girl you saved during the robbery?"

"Why yes she is, Missie," said a surprised Doaksie. With a painful look he added, "That was a bad day."

"Yes it must have been. Sorry to bring it up," she said.

"That's O.K. Missie," said the Sergeant with a smile. "It's all bridge under the water now."

She smiled and corrected him, "Water under the bridge, you goose!"

"Of course, of course. That's what I meant to say," said Doaksie.

"Show me where the Christmas tree is, will you?"

Entering the hospital again, they made their way down the main corridor at the end of which stood a large and imposing, beautifully decorated tree.

"I'm very impressed," said Clare.

Although staring in the general direction of the tree Clare's mind was elsewhere trying to identify what was and what wasn't a worthwhile piece of the jigsaw.

After a good thirty seconds or so Doaksie asked. "Everything alright, Ma'am?"

"Just having a little ponder, Doaksie," she said.

Noticing a nearby basket full to the brim of cellophane, decoration wrappers and odd bits of tinsel, she rummaged through the oddments and found a small piece of material about one inch by a half inch.

Turning to Doaksie she said, "Tell me did your friend, er what's her name?"

"Janice," he answered.

"Has she been working on the tree just now?"

"Yes, I believe so but you need two really. You know... for safety. Holding the ladder etcetera."

"Yes, yes. So........working alone and just recently?"

"Yes, I think so," answered the perplexed Doaksie. "Anything wrong?"

She smiled at him and, putting the piece of material in her pocket, said, "No, not a bit."

****

Back at the station Clare was disappointed to learn that there were no missing persons, from the London area fitting Andy's description. She picked up the phone receiver and dialled Directory Enquiries. "Hello? Can you find a number for costumiers, *Worths of Mayfair* please? Thank you."

Upon being given the number she rang it and once connected, asked for the manager of the establishment.

"Hello. This is Detective Sergeant Clare McKee of the Yorkshire C.I.D. I would like your help in locating the name and address of a person whom I believe rented a costume from you a few weeks ago."

The manager replied in a plummy West End accent that Clare had come to recognise from her time in the capital city. "Certainly Sergeant," he agreed. "I'll help if I can. We do have a large clientele but he should be in our records."

"I have a first name of *Andy,*" she told him, "no surname. This chap rented a dark suit and cape from you, probably just before Halloween."

"Ah! Good, you've found him!" said the manager excitedly. "We know him well. Never had him down as a thief though. We do get thefts every now and again but this chap is an old customer. Respectable sort really we thought. One can never tell though, can one? When can we have it back? Is it damaged? It's one of our better costumes y'know. Very good material."

"Don't worry, we have your costume for you but will have to keep it for a while as it is evidence in a murder enquiry," she informed him.

"Murder? Oh my word! Who.........?"

Avoiding further questions she cut in, "Do you have a name and address for him?"

"Y-yes!" stuttered the shaken manager. "His surname is Clayton. Lives with his brother and wife I believe. Their address is as follows. Do you have a pen?"

"Go ahead," said Clare and jotted down the details. "Thank you. Thank you. Yes, we'll be in touch. Goodbye."

Reading from her scribbled notes she dialled the number the costumier had given her.

Moments later Norris and Sgt. Doakes entered the police station.

"Get the kettle on, Doaksie," ordered Norris. "Let's have a decent cup of tea. That stuff they serve up at the hospital is as weak as gnat's pee!"

Turning to Clare he said, "Oh, I didn't see you there, Sergeant. Any progress?"

Acknowledging the two with a wave she continued her phone conversation. "Why didn't you report him missing?" Then, "Oh I see. Well thanks for your help Mr. Clayton. Yes, I think it will be O.K. but let me check with the doctor first, will you? Thanks. Look forward to meeting you."

Hanging up the phone she informed Norris, "We have a name and address for our Count. He's a civil servant from London."

"Really?" replied Norris somewhat unimpressed. "Why didn't he confine his activities to down there? Kill his own, not come up here and start on ours!"

Clare shook her head and sighed at the Super's attitude. "Well at least we can rule out his alter ego," she said.

"Doesn't mean to say he's not the serial killer though, does it?" asked Norris.

"That's true," agreed Clare, "but I think enough information has come up to throw sufficient doubt on that theory."

Before he could comment she asked, "Do you know of a taxi company in town that primarily uses red cabs?"

"Yes," said Norris. "There's one called *Reddy-Cabs*. A new firm just been set up a few months. Why?"

Clare told Norris, "I think I have put this thing together Sir, and if I'm right you'll have an arrest this afternoon."

"As far as I'm concerned we already have our killer. That crackpot masquerading as Nosfer-bloody-ratu!"

"No Sir!" said Clare. "That's what we are supposed to think. He didn't do it. I'm certain. Don't worry, I have a good idea what's going down."

Norris groaned, "Oh God! Don't make this any worse than it is, eh? Are you sure? I mean are we on solid ground with this?"

"I'd say so," she replied confidently. "Don't worry yourself. Collars will definitely get felt today I promise. But I'm going to make sure you feel the right ones. Now I need Doaksie to get changed into his *civvies* and come with me," she said.

"What? Why? Where to?" asked a somewhat bewildered Norris.

"To see some of his old friends," she answered. Then to the Sergeant, "Hurry up and get changed Doaksie."

"Yes Ma'am," he replied. "Up, indeed, I shall hurry," before disappearing into the police changing rooms.

Before Norris could ask for an explanation Clare explained "When I have everything in place I shall phone you on your mobile phone Sir, and if it all goes to plan we will meet at the hospital. I would suggest a small detachment of officers and at least one police van to accommodate from one to four persons."

"What's going on?" demanded Norris.

"Detective work," she told him. "I'll do the detecting and you do the arresting. Remember? Now, are you sure there are no more red cabs you know of? Is it just the one firm?"

"Just the one, I'm certain."

"Excellent!" said Clare just as Doaksie appeared wearing an old pair of jeans and 'Sloppy Joe' jersey.

"Why thank you Missie. It's nothing special really."

"Not you, you twit!" rasped Norris. "She was talking to me."

Confused and with an air of dismay Doaksie muttered to Clare, "I didn't know you even liked him."

"Oh - Come on!" said Clare grabbing Doaksie by the arm and pulling him towards the door.

"But don't you need any back up?" shouted Norris.

"No! Not yet!" shouted Clare over her shoulder. "I want to catch them, not warn them off! Stand by your phone."

Clare and Doaksie climbed into the unmarked police car and drove off leaving the Superintendent scratching his head. "*Them, eh?*" he thought.

****

The unmarked car pulled up a few yards away from *Reddy-Cabs* office and before getting out Clare asked, "Doaksie, those villains whom you had trouble with a year ago; if you were to bump into them, would there be anything at all you would recognise?"

"Oh yes, Missie. Easily. I'd recognise the lot of them."

"You would?" asked Clare incredulously. "Why did you not say this before?"

"I did Missie, but they wouldn't believe me. I should know, shouldn't I? I mean I was there!"

"Yes, yes!" said Clare excitedly. "Tell me how you would recognise them?"

"Simple. They were all wearing face masks!"

"What?"

"Well I mean to say, how many people go around wearing face masks?"

Clare sat back in her seat and groaned, "You soppy old sod! When did you say you are retiring?"

Doaksie remained happily oblivious to her words.

Although her elation had been premature, she nonetheless couldn't help smiling at his silly logic. "Doaksie, you're a sweet old thing but you are so dizzy at times."

"Thank you."

"Now when we get inside Doaksie, if you do feel you recognise anyone, do not say anything until we leave. O.K?"

"O.K. Missie."

Handing him a pair of sunglasses she said, "Here. Wear these."

"But there's no sunshine. It's snowing!"

"You'll look cool. Trust me."

Clare assisted Doaksie as he shuffled into the office. Addressing a scruffy looking man behind a desk she said, "Zdravo! (Hello!) Izvinite ! (Excuse me!)"

The man appeared a little surprised. Looking her and Doaksie up down he asked in a somewhat fractured English accent, "You are from the old country?"

"No. My boyfriend was in the Army in Bosnia years ago and he taught me one or two words," she told him.

"How you know I from Bosnia?"

"Oh, I think someone heard your accent some place. Also someone described you as a scruffy lot. No dress sense y'know? Not dirty really but dishevelled, untidy. No sense of fashion. You wear western style clothes but they look out of date. Not trendy or 'with it' are you? Yes, I think scruffy describes you well enough."

"Scroofy? What iz 'scroofy' pliz?"

"Not all Bosnians you understand. Just you lot who work here!"

Hearing the conversation a rather large younger man appeared from the back room chomping, open mouthed, on a sandwich. He stared at Clare for a moment and, with blackened teeth for all to see, masticated his lunch in the disgusting cement mixer that was his mouth. One swallow cleared the contents enough for him to whisper to the man at the desk.

"She is taking the p*ss!"

Clare smiled as she saw the man at the desk react to the other man's halitosis. *'Not surprised with those teeth'* she thought.

"Ha Ha!" said the man at the desk. "You are having the joke? You English with the crazy humour, eh?"

"Yes it was just a bit of fun," said Clare. "Getting to the point, I need a taxi for a dozen girls, in about one hour. Can you manage that?"

"What kind is *dozen*?"

"Twelve girls. Sorry, I should have said twelve girls. We are nurses at the hospital and we are going out to celebrate finishing our training. So we shall need you to take us to different pubs and clubs and bring us home at the end of the night. Can you accommodate us?"

The deskman said eagerly, "Yes, yes. We can do. No big bus but we got taxis. We like nurses. What time you want?"

"That's good," said Clare. "Separate taxis are better. Can we be picked up at the hospital car park in about an hour?"

"Wow! You wanna start early on your party, eh?" said halitosis breath. "Sure, we can do that. You wanna give me a deposit? You know we gotta commit all our cabs and you might take another instead. You know what I mean? Like a big joke? We don't take the chances."

"That's fair enough," said Clare. "Here's a fifty pound note on account. Is that O.K.?"

Holding the note up to the light the scruffy deskman said, "Yeah, yeah. Is O.K."

"Right. I'll see you later then, "she said with a smile.

As Clare took Doaksie's arm and led him shuffling to the door, the large man nipped ahead of them and held the door open for them.

"See you later," he said a little out of breath.

"Fat pig!" mumbled Doaksie, a little too loudly.

"Hey! How you know I'm fat?"

Doaksie could only fumble a reply, "ER, you sound fat!" he said.

"I thought you was blind?" the man shouted.

Caught off guard all Doaksie could think of to say was, "I am!"

Thinking quickly Clare tapped her head and explained, "He's a patient."

Satisfied with her visual explanation the man calmed down. As they walked out of the door the man shouted after them, "Hey! You need taxi now?"

"No thanks," said Doaksie. "I'm just off to take my driving lessons!"

Both men in the taxi office laughed out loud as *Nurse* Clare escorted her shuffling charge down the street.

"Crazy Inglish!" said the fat man.

"Good contacts!" said the other man.

Once inside the car Clare said, "Doaksie, I nearly had kittens in there!"

Her partner just laughed as he removed his sunglasses and started the car.

"Well? Anything familiar?" she asked.

"Yes, there was!" he affirmed. "Y'know with the accents ....and the smell!"

He just laughed and told her, "Sorry I can't be more definite."

"Don't worry," Clare said, "It's all going well. Now quickly. To the hospital!"

As the car sped off she quietly rebuked Doaksie by repeating his ridiculous answer to the man, "You *sound* fat! Lord, give me strength!"

Doaksie just laughed. "I know why you had me wear the sunglasses, Missie."

"Do you?"

"Yes. So I could check them out without them recognising me!"

"That's right. But did it work?"

"I couldn't swear, but if they were the ones, I don't think they recognised me!"

"No. They probably beat up that many people they wouldn't remember each one. Now to see your friend Janice."

"Why Janice?"

"I'll bet you a pound to a pinch of snuff she's involved!"

"Oh dear! She seemed such a nice girl too."

"You can't judge a book by the cover," said Clare.

"But if that's the case, shouldn't we have seen her first? Now they will warn her."

"I took a chance knowing, that while on duty, hospital staff are not allowed to carry mobile phones. Besides I wanted your reaction to these guys first."

Clare contacted Norris on her mobile phone. "Three foreign nationals will arrive at the hospital car park driving *Reddy-Cab* taxis at approximately four p.m. I want them all detained."

"What's the charge?"

"Anything you like for now," she said. "You decide."

"Suits me!" replied Norris.

After a short drive through the snow covered streets filled with bustling shoppers, Clare and Doaksie arrived at the hospital. In the car park, the rich tones and sweet harmonies of a group of heavy coated and ear-muffed carol singers all blended perfectly into a Dickensian Christmas scene. With snowflakes falling in the late afternoon light and the carollers' music punctuated by clouds of white breaths, Clare couldn't help but take a moment to admire the scene.

She thought, '*What a magical time of year this was. How nice it would be to share it all with someone. How sad for those who don't.*'

Quickly getting out of the cold air, they shook loose snow flakes from their garments in the hospital entrance. Then, a brief walk along a corridor festooned with Yuletide trimmings, they entered the secure unit and joined the doctor and guard at Andy's bedside.

She addressed Andy with a smile, "Hello again, handsome."

"Hello….."

"Clare," she reminded him.

"Clare," he said with a warm smile.

"Feeling better?"

"The same. Tired and confused."

"Well you'll feel a lot better when the drug wears off and as for the confusion, when I have explained a few things to you, I expect to see a dramatic improvement."

"Why are you being so nice to me?" he asked. "I have already admitted the murders."

Taking hold of his hand she said, "But you didn't. Don't you remember? I told you that you had been drugged."

"So I killed under the influence of drugs? Is that it?"

"No. You didn't. You are a victim in all this as I hope to demonstrate."

"I can't tell what's real and what isn't. Did I kill or just dream it?"

"Don't worry, you are not a killer."

"If I could only believe that's so, it would be a great weight off my mind."

A pair of rich, dark brown eyes held the gaze of two beautiful deep blue ones, "I don't want to be a bad person. Please help me," he pleaded.

"You are not and I will, I promise." said Clare.

"I feel so relaxed with you," he said. "I don't feel like a killer but I thought I ……"

"Listen to me. You are a decent man who was duped into being a fall guy. And what is more Andy Clayton, of 10, Stirling Place, London W.1 and civil servant of the borough of Hounslow; the reason I am being nice to you is because I like you and I like you even more knowing you are neither a murderer or a vampire. Does that answer your question?"

Squeezing her hand he said, "And I like you Clare, because you are making me feel good about myself again. You're giving me hope."

"Good."

"You're not a dream are you?"

Squeezing his hand she replied, "No, I'm real Andy."

"Plus, you are incredibly beautiful!" he said.

This caught Clare a little off guard despite it being exactly what she wanted to hear.

"He's improving!" said the doctor with a little smile.

Just then Norris barged into the room. "Right!" he said. "I have men and the *paddy wagon* positioned out of sight in the car park. We're all set to go. You had better tell me what your 'battle plans' are Detective Sergeant. I can't go arresting people just on a whim!"

"Why not?" said Clare laconically. "You were prepared to arrest Andy here on the slimmest of evidence?"

"It was a hunch. You're allowed to have hunches, why not me?"

"Because mine are based on intelligence, not making arrests for the sake of it! Now just take a seat, Sir, and watch a bit of detecting!"

Turning to the doctor she said, "Can you ask the Path Lab for another pint of 'O' positive blood please? I know we don't need it but ask anyway and make sure Nurse Janice brings it will you?"

"O.K. Sergeant," said the doctor.

"What's going on?" demanded Norris.

"Be patient, Super," said Clare.

Noticing Clare holding Andy's hand Norris felt obliged to comment. "Detective Sergeant?" he called, crooking his index finger in order to beckon her over to him. He whispered in her ear, "You wouldn't be about to start fancying this character would you?"'

"What's it you?" she asked.

"Ha! So much for the clear-headed professional!"

"The case is at the forefront of my mind. If I were to harbour any personal thoughts in that area, I would shelve them and deal with them as a separate issue."

"O.K. just as long as I get an arrest soon, but I hope you know what you're doing."

"Don't worry, you will have an arrest one way or another. If this guy is the culprit, that's my loss."

In a rare moment of compassion and understanding, Norris told her, "Look Clare, please don't let a fancy Dan like this guy turn your head. You're smarter than that!"

"I am in control of my emotions," she insisted.

Norris asked her, "Have you ever noticed how some real evil killers also happen to be good looking swines? You know, like Ted Bundy for instance? Or what about Peter Sutcliffe, the Yorkshire Ripper? It makes one wonder that even *Jack the Ripper* might not have been too hard to look at? What I'm saying is don't get fooled by looks. Are all murderers ugly and all good guys handsome? Do villains wear black hats and the heroes wear white? Just think about it!"

"I am aware of the phenomena you describe. But don't worry, I can be quite detached." Then with great emphasis added, "Don't worry. If this guy is guilty then he's going down!"

"Good enough!" Norris said.

Moments later the doctor returned with Janice carrying the pint of 'O' positive blood. Upon both entering the secure room the guard closed the door and stood in front of it barring access or egress.

"Ah! The very person!" said Clare. "Take a seat will you?"

Instantly recognising her, Andy cried out, "Janice! Where have you been?"

Janice offered no acknowledgement. Puzzled, she asked the doctor, "Don't you want me to set up the drip?"

Raising her voice Clare said, "Janice. Give the doctor the blood and sit down!"

It was an order not a request.

"What is all this?" demanded Janice.

Ignoring her Clare pointed to Andy and asked her, "Do you know this patient?"

"I've seen him around," she replied.

"You've done more than that, haven't you?" asked Clare. "It would take more than putting your hair up in a bun to disguise yourself!"

"Look, I just came here to bring this blood. What is all this?"

"All this," said Clare, "is your opportunity to come clean and tell us how and why you did it?"

"Did what?"

"Murder those two girls last month!"

"What are you talking about?" Janice shouted. "You're off your head woman!"

Clare informed her, "If you help me with this, your sentence could be lighter but if you don't, the courts will show no leniency at all! Well? What's it to be?""

"Get lost!" spat Janice. "You haven't got a thing!"

"Somehow I thought you would take that line," said Clare. "O.K. I'm not wasting time, I will not only tell you how you did it - I'll have a damn good shot at why!"

All eyes in the room were trained on Clare she related her findings. The faint sounds of joyous carols could be heard from outside providing a weird contrast of a tale of evil against a background of love and goodwill.

"Well, sit back folks and listen to this for a Christmas tale." Clare said. "A promising young civil servant, one Andy Clayton, resident of London, loses his wife in a car accident. The distressing effect of his loss causes deep depression and his doctor puts him on a course of Valium to combat this condition. He moves in with his brother Mike and his wife to be looked after.

After weeks and weeks of being ill, feeble and bedridden, his health gradually improves due to the care and attention from his relatives and the prolonged course of anti-depressants. Before long he is able to resume work, and his concerned family encourage him to get his life back on track by socialising more. Since childhood Andy has been teased about his larger than usual canine teeth and because of this and his dark good looks his brother has the idea of entering him in local competitions for Dracula look-alikes. This goes down well in the local pubs and bars and the social life does indeed help Andy to return to some level of normality after his tragic loss.

Finally coming off Valium after two years or so, Andy has adjusted to his loss. Wishing to put it all behind him, he decides to re-start his life anew by having a four-week holiday. Firstly going to attend the Goths Festival at Halloween in Whitby then over to Rumania where a similar festival is held. Then while over there his intention was to visit a local dentist whose fees are noticeably cheaper on the Continent than in U.K. and there to have his canines either filed down or removed. So, it was to be a last fling with the Dracula look-alike thing, a cheap dental job then back home in London for Christmas, after which he intended to take leave of his brother and return to his own house which had been tenanted during his recuperation. So far so good, eh?"

"You'll have to tell me how you arrived at all this McKee," said Norris.

"Easy," she said. "His Dracula costume came from an outfitters in London. I simply phoned them, they gave me a name and address and I contacted his brother Mike who corroborated all I have just described to you."

"Mike? You spoke to Mike? I remember! I remember!" said a startled Andy.

"Good," said the doctor. "That means you'll soon be back to normal."

Norris chimed in, "Well, as you say, so far so good. Now tell me why he is not the killer."

"All in good time," said Clare. "I'm setting the scene as it unfolded chronologically. Now folks, Andy arrives in Whitby, on a three-day rail ticket, which indicates his intention to stay only for the duration of the festival. It is at the festival where he meets Nurse Janice here, and that's where his trouble begin."

"Bull!" spat Janice.

"Be quiet you!" said Norris.

Clare went on, "Poor old Andy here, instead of having fun and re-starting his life after his tragic loss and his ensuing illness, now descends into a living nightmare. It turns out that our lovely, caring nurse here is part of a gang... the same gang that Sergeant Doakes stumbled onto in the course of an attempted robbery at the dispensary about a year ago, with most unfortunate consequences for him and the hospital security guard."

"What?" gasped Norris. "You sure about this?"

Holding up her hand to the Super in a gesture to be allowed to continue, Clare went on. “I don't know how Janice met the gang, perhaps they targeted her because she works in a hospital, but knowing she had access to the drugs in the dispensary was too good an opportunity to pass over. They thought they could have Janice unlock the drugs cabinet for them, grab what they wanted and slip out unnoticed. Unfortunately for them Doaksie decided to call in for a brew with his pal Joe the night guard. Doaksie was beaten into a coma and old Joe took a real thumping he could have well done without.”

“Janice!” cried Doaksie. “I saved you! I saved you!”

“Sorry Doaksie. It just wasn't so!” said Clare.

“You mean she wasn't in any danger?” asked a stunned Doaksie.

“Not until you showed up,” said Norris. “It looks like you got your award under false pretences didn't you? You ought to give it back!”

“Don't be so nasty Superintendent!” said Clare. “He wasn't to know she was in on it.”

“O.K. get on with it!” snapped Norris. “What happened then?”

Clare continued, “The unsuccessful gang then must have abandoned the idea of robbing drugs as from then on security was doubled and more cameras were installed. So instead they came up with another money making scam, again with the help of Nurse Janice here.”

“Which was?” asked Norris.

“Selling rare blood groups!” she answered.

Surprised mutterings issued from Norris, the doctor and Doaksie.

“Yes,” continued Clare, “Janice requested a transfer to the Path Lab where the blood is kept, but because of the recent break in, all security had been improved so much it prevented any chance of swiping the rare blood groups. So, no more cracks at the drugs room and no chance of raiding the Path Lab for blood so, what to do?”

Clare's audience hung on every word as her fantastic but entirely logical tale unfolded.

“So, they decide that the hospital records office would be less of a problem to infiltrate and after rifling through the records Janice soon discovers a list of donors in the area who have rare blood groups. The sad shame about it is these people, who out the goodness of their hearts allowed themselves to be listed to help others, made themselves potential murder victims! When Andy here pops up as a Dracula look-a-like, the gang develop a warped plan to murder them, drain then sell their blood and put the whole blame on the dubious tale of the vampire returning to the town.”

“Bloody hell!” said Norris. “That's diabolical!”

“And I say you are off your head, woman!” said Janice who by now had lost a considerable amount of colour from her cheeks

“So carry on,” said Norris eagerly. “How did they do it?”

"Simple," said Clare. "Bloody devious, but simple. Janice trawls the Goths festival for anyone she knows to be on the rare blood group list. She befriends one and suggests they go up to the old abbey cemetery where there is more festival fun going on. She slips the date rape drug Rohypnol into her drink and, upon passing out, she is joined by the gang members who, with Janice's help, locate the carotid artery, insert a catheter and begin the process of draining her of her rare and valuable blood to sell on the black market. The girl's body is found draped over the tourist attraction grave of Dracula and the rumours begin."

Norris piped up, "Well doing her out in the open is a bit silly. What if they were seen? Why not kill her somewhere less risky?"

"Ah!" said Clare. "It was probably the most convenient thing to do. It was important that folk saw Dracula with the intended victim. If witnessed they could always say they found her like that and point old Drac out as the culprit. He would honestly claim not to remember, because she had slipped the drug into his drink also!"

"Devilish!" said Norris.

"O.K." said Clare, "now, if murder wasn't evil enough, the next part defies belief as they go about setting up Andy for the fall for murders to come! We have established he had been befriended by Janice, who is fairly attractive in an obvious sort of way, and after learning of his recent unhappy history in London, the stage is set. He is the perfect candidate. Knowing his history of medication Janice knew full well of the adverse effect of adding Rohypnol to his system. Amnesia. If he were arrested for the murder and tried to claim amnesia, it would simply look like he was offering a lame excuse. O.K., so that, we know. What is even more sinister is that if Andy could be brainwashed into believing he was a vampire, they could commit even more murders. Then if he was caught, of course he would appear as a nut-case and presumed guilty. So Andy, who has also been plied with drug-laced alcohol, is persuaded back to Janice's flat and there begins the process of brain washing him into believing he is the re-incarnation of the fictional vampire. The combination of alcohol and Rohypnol, to say nothing of his earlier dependence on Valium, leaves Andy totally confused and therefore wide open to the gang's evil suggestions that he is the reincarnation of the old vampire and is responsible for murder."

"It sounds too uncannily weird not to be true," said the doctor. "Amnesia can readily develop when too much Rohypnol is in the system for a prolonged period. The Valium and alcohol would only worsen his condition. No wonder his memory is shattered!"

"Which is what her gang intended," said Clare. "If they could supplant new memories for old, he would be the prime suspect in the murders, as he himself would believe he was responsible.

"You must be one evil cow to come up with this!" said Norris to Janice.

Clare continued, “When the selected girl was lying bleeding to death, that's when the drugged and confused Andy now easily open to suggestion, was told that he had killed her. That way they could continue murdering people who had rare blood groups, which they intended to sell, and had a fall guy already in place should things start becoming too hot for them.”

“The best fall guy in the world,” said Norris, “One who actually believes he did it! The evil b*stards!”

“The only thing was that in his confused state Andy, who now was convinced he was Dracula, still had a decent impulse to correct the misdeeds. Back at the flat he slashed his wrist in a fit of remorse. The fact that Andy is left-handed and it was his right wrist that was slashed indicates this. But one of the gang, don't know who, managed to bind it up. Not out of kindness or decency, but because *they* would decide when it was time for Andy to die... after more killings!”

"How do you know he did that at the flat?" asked Norris.

"Simple," said Clare. "His blood group is 'O' positive and wasn't found on the headstone until after the second killing and his second suicide attempt. So his first attempt, I suspect, would have been at the flat."

"Oh, er, yes," said Norris, "Simple."

Clare continued with her summation of events, secretly revelling in the Superintendent’s ignorance. "For the next few weeks he was kept at Janice's flat. She stole his bank card and made use of his funds to stay off work and keep an eye on him, continuing his brainwashing, his dependence on her and forming a bond. But during this time the gang, who would engage in any illegal venture to get rich quick as their previous antics had shown, realised there was not enough money in the sale of blood as they could not supply the amounts needed quickly enough. They couldn't steal it in big enough quantities from the Path Lab and each murder could only supply six to eight pints at a time. So this new venture didn't really have a viable future and had come to an end. To cover their tracks over the first girl’s murder, they had to commit a second one. The first murder being attributed to the arrival of the infamous vampire at the Goths festival, it was easy to blame another murder on the same suspect. Again Janice located a likely target from the blood donors list, befriended her and doped her drink with the date–rape drug Rohypnol. Having passed out she suffered the same fate as the previous victim, drained of blood and dumped on Dracula’s fictional grave perhaps even with Andy there to re-enforce the idea in him that he was responsible for that murder also."

"Why drain the second girl's blood if they knew they couldn't sell it," asked a confused Norris.

"Really Sir!" said Clare in mock exasperation. "You must keep up!

They could sell it but just didn't have enough of a supply. Besides, they had to show the same modus operandi to reinforce the ideas that it was the same guy who committed the first murder. To confirm without doubt Andy was indeed the murderer."

Norris just looked at her red-faced, "Yes, Yes. Carry on," he said impatiently.

Clare continued, "In any case, it was time to sever any connection with Andy/Dracula and so he was installed into the small hotel a couple of days before his arranged suicide. Probably driven to the cemetery by the *Reddy-Cab* thugs, it was then that they encouraged Andy to commit suicide. He had wanted to before when he was convinced he killed the first girl, and now he thought he had killed a second he wouldn't have needed much encouraging. Perhaps he couldn't manage it using his already injured right wrist so they slashed his left wrist for him!"

"He didn't do it himself?" asked Norris.

"I would say not," affirmed Clare. "Don't forget he was doped up and probably needed help anyway as his right hand was already injured. So to make sure the job got done, either Janice or her evil cronies obliged him by slashing his good left wrist. However, due to it being a freezing cold night he didn't bleed to death as his vessels would be somewhat constricted. Right, doctor? Possible?"

"In such cold temperatures, very probable!" he replied.

"For good measure the decision was made to help him on his way by one of the gang obligingly smashing him over the head with a shovel or some implement. Believing the cut wrists and the whack on the head would 'do for him' they left the scene, convinced the police would assume this was the man they were looking for, some nut case who had committed suicide in a fit of remorse over the murders. As far as the gang were concerned, they had tied all loose ends up neatly only, as I said, the low temperature saved his life due to the cold restricting his blood loss and thereby reducing his metabolic rate. And so it was that he was found barely alive the next time the guard did his patrol. The fact he did not die of his injuries is pure good luck. I don't doubt for one moment that the gang would be satisfied his memory would not return. They wouldn't take that chance and so I say now that until they are arrested, Andy's life is still in danger!"

Turning to a white faced and obviously shaken Janice, Clare asked, "Did I leave much out?"

Visibly shocked, Janice answered feebly, "No, not much. Are you bloody psychic?"

With a triumphant sigh Clare said, "Maybe. Are you psychotic?"

"That's incredible!" said Norris. "What led you to suspect her in the first place?"

"Oh a few things that looked a bit funny," Clare replied. "The two different blood groups got me thinking, and why blood was taken from the carotid instead of the jugular. That showed some medical knowledge and indicated a purpose. Then just by luck I saw her mollycoddling our boy in the hotel. What clinched it for me was that his costume had the retailers tag removed from it. It must have been an afterthought on Janice's part otherwise she could have done it earlier. Obviously it had been removed in the hospital and very recently because I found it moments later in the waste basket with all the cuttings from the Christmas decorations that Janice had only moments earlier had been working on. And that she had volunteered to do the decorations as well as work in the Lab meant that she could keep close tabs on what was happening to Andy. He was meant to die after the second murder. He didn't and was still alive which meant his memory of the murderous events might return and thus finger the gang. An attempt would have to be made on his life soon, and I believe Janice has just been biding her time waiting for an opportunity."

"Why not suspect Andy?" asked Norris.

"Oh a few things," she said. "The cuts on the wrists for one. A cut to his right wrist indicated a suicide attempt but cuts to the left wrist suggested assistance – an attempt on his life. Luckily I saw him myself with Janice just before his second suicide attempt and something didn't look right between him and her. I also saw her in conversation with the *Reddy-Cab* driver. She paid Andy's hotel bill, out of his own money admittedly. That didn't look right either, and my intuition told me to think about a possible connection between this case and Doaksie's. The rest fell into place when I found that clothing tag and heard Andy's brother's story. Simple really."

"Simple?" asked a stunned Norris. "I would never have pieced all that together. I think you *are* bloody psychic!"

"I'd solve a lot more crimes if I were," said Clare. "No just observation and attention to detail. Good old fashioned coppering, y'know?" With a wink she added, "Plus a bit of intuition! Anyway, that's my assessment. What have you got?"

"I'll have your version!" affirmed Norris.

"Good," she said, "I'm sure if you search her flat and the taxi firm's accommodations you will find some good evidence."

"Like what?" he asked.

" 'A' negative blood perhaps and possibly Andy's bank card, but if that can't be found, we simply have to look at the bank's CCTV records of which branch the money was taken from."

Turning to the nurse she asked, "Will it show Andy's face withdrawing his own money or yours?"

With a sigh she admitted, "Mine."

"So you're holding your hands up to it are you?" asked Norris. "We can make all this stick you know but your confession will help, and if you're sensible you will finger the gang for us. You're not going to take all this on your own are you? A guilty plea is always appreciated by the courts due to the time and costs so it will go in your favour when you are sentenced. You have ten seconds to think about it. What's it to be?"

"O.K." Janice said dejectedly. "It was like 'Miss Clever Clogs' said. Me and the *Reddy-Cab* gang did it but I didn't kill them. That wasn't me!"

"Oh really?" asked Clare. "Who would best know how to locate the carotid artery, you or your cohorts?"

The sick look on Janice's face confirmed Clare's brilliant analysis of the case.

"The courts will decide," said Clare.

"Brilliant!" said Norris. "We have our confession."

Clare corrected him, "It's an admission of complicity in murder, but either way she's all yours, Super. And now it's four o'clock. Your next 'arrests' should be entering the car park any minute now looking for a big fare."

"O.K. I'm on it!" Norris said and dashed out side to confront the villains.

Right on time, the three *Reddy-Cabs* gently pulled up into the hospital car park. Almost immediately pandemonium broke loose as police cars that had lain in wait screeched to a halt, closing off the exit and thus boxing in the three cabs. As a dozen officers pounced on the villains who instinctively tried to fight their way free, the ranks of the carol singers disrupted in panic. The car park rang out with their cries of shock and the wild shouts from police and villains.

Despite being outnumbered, the taxi gang fought fiercely but were quickly subdued by the overwhelming administering of several painful cracks on the head from teak and mahogany billy clubs. Handcuffed then quickly manhandled into a large paddy wagon, they were driven away.

Following behind were four police cars, one of which transported the evil nurse Janice to await her fate in the courts.

Back in the secure unit, Clare told the constable guarding Andy, "Well, I guess you are relieved of duty. Off you go."

"Thank you, Ma'am," he said.

Turning to the doctor she smiled and asked, "What's the prognosis for old Dracula here, Doc?"

"Well, his memory will take a while to return fully but we are confident of a rapid improvement now. We ought to keep him for a couple of days more under observation."

"I want to thank you, Clare," said Andy. "Your boss had already found me guilty. Why, I even thought so myself. You're the only one who could have helped me and you did. I think you're wonderful!"

"To begin with, he is not my boss and if he had been considered bright enough to deal with this case then I wouldn't have been brought in to investigate.”

“And so modest too!” said Andy with a big grin. “But you are a wonderful copper, and a pretty wonderful woman as well, I might add.”

Smiling back at him she said, “Yes Andy. You may indeed add.”

She leaned forward and kissed him on the cheek. “I think you are pretty special, too,” she said.

"You do?" he asked with a hopeful look.

"Of course," she answered. "You're a handsome so and so but not vain I think. And only a decent person would attempt suicide if he thought he were responsible. No, you're not a bad sort."

"You're a pleasant surprise, too," he said. "A great looker but with brains, too!"

They both laughed.

"Well then," Clare said, "I guess we make a fine pair."

They shared a quiet moment just staring into each other’s eyes.

Eventually Andy asked, “What will you do now, Clare? Will you leave?”

“No, not right away.”

“I hope I shall see you again.”

“I have a bit of leave coming,” she said. “What with Christmas and Doaksie’s retirement party coming up, I think I should stay at least for that.”

“Oh yes! Please do,” said Andy enthusiastically. “That would be great!”

“Tell you what. You rest up and work with the doctor here and when you're able to we could take a look round this pretty little town. I'm going to be busy writing my report and preparing for the court case, whenever that will be, and you will be busy getting better.”

“Deal,” he said.

“O.K. me and Doaksie are off back to the station now.”

As they made to leave the room Clare blew Andy a kiss and Doaksie gave him the 'thumbs up'.

The doctor piped up, “Under the circumstances, I think you could visit any time you like.”

“Thanks Doc,” said Clare. “As a matter of fact I shall be busy for a day or two but can I phone his brother to say he and his wife can come up to visit? They will have to arrange to take him back down to London with them anyway.”

“Of course,” said the Doctor, “That's a great idea.”

With that Clare and Doaksie left the building and drove back to the station.

****

Two days later, Clare's mobile phone rang and a voice on the other end said, "Is that Clare McKee, please?"

"It is. Who am I speaking to?"

"Hi. This is Michael Clayton. Andy's brother."

"Oh hello. Nice to hear from you again."

"My wife and I came up yesterday. What a relief to know he's O.K."

"Yes it must have been quite a shock for you."

"We thought all this time he was in Rumania enjoying himself, but all this! And after all he has been through already!"

"Well I'm sure he's in good hands now. Will you be leaving soon?"

"Far from it. We are staying in town over Christmas. London is pretty crazy just now and Whitby is so picturesque with all the snow."

"Yes it is lovely, isn't it?"

"Look Clare, would you like to join us for lunch? My wife and I are doing some Christmas shopping and it would be lovely to meet you to say 'thank you' for all you have done."

"Oh that's not necessary."

"Now don't be modest. We're extremely grateful and I know Andy is. He's never stopped talking about you since we saw him."

"And how is he now?"

"Come along to lunch and you can see for yourself!"

"Ah! He's been allowed out of the hospital?"

"Yes, under our care. He's improved such a lot. Please come."

Within twenty minutes they all met in one of Whitby's swankiest restaurants.

Andy's beaming smile at seeing Clare exposed his canines and instinctively he covered his mouth with a hand. Realising what he had done he took his hand away and pulling a silly face snarled at Clare in a mock terrifying manner. They all broke up laughing, but Clare was a little shocked to realise she had blushed, quite markedly. After swift but polite introductions, they all took their seats and began a happy chatter as a magnificent Christmas lunch was served.

"The food is so rich!" said Jodie, Mike's wife. "But Mmmm – so good!"

"Ah, let yourself go," said Mike topping up everyone's wine. "We're celebrating and not just Christmas either!"

"The diet is on hold until new year," said Jodie with a laugh. "To heck with it!"

Clare couldn't have wished for better company than Mike and Jodie. She took an immediate shine to them, but found herself looking more and more at Andy.

"He is a handsome bugger, isn't he?" said Mike. "I had to make do with the brains while old Andy here had to put up with the looks!"

"Well I can do something about them," Andy said. "As soon as I'm able to, I am off to a good dentist to have these fangs filed down or removed. They have always bugged me!"

"Oh I dunno," said Clare. "It gives you a certain animal appeal!"

She immediately blushed again when she said it.

'Oh my God! Why did I say that? What impression am I giving?'

To her great relief everyone just laughed it off.

"Do you think you might relocate to London sometime Clare?" asked Jodie.

"Well that was the idea of joining the C.I.D."

"Good! It would be lovely to see more of you. You know we can't tell you enough times how grateful we are for your help."

Taking Clare's hand Andy said, "And I certainly appreciate you Clare. I owe you my life at least, and my sanity. It could have been so much worse for me."

She tossed her shoulder length blonde hair back and, with an impish giggle, said, "It must have been fate. Eh? What do you think?"

Andy and Clare's prolonged gaze into each others eyes whilst holding hands was more than enough of a cue for Jodie,

"Right!" said Jodie. "Shopping – phase two!"

"Oh good Lord!" moaned Mike. "Back into the fray!"

As they got up to leave, Andy said to Mike and Jodie, "I think all the dashing around the busy shops would be a bit too much for me. Do you two fancy going it alone? Clare and I could just take a nice walk instead."

"Of course, of course," said Mike with a hearty slap upon his brother's back. "You both get some chill time why don't ya?"

Clare linked arms with Andy and pulled out her mobile phone.

"Who you calling?" asked Andy.

"Transport," she said. "I know a nice quiet and picturesque spot we can stroll around without too many people."

"Where's that?"

"You'll see."

****

A few minutes later the transport, in the shape of a police car with Doaksie at the wheel, had driven up the steep hill to the Abbey cemetery.

With snow on the edges the headstones and decorating the leaves on the trees, the whole scene looked like a Yuletide picture postcard.

Upon seeing the old curate come out of his lodge up ahead, Doaksie hailed him, "Get the kettle on then, eh? I'm parched."

Then to Andy and Clare he said, "You take your time. Him and me will have a yarn for a bit."

"Oh! It's you two!" said the curate recognising Andy and Clare. "I suppose an apology is due. Well you can't blame me really, can you? I mean he does look a real dodgy character!"

The couple laughed.

"Now, now!" said Doaksie," You ought to know better. We do not go on appearances, do we?"

Slightly embarrassed but smiling, the curate said, "Of course," and offering his hand to Andy said, "No hard feelings eh, mate?"

Accepting the handshake Andy replied, "None at all old chap."

"Dodgy character indeed!" said Clare. "Would you believe Andy is nothing more than a mild mannered civil servant? They don't come much more un-dodgy than that!"

All four grinned cheerily at the mild rebuke.

"Let's go for that cuppa," said Doaksie to the curate.

"See you later," Andy said.

Arm in arm the couple crunched the snow underfoot treading their way along the path.

Suddenly Andy said, "Shh! Look over there. A robin!"

"Oh how lovely!" said Clare.

"This is picture perfect," said Andy. "Just look at us walking among snow-laden trees and red robins."

They stopped to look at the beautiful Christmas scene they were in.

"So tell me Clare. Is this where we end on a happy note or is it the start of something really special?"

"What do you want it to be?" she asked coyly.

With that he took her face in his hands and kissed her passionately.

She responded by hugging him close to her and returned his kiss with as much passion.

He kissed her luscious lips, her cheek, her forehead. He couldn't stop kissing her.

When he stopped to catch his breath, she took over and kissed him all over his handsome face.

They stood there breathless then both burst out laughing.

"I guess we've answered that question!" said Andy. "Let's go and do this somewhere warmer."

Hugging each other they returned to the car.

Looking out of the curates lodge window, Doakise gulped his tea and opened the door.

"What a nice couple they make," said Doaksie. "And you thought he was a vampire! Ha!"

The curate said, "Well whatever he is I wouldn't have had him down as a blinking civil servant! What exactly does he do in the civil service anyway?"

Doaksie replied, "I think he's something to do with the Inland Revenue people. You know....income tax."

The curate nearly choked on his tea. “What?” he spluttered. “Inland bloody Revenue? Income Tax?”

“Yes. Why?”

I knew it!”

“Knew what?” asked Doaksie.

Catching his breath from partly inhaling his tea from the shock he said, “A taxman! I was right all along.”

“No,” Doaksie corrected, “you said he was a vampire!”

Tapping his nose the curate replied, “Ah! I knew he was a blood sucker of some kind!”

The End

Lightning Source UK Ltd.
Milton Keynes UK
30 October 2010

162172UK00003B/9/P

9 780984 461561